Terra Incognita

A Novel About the Crypto-Jews of Spain

LIBI ASTAIRE

ASTER PRESS

Published and distributed by:
Aster Press
Kansas-Jerusalem
www.libiastaire.weebly.com

To:

Faigel Safran, who commissioned this story for *Mishpacha Magazine*
- and to all the staff of *Mishpacha* -
thank you.

And to:

My father -
May his soul be bound up in the Bond of Life.

Fear not, for I am with you. I will bring your children from the east,and gather you from the west. I will say to the north, Give them up. And to the south, Do not hold them back. Bring My sons from afar, and My daughters from the ends of the earth.

- Isaiah, 43:5-6

The Ingathering shall be for the Children of Israel who are called Jacob, and also for the Anusim *who are of their seed.*

- Don Isaac Abarbanel, rabbi, diplomat, and exile from Spain

PART I: PEACELAND

CHAPTER 1

C lara? Where are you?"

Anna groped for a chair to steady herself. The room was twirling around again, and as it twirled the walls receded into the distance. If she could just grab on to the chair before it twirled away from her, too, she would be all right. She stretched out her arm and readied her fingers to curl around the wooden back of the chair, worn smooth from the passage of many years. The table, the oven, and everything else in the kitchen were giddily whirling around, as though dancing to some mad music that only they could hear, but she could see the chair so kindly. No, *kindly* wasn't the right word. What was the word she was looking for? Was there a word that could describe what she saw as she gazed at this chair that had been such a faithful friend to her for so much of her life?

She remembered the day that Uncle Manel, who had made the sturdy pieces of furniture himself, unloaded the chair and its five companions from his wagon. "These will get you started," he had said with a broad smile.

"With the good L-rd's help, I'll live to see the day when the young couple will need to order six more," her grandfather had said, also smiling.

Everyone had laughed, except her. She was only seventeen when she became engaged, and she was scared to death of becoming a bride. She was even too embarrassed to watch as Uncle Manel and her father carried the chairs into her new home.

As it turned out, she never did need to order more chairs. Her first child, a boy, left the world just a few moments after he arrived. When she was strong enough to sit up at the table, Miquel, her husband, had led her to the kitchen and gently helped her into her chair, the one with the carved wildflowers. The other chairs had a simple scroll design carved into their heavy wooden backs. But she was Uncle Manel's favorite, and her chair, with its wildflowers, reflected the special bond between them. They shared a love of taking long walks in the Catalan countryside, and since he and his wife didn't have children of their own, Uncle Manel passed on all his knowledge to Anna. He taught her the names of all the bushes and flowers that burst into color every spring, filling the air with their heady perfume.

There was yellow broom, a scrappy bush with yellow flowers that only a native could love. Those were Uncle Manel's words: "that only a native could love." And they were natives, he had assured her. They had lived in this little valley for generations. Anyone could appreciate the delicate pink and yellow cistus flower, or the clumps of lavender, rosemary, and thyme. Even someone from Barcelona, who just came to their valley for a Sunday afternoon to enjoy a picnic lunch in the countryside and snap a few photographs, could smile at a cistus and admire its crumpled beauty. But there was nothing delicate or sentimental about the yellow broom.

"In some places of the world," Uncle Manel had told her during one of their walks, "they consider our yellow broom to be a weed that must be rooted out. Destroyed."

"Why?" she had asked. She must have been seven years old at the time, perhaps even eight.

"They are afraid that it will take over the entire countryside," Uncle Manel explained. "They are afraid that it will eat up all the soil's nutrients and leave nothing for the other plants. But don't believe it, Anna. The yellow broom takes over only when the soil is already eroded, when it has been depleted of its natural vitality by greedy kings and ignorant farmers. When the soil is healthy — when crops are planted with wisdom and in moderation — the yellow broom will live peaceably alongside its neighbors, making its own unique contribution to the countryside. Do you understand?"

The little girl had nodded her head, even though she didn't really understand. The elderly Anna nodded her head, too, as she recalled the memory. Now she did understand. When her mother was in the hospital, a few weeks before she passed away, she had explained everything. But why was she thinking of her mother and the yellow broom and Uncle Manel? All of it had happened so long ago. Her grandfather and grandmother, her mother and father,

Uncle Manel and Aunt Nuria, they were gone. All that was left from those days were her two brothers and Miquel. And Clara.

That was it. She wanted her daughter, Clara. She wanted to tell Clara about the chair. She wanted to tell Clara to hold on to the chair, tightly, because the world was slipping away. People were starting to complain about the yellow broom again. She had heard it on the radio. It was someone with a funny name — not a native — and he was saying that the yellow broom had to be destroyed before it took over the world. She had to warn Clara not to listen. Or was she supposed to warn Clara to listen? She was getting all confused.

But where was she? Where was her Clara? She had been in the kitchen just a few minutes ago. Anna was sure of it. It was so like Clara to wander off, just when she had needed her. Not that she was complaining. She was grateful to have a child. She had waited so many years. Miquel had put the four extra chairs up in the attic because it made her sad to see the empty places at the table. She could still remember the day when he brought one of them back down. They were so happy.

So what if she was no longer a young bride who blushed at every little thing? She had a daughter. She had someone to walk with in the countryside, someone she could teach all the names of the flowers. She had someone to help her in the kitchen, before the holidays, when there was so much to do. Just this morning she had phoned Clara and told her to come over.

"Remember? We need to bake the cakes today," she had said.

"I'll be over at nine, Mama."

Clara Bonet sat on the porch. It was only eleven o'clock in the morning and already the day was boiling hot. She didn't know how her mother stood it in that stuffy little kitchen, especially when the oven was going.

She would have to convince her parents to put in an air conditioner, at least in the kitchen. Enough with being stubborn. At their age this heat was dangerous. Should she bring it up now? Maybe not. Why spoil things by starting an argument over an air conditioner when they were having such a nice morning? She enjoyed these times, when she and her mother worked together in the kitchen.

"Mama, why don't we make a lemon cake this year?" she would tease.

"Lemon cake? In the fall? Who ever heard of such a thing?" her mother would reply. "Really, Clara, I don't know where you get such crazy ideas. Certainly not from Papa and me."

Her mother would make a big show of being exasperated with her only child, but Clara wasn't fooled for a moment. She knew that her mother waited for these moments, these little exchanges that took place between a daughter and her mother. It didn't matter that what had once been a real question had turned into ritual as the years passed. Making cakes for the upcoming fall holiday wouldn't be the same without her suggesting that they make a lemon cake this year and her mother looking appalled at the suggestion.

But why was making a lemon cake in the fall such a crazy idea? she had always wondered. Someday she would have to ask.

"Clara?"

The sound of her mother's voice slowly pulled Clara out of her reverie. She crinkled her nose. Something was burning.

Clara hurried into the kitchen. A thin wisp of smoke was escaping from the oven and floating out of the open window. It was odd that both of them had wandered off and forgotten the cakes. All the work of the morning would be for nothing. But her mother had called her, hadn't she? Where was she then?

Clara looked around the room. For the first time she noticed that her mother's chair had overturned and her heart froze.

"Mama?"

The silence sent tingles down her spine. Clara rushed to the heavy kitchen table and peered underneath it. Why was her mother lying there, her eyes staring into the dark brown expanse of wood?

"Mama, are you all right?"

She knew it was a stupid thing to say. Of course, her mother wasn't all right. Her mother didn't spend her mornings lying under kitchen tables. If only her mother would turn to look at her, with that droll look on her face, and say, "Clara, I don't know where you get such crazy ideas." But her mother didn't say a word. She just kept staring up at the bottom of the kitchen table, as though she was seeing an entire world etched within its dark surface.

"I'll call the doctor, Mama. I'll call Josep, too. I'll tell him to go out to the fields and pick up Papa. Don't worry. Everything is going to be fine."

The phone calls were made. The oven was switched off. Clara wet a dish towel and placed it over her mother's forehead. She didn't know what else to do. She was afraid to move her mother. What if she had broken a hip? If only she would speak to her.

Maybe she should put a pillow under her mother's head, while they waited. Surely that wouldn't hurt. Clara took her mother's hand in her own and said softly, "I'm just going to bring you a pillow. I won't be long."

Clara was about to let go of her mother's hand when she felt a slight pressure, just a hint of a squeeze. Communication had been made, but what was her mother trying to say? "Thank you?" "Don't worry, it's not as bad as it seems?" "Don't leave me?" Her mother squeezed her hand again, this time more tightly. Clara lowered her head so that she could see her mother face to face.

"I'm here, Mama. Is there something you want to tell me?"

Anna nodded her head ever so slightly. Her lips began to work. Clara held her breath, afraid that even the slightest noise would prevent her from hearing her mother's words.

"Ba...room."

Clara heard the sound of a car driving up to the house. The engine turned off. A car door opened. Then it slammed shut and footsteps approached the front door. She waited. Would there be a knock, or would her father stride into the room and take charge, the way he knew how to do so well, and relieve her of the responsibility of acting brave and strong when all she wanted to do was collapse into a corner like a crumpled flower that has been out in the sun for far too long?

There was a knock.

"It must be the doctor, Mama. I have to let him in."

Her mother refused to let go of her hand. She could see that tears had begun to well up in her mother's eyes and that her mother's lips were moving, clumsily but with determination. "Ye...lel...ow... ba...room. Un...duh...ste...and?"

There was another knock, this time a bit louder. Clara had to answer the door. She had to let go of her mother's hand. She had to say something.

"Yes, Mama, I understand."

11

Her mother's hand loosened its grip.

"I'll be right back, with the doctor."

Clara stayed by the door to the kitchen so that the doctor could attend to her mother without interference. Her mind was already moving forward to the next stage: the stay in the hospital. She would have to pack a bag for her mother and some food for her father. Her father would go with her mother in the ambulance. She would follow — her husband Josep would drive her — with the little suitcase and the food. Would they let her father stay overnight, or would he have to make the forty-five-minute journey by train to Girona, the nearest city with a hospital, every day? If he stayed overnight, she would need to pack a suitcase for him as well.

"Mrs. Bonet? May I use your phone?"

"The phone? Yes, of course."

She overheard the doctor order an ambulance. After he hung up the receiver, there was only silence.

"Will my mother need to stay in the hospital a long time?" Clara asked him.

"I'm sorry, Mrs. Bonet, but your mother has passed away."

Clara stood next to her father as the ambulance team lifted Anna's lifeless body into the car. Her husband and her eldest son, Arnau, were also there. No one said a word, and since they weren't the sort of people to wail and scream a heavy silence hung over the little group.

The big doors swung shut and the ambulance made its way down the dirt road, slowly so that the car wouldn't bounce too much down the bumpy path.

"I should have paved that road long ago," Miquel said. "Your mother was always asking me to do it."

Clara glanced at her father, whose eyes were fixed on the dirt road. The next few days were going to be very hard, for both of them. For now, though, they stood quietly, as though sheltered together within a protective bubble that shielded them from the worst of the pain, and watched as the ambulance grew smaller and smaller, until finally it disappeared. It was Miquel who broke the spell.

"We should call Vidal. He'll want to know."

CHAPTER 2

W here's the gate for Memphis?"
"Straight ahead, sir, and follow the signs."
"Rome. Which gate?"
"Straight ahead and follow the signs to the train. Get off at Concourse E."

"Barcelona?"

"Main terminal, sir. Follow the signs to the train."

By the time Vidal Bonet arrived at the gate for Barcelona, the waiting area was nearly full. He quickly scanned the space, not because he actually expected to see anyone he knew but because that was his way. One never knew when an opportunity would present itself, or an obstacle for that matter, so it was better to be prepared and on the lookout than to be taken by surprise.

There were still a few scattered seats available, including one near the far wall, where one could look through the large windows and see the planes waiting on the Atlanta airport's tarmac. A group of American college students were camped out by the wall, probably on their way to Barcelona to study for a year in one of the city's many universities. Their animated chatter could be heard clear across the room.

He would not sit with them, and not just because he was already twenty-five years old and had just completed his graduate studies. He was sure that even when he was twenty and a college student himself — not in Barcelona, but at the University of Girona — he had never talked so loudly. That didn't mean he couldn't argue passionately about a subject when it was dear to his heart, but where he came from, people argued quietly and behind closed doors.

He glanced at the sign above the check-in counter and then down at his new, state-of-the-art wristwatch. There was still more than an hour's wait before the plane to Barcelona was scheduled to board. He could get some work done, if he chose his seat well.

13

His restless eyes scanned the area again. Besides the students, most of the people looked like they were Americans going to Barcelona for an end-of-summer holiday. There were certainly plenty of opportunities in this little area to do some market research. It was a gold mine — American tourists visiting Catalonia were exactly the people he wanted to capture with his new business venture. And yet this really wasn't an appropriate time, not when he was on his way home to attend his grandmother's funeral.

This wasn't how he had expected to make his return home. After two years of studying for his MBA at a top business school, and graduating with honors, he had visualized a grand homecoming awaiting him. His two great-uncles, Uncle Pau and Uncle Biel, had financed the venture along with his grandfather. Being frugal people, his great-uncles had wanted Vidal to attend a business school in Barcelona, where there were several fine institutions. It was his Grandfather Miquel who had insisted that the young man go to the United States.

"If you want to do business with the Americans, you have to learn how they think," he had said, "and the way to do that is to live beside them, day by day. Going to school in a place like New York City is an opportunity of a lifetime. It may be more expensive, but it will pay off in the long run."

After Vidal received a prestigious scholarship, the matter was settled. One didn't say no to such an honor.

"The whole village is pinning its hopes on you," Uncle Pau had told him when the little family group went to the Barcelona airport to see him off.

"There are many distractions in a big city like New York," Uncle Biel had added, "but we know you will take your studies seriously and won't let us down."

Then his grandfather had pulled him over to the side and whispered in his ear, "That's just like your grandmother's side of the family, always so serious. So I'll give you my two cents' worth of advice as well: don't forget to have a little fun."

He hadn't disappointed his great-uncles. For two years he had worked hard and graduated near the top of his class. More importantly, he had succeeded in coming up with a business plan for revitalizing his village.

It was serious business, having a whole village depend on you, even when the village was no larger than a speck on the map. His great-uncles would want to know all about the plan as soon as he arrived, but if he knew his grandfather — and he did — the great-uncles would have to wait. It would be just like his grandfather to have a huge, brightly painted "Welcome Home" banner made and string it across the square. Nor would it be farfetched to believe that Grandpa Miquel would hire musicians who would strike up a triumphant noise as Vidal's car pulled into the village, which consisted only of the little square and the farmland surrounding it.

Uncle Pau and Uncle Biel would be forced to sit at the head of the long table that had been set up in the square especially for the occasion, where they would look extremely uncomfortable throughout the congratulatory speeches. Vidal would have to pretend to be embarrassed by all the fuss. People in his village prided themselves on being down-to-earth working folk who didn't go in for sentimental foolishness or showy displays of emotion. This is why, even though Grandpa Miquel had lived in Sant Joan Januz for more than fifty years, ever since he had married Grandma Anna, he was still considered a "Spaniard," and not someone who had his roots in Catalonia.

Vidal smiled. Sant Joan Januz, little as it was, had been his entire world when he was young. Then he had gone off to university in the "big city" of Girona, which wasn't more than a dot on the map of the world itself. Now here he was, a world traveler, dressed in an expensive business suit and carrying a laptop, just like businesspeople from New York and London and Berlin. What would it be like to return home? When his family made a fuss over him, would he be embarrassed because he was the center of attention or because it was all so very provincial?

Then he remembered. There wouldn't be any party. Vidal was coming home to attend his grandmother's funeral.

"How can people live in such a place?" Arnau Bonet muttered under his breath as his car rolled to a stop.

Though it was well past the time for the morning rush hour, the traffic wasn't moving. Either there had been an accident on the highway, or there was roadwork up ahead. Whatever the reason,

15

Arnau unexpectedly found that he had time to take in the view of Barcelona that stretched out below him.

It wasn't a sight that inspired him. He never could understand why some people preferred to live in the crowded city, piled up one on top of the other. Of course, he knew all the arguments in a big city's favor: the constant stimulation, the cosmopolitan atmosphere, the exchange of ideas. Another factor, and a compelling one, was being able to keep up to date with who just opened an art gallery, who was the new curator at the museum, who had been appointed art critic of the newspaper. Yet he wouldn't exchange his little studio in Sant Joan Januz for all the galleries and cafes in

Barcelona, even if it meant his paintings remained undiscovered.

The traffic began to move, slowly at first and then it picked up speed.

"Look, Papa! A dump truck!"

His four-year-old son, Manel, had his nose glued to the window. Arnau looked over at the side of the road where workers were widening the highway to add more lanes.

"Why are they digging up the road?"

"I don't know, Manel. I guess some people think they're making the world a better place when they tear up what came before them."

Arnau grasped Manel's hand tightly as they walked through the arrivals area of the Barcelona airport. A sign indicated that flight 114 from Atlanta had landed safely and on time. He was glad they wouldn't have to wait long in the crowded terminal.

Manel, for his part, was looking around the busy terminal with eyes filled with wonder. He had never before seen so many people, or suitcases. He looked longingly at the metal carts that the grown-ups were pushing with such importance. It seemed a shame to waste a good cart on transporting luggage when a little boy would appreciate a ride so much more. He would have asked his father to get a cart so he could have a ride, if he didn't have something even more important on his mind.

"Papa, where is the airplane?"

"It's on the runway."

"Why does it need to run away?"

16

Arnau smiled. He was glad he had thought to bring Manel with him. With luck, his son would keep his brother Vidal busy with a thousand questions. Otherwise it would be awkward, the long drive back home, since the two brothers never did have too much to say to one another.

"The runway is where the airplanes go before they take off and after they land. Once they land, they park outside the terminal and all the people get off the plane and come inside. The people then come here to pick up their luggage."

"And a cart."

"And a cart, if they have a lot of luggage."

"Will Uncle Vidal have a lot of luggage?"

"I don't know. We'll have to wait and see."

Arnau felt a tap on his shoulder and turned around. It was Vidal. The two brothers embraced. For the moment, at least, they were genuinely happy to see each other. Then Arnau introduced Manel to Vidal.

"You have a cart! I knew you would!"

Vidal knew exactly what to do. He lifted Manel up high and then plopped the boy on top of his suitcase.

"Hold on tight."

"I will, Uncle Vidal."

The two sped off in the direction of the parking lot. Arnau followed behind them. That's the way it had always been, for as long as Arnau could remember. Although he was the elder of the two by three years, it was always Vidal who was racing ahead.

"Well, let him run," Arnau muttered under his breath. "He'll have to stop sometime. I have the keys to the car."

Vidal and Manel were the best of friends by the time the car sped past Barcelona. It didn't hurt that Vidal had kept Manel's present — a plastic pencil box shaped like the Statue of Liberty — in his jacket pocket so that he could give it to his nephew when the opportune moment arose. That moment didn't take long in coming. Manel wasn't shy about asking for what he confidently assumed to be his due, as Vidal's first and only nephew.

Manel wanted to know all about this statue. Why was she green? Why was she wearing a crown? Was she a queen? When he found out that once it had been possible to climb all the way to the top and look out of her head, he was momentarily silent. This was

17

a brand-new idea for him, being able to see the world through someone else's eyes, and he didn't know what to make of it.

"It's like the statue of Christopher Columbus in Barcelona," Arnau interrupted. "I'll take you there one day."

Vidal smirked.

Arnau felt the muscles in the back of his neck tense up. Should he take up the bait? Manel decided the issue for him by asking a question on another subject entirely: what was it like to ride in an airplane?

That topic kept uncle and nephew busy until they passed a sign signaling the turnoff for the Costa Brava, Catalonia's famed resort-studded coastline. The landscape was already beginning to change. The Pyrenees Mountains, which had been hovering in the distance, were becoming more pronounced. Factories had given way to the fertile farmland that had once been a primary source of Catalan wealth, before the tourists arrived. Arnau felt he could breathe again. He stole a glance over at his brother, to see how Vidal was reacting to the landscape, which must be both familiar and new after an absence of two years.

Vidal was also looking out the window, surveying the hills and farms. Yet he was far from relaxed. He intently took note of the sign for the Costa Brava, which was gaudily painted and looked terribly outdated. Perhaps the middle-aged tourists from Europe who flocked to the resort towns didn't care, but he thought he might dash off a note to the tourist board anyway.

By the time the highway sign for the Girona turnoff loomed ahead, Manel was fast asleep and Vidal was still lost in thought, making mental notes. Arnau was relieved that he didn't have to talk.

A few miles past Girona, the car turned off the highway and headed west, into the hills. There was no sign to mark the way. People either knew that this was the road to Sant Joan Januz or they didn't, and most didn't.

"But that will change," Vidal whispered softly.

"What?"

"Nothing. I was just thinking."

Arnau shrugged and returned his attention to the road. From the highway, the side road that he had taken didn't look as though it led anywhere, except perhaps to some farmer's field. Indeed, as the car traveled west, toward the mountains, it passed by several fields dotted with bales of hay that were all neatly rolled up into balls. What the eye couldn't see, because the terrain was perfectly flat, was that after several miles there was a sudden dip in the landscape, a kind of entranceway into a hidden valley within the valley, which was a little world of its own.

As it descended, the road narrowed to just one lane that ambled between a twin guard of tall trees. The trees' leafy branches reached out to one another and formed a green canopy that both protected the traveler from the hot sun and guided him deeper into the rural terrain.

The next landmark, not that the passengers in the car needed one, was the narrow stone bridge that spanned the lethargic waters of a small stream below. Then there was a bend in the road, and the village of Sant Joan Januz suddenly appeared at Vidal's right — and just as suddenly disappeared from view. It was so quick that there wasn't even time for him to fully internalize the fact: *I'm here. I'm home.*

Instead of continuing on to the fields and farmhouse that belonged to their grandfather, the car turned onto a different dirt path. In the distance stood a huddle of cars and trucks, a sort of makeshift parking lot. A few minutes later, Arnau's car joined them, and he pulled the car to a stop.

Arnau glanced into the rearview mirror. Manel was still fast asleep. His gaze shifted to Vidal, who had closed his eyes for a few moments and was leaning his head against the back of the seat.

"Are you feeling all right?"

Vidal wearily opened his eyes. He forced himself to shake off the tiredness from his long overseas flight and sit upright. "I'm fine."

The small crowd parted to let the two brothers pass through. Arnau, who held the still half-asleep Manel in his arms, took a place next to his wife, Joanna, and behind his mother. Vidal, the returning son, quietly greeted the small circle of mourners: his mother first and then his grandfather and then his two great-uncles.

They all felt awkward, knowing that the whole village was watching them. It was a relief when Uncle Pau, always the practical one, glanced at his watch and then over at the gravediggers, who were standing off to the side, and said, "We should get started."

The burial had to be performed quickly. Unlike the other villages in the area, Sant Joan Januz had its own customs when it came to sending a member of its community off to his or her eternal rest. They didn't bury the person in a coffin, for instance, as was required by Catalan law. They had to bribe the gravediggers, who were employed by the local council, to look the other way while they quickly lowered the deceased person, who lay on a plain board and was covered only by a white shroud, into the ground.

No one knew where the custom had come from, just as no one knew why they still observed it. It was just something they did, like washing their hands after they left the cemetery and covering the mirrors in the mourners' house. After every funeral — not that there were that many, since the village was so small — Uncle Pau and Uncle Biel would shake their heads and one of them would say, "What a waste."

"Indeed, it is," the other brother would agree. "First the family has to pay for the coffin, then they have to pay the gravediggers to ignore the coffin, and then they have to pay the gravediggers to cart the coffin away."

"If at least the coffin was used..."

"Sssh!" Grandmother Anna would interrupt. "That's not how we do things."

And that would be the end of the conversation. But who would say "Sssh!" now? Vidal wondered.

"Vidal?"

Vidal realized that his father was standing before him, waiting to give him a shovel. He mechanically took it from his father's hands and shoved it into the dirt. But he couldn't look down as he emptied the shovel of its contents. Instead, in his mind's eye he gave his Grandma Anna a kiss on the cheek, and then he handed the shovel to the next person in line.

Clara gave a sigh of relief as the sun dipped below the hills and disappeared from view. The long day was finally coming to an end. Her uncles had already gone home. Soon she would be able to close the door and go to her room and rest. Tomorrow she would feel better, she hoped, and be able to give her son Vidal more attention. She would make him a nice meal and bake one of his favorite cakes. Then they would talk, and he would tell her all

20

about New York and school and the friends he had made and his big plans for the future. It would be like the old days, when he would come running home from school with his head full of all sorts of ideas. He would fill the kitchen with life and laughter and energy and excitement, and then maybe she would forget about how sad and empty she was feeling.

She glanced over at her father, who was sitting beside her on the front porch.

"Papa, why don't you spend the night here? There's an extra bed in the sewing room."

"I have my own bed, in my own home."

So stubborn. Were her parents always like that? Or was the stubbornness part of getting older?

"Why doesn't Vidal sleep over at Grandpa's home tonight?" Arnau had come out onto the porch with his wife.

"Because Vidal is exhausted." The words flew out of Clara's mouth and hit their mark. Arnau winced. Clara felt guilty. But why did Arnau always have to express his opinion when no one had asked for it?

"If he's exhausted," Joanna started to say, "why does it matter where he sleeps?

Arnau motioned to her to be silent. Joanna strode over to the car and waited beside it, with her back to the little group on the porch.

"Have you seen Manel, Mama?" asked Arnau. "It's past his bedtime. We have to get home."

"I didn't mean to snap at you."

"I know."

Arnau walked onto the front lawn, where there were several trees good for climbing, a latticed pergola, and other excellent places for a small child to hide. "Manel!" he called out. "Ma-a-a-nel!"

"I'm here!"

They all looked up. Manel was looking down at them from a second-story window.

"What are you doing in the attic?" Arnau returned to the porch. He wasn't pleased that Manel had wandered into the attic without telling anyone.

"I'm writing a letter. With Uncle Vidal."

"It's time to go home."

Vidal appeared at the window. "We'll be down in two minutes." Vidal and Manel disappeared from view.

"You and Vidal used to spend hours playing in that attic," said Clara.

Arnau shrugged. "I don't remember."

A few moments later the screen door squeaked open, and Manel raced onto the porch, tightly grasping an envelope in his hand.

"Grandpa, you have a letter!"

"I do?" Miquel wasn't in the mood to play childish games, but a smile, which apparently had a mind of its own, played upon his lips of its own accord. "I wonder who it's from."

"You'll have to guess," said Manel, as he shoved the letter into his great-grandfather's hands. "And you'll have to guess how I wrote it."

"You already know how to write letters, Manel?" Miquel asked. "You must be a very clever boy."

"The machine wrote it. It has keys, just like Papa's computer. But there's no screen and you don't have to plug it in. And it makes a noise when you press down on the keys, like this: Clack, clack, clack, clack — ding. Clack, clack, clack, clack — ding."

"And the 'I' key is broken, Grandpa, so we need your magic hands to fix it." Everyone turned to look at Vidal, who had appeared in the doorway.

"Uncle Vidal says I can have his... What's it called, Uncle Vidal?"

"Typewriter."

"His typewriter. That's what people used, Grandpa, a long time ago, before there were computers, to write letters. But it's a little broken, so can you fix it?"

"I don't know," replied Miquel. For some reason his eyes had become misty as he gazed at Vidal, who was standing in the doorway holding an old toy typewriter in his hands. The typewriter had been a birthday present from him and Anna. That had been during the phase when Vidal was going to be a famous explorer and "needed" a typewriter so he could record his explorations for posterity. For the first time Miquel noticed that Vidal and Manel were very alike.

"Please? If you fix it, I can write you lots of letters."

22

"I can't promise, Manel. It's been a long time since a little boy has asked me to fix a typewriter."

"We'll bring it with us to Grandpa's house and take a look at it in the morning," Vidal said to Manel. Then he turned to his grandfather. "Do you want me to drive?"

Miquel noticed now that in addition to the typewriter, Vidal had brought outside an overnight bag. Obviously, Vidal intended to stay with him, and Miquel knew there was no longer any point in putting up a fuss since his grandson was as stubborn as he was.

"I'm not letting someone who has been up for twenty-four hours do anything for me," said Miquel, as he got up from the chair. "Understand?"

"Yes, Grandpa," said Vidal.

"Clara, get some rest. I'll talk to you in the morning."

"All right, Papa. Come here for breakfast."

The little group started to gravitate to the cars.

"And don't stay up all night talking to your grandfather," she said to Vidal as she gave him a quick hug. "You both need to get some sleep."

By the time Miquel's car pulled up in front of his house, it was shadowed in darkness. Miquel wished he had thought to turn on a light in the kitchen before he had left for the cemetery. But that was a whole lifetime ago, and who could be expected to think so far in advance?

"Why don't you sit on the porch for a few minutes, Vidal, and watch the fireflies come out. You used to like to do that when you were a little boy. Remember?"

"Are you sure you don't want me to go inside with you?"

"There are some journeys that a man has to make by himself, and this is one of them."

Miquel opened the front door and took a deep breath. He flicked on the light switch and glanced around the parlor, which served as the "formal" sitting room. It was rarely used, so its emptiness felt natural and didn't bother him. The kitchen, whose shadowy entranceway stood at the far end of the hallway, was another matter. That was where he and Anna had lived most of their lives, and he would have preferred to avoid entering it on this, his first night of official widowhood. However, Vidal might want a hot drink before he retired for the night, and there really wasn't any reason to be afraid.

Afraid? Was that what he was feeling? Is that why he was hesitating to switch on the kitchen light? And what was he doing, all of a sudden, thinking, analyzing his feelings? He never would have described himself as a thinker. If anything, he defined himself by his magic hands that could fix anything.

A thought occurred to him as he recalled what Vidal had said earlier about the typewriter. Its "I" key was broken. That's how he was feeling, like his I key was broken. The best part of his "I," his persona, had been the part that was attached to his wife, Anna. And now it was gone.

He was starting to feel depressed again, and he didn't like the feeling. If that's what thinking did to a person, it was better not to do too much of it. Besides, he had work to do: make a hot drink, fix up Vidal's bed. Tomorrow he would take a look at the typewriter.

He looked down at his hands. As long as he could use them, he could still be of use. No, there was no reason to let his grief run wild, he decided, and he switched on the light.

Vidal could hear his grandfather moving around inside the house. It sounded like the old man was doing all right. He allowed himself to sink down on the top step of the porch.

He had valiantly battled sleep all day, but now it was starting to gain the upper hand. Through the small slit in his half-shut eyes he could see, over by the flower bed, three fireflies dancing above the geraniums, flicking their tiny lights on and off. He had forgotten how much he loved the quiet beauty of his home.

"It's too bad," he murmured sleepily, "that it all has to be destroyed."

CHAPTER 3

C lara hesitated outside the closed door. Should she knock? Or should she let Vidal continue working undisturbed?

"Is there any more olive oil?"

Clara turned. Her daughter-in-law, Joanna, stood before her, holding an empty bottle of olive oil in her hand like she was a prosecuting attorney presenting a piece of evidence at a trial.

"Did you look in the pantry?"

"Yes."

Clara wished she could look her very smart and always so organized daughter-in-law straight in the eye and say, with dignified self-assurance, "Well, my dear, if that bottle is empty and there aren't any more bottles in the pantry, then of course there isn't any more olive oil." Instead, she averted her glance to some vague spot halfway down the hall and mumbled, "I guess I've run out."

Joanna gave a loud knock on Vidal's closed door. "Lunch is ready. We're waiting for you." Joanna returned to the kitchen, where the rest of the family was gathered.

Clara still wasn't used to having such a crowd every day for lunch, which was the main meal of the day in their farming community. Before her mother had passed away — was it really just two weeks ago? — her father and Uncle Pau and Uncle Biel had gone to her mother's house for lunch. Her husband and Arnau came to her home to eat, but Joanna had stayed home to be with Manel. Vidal, of course, was still in New York. Once she invited her father to eat at her house, she had to extend the invitation to her uncles, who were also widowers. And once the rest of the family was gathered around her kitchen table, it didn't seem right to leave out Joanna and Manel. So instead of having to prepare a full meal for just three people, she had to prepare enough food for nine, and so was it any wonder if she ran out of something — like olive oil — every now and then?

"Why are you standing in the hallway, Mama?"

Clara turned again, this time to look at her son Vidal. The house had been so topsy-turvy during the past two weeks that she hadn't had a chance to have a real talk with her son. But that wasn't why she was standing in the hallway, and so she said, "If you're in the middle of work, you don't have to stop now. I can put aside some food and heat it up for you later."

"Everyone's in the middle of work. Let's go to the kitchen."

The hearty vegetable soup was eaten in near silence. It did its intended job of taking the edge off everyone's hunger, and after the course was finished, the little group, which still wasn't entirely used to the new routine, began to relax. The salad course was skipped since there wasn't enough olive oil to make a proper dressing. Clara apologized, but everyone assured her that no one cared, a response that for some reason left her feeling more depressed than reassured.

As the chicken cutlets and garlic-roasted potatoes were passed around, Josep asked how things were going in the fields, where the last of the grapes were being harvested. Since not much had changed since the day before, Miquel and the uncles didn't have much to say, other than that the harvest was going as usual. Then it was Miquel's turn to inquire about how things were going at the workshop, where Josep made handcrafted pieces of furniture, assisted by Arnau, who had been forced to relegate his artwork to hobby status once he had a family to support.

Josep also wasn't much of a talker. His main conversations in life were with the planks of wood that entered his workshop as simple, unassuming creatures of nature. With his artist's eye, he could immediately size up each piece of wood's potential and then coax and cajole the inert matter until it revealed its true essence and emerged as an object of exquisite beauty. His work graced the homes of some of Catalonia's more discerning admirers of handcrafted furniture, but he wasn't particularly interested in the commercial aspects of his business. Since he also wasn't particularly interested in finding the words to articulate what went on during the creative process, he didn't have much to say in response to Miquel's question and so he simply said, "Fine."

Josep did think to compliment his wife about the food, and that kept the conversation going for a few minutes as everyone told Clara how delicious the meal was. Then there was another short silence, while Clara and Joanna cleared the dishes. Finally, the fruit bowl appeared and made the rounds while Clara poured out the freshly brewed coffee, which was drunk black and with several heaping teaspoons of sugar. Miquel, coffee cup in hand, settled back in his chair and cast a contented eye on his younger grandson.

"Well, Vidal?"

"Yes, Grandpa?"

"When are we going to hear about this business plan of yours?"

"I've almost finished reconstructing all the slides."

"It's too bad your computer crashed and you lost all the data," said Clara.

"If you'd made a backup," said Arnau, "it wouldn't have happened."

"And since when does my brother the artist know about computers?"

"Arnau is thinking about making a website for his paintings," Clara quickly interjected. "That way he can publicize his work without having to leave the village."

"It was once common for people to believe that a website is the answer to all of one's marketing problems." Vidal commented, professorially. "However, research during the past decade has shown that such thinking is flawed. A website is just one marketing tool of many, and it can never entirely replace traditional practices such as advertising, a public relations campaign, and getting out and meeting one's potential customers."

"We're not interested in Arnau's marketing problems," said Uncle Biel. "We want to hear about your plan."

Joanna tapped her teaspoon against the inside of her coffee cup.

"What Uncle Biel means," Clara interjected a second time, "is that we are interested in helping Arnau sell his paintings, but at the moment..."

"We know what Uncle Biel means, Mama," said Arnau. "There's no need to explain."

"Did I say something wrong?" Uncle Biel asked his brother Pau. Since Biel was a little deaf, he often spoke more loudly than was necessary and his whispered question was heard by everyone at the table.

"Oh, do be quiet, Biel," said Uncle Pau.

27

"What did I say?" Uncle Biel persisted.

"Sssh," Uncle Pau whispered, equally persistent as he pushed the fruit bowl in Biel's direction. "Have another apple."

Uncle Biel humbly accepted the chastisement and took an apple from the fruit bowl. For a few moments, the sound of his crunching filled the room. Then Miquel tried to steer the conversation back on course, by saying, "We can understand, Vidal, why you'd want to put on a big show when you present your idea to the rest of the village. But we're family. You don't need to impress us. Just tell us what you've come up with, in simple words for simple folk."

"I'm sorry, Grandpa, but it's not a question of impressing people. It's a question of presenting the argument logically and coherently, so that everyone will understand the issues involved."

"Which are?"

"One, what the problem is. Two, what the available options are for solving that problem. And three, the reason why my plan is the best solution."

"Will there be a test at the end of the presentation?" asked Joanna.

"I think everyone in this room understands the problem," said Miquel, ignoring Joanna's comment. "The young people want jobs. Good jobs."

"They aren't content with farming a small plot of land anymore," added Uncle Pau.

"What you say is true," said Vidal, "on a superficial level."

Miquel and Pau exchanged a quick glance. Then Miquel asked, "What do you mean, 'superficial'?"

"This is exactly why I need to introduce the plan in a formal presentation. So that everyone will be able to follow the argument from Point A to Point Z. At the end, people will be able to ask as many questions as they like. All I'm asking for is the opportunity to present the plan in the way that I feel is best."

"All right, Vidal. You win. But how much more time do you need?"

"I can be ready in two days."

"Fine. Your uncles and I will let everyone know."

Two days later, Vidal carefully placed his notes and slides into his briefcase, checked his appearance in the mirror one last time, and drove over to the square, where his family and the rest of the village were already gathering. He couldn't have asked for a more perfect night. A refreshing breeze meandered across the valley, bringing with it the first hints of autumn. Overhead, a nearly full harvest moon cast its benevolent glow upon the little village, which was looking unusually festive for an ordinary weeknight thanks to a string of colored lights strung around the square — a last-minute suggestion of Grandpa Miquel. Another one of Miquel's suggestions had been to have Clara phone all the ladies and invite them to bring along one of their favorite desserts to share with their neighbors and friends. "There's nothing like a piece of homemade chocolate cake to sweeten the mood," Miquel had explained to Vidal, who readily gave his assent to the suggestion.

"But, Papa, all the ladies are busy enough cooking and baking for the holiday," Clara had protested.

"If they're already in the kitchen, one more cake won't make any difference."

Miquel had been right about the women in the village, who happily agreed to make a contribution. He was also right about the dessert table. It made a natural welcoming point, and people gladly accepted the invitation to admire, and sample, the cakes and pastries and other delights.

As Vidal stood at the far end of the square and watched the scene, he smiled with satisfaction He was also pleased by his own contributions to the evening. Earlier that day he had recruited several of the village's teenage boys and turned the assembled group into an enthusiastic team of workers. After evaluating their various talents and capabilities, he had instructed some of them to build a small stage from discarded pieces of wood from his father's workshop, while others were sent scavenging around the village for metal folding chairs, plastic garden chairs, and wooden benches. A young man with electrical knowledge went with Vidal to his grandfather's home, where an overhead projector and screen were stored, and helped him transfer the equipment to the square and set it up. By the end of the afternoon, under his leadership and management, the square had been transformed into a passable outdoor auditorium.

Assemble, lead, manage. Those were top-notch action words for writing a successful business resume. But on this night Vidal had bigger dreams than that. In a few minutes he would present his plan for the development of Sant Joan Januz, the first major step of his business career. True, that milestone wasn't going to take place in the plush offices of some billion-dollar multinational corporation. Yet Vidal had read enough biographies of successful businessmen during the past two years to know that best sellers were made of stories exactly like this — humorously charming anecdotes about a person's humble beginnings. And nothing could be humbler than this little square with its twinkling colored lights, hodgepodge of mismatched seats, slightly sloping wooden stage, and yellowing fabric screen that had a slight tear in the lower right-hand corner.

A burst of laughter returned his thoughts to the present. A few farmers were speaking with his grandfather, and the laughter had come from their little circle. Vidal noted that his grandfather was going all out in playing the role of amiable host. For that's what Miquel was doing, as he greeted this one with a cheerful inquiry about the harvest and that one with a hearty congratulations on a new grandchild or tractor. It was a performance that no one else in his family could have pulled off with such casual aplomb, and Vidal was grateful. He knew that his grandfather was still grieving over the loss of Grandma Anna. The show of conviviality could be due to only one thing: love for him, his grandson.

Miquel spotted Vidal standing in the shadows and waved. He made his way through the crowd, patting neighbors on the back and shaking hands, and walked over to where Vidal was waiting.

"I've warmed up the crowd," Miquel said with a reassuring smile. "They're all yours."

CHAPTER 4

B eginnings are always the hardest, but apparently no one ever mentioned that fact to Miquel, who had volunteered to give the evening's opening remarks. Vidal was certain that his grandfather had never taken a course in public speaking or read any books on the subject, yet Miquel was relaxed as a seasoned politician. He started with a good story that ended with a reasonably funny punch line, and the crowd good-humoredly laughed in response. Having accomplished his mission of putting the audience at ease, Miquel seamlessly switched gears and proceeded to make a smooth transition to the main event of the evening, Vidal's presentation.

"Now as most of you know, two years ago my grandson Vidal also set off for the New World. But unlike Christopher Columbus, he knew where he was going, which was a good thing, because..."

While his grandfather talked, Vidal allowed himself a quick look at the audience. There was a good turnout, and he could see that the people were smiling, reflecting back the smile that was on his grandfather's relaxed face. "Smile!" he hastily scribbled at the top of each page of his notes.

"...And because I know that you're all anxious to hear what he has to say, I'm now going to turn over the microphone to Vidal. Vidal?"

Polite applause accompanied Vidal as he walked over to the podium. Unlike his grandfather, Vidal wasn't a natural when it came to speaking before a crowd, though he had worked hard to acquire the skill. While he straightened the pages of his notes, which didn't really need straightening, he put into practice what he had learned at business school. *Plant your feet firmly on the ground,* he silently intoned as he shifted his weight so that it was perfectly balanced between his two feet. *Take a deep breath. Let out the deep breath. Look at the audience. Nod to a few of the people. And...what else?* He glanced down at his notes. *Smile.*

Vidal smiled, took another deep breath, and plunged in.

31

"Friends, we all know why we're here this evening. Sant Joan Januz, the village where many of us were born, and which all of us love, is dying. I apologize if my diagnosis of the problem sounds blunt, but I don't have to tell you what happens after our young people graduate from high school. They go off to a university in Girona or Barcelona, and most of them don't come back. If this trend continues, in another decade there will no longer be a Sant Joan Januz. So if we want to keep our village alive, we must act now, while there is still a village left to save."

"Here! Here!" Miquel called out and clapped his hands.

A few others followed Miquel's lead and clapped their hands, as well. Vidal acknowledged the show of support. Though it was obvious that the support had been manufactured by his grandfather, what was important was that the ice had been broken and he hadn't fallen through it. He took another deep breath and went on.

"Yet how can it be, I ask you, that Sant Joan Januz is dying? Our village is located in the province of Girona, one of the richest provinces of Catalonia, and Catalonia is the wealthiest region in Spain. Practically every other city and town in Catalonia is experiencing a period of unprecedented prosperity. Why is this prosperity passing us by?

"I know what many of you are thinking. You're saying to yourselves, 'It's because we don't have more jobs.' You're thinking that if we only had a factory or a packing plant, all our problems would be solved. The young people would stay put, and life would go on as before. But I would like to challenge that assumption for just a moment and ask you to consider a new thought: Our problem isn't that we don't have more jobs. Our problem is that we don't have more dreams.

"I can already hear your objections. You're thinking that the people of Sant Joan Januz are simple, hardworking folk who don't have time to waste on something as frivolous as a dream. And maybe that was true for the older generation. I don't know. But what I do know is that young people today need more than a job and a paycheck. They have a need to make their mark on the world, to use their talents to the fullest, and to feel that they are a part of something that is noble and inspiring and worthwhile. It is a longing of the soul, which is just as real as a longing for food and shelter.

32

"Unfortunately, Sant Joan Januz doesn't fulfill that need. Our village floats through time without any vision or purpose or meaningful connection to the outside world. But when a village just drifts along, is it any wonder that so many of its young people drift away?"

In his notes Vidal had written, "Pause here," and so he paused there. He stole a quick glance at the assembled crowd to see what sort of effect his words were having. He had to admit that some of the people were looking bored. But some — and not just his grandfather — were thoughtfully nodding their heads in agreement. It was a start. He only needed a few key families to support his plan and the rest would follow. He took another deep breath and forged ahead.

"What can help us regain a sense of purpose? Is there a business venture out there that can provide us with an inspiring vision for the future? I believe there is. But before I tell you what it is, let's take a look at Sant Joan Januz's unique strengths and weaknesses to better understand how we got into this state and what we need to do to pull ourselves out of it."

Vidal switched on the overhead projector, which was at least thirty years old. That afternoon he had tested the projector several times, and it had worked. But at this crucial moment the machine's motor refused to obey. It sputtered and whined, as though it was deeply aggrieved at being wakened from its slumber yet another time that decade.

Although he didn't show it, Vidal was displeased by this display of lazy insubordination. After all, sending an electric current to one light bulb located under the projector's glass plate wasn't exactly a demanding task. But there was nothing he could do, even though he was a promising young executive who knew how to assemble, manage, and lead a team. Unlike the teenagers he had led that morning, who had positively responded to his words of encouragement and promises of a free lunch, a machine couldn't be coaxed or bribed into becoming a team player.

The audience waited patiently while Vidal fiddled with the projector's knobs and wires. They were farmers, for the most part, and a broken piece of machinery was an accepted part of life. Only one person in the audience seemed to be disturbed by the unexpected glitch.

33

"Do you think you should help Vidal fix the projector, Papa?" asked Clara.

"He looks like he's got the situation under control," Miquel replied with a touch of pride. "Vidal's not the type of person to let some malfunctioning piece of machinery throw him off balance."

"But this is supposed to be his big night," Clara protested.

"Which is why it will do more harm than good if I leap up on that stage and take control."

"If he wants help, he'll ask for it," Josep added.

Clara sank back in her chair and closed her eyes. She told herself that her father and husband were right. There was nothing to worry about. In just a few minutes everything would work out for the best. Either Vidal would fix the projector or he would ask her father for help. There was nothing to worry about. Really. Vidal wasn't in any danger. There was no connection at all between her son standing on a stage and what had happened to her when she was a child. There was absolutely no reason for her hands to turn cold and clammy, just as that queasy feeling in her stomach was totally uncalled for. As for the pounding of her heart and the feeling that she couldn't catch her breath, it went without saying that extreme reactions such as these were completely unwarranted.

She stealthily wiped away the beads of perspiration that had popped out on her forehead, hoping that no one was aware of her mounting anxiety. It was ridiculous to let some vague memory floating around in her head have such a power over her emotions. At least she hadn't passed on these fears to her children. But she wished Vidal would fix the projector already so that the presentation could continue and drown out the little drama that was currently playing before her closed eyes.

She was a small child, in the first grade of the regional school that served all the farming communities in the area. Her teacher had chosen her to sing a solo in the school play, and she decided to keep it a secret from her mother so that she could surprise her. When the big day arrived, Clara stood on a stage, just as Vidal was standing now. Clara had thought her mother would be proud of her for being chosen, for being singled out, but after the performance her mother gave her a sharp slap on the face.

"Never attract attention again," her mother said sternly. "Never do anything that will make you stand out from the others. It's dangerous. Understand?"

Clara didn't understand. What could be dangerous about appearing in a school play? She wanted to protest that it wasn't fair of her mother to get angry. Any other mother would have been proud. But when she looked up, Clara was surprised to see that there wasn't a trace of anger in her mother's eyes. All she could see was terror.

As Clara got older, the list of "nevers" got longer. There were also plenty of "don'ts," but a "don't" was different than a "never."

"Don't go out to play until you finish your homework." "Don't wipe your mouth with your sleeve." "Don't imitate the way your teacher talks."

When her mother would say these things, she was calm. Sometimes her mother would even hide a smile when she said them. That never happened with a "never."

"Never leave a lit candle by a window."

"Never make fun of a priest."

"Never let a stranger come into the kitchen."

When her mother rebuked Clara with a "never," she would get all tense and rigid. Later, after her mother returned to her usual self, Clara would try, unsuccessfully, to pry an explanation from her mother's sealed lips. All her mother would say was, "Someday you'll understand, when you're grown up. In the meantime, keep your eyes open, Clara, all the time. Even a little piece of wire strung across the path can make a person stumble and fall."

For a while, Clara did keep her eyes firmly fixed on the ground, always on the lookout for that elusive piece of wire. When it failed to materialize, she gradually lost interest and forgot about it. Yet, without her being aware of it, her mother's words had entered into her internal landscape, where her inner eye remained at its post, always on the lookout, always expecting the worst, always anticipating the sudden appearance of some unspecified yet very palpable dread.

Josep glanced over at Clara. He saw that she was growing paler with each passing second. This wasn't the first time she had experienced a panic attack, and even though he had never been able to understand what caused his wife's distress, he recognized the signs.

35

"Breathe, Clara," Josep said quietly. "Take a few deep breaths and it will pass."

Clara heard Josep's words, and she wanted to be reassured by them. She had hoped that the terror would depart from her world after her mother passed away. When Vidal announced that he wanted to present his business plan in the village's square and make a big public event out of it, she had wanted to say to her son, "Stand out. Succeed. Attract all the attention in the world."

She couldn't get the words out of her mouth. She was too much her mother's child. She didn't try to stop him and she kept her worries to herself, but now those worries were tumbling out, indistinct and impossible to name, yet all the more terrifying because of their vagueness.

Breathe. It will pass, she silently told herself. But there was another voice inside her that insisted on having its say. "It will never pass," the familiar voice whispered. "Never."

After a few minutes of pretending that he knew how to fix the projector, Vidal admitted defeat and switched it off. He decided that if corny jokes worked for his grandfather, he would try the same tactic to get him out of his predicament.

"Friends, my intuition tells me that you're all wondering the same thing. How many business school graduates does it take to change the light bulb of an overhead projector?"

The crowd laughed, exactly on cue.

"Since I happen to be one of those graduates, I can tell you the answer: none. Business school graduates never do any actual work themselves. They hire other people to do the job for them. Mr. Garcia, are you sitting out there?"

Eduard Garcia owned the village's general store, a combination grocery and hardware store. Because he enjoyed the challenge of repairing things more than he enjoyed selling boxes of cereal, he kept his store stocked with just about anything that a handyman might need. Vidal's grandfather was one of his best customers, thanks to Miquel's own love of fixing things. But the relationship between the two men wasn't just that of a buyer and seller. They had been good friends for years.

Vidal had often accompanied his grandfather to the general store as a child. Eduard Garcia would invite the two of them into the store's back room, where all sorts of interesting things were stored. He would then lead Vidal to four wooden kegs that sat against the room's far wall. One keg was filled with candy, one was filled nails, and one was filled with dried beans. Eduard Garcia would tell him, in a very serious tone of voice, that he could put his hand into whichever keg he wanted — the candy or the nails or the beans — and take out a handful to enjoy while the grown-ups talked. Naturally, he would always choose the candy, although he did often wonder what was in the fourth keg — the one that Eduard Garcia never opened.

For all these reasons, Vidal knew that he could count on Eduard Garcia to come to the rescue. Of course, his grandfather could have fixed the projector, but Vidal had quickly calculated that asking the store owner for help was the smarter move. He knew that the village viewed him as "Miquel's grandson," rather than a person and a future community leader in his own right. Although he hadn't minded receiving assistance from his grandfather to get the evening off on the right foot, he didn't want it to appear that he needed his grandfather to help him out every step of the way.

"How much are you going to pay me to fix that old contraption of your grandfather's?" Eduard Garcia called out in reply.

"We'll discuss that in your office," Vidal answered.

Despite the feebleness of the joke everyone laughed again, a fact that Vidal noted with satisfaction.

The recalcitrant piece of machinery was no match for Eduard Garcia, who quickly discovered the problem and repaired it. After giving a few final groans of protest, the projector resigned itself to its fate. The light switched on and the crowd applauded. Eduard took a little bow and then returned to his seat.

Vidal picked up the first of the transparent slides he had prepared for the presentation. Only one word was written on it. After two years of intensively studying Sant Joan Januz, he strongly believed that this word said it all. Contained within its nine letters were both the village's problem and the solution. It also contained within its nine letters a mystery that he had not been able to solve. But that would have to wait.

"As I was saying earlier, before we can evaluate any proposed solution to our village's problem, we first have to understand our strengths and weaknesses. And I believe that both can be summed up in one word, which is..."

Vidal placed the slide on the illuminated glass, and the projector bounced the word up onto the yellowing screen behind him.

"Location."

Vidal paused, and not because his notes instructed him to do so. He had rehearsed his presentation many times, and every time he did so this one word, floating in a sea of white space, took his breath away. To him, the word's very form suggested a long and elegant tall ship sailing to some unknown destination. It was like a little world, full of mystery and complete unto itself, and yet waiting for some worthy and intrepid navigator to take command so it could share its secrets.

Some philosophers might posit that man's most basic question, when embarking upon the voyage of self-discovery, was, "Who am I?" Once that question was answered, the rest would follow. But after two years of thinking deeply about the matter of identity, whether it was the identity of an individual or a village like Sant Joan Januz, Vidal dared to disagree. The real first question of existence, he now believed, was "Where am I?" But he was getting distracted, and this wasn't the time for philosophical musings.

"There's a popular saying that only three things matter in the real estate business: location, location, location. So let's take a look at the connection between location and prosperity in Catalonia and see how it relates to our little village."

Vidal removed the first slide and replaced it with the next one, which said:

TOURISM

1950s: Hollywood discovers the Costa Brava.
1960s: The packaged tour is born.
1990s and beyond: The return of the luxury traveler.

The audience didn't need to be reminded that Catalonia's tourist industry was a hen that lay golden eggs to the tune of more than nine billion dollars a year. The industry had totally transformed the Costa Brava, which once upon a time had been a quiet strip of coastline dotted with sleepy fishing villages. Yet it wasn't just the Costa Brava's resorts that were raking in the money. The Catalan countryside had an ample supply of small towns that had preserved their medieval character. Former castles and well-preserved farmhouses were now enjoying a second life as upscale retreats for the wealthy tourist who didn't mind paying a small fortune to get away from the cares that enabled him to travel through life first class.

"And where was Sant Joan Januz while all this money was pouring into the Costa Brava?" Vidal asked the audience. "It was sitting here, in this valley, miles and miles away from the nearest beach.

"And where are our historic places? If anyone out there has a map that says where these treasures are buried, I wish you'd share it with us. But the truth is that we don't have a castle, or a deserted monastery. We don't even have a Romanesque church, which is amazing, really, because every village in Catalonia has a Romanesque church, or at least the ruins of one. So in addition to the inconvenience to our souls..."

That remark got a chuckle from the crowd, as Vidal knew it would. The villagers of Sant Joan Januz didn't have much use for religion, or at least the official religion of the Catholic Church. As farmers, their eyes were constantly looking upward, and they weren't ashamed to say a few words to their Father in heaven when the weather was misbehaving. A serious illness also called for a few private words with the Creator. But they had no need for formalized rites, or a formal place of worship.

"...our pockets are feeling the pain. We can't make money from the tourists interested in seeing historic sites, because there's nothing here to see. But tourism isn't the only industry that can make a village rich, so let's take at look at some of the other industries that have turned Catalonia into the wealthiest region in Spain."

The next slide was labeled "INDUSTRY & TRANSPORTATION," two topics that the people sitting in the audience were familiar with.

The village belonged to an agricultural cooperative that had been set up in the early 1900s, along with other cooperatives in the region. The cooperatives were responsible for organizing the logistics of getting the farmers' crops to the marketplace, amongst other things, and in most places the trucks came into the village to pick up the produce. But things worked differently in Sant Joan Januz.

For as long as most people there could remember, Miquel made the rounds of all the individual farms and then transported the village's produce to a village in another valley, where it was picked up by the cooperative's truck. It was a system that worked well enough for the farmers, but Vidal had discovered a fatal flaw: It allowed the farmers to remain in their own little time warp. Since Miquel didn't mind being jostled as he made his rounds, the farmers of Sant Joan Januz were able to amble down their dirt roads as their ancestors had done before them, and ignore the super-modern transportation infrastructure that was springing up everywhere else in Catalonia.

"Where was Sant Joan Januz when the rest of Catalonia first built its high-speed train tracks and superhighways?" Vidal asked the audience. "It was sitting here in this valley, miles and miles away from the nearest railway station or even a four-lane road. And where are we today, when Spain is building its brand-new high-speed railway system, the one that will connect Spain with the rest of Europe?"

Vidal didn't have to answer his question. The new trains, which promised to travel at lightning-fast speeds, had been written up in the local newspapers more than once. Everyone knew that they were coming — and that they weren't coming to Sant Joan Januz.

"But our remoteness doesn't just affect our ability to transport goods," Vidal continued. "It has other consequences. New industries are being developed in Catalonia, such as biotechnology and biomedical research. As I speak, our government is creating something called a 'bioregion,' a centralized location for all these new industries. But it's being built in Barcelona, and not in Sant Joan Januz, and the reason for that decision is simple. A big city like Barcelona has universities and hospitals and research centers, and we don't. So, my friends, we have to face the facts. We sit surrounded by a sea of wealth, but because of our location there isn't a single drop for us to drink."

What Vidal didn't mention were his private thoughts about Sant Joan Januz. The more he studied the mystery of the village's location, the more it seemed to him that his ancestors had

40

purposely looked for the most isolated spot in Catalonia that they could find. Why would they have done such a thing? He had spent countless hours pondering that question, but the answer refused to reveal itself. He had decided to pose the question to his Grandma Anna when he returned to Catalonia. Everyone considered her to be the matriarch of Sant Joan Januz, and so Vidal assumed that she would be able to tell him about the village's history. Unfortunately, his interest in the past had been kindled too late.

"So this is our weakness," he continued. "Earlier, though, I mentioned that our location is also our greatest strength. How can that be? you're all probably wondering."

Joanna glanced at her watch. She was bored. She also had better things to do, such as prepare for an important job interview in Girona that was coming up soon.

Before she married, she had worked for a former professor of hers at the University of Girona, where Joanna had received a bachelor's degree in history. Like many of the young people that Vidal had mentioned in his presentation, she had intended to stay in Girona after completing her studies. That all changed after a visit back to Sant Joan Januz.

Her parents had asked her to come back to the village to "meet" Arnau Bonet. Since they had both grown up in Sant Joan Januz and were around the same age, they hardly needed an introduction. But she knew as well as everyone else in the village the true purpose of such meetings.

She had been sure that nothing would come of it. To her surprise, she discovered that the years had changed him, or perhaps her, or perhaps both of them, and they now had much in common. Once that fact was established, the two families moved quickly to steer the two young people to the mutually desired outcome. After the wedding, she continued to commute to her job in Girona, but that came to an end when Manel was born.

To please her husband, she agreed to stay at home until Manel went off to kindergarten. Though she often felt stifled by life — or rather the lack of life — in the village, she tried not to complain. What bothered her more than the boredom was the way Arnau's family refused to recognize his talent. He, too, was being stifled. So when she received a phone call from her former professor, who had switched jobs and was looking for an assistant, she listened with interest.

"This project is a wonderful opportunity for both of us," said the professor. "When does Manel start kindergarten?"

"Next year."

"Twelve more months in Sant Joan Garraf ? I don't know how you do it and stay sane."

"It's Sant Joan Januz, and I've already reached the half-crazy point, so now my goal is maintenance."

"Joanna, why don't you come into town one afternoon next week? I'll check out the day-care centers here in Girona. There must be a way to make this work for all of us."

The mention of a day care center in Girona gave Joanna new hope. Lots of children went to day-care centers. Some educators even said that children who went to preschool were better prepared for regular school than children who stayed at home. And the fact that the tradition of Sant Joan Januz was for young mothers to stay at home didn't mean a thing. Most of the young people left the village before they married and started a family. Only she had been foolish enough to come back.

Joanna glanced over at Arnau, who also looked bored. "Why don't we leave?" she whispered.

"We can't."

"I can pretend that the baby-sitter called and we have to go home."

"We can't."

"Sssh!" Uncle Pau, who was sitting in front of them, beside Uncle Biel, turned around and motioned toward the stage, where Vidal had already placed the next slide on the overhead projector.

Joanna stopped talking, but her thoughts were not so easily hushed. "We can leave," she wanted to say to Arnau. Then she added a thought for herself. *And we will.*

Vidal had arrived at the crucial point of the evening. Up until then, no one could really disagree with the main thrust of his argument. There were, though, a few people in the audience who had a different opinion as to the cause of the village's stagnation. One of those people was Luis Adarra, Joanna's father. The real problem, in his view, was something else that Vidal had mentioned, but glossed over: a lack of vision.

As far as Luis was concerned, if the village was in trouble a person didn't have to go to business school in New York to find out where to place the blame. The fault lay right at home, with the village's leaders, which happened to be Vidal's family. They had run Sant Joan Januz for as long as anyone could remember. Forty years earlier, for instance, Luis had tried to start an electronics factory in the village. His plan had been opposed by the ruling triumvirate of Miquel, Pau, and Biel. The old-timers in the village sided with them. Once that happened, just about everyone else followed suit, and the factory was voted down. Luis went back to helping his father in the fields.

There had been hard feelings on Luis's part, but the passing years softened them. Whenever something needed repairing at the Adarra home, Miquel was there to lend a hand. His wife, Anna, always sent over a cake before the holidays. It was hard to hold on to a grudge. Years later, when Luis's two sons left the village to find work in faraway cities, the repressed anger bubbled up again, but it subsided after a match was suggested between his daughter Joanna and one of Miquel's grandsons. At least Luis would see some of his grandchildren grow up. The Bonet boys weren't about to leave Sant Joan Januz, where they were the designated crown princes, for a place where they would be treated just like everyone else.

While Luis was preoccupied with his thoughts about the past, Vidal was forging on with his plan for the future. The slide projected onto the screen listed a series of paired words that showed how an apparent negative could be turned into a perceived strength:

Remote — Pollution-free
Isolated — Quiet
Small — Accessible
Unexciting — Peaceful

"Peaceful." Vidal lingered on the word. "Before I left Sant Joan Januz, I didn't appreciate what a precious commodity peace is. But after living in New York City for two years, I can tell you that people crave peace, and they're willing to spend good money to obtain even a little bit of it.

"But when I say peace, I'm not talking only about peace and quiet, although fulfilling that need is certainly part of my plan. What I would like you to do is to think bigger, for just a few moments, and follow me, as I lead you on a journey to an entirely new vision of what Sant Joan Januz can offer the world. Yes, you heard me correctly. The world."

A photograph of the Earth suspended in outer space appeared on the screen.

While preparing for the presentation back in his dorm room in New York, Vidal had debated whether or not to include this slide. Everyone had seen this "blue marble" photograph of the Earth many times, and perhaps the image had become trite. As always, he consulted with his roommate, a young man from Saudi Arabia named Talal. Since the Americans couldn't pronounce that name without giggling, Talal went by Al instead. By either name, Vidal considered his roommate to be a gift from heaven.

Although the Saudi family's serious wealth came from oil, Al's father was a highly successful real estate developer who specialized in building high-end resorts. Al had worked with his father for a few years before attending business school, and so he already had some solid experience in the tourism industry. From the beginning, Al had willingly shared his knowledge with his inexperienced roommate, and the two had spent countless hours analyzing every detail of Sant Joan Januz and Vidal's presentation.

By the end of their second year of business school, Al was practically as familiar with Catalonia and the village as Vidal, who scrupulously wrote down each of his mentor's suggestions in the margins of his notes.

"Include the photograph," said Al. "When your village accepts your plan, it will be a historic moment, like when Neil Armstrong landed on the moon. I can see the headlines now: One small step for mankind; one giant leap for Sant Joan Januz."

Vidal laughed. Al was always coming up with funny comments, which despite their humor always had a grain of truth in them. When Vidal considered the matter, it did seem to him that sending a spaceship to the moon was in some ways easier than the job he had before him. The whole country had been behind the United States' space program. All the scientists had needed to do was work out the technical details. He, on the other hand, had to get his entire village to change their way of thinking.

"And that will require a giant leap on their part," Vidal commented morosely.

"It was a joke," Al chided. "Don't take everything I say so seriously."

"When your father is a billionaire, it's easy to laugh."

"I keep telling you, Vidal, we're going to make you a billionaire, too. So cheer up."

"The photograph stays in?"

"But only for three seconds. Then move on to the next slide."

Vidal could still hear Al's instructions ringing in his ears, though his former roommate was now half a planet away. When the three seconds were up — Vidal knew, because he counted — he removed the photograph of the Earth and pulled out the next slide from the folder. He was entering the do-or-die mode.

"My friends," he said as he placed the slide on the glass plate of the projector, "welcome to Peaceland, a whole new concept in global tourism."

Vidal knew that quite a few eyebrows were being raised in the village's little square at that moment, a natural reaction since probably no one in the audience had ever heard of "peace tourism." Despite its newness, Vidal's research had shown that peace tourism was already being successfully implemented in several parts of the world. More to the point, it was also generating nice profits.

"The idea," Vidal explained, "is as simple as it is powerful. People have a need to relax. People have a desire to make the world a better place. Build a vacation resort and create activities that will satisfy both of these needs and you will attract wealthy and socially responsible tourists from both Europe and the United States.

"But what does Sant Joan Januz have to offer the wealthy person who wants to make the world a better place, you might wonder? Again, the answer is as simple as it is powerful: we can help bring peace to the Middle East."

"Sure, it's a gamble," Al had replied in answer to Vidal's hesitations. "But people can't think big when they're still a little

45

chick trapped inside a shell. First you have to crack open the shell — with a hammer if that's what it takes."

"But bringing peace to the Middle East? Isn't that a little ambitious for a farming village?"

"Not at all. Spain has something no other country in the world ever had — La Convivencia, the Coexistence — that great period in history when Muslims, Jews, and Christians lived together in perfect harmony."

"It wasn't so perfect."

"Vidal, if you want to quibble over historical details become a history professor. But if you want to make a fortune in tourism, you have to sell the dream. La Convivencia lasted from the 700s until 1492. Of course there were disagreements from time to time. But your Peaceland resort is going to be about the positive. It's going to recreate the atmosphere when people from these three religions did get along — when they put their brains and pocketbooks together to conquer the seas and establish a new world ruled by the principles of respect, tolerance, and liberty for all."

"Columbus wasn't interested in any of that, and neither were Ferdinand and Isabella. They all just wanted to get rich."

"And if you want to get rich, you'll listen to what I'm telling you: focus on the positive. So what if Ferdinand and Isabella were some of the most intolerant people ever put on this planet? G-d had other plans for that little continent that Columbus discovered. It was His will to create a haven of tolerance and peaceful coexistence, and that's what you should focus on in this peace village you're going to build."

"Okay, so let's say I do what your father suggests. I build a museum in Sant Joan Januz that's about this time in history when there was coexistence, and I organize workshops in art and music so that the visitors can create their own little works of art on the topic of peace. And there are tours to the religious sites — the Jewish quarter in Girona, the Moorish castle in Tortosa, and the monastery in Montserrat..."

"Don't forget about the relaxation component: An afternoon at the Costa Brava to swim in the sea, horseback riding and cycling in the Catalan countryside..."

"And shopping. No, I haven't forgotten the relaxation component. But I still don't see what all this has to do with bringing peace to the Middle East."

"That's because you've forgotten about the lectures," said Al. " 'Visions of Peace as Brought Down by the World's Great Religions.' 'How to Create Connections between Diverse Communities.' 'Ten Steps to Inner Peace.' The peace lectures are an integral component of the vacation package."

"But how does talking about peace create peace, especially when the talking is being done in Catalonia and the fighting is being done in the Middle East?"

"*Tracht gut vet zein gut.*"

"What?"

" 'Think good, and it will be good.' It's a Yiddish saying. I think some big rabbi said it."

"How do you know Yiddish, Al?"

"If you want to succeed in the international business world, a Yiddish phrase book will be one of the wisest investments you'll ever make. When Jews hear an Arab speak Yiddish, they go wild. It will be the same with you. And this 'think good and it will be good' mantra is powerful. It really works."

"You mean I'm supposed to tell all these CEOs and Harvard Business School graduates that if they sit in a circle and meditate on the word peace, they'll actually be doing something to change the world?"

"Look, Vidal, between you and me, seriously wealthy people may like to think that they're interested in saving the world, but they aren't interested in sleeping on a lumpy mattress or eating lousy food for anything, not even an ideal, and they're certainly not going to risk their lives for one. So they're not going to use their vacation time to rough it in a refugee camp in Gaza or spend the night in a bomb shelter in Sderot to find out what's really going on in the Middle East. You, however, will be offering them the opportunity to make a positive contribution to world peace while relaxing in the sort of luxury accommodations they are accustomed to staying in whenever they travel around our troubled little planet. My father is an expert in building these places."

"I know what your father is going to contribute to the project. What's my contribution to world peace going to be?"

"The copy on the brochure?"

"That's right. The copy on the brochure."

Al thought for a few moments, and then he stood up and fixed his gaze upon an imaginary, but apparently rapt audience. "Explore the land of *La Convivencia* with Peaceland. Gain new insights into the positive, peace-building aspects of the world's three great religions. Learn how to build bridges — peace bridges — between diverse peoples and cultures. And discover how these tools can be used to build a model for peace in the Middle East."

"You really think that these people will work to build bridges between the Palestinian and Israeli people after they return home?"

"What they do when they return home is up to them. But this isn't a scam. If your Peaceland can teach people to think good — to think positively about others — then you will have done something good. You will have done something good for the world and for world peace."

"So by teaching people to think good — to think positively about others — our little village of Sant Joan Januz won't be just another player in the already overly crowded field of international tourism. Our village will be a unique vessel for exploring a new world: a world called Peaceland."

Vidal had come to the end of his presentation. He knew to wait a few moments to let his final words sink in. Yet there was something unsettling about the silence coming from the other side of the little stage. No one coughed. Not a single chair creaked. It was just very, very quiet.

Think good and it will be good, Vidal silently intoned. Silence wasn't necessarily a bad thing, especially not if it meant that the audience was thinking about what he said. After all, it took time to absorb any new idea, even a good one. He waited a few more moments. Then, forcing a smile onto his face, he looked into the darkness and asked, "Any questions?"

CHAPTER 5

T ime is a curious traveler. It leaps and creeps at will, sometimes dashing ahead with dizzying haste while other times dawdling at a speed that would make a snail lose its patience. Vidal had spent two whole years analyzing in detail every tract of land and quirky custom of his tiny village. He had spent countless hours agonizing over every image and word of his presentation. Yet now that it was over, the time he had spent in New York seemed to have passed as quickly as the blink of a firefly. On the other hand, as he stood on the stage in Sant Joan Januz and listened to the silence, each second seemed to crawl by like a wounded elephant — heavy, awkward, and too large to ignore.

"Are there any questions?" Vidal asked again. Even an objection would have been preferable to the hush that had settled over the square. Or so he thought, until he saw the half-shadowed figure of a man rise shakily to his feet. Like an elderly knight of old preparing his worn but still lethal lance for battle, this aged but still imposing figure thrust his outstretched arm toward Vidal and angrily shook his tightly clenched fist.

"Questions?! There's just one question that concerns me, young man. Have you gone mad?"

Vidal turned white, but he was too stunned to know what pierced him more: the stinging words, or the fact that the words had been hurled at him by his grandfather. The crowd was also surprised by this unexpected turn of events. There was no mistaking the fact that Miquel was angry — very angry, almost crazily angry, practically-ready-to-explode angry. And so even if there had been many questions just a second before, there now was only one: what was going to happen next?

Vidal tried to think of something to say, some light and easy reply that would defuse the situation, but Miquel's accusation was uncharted territory. Vidal and his roommate had come up with dozens of questions the villagers might ask about the plan, but they were questions of a technical nature: questions about financing the project, projected income, and so forth. They had never discussed the possibility that someone — and certainly not his grandfather, of all people — would angrily accuse Vidal of being insane.

Although Vidal didn't consider himself to be a religious person, he did remember something his grandmother Anna had taught him when he was a small child: There's a G-d in the world. When you're in big trouble, you can ask Him for help. Since Vidal felt himself to be in big trouble, he availed himself of his grandmother's advice and uttered a brief but intense prayer.

I don't want to get into a fight with my grandfather, he silently pleaded. *So please, G-d, give me the right words to say.* To his great relief, the words came to him in an instant. Their truth was so apparent that Vidal instantly relaxed, confident that his prayer had been answered.

"Yes, Grandpa, I have gone mad," Vidal replied with a smile. "But this madness of mine is a good Catalan failing, and it's one that you taught me to admire. It's the madness of Christopher Columbus, who was determined to find a route to the Far East by sailing west, across the sea. It's the madness of our own King Jaume I, who was determined to transform the muddy waters of the Barcelona shoreline into a prosperous international harbor. And it's the madness of all those other kings and explorers you told me about when I was a child, who dared to contradict accepted notions. They discovered new worlds thanks to their hard work and persistence, but also because of what their contemporaries most likely described as their totally mad and improbable dreams."

The words did their work. King Jaume I, the medieval Catalan king who created a Golden Age of culture and prosperity, was a revered figure in Catalonia. Christopher Columbus, although not a native son, was so intertwined with the glory period of Catalonia's history that his name also evoked positive feelings of admiration. By linking his Peaceland project to the deeds of these luminaries, Vidal achieved in an instant what he had failed to accomplish in an hour: credibility, Catalan-style.

Of course, this didn't mean that all objections had vanished into the cool night air. The crowd had plenty of questions, and now that they had awakened from their dazed slumber, the people lined up to voice their concerns. But the danger had passed, and the atmosphere had returned to one of neighborly congeniality, where questions were politely asked and just as courteously answered. For this Vidal was prepared. Indeed, he and Al had prepared information packets for the villagers to take home and peruse at their leisure. And so after half an hour Vidal suggested that the meeting be adjourned and that they would meet again, after the holiday, to discuss the proposal in more detail.

While Vidal was deftly fielding questions, the tall figure standing in the center of the audience reluctantly retook his seat. Clara wanted to say something to her father, but she was too shocked by what had happened to utter a single word. Even if she had been able to speak, it wouldn't have helped. A wall of impenetrable silence stood guard around Miquel, repelling any attempts at communication.

But Miquel's reticence was not the silence of a simple soldier who was embarrassed at having been vanquished in battle. It was the silence of an experienced warrior who had shrewdly sized up the situation and decided that it was better to wait. His pointed barbs would better hit their mark at another time and place.

Clara had never been an early riser, and so she rarely saw the radiant unfolding of a brand-new day. The only reason she saw the sunrise on this particular morning was because she hadn't been able to sleep the night before.

She had tried her usual tricks when insomnia struck, but she was too wound up for them to work. Neither the meandering novel nor the mug of steaming herbal tea could still the rush of emotions that crashed over her taut nerves like waves smashing into a rocky shore. And so, unable to tolerate yet another hour of restless tossing and turning, she decided to put her pent-up energy to good use and wash the house's windows. She hoped that the work would tire her out enough so that she could finally get some rest. Even if it didn't, she would at least have something to show for her night spent in sleepless purgatory.

Sleep continued to elude her as she rubbed the kitchen windows until every last grimy streak surrendered in defeat. While she was tackling a big window in the living room, the first rays of sunlight appeared on the horizon. She stopped her work to watch as the pale light took on a rosy hue. The sight of the quickly

51

changing canvas filled her with mixed feelings. True, the long night was over, but what would the new day bring?

"It will bring what it will bring, Anna. What happens over there isn't for us to decide."

That was the voice of her father speaking, but a much younger Miquel, when Clara was a little girl.

"But all those innocent people. They're going to be killed." Anna was reading a newspaper and tears were falling from her eyes and onto the page.

"Who's going to be killed, Mama?"

"Clara, what are you doing here?"

"I want a glass of water."

Her mother filled a cup with water and placed it in her hands. "Go back to bed, Clara. Right now."

"Who's going to be killed?"

"Clara, do as your mother says."

Clara had gone to bed, but not to sleep. When all was quiet, she grabbed the little flashlight her great-uncle Manel had given her as a birthday present — he gave it to her just a few months before he passed away — and snuck back down to the kitchen. The newspaper that her mother had been reading was still sitting on the kitchen table. Clara flicked on the light and read the story that occupied a large part of the front page. It was something about a war that might happen in the Middle East. Someone named Gamal Abdel Nasser, who lived in Egypt, was threatening to drive all the Jews who lived in Israel into the sea.

When she had tired of reading the article, Clara carefully refolded the newspaper so that her parents wouldn't suspect that it had been disturbed, and tiptoed back to her bedroom. She agreed that it would be very sad if all the Jews — and especially the little children — had to die. But since she didn't know any of them, she found it hard to be as upset as her mother had been.

"If it was my family, I would cry," she decided as she climbed back into her warm bed. And with that thought she had drifted off to sleep.

But why was she thinking about that now? Clara didn't know, but lately it seemed as though her thoughts had a life of their own. While she had so much to worry about in the present — especially now, when it looked like her father was going to veto her son's plan — her thoughts traveled across time like carefree tourists who had nothing better to do than travel to the most obscure places. Yet she didn't have any more energy to give to her errant reflections because all of a sudden her limbs felt tremendously heavy. She sank into the armchair that sat beside the window and watched passively as the quickly rising sun burst into view, searing the placid sky with its blistering red flames.

"Why is the sun so angry?" she murmured as sleep finally overcame her.

The house was filled with the smell of freshly brewed coffee when Clara awoke. She glanced at the clock. It was a few minutes after eight o'clock. Had she really been asleep for just a little over an hour, or was she still dreaming? She stood up, and the weariness of her still exhausted body assured her that this was no dream.

Apparently the new day was already underway, without her assistance. When she entered the kitchen she saw that her husband Josep was putting his breakfast dishes in the sink and Vidal was reading a newspaper. His half-eaten omelet was still sitting on the table.

"Are you feeling all right?" asked Josep.

"I'm just a little tired." Clara knew that no one in the room was fooled by her remark. She had long since passed the age when she could stay up all night and not show it on her face the next morning.

"Can I make you an omelet, Mama?"

"Don't be silly. Finish your breakfast, Vidal, before it gets cold. And I'll do the dishes, Josep. You have to get to work."

"Why were you sleeping in the living room?"

Clara knew that her husband's question wasn't an accusation. Still, it annoyed her. Was she really the only one in the family who had been upset by what had happened the night before? Maybe so, since both her husband and Vidal looked like they had gotten a good night's sleep. Well, if they wanted to pretend that her lack of sleep was more important than her father being angry at Vidal — if they wanted to pretend that they didn't understand what that anger meant — she could pretend, too.

"I wanted to get a head start on the cleaning before the holiday," she said with a forced cheerfulness. "My mother always used to get up at the crack of dawn at this time of year. I must have fallen asleep while I was cleaning the windows in the living room. But see how nice the windows here in the kitchen look, or didn't you notice?"

"They look very nice," Josep replied noncommittally. "Do either of you need the car today?"

"I was thinking I might go to Barcelona," said Vidal, "if no one else needs the car."

"Clara?"

Clara thought it was odd that Vidal wanted to go to Barcelona, and odder still that Josep didn't question Vidal about his proposed trip. Her husband had never let the boys take the car on long trips unless they had a good reason. But she was too tired to question Vidal herself, and so all she said was, "I do need to do some grocery shopping. Otherwise I don't know what we're going to have for lunch, and you know how particular my father is..."

Josep glanced over at Vidal, who was staring stonily into space. Clara followed her husband's gaze. The reason for Vidal's trip to Barcelona was now clear. He wanted to avoid another confrontation with her father.

"Of course, if you have something important to do in Barcelona," she said quickly, "I'm sure I'll be able to find something in the pantry."

"Why don't you make a list of what you need now, Clara?" said Josep. "That way Vidal can go to the store while you're having your breakfast. Then he can drive to Barcelona. And while you're there, Vidal, I need you to pick up some varnish and a few other things."

"Sure, Papa. Just tell me what you want me to buy."

While Josep wrote down a list for Vidal, Clara poured herself a cup of coffee and glanced out of her newly cleaned kitchen window. She noted with relief that the sun's color had returned to the familiar pale yellow. A crisis had been averted, at least for one more day.

It was already after ten o'clock when Vidal entered Eduard Garcia's general store. For a farming community, that was practically the middle of the workday and a time when the store was usually empty. Eduard noted both the late hour and the fact that it was Vidal who was doing the grocery shopping for the Bonet family, and not Vidal's mother. But he didn't pry into the private affairs of his customers, and so said nothing other than to return Vidal's greeting of "Good morning."

"Do you have any whole-wheat pasta, Mr. Garcia?"

"There should be some halfway down the second aisle, bottom shelf on your right."

Vidal disappeared down the aisle and came back to the counter a few moments later. "Found it. And thanks again for helping out last night with the overhead projector."

"Don't mention it."

Vidal waited, hoping that Eduard Garcia would say something about his Peaceland project. He had always admired the store owner for his uncomplicated wisdom. His opinion mattered to Vidal. But Eduard Garcia chose to ignore the invitation to speak about the project and instead mentioned the special he was running on disposable foil baking pans.

"Your store is selling disposable pans?" Vidal asked, feigning good-natured surprise and an interest in the subject that he didn't really have. "I didn't think you ever threw away anything."

"My wife tells me that they come in very handy at this time of year, when the ladies are busy cooking and baking for the holiday," the store owner explained. "And there's less cleaning up after the meal." He paused for a moment and then he added, "I suppose the meal will be at your parents' house this year."

"Yes."

"Well, that's how it is. Things change."

Yes, Vidal silently agreed. Now that his grandmother had passed away, the holiday meal would be held at his parents' home, instead of the home of his grandfather and grandmother. Change was part of life — for families and for communities. If Eduard Garcia could see that, why couldn't his grandfather?

"You'd better patch things up with your grandfather."

For a moment, Vidal had the eerie sensation that Eduard Garcia had been reading his mind.

"And it would be best if you did it before the holiday," he continued. "There's no profit in dragging an old quarrel into a new year."

"Any suggestions for how I can do it?"

"You might have to forget about that plan of yours."

Vidal was silent.

"Look, Vidal, we're quiet people. We're quiet people who like to live quiet lives."

"And if the younger generation is different?"

"Things change?"

"You said it yourself, Mr. Garcia, just a few minutes ago."

"I don't know what to tell you, Vidal. You dropped a bombshell on us last night with this Peaceland idea of yours."

"I knew the idea was powerful, but I didn't think it was going to be explosive."

"Maybe it's a good idea. To be honest, I don't know much about these things. But it's an idea for somewhere else. Hi-rise hotels don't belong here in Sant Joan Januz."

"If that's your objection, I agree with you one hundred percent. That's why the architectural plan explicitly states that the buildings won't be more than five stories high. The whole idea is to peacefully integrate the resort's infrastructure into the natural surroundings. It's all in the information package I handed out last night."

"That may be so, but your grandfather said..." Eduard Garcia paused.

"What did my grandfather say?"

"That you're going to build a casino." While Vidal and Eduard had been talking, a farmer named Jeroni had entered the store and was looking at the rolls of duct tape. It was Jeroni who added the information about the casino.

"What?" Vidal was too shocked to say anything more.

"That's what your grandfather told me this morning," Jeroni replied. "As part of Phase Two."

"What Phase Two?" Vidal looked from Jeroni to Eduard. "What else did my grandfather say?"

Jeroni was about to say something, but a sharp look from Eduard convinced him to return his attention to the rolls of duct tape.

"I don't want to step into the middle of a family fight," said Eduard.

"This isn't a family fight. The Peaceland project concerns the entire village."

"How many of these baking pans do you think your mother will want?"

Josep carefully examined all four sides of the wardrobe and shrugged his shoulders. It wasn't that he had found fault with his son's work. Arnau had faithfully reproduced the eighteenth-century Tuscan landscapes that the wealthy American client had asked for, as well as the intricate latticework designs that were popular during that era. In the eyes of some people, the work would be considered exquisite, but painted wood furniture didn't appeal to Josep. It pained him to see the natural beauty of the wood camouflaged in this manner. But projects such as this one gave Arnau a respectable paycheck every month, as well as something more interesting to do than merely cover a wardrobe or buffet with a few coats of varnish. Josep had therefore added reproductions of antique Italian furniture to the workshop's product line.

Of course, Josep was aware that even this large order for furniture painted in the Italian style couldn't dispel his son's dissatisfaction with his job. That dissatisfaction was never voiced, but its presence could be felt by the pervasive lack of joy that had entered the workshop not long after Arnau's arrival. Josep sympathized with his son. He knew it was hard for an artist to repress his vision and spend the better part of the day copying another person's artistic creations. But Josep was also making a sacrifice. He greatly missed the days when an air of harmony had reigned over his simple one-room empire, and he had felt at peace with his world. But until something changed, he had resigned himself to making the best of things. The workshop would continue to produce hand-painted furniture for as long as Arnau needed the work, and Josep would continue to shrug as he placed a check mark inside the "completed" box on his clients' order forms.

"I'm sorry I'm late, Papa. Manel woke up with the stomach flu. It's been quite a morning." Arnau took off his jacket and hung it on the coat rack standing by the door. Then he went over to the desk to take a look at the production schedule for the day.

"He's better?" Although Josep asked the question out of concern for his grandson, the truth was that he wouldn't have minded if Arnau took off the entire day to look after Manel.

"He's enjoying the attention now, and he ate some breakfast." Arnau looked over at some pieces of unpainted furniture that were standing to the side of the room. "What's next, the buffet or the highboy?"

"Whichever you prefer," Josep replied. "By the way, the wardrobe came out very well."

"I know you hate it."

Josep couldn't help but wonder at the difference between the two sons he had brought into the world. Whereas Vidal had an instinctive knack for sweetening life's stings, Arnau's natural habitat was the black cloud that stubbornly refused to acknowledge the existence of the proverbial silver lining.

"I'm not an admirer of this style of furniture, but I can recognize good work when I see it," said Josep. "You did an excellent job. Thank you."

Arnau shrugged and then shuffled through some papers. Josep had to smile, since he recognized the gesture. For both of them the shrug was a way of saying, "Thanks, but it doesn't really change anything."

"We're running low on paint," Arnau commented, still looking at the computer printouts. "There's no sienna in stock, or sage."

"I know. Vidal is going to Barcelona today, and I've asked him to pick up a few things. Here's a copy of the list I gave him. If you have anything to add, you can probably still catch him before he leaves."

"Why is he going to Barcelona?"

"I have a lunch date with Christopher Columbus. He's very excited about my Peaceland project, and he asked to hear more details." Vidal stood in the doorway to the workshop. "You're invited to come along, Arnau, if you're interested in hearing more about it."

"Sorry, but I have other plans." Arnau turned to Josep. "Grandpa called me this morning. He said he had something he wanted to talk to me about so he's going to have lunch with me and Joanna today, at our house. Can you tell Mama?"

"I'll call her." Josep glanced at Vidal, who was still standing in the doorway. He noted that Vidal was smiling, but there was something unnatural about the way he looked. It reminded Josep of those old porcelain dolls that one sometimes ran across in a flea market. Their sweet smiles remained frozen on their faces, even though they no longer had anything to smile about since they had long ago been abandoned by their youthful owners. "Was there something you wanted, Vidal? You can come inside for the same price of admission."

"I can't read this word." Since Vidal had refused his father's offer to come into the workshop, Josep walked over to him. Vidal showed him the list of supplies that Josep had prepared earlier that morning.

"Casein paint," said Josep. He wrote the word casein more clearly. "Arnau needs it for the murals he paints on the furniture."

Vidal took back the list and put it into his coat pocket.

"Drive carefully, Vidal," said Josep. "Keep your thoughts on the road, okay?"

Miquel was in a cheerful mood as he walked up the path leading to Arnau and Joanna's house. Manel, who had been waiting impatiently by the living room window for his great-grandfather's arrival, ran outside to greet him.

"Grandpa, I'm sick! Do you want to see how many numbers I have on the thermometer?"

"I heard you were unwell, but first let's go inside and say hello to your parents." Miquel took Manel's hand and they walked up the front steps together. They were still standing on the front porch when Arnau's car pulled into the driveway. Manel waved to his father with his free hand.

"Papa! Grandpa's here!"

"That's quite an announcement," Miquel commented. "If you had been a little boy during the time of King Juame, you might have served at court as the king's royal page."

"What's a page?"

"He's someone who announces when the king is about to arrive. Like this: 'Make way for the king! Make way for the king!' "

Manel giggled with delight. "I wish you would eat lunch at our house every day."

"Maybe that's not such a bad idea," Miquel replied softly.

Joanna came onto the porch just as Arnau joined Miquel and Manel. "Lunch won't be ready for another fifteen minutes. I hope no one is starving."

"Not me," said Miquel. "But since we have a little time, why don't you show me around your studio, Arnau?"

Arnau and Joanna exchanged quick glances. Miquel hadn't shown any interest in Arnau's artwork for years.

"I know what the two of you are thinking," said Miquel, who hadn't missed a thing. "You're wondering what the old man is up to now."

"No one is wondering anything, Grandpa," replied Arnau.

"If that were true, you'd be fools," said Miquel.

"All right, so what are you up to?"

"Lately — what with your grandmother's passing away, and the holiday coming up, and other things — I've been doing some thinking. And I've decided, Arnau, that it's not right that I haven't taken more interest in your work. Maybe there's more that I can do to help you out."

Miquel had been right. Arnau and Joanna weren't fools. If Miquel was suddenly taking an interest in Arnau's artwork, they both knew that it had nothing to do with the death of Grandma Anna or the upcoming holiday.

It was already late in the afternoon when Vidal arrived for his "lunch date." Unlike his brother, Vidal thrived in a big city like Barcelona. If Sant Joan Januz was comforting as a rocking chair on the front porch, and Girona was solid as a stately middle-aged matron, Barcelona was like getting the keys to the car for the first time. It was all energy, motion, and the thrill of unexplored potential.

He was counting on the city's upbeat energy to recharge his batteries, which had been seriously depleted during the past twenty-four hours, and so after he did the errands for his father, he headed for La Rambla — the rambling, rambunctious, tree-lined avenue that cut through the city's center like a motorboat slicing a path through the sea. He allowed himself to be serenaded by the street musicians and enticed by the shopkeepers displaying their overpriced wares, but his real destination was a place that both epitomized everything the city stood for and yet stood apart from it: the bronze statue of Christopher Columbus that rose majestically over Barcelona's harbor.

The statue stood on the spot where the explorer had landed, in triumph, after his discovery of the American continent. That moment of triumph had been preserved for posterity in the 1890s, a time of prosperity for Catalonia and an era when the Catalan people believed the explorer was one of their own. Although the inaccuracy of that theory was later proved and accepted, another theory was not so easily forgotten: the whispers that Columbus was a descendent of New Christians — Jews who had converted to Christianity during the Middle Ages to escape poverty, humiliation, and sometimes even death, but who had stubbornly remained loyal to the Jewish faith. The "proof " of the explorer's Jewish roots, some people would jokingly say, as they pointed to the statue, was that Columbus wasn't facing Barcelona, where he received a triumphant welcome from the monarchs Ferdinand and Isabella. Instead, he was gazing out to sea — the Mediterranean Sea — and that Promised Land that lay to the east: Israel. But neither the statue's confused identity nor the ambiguous interpretations surrounding it bothered Vidal. He couldn't have cared less about the explorer's roots. His interest was in the man's triumph.

And so after ascending to the top of the statue in the monument's small and stuffy elevator, Vidal stepped out onto the narrow observation deck and took a deep breath. From one side, he had a clear view of the Mediterranean, whose calm waters stretched out below him for as far as the eye could see. From the other side, the entire city of Barcelona unfurled like an urban scroll at his feet.

"Empires aren't built by the fainthearted," the explorer seemed to be whispering into his ear.

CHAPTER 6

L unch that day was a quiet affair, at least in terms of the number of real people sitting around the kitchen table. They were only four: Clara, Josep, Uncle Pau, and Uncle Biel.

The shadows were another matter.

As her glance darted from one empty chair to another, Clara's thoughts traveled anxiously between Vidal, who was somewhere on the way to Barcelona, and the conversation that was taking place at that moment between her father and Arnau at Arnau's home. Something had changed that morning, and even though a mother was supposed to have a special intuition about her children, today the radar screen was blank. She only knew that the Vidal who had left the house in the morning to pick up some groceries was not the same Vidal who came back.

"Not every crack in a house's wall is dangerous, Clara."

There went her thoughts again. Unlike at airports, there was no border control for the mind. No one was there to give her thoughts a rigorous security check before deeming them safe to travel. And so she found herself back in her childhood, having a talk with her father.

Something had happened — she didn't know what — and her parents had argued. From her bedroom she could hear their angry voices, and she felt very scared. Later, when her father had come in to check on her, he had reassured her that despite the argument everything was still all right.

"Not every crack in a house's wall is dangerous, Clara," her father had said. "It's only natural for people to have an argument from time to time. That doesn't mean that they don't still love each other. The foundation of our house is strong and solid."

That's right, Clara silently reassured herself. Arguments were a natural part of life. And the ties that bound their family together were strong. Her mother had always worked hard to keep the family together, despite the extra effort it entailed. Uncle Pau and

Uncle Biel and their wives came to their home every Friday evening and every holiday for the special meal. Even though the aunts had offered to share the burden, her mother wouldn't hear of it. It was enough that the poor women didn't have any children, her mother had always said.

Clara's stream of consciousness rolled to a halt. She hadn't thought about her aunts in a long time. They had been tragically killed in a train wreck. She didn't remember the details. It was odd, though, to think that her mother was now gone as well, and that she would have to take on the role of keeping the family together.

The foundation is strong, she repeated to herself. But as she looked around the table, the empty places staring back at her left her feeling far from encouraged.

"Shall I help with the dishes?" During the few minutes that it had taken for Arnau to walk his grandfather to his car and return to the house, the table had already been cleared, a tribute to Joanna's efficiency. But Arnau was in no hurry to return to the workshop.

"I'm almost finished," Joanna replied. "There's some coffee left, if you'd like another cup."

Arnau accepted the offer. While he poured the coffee into his mug, he noted that he wasn't the only one who was feeling unsettled by his grandfather's visit. Joanna was giving the forks a particularly vigorous rub with the scouring pad. Something was obviously on her mind as well.

"What are you thinking?"

"He's not moving in with us."

"What?"

"Don't be naïve, Arnau. People don't wake up in the morning with a burning interest in modern art. It's not the flu."

"I don't follow you. I thought the topic we discussed over lunch was arranging an exhibit of my paintings in Barcelona."

"And why is your grandfather interested in helping you now?"

"Because he's angry with Vidal."

"Exactly. And if he's angry with Vidal, where is he going to go?"

Arnau stared at Joanna. Too much had happened during the past twenty-four hours that didn't make sense, and now Joanna was adding another wrinkle to the already frayed garment. Had she caught some subtle hint that Arnau had missed, or had her dislike for his grandfather made her misinterpret an innocent remark?

For his part, he was still trying to unravel the cause for his grandfather's unusual behavior. It was one thing not to like Vidal's plan, but to turn so completely against Vidal, and to do it in public, just wasn't the way things were done in the family. Then there was the phone call from Joanna's father about the campaign against Vidal's project that Miquel was waging in the village. It sounded like the old man was doing everything in his power to make sure that the plan would be rejected. Yet when his grandfather had sat with them at lunch, he hadn't said a word about Vidal or the plan. It was as if they didn't exist and never had and all Miquel cared about in the world was Arnau and his art.

During lunch the thought had occurred to Arnau that perhaps something had snapped in his grandfather's mind. He had quickly dismissed it, though. It was unthinkable that his grandfather would ever be anything but the perfectly healthy, larger-than-life figure that had dominated the family for all of Arnau's life.

"I don't understand what you're getting at, Joanna. Why does my grandfather have to go anywhere?"

"He can't live on his own in that house for much longer. Your mother is too much of a worrier. Not that I blame her after the way your grandmother became ill so suddenly."

"So he'll move in with my parents."

"And Vidal?"

Arnau had to admit that Joanna was on to something. To complicate matters further, there wasn't just his grandfather to worry about. There were also Uncle Pau and Uncle Biel. The family had a responsibility to take care of the older generation. That job would be harder if some of the family members were involved in a feud. On the other hand, his grandfather and great-uncles were still healthy, and they weren't complainers who indulged in self-pity.

"That's the difference between our generation and yours," his Uncle Biel had once said in his typically forthright and undiplomatic manner. "We're tough, like the yellow broom. You young people take after the cistus. You crumple and give up as soon as the fight gets too hot."

But it would take more than a few hints from his mother to convince any of them to give up their independence and move into someone else's home. As for his grandfather initiating such an idea, the thought was ridiculous.

"Joanna, I think you're making too many faulty assumptions. Vidal will make peace with Grandpa. They'll probably be the best of friends again by next week."

"Maybe they'll make peace, but he'll leave the village if his plan is voted down."

"Vidal?"

"Well, what will he do in Sant Joan Januz? Work in the fields? Drive to Barcelona once a month to pick up paint for your father and be grateful for the work?"

"What Vidal decides to do is his own business."

"Your mother will be furious if Vidal leaves, and your grandfather knows it. That's why he's suddenly remembered that he has another grandson. You're his Plan B, Arnau. Don't be fooled by his glib words."

Clara slowly walked across the length of her living room, measuring the space with her footsteps. If the meal for the upcoming holiday was going to be held at her home, she wanted it to be nice. That meant having the meal in the living room, not in the kitchen. But the long dining table was in the kitchen, which happened to be the larger room, and she wasn't sure if there would be enough space in the living room to seat everyone comfortably.

"Wouldn't that job be easier if you used a tape measure?"

Clara looked over at the large window she had cleaned early that morning and which was now open to let in the late-afternoon breeze. Through the window she saw her father standing on the front porch. Or at least she thought it was her father. Her mind had traveled from the present to the past so many times that day that she wasn't sure if what she was seeing was really her father or an apparition.

"If you invite me in, maybe I can help you with whatever it is you're doing."

"Sorry, Papa. I didn't see you out there." Although the door was unlocked, Clara went to open it for her father and escort him inside.

"Now, what was it you were trying to do?"

"Do you think my kitchen table will fit in here? I was thinking of serving the holiday meal in the living room."

Miquel surveyed the space with an air of authority. "It will fit, but why go to all the trouble? We're simple people. Your kitchen will do fine."

"I want the meal to be nice."

"Your mother always had the meal in the kitchen, and no one ever complained about it not being nice."

"I know, Papa."

"The main thing is the food. That's why I've brought you this."

Miquel handed her a binder, which Clara recognized at once. It was the one that held all of her mother's recipes. Clara had decorated the cover with pictures of wildflowers when she was a child, but that didn't interest her at the moment. It was the pages inside that she cared about. On each page was a recipe, written in her mother's neat and precise handwriting.

Several of the pages had become stained over the years, and Clara remembered when some of them made their first appearance. There was the time, for instance, when she had grabbed the top of the potato-and-string bean-casserole page with her chocolate-smeared hands, leaving behind a border of small, dark fingerprints. Yet even the pages that hadn't been adorned by her youthful "artwork" had a story to tell. For those who knew how to decipher the code written in tablespoons and measuring cups, the pages of the little book contained a faithful history of the most treasured moments in the family's life.

"Thank you, Papa."

"Clara, there's something I've been meaning to ask you."

"Yes?"

"That day, when your mother..."

"Yes, Papa?"

"Did she say anything? Before the doctor arrived? While the two of you were alone in the kitchen?"

"I know she must have been thinking about you, Papa."

"Well, of course, she would have been thinking about all of us. That was your mother's way, to always be worrying about others. But she didn't say anything?"

"No."

66

Miquel was silent for a few moments. Then he walked over to the open window and looked outside. "Serve the meal in the kitchen, Clara. Anyone could look through this window and see us while we're eating. There's no need to make a public display of ourselves."

"You didn't mind making a public display last night." Clara didn't know where the words had come from, or how she had dared to speak to her father in such a manner. Once again she had the odd sensation that she didn't know if what she was experiencing was real or a dream.

"That was different," Miquel replied coldly. "We didn't send Vidal to business school to dream up foolish ideas, or to waste the family's money. Common sense should have told him that we would never agree to open our home to hordes of strangers. We're quiet people who like to live quiet lives."

"But Vidal said the resort would be built on the other side of the square. Why can't we at least give it a try?"

"As far as I'm concerned, the matter is closed."

Clara watched through the open window as her father strode down the driveway and got into his car. He drove off without giving her the customary wave good-bye.

"The foundation is strong," she murmured for about the twentieth time that day.

She looked down at the binder that was still in her hands. Her mother would have known how to handle the situation. Unfortunately, her mother hadn't included a family recipe for making peace in her little book. Nor was there one that would satisfy the hunger of a young man who had big dreams.

But whose fault was it that Vidal wasn't the type to be satisfied with a quiet country life? Who had filled the young boy's head with stories about King Juame and Christopher Columbus? Only her father. Her mother's side of the family had desired a kingdom no greater than the countryside that lay just outside their front doors.

Clara glanced down at the binder. The pictures of the wildflowers that she had pasted on the cover had faded long ago, but they were still a reminder of her mother's favorites: the rosemary and rose garlic, which were staples in her mother's kitchen; the brightly colored cistus and the elegant Jerusalem sage; and, of course, the yellow broom.

67

The sight of the bushy shrub, still a defiantly cheerful yellow despite the passage of the years, jolted something in her mind. She now remembered that her mother had said something before the doctor arrived. But her father had already driven off, and she felt no desire to call him back. Besides, it probably didn't matter. Her mother most likely had been confused during those last moments. Why else would she have been thinking about yellow broom and not about the family?

CHAPTER 7

I t was already dark when Vidal's car turned onto the road that led to Sant Joan Januz. Yet despite what the pitch-black color of the heavens suggested, the hour really wasn't so late. From time to time, a small square of yellowish-white light signaled that a farmhouse lay in the distance and that its inhabitants were not yet asleep.

Not asleep, but were they awake? Vidal wondered. Or was it Barcelona that was dreaming? When he was in the city, the answer seemed so clear: life was growth, change, transformation, a continual moving forward. Sant Joan Januz was dying. He had to do something to revive it, even if that meant going in a direction that was against his grandfather's wishes.

But now that he was back on the road leading to Sant Joan Januz, a kind of sleep descended on him, as it always did when he left the highway behind and descended into the valley. Just as he heard the night breeze leisurely making its way through the rustling leaves, he heard a voice whisper to him to relax and let things be. The same sun rose and set every day. A tree might grow taller and stronger, but at the end of the day it was still a tree. What did it matter if this year's world was remarkably similar to the world that had existed a decade before, or a century?

The whole appeal of Sant Joan Januz was that it didn't change. People were born, people died. When it was planting season there were always farmers who rose with the sun, and when it was time to harvest their crops they didn't leave their fields until the sun dropped below the horizon. Life was safe, predictable, and rooted in a cycle that had been set in motion at the dawn of time. Who was he to disturb it, especially when disturbing that fixed rhythm meant going against his grandfather? Why should he make a change, if that change also meant a change in the relationship with the people he loved?

The village is dying, he reminded himself. The sun might continue to rise and set, but in a few years time it would rise and set on a world that would have one less dot on the map. Perhaps his grandfather wouldn't be there to see that day, but he would.

"It's my village, too," he whispered as the headlights of his car illuminated the faded sign for Eduard Garcia's general store. Feeling too restless to go home, Vidal parked the car and continued his inner conversation in the little square. As he expected, no one else was there, and the square looked even more forlorn at night than during the day.

He sat down at the lone cafe table that was the property of the general store. Once there had been several more to keep it company, but for the last few years the round plastic table, with its tall umbrella sticking out of its center, was the only sentinel standing guard over the "commercial center" of Sant Joan Januz. Not that there was much to guard. Eduard Garcia's food and hardware emporium was by far the largest store in the square and the only one that did a passable business. The others, the clothing and notions shop owned by Ferran and Carme Rodriguez and the shoe store owned by the Lunel family, were struggling.

The square came to life only on market days, which took place on Monday and Thursday mornings. Villagers who had something to sell set up small stalls and displayed their wares. Regina Adarra, Joanna's mother, came with her homemade jams and preserves when it was the season. Families that had grown too much produce in their home gardens sold their extra fresh fruits and vegetables or bartered for the produce of another. It was all very easygoing and neighborly, and for those few hours the square hummed with activity. Then the stalls were returned to their storage places, the shops emptied, and the one lone cafe table with the closed umbrella returned to its lonely occupation.

As Vidal sat and listened to the quiet, the square seemed to stretch before him like a blank screen waiting to be filled with color and life. Not the color and life of a casino, of course. He had never had any intention of sullying the pure sky above Sant Joan Januz with a blazing rainbow of neon lights. In fact, the irony of the idea made Vidal smile. Vidal was the member of the family who was the least interested in the card games that took place every Friday night. It was his grandfather who removed the deck of cards from their storage place with a flourish and enthusiastically presided over the game.

70

Vidal could see so clearly how this little square would look after the resort was built and the first tourists arrived. As if he were watching a promotional DVD for the resort, he could see a small crowd of visitors enjoying their evening meal at the deluxe restaurant that had been opened by one of the village's families. Other tourists were strolling past the galleries and shops that were stocked with high-quality merchandise that had a distinctive Catalan flavor. Beatriz Rodriguez, the daughter of the people who owned the clothing store, was selling her handmade jewelry from one of the boarded-up shops. His brother Arnau had opened an art gallery. A gourmet-food store was selling Regina Adarra's preserves and other homegrown delicacies that came straight from the villagers' farms. Everyone in the village would benefit from his plan. So why was his grandfather so vehemently against it? What was his grandfather afraid of?

For his grandfather was afraid, Vidal suddenly realized. His plan had inadvertently hit a raw nerve. But why? What had he said during the presentation that had shaken his grandfather so badly that afterward he had stomped off to his car and angrily ignored Vidal's attempts to talk to him? And why did he feel it was necessary to immediately start a whispering campaign so that Vidal would be totally discredited in the eyes of the villagers?

"What is he afraid of?"

Vidal asked his question of the silent night sky without really expecting a reply. But when he heard a car pulling into the parking lot behind Eduard Garcia's store, Vidal silently hoped that he would be answered. Perhaps the car belonged to his grandfather, who was somehow aware that he was sitting there and wanted to talk to him.

Instead, Vidal heard the muffled voices of a man and a woman as they got out of the car. From where he was sitting, he could see them clearly — it was Ferran and Carme Rodriguez, the owners of the clothing store — but they didn't notice him, probably because they didn't expect anyone else to be there at that time of night.

Mr. Rodriguez, who was carrying several heavy boxes, unlocked the door to his store. He allowed his wife, who was also carrying several boxes in her arms, to go inside first.

"I'll get the rest of the boxes," Mr. Rodriguez called out to his wife, and then he retraced his steps across the square.

71

"Need any help?"

"Vidal! You startled me."

"Sorry."

"What are you doing here? If I'm not mistaken, Mrs. Perez's ice cream shop closed down seven years ago after she tripped over a tub of homemade lemon sorbet and broke her hip."

"And the village hasn't been the same since, in my opinion."

"I'm inclined to agree with you there."

"Have you been stocking up on new merchandise for the fall?"

"That's right. Mrs. Rodriguez and I like to go into town and look around before everything gets picked over. Though sometimes I don't know why we bother to keep the store open. Most people go to the larger towns to do their shopping. They just come to us for the odds and ends. But I'd better get going, before Mrs. Rodriguez starts worrying about what's happened to me."

"Let me help you with the boxes." Vidal started to get up from his seat, but Mr. Rodriguez stopped him.

"If you want to help my family, get that plan of yours passed."

"So you'd like to see a resort built here?"

"I don't know anything about this peace tourism business. That's your headache. But if you can lure the tourists to Sant Joan Januz, I know of several people who would be interested in setting up shop in this square. They're behind you."

"Thanks. That's good to know. But I understand there are other people who feel differently."

"Your grandfather and great-uncles are farmers. They have a cooperative that sells their produce, so they can afford to be picky about what sort of industry we bring into the village. But if they had to depend on the number of people who spend money in this square, like me, they would feel differently about building a resort in Sant Joan Januz. And as for those casinos..."

"You can be honest with me, Mr. Rodriguez. I'd like to hear your opinion about what my grandfather is saying."

"Probably I shouldn't say anything, but you should know that people are talking about your grandfather. Not in a bad way, but they're concerned. Things can happen to the mind, you know."

"No, I don't know. What do you mean?"

72

"I had to put my mother in a nursing home toward the end, after her mind went. It happened not long after you left for New York. It was a sad day for all of us, but my wife and I couldn't take care of her by ourselves anymore."

"I'm sure you made the right decision. But what does this have to do with my grandfather?"

"Everyone knows how fond your grandfather is of you. So why is he acting this way? It just isn't normal. Some people are thinking that maybe it has to do with the way your grandmother went so suddenly. It had to have been a shock for him. It could have done something to his mind."

"That's what people are saying?"

"Don't be offended, Vidal. What people are saying isn't important. None of us are doctors, and I'm sure your family has everything under control and there's no reason for anyone to interfere. But what I am trying to say is that people aren't paying attention to your grandfather's talk about those casinos. They're ready to hear more about your plan. So if I were you, I'd start making the rounds and talk to people in their homes. And when you do it, Vidal, talk less about how your millionaires are going to bring peace to the Middle East and more about what's in it for us. The people want to know how many postcards you think we'll be able to sell, if you know what I mean."

Vidal stopped his car at the end of the dirt path that led up to his grandfather's farmhouse. During the short drive he had quickly gone over the events of the past few weeks, trying to recall if there had been any other incidents that would add proof to what Ferran Rodriguez had said in the square. He couldn't think of any, although he had to admit that he had been so busy preparing for the presentation that he hadn't paid too much attention to anything else.

What he wanted to do was confront his grandfather with the facts about what his day's work had accomplished. In his imagination, he could see his grandfather's reaction. His Grandpa Miquel would raise himself to his full height and pronounce, in his sonorous voice, "So that's what they think, is it? Well, let me set the record straight, young man. The reason I object to your plan is because..."

Then, once the reason was out in the open, the two would sit down at the kitchen table and go through all the points pertaining to his grandfather's objection, one by one. All the misunderstandings would be cleared up. Things would go back to the way they were.

Perhaps that's what he should have done in the first place. Surprising everyone had been the idea of his roommate. But for all his expertise in marketing, Al didn't know his family and understand all their little quirks. Still, what was done was done and couldn't be changed. The present, though, could be repaired, and he was ready to talk to his grandfather right then.

But the house was dark. Apparently his grandfather had already gone to sleep. It wouldn't be right to disturb him.

Vidal started up the car engine, but before he continued on his way home he took a parting look at the farmhouse, whose dark, shuttered windows stared blankly into the night. Their vacant gaze made him uneasy. From somewhere in his tired consciousness a chorus of voices began to sing him a confused lullaby:

Things change.
You dropped a bombshell on us last night.
Things can happen to the mind, you know.
Things change.

"It can't be true," Vidal whispered softly, in refrain.

Miquel watched as the car backed out of the driveway and drove off. Although he hadn't seen who the driver was, he had recognized the car and knew it must have been Vidal. He decided to wait a few more minutes, in the dark, to make sure the car didn't return.

It was odd feeling like a thief in his own house, watching from behind the half-opened slat of the wooden shutter, afraid that someone outside would see he was there. It was odder still feeling threatened by the unexpected appearance of his grandson Vidal, a surprise that would have given him pleasure just a few weeks earlier. Yet how many times had he heard his wife warn their daughter Clara to watch out for the piece of wire spread across the path? Even the thinnest piece could make a person stumble and fall, Anna had always said. He now realized just how true those words were. A person never knew where the danger would come

74

from. The fact that it had come from such an unlikely source — his own grandson — didn't make the danger any less severe.

The clock ticked away the seconds. When he felt that enough of them had gone by, he let the slat fall back into place and turned away from the window. He noted that the room looked different in the dark. Furniture that seemed to be the right size in the light now looked heavy and ominous. From the corner of his eye he saw a picture hanging on the wall, and he realized that he couldn't remember what it was. He didn't like that.

Perhaps he was getting older, but he wasn't going to surrender his memory without a fight. He switched on a light and went over to the picture.

It was a collage of family photographs from throughout the years. Clara had put it together, he recalled, but he couldn't remember if it had been an anniversary present or a birthday present for his wife. He also couldn't remember when the last time was that he had actually looked at it. Now that he did look, he saw that in the center of the collage was a large photograph from his wedding. He and Anna were standing in the middle of the group portrait of the family as it had looked more than fifty years ago. He stared at the faces of his parents and grandparents. Anna's family was also there.

There were other photos: Clara as a child; Clara's wedding, when it was his and Anna's turn to pose as the smiling parents; Arnau and Vidal as children. But it was the photo of his wedding that his eye kept turning to. Everyone was smiling, and why not? It had been a happy marriage. He had done his best to be a good husband and father. When it came time for him to join the older generation in that other world, he was confident that they would be satisfied with what he had accomplished in those areas. As for the other things...

He looked intently at the smiling faces of Anna's relatives, those who had once been the heart and soul of Sant Joan Januz. His wife Anna was also smiling at him. "Yes, why not smile?" they seemed to be saying to him. "The future is going to be fine. We know we can rely on you."

"Forgive me," he whispered as he stared into their trusting eyes.

75

CHAPTER 8

The sun beat down on the car's roof as Vidal drove down yet another dusty back road. It had been a long and frustrating week. After meeting with almost half of the village's families, and talking about his vision of the village's future until his voice was hoarse, he realized that the picture that was emerging was not encouraging. A third of the families were solidly behind him. A third of them were just as solidly against. The rest were solidly committed to sitting on the fence.

A person didn't have to be a clairvoyant to know where the opposition was coming from. Overnight Miquel had emerged from the cocoon of his close family and turned into a social butterfly; flitting from one farmhouse to another, he was gaily spreading ominous rumors wherever he went. And apparently what Ferran Rodriguez had said about no one taking seriously his grandfather's talk about casinos and other social ills wasn't completely true. Vidal was learning that even if people weren't accepting all the details, many of them seemed to have accepted the underlying, cautionary message: the planned resort spelled disaster for the village. It had to be voted down.

And so, if at the beginning of the week Vidal had hoped to be received in people's homes as the savior of Sant Joan Januz, he had grown used to being greeted with all the enthusiasm that a skeptical farmer reserves for the traveling salesman touting a bottle of snake oil. Still, he was determined to keep on fighting. If he couldn't entirely undo his grandfather's work, at least he could poke a few holes in the colorful yarns his grandfather was busy weaving — and fill those holes with a few cautionary doubts of his own.

"Voting against Peaceland means voting for the death of Sant Joan Januz," Vidal reminded those who were still undecided.

And it was true. Despite the opposition, so far no one had come up with a better idea. If his plan was voted down, where would they be the morning after the vote?

76

Vidal instinctively glanced down at his watch to check the LED display. It was something he did whenever a troubling "where" question bubbled up in his mind. And as he did so, he couldn't help but note that where he was now was a different place entirely than where he had been when he had first seen the watch.

He had bought the watch in New York in a spirit of optimism, after his grandfather had insisted that he buy himself a nice graduation present. From the moment he saw it, he knew that the watch had been designed for someone just like him. Not only did the watch show the time, but it also came with all sorts of features that enabled a person who was going places to keep track of that journey. Should he ever decide to go on a sea voyage, for instance, the watch had a tide graph to tell him if it was high tide or low. The watch's barometer could warn him of any approaching storm. Once the storm broke, the thermometer would let him know how hot or cold the winds were blowing. And if a gust of wind should send him tumbling overboard, the watch's depth log would record his path, while its depth gauge would tell him just how deeply he had fallen into the sea's dark waters. That same depth gauge would, of course, chart his eventual rise back up to the top.

Admirable as the seafaring features were, they weren't particularly helpful in Sant Joan Januz, which sat contentedly moored in its landlocked valley. The watch's digital compass was another matter. The more he felt alone and at sea due to his grandfather's unexpected and roundabout opposition, the more he found the compass to be oddly comforting. He wasn't a lost speck traveling blindly and unnoticed through the world. He was traveling somewhere, at least according to the solar-powered LED display of his watch, which faithfully charted the changing directions of his zigzagging path.

It was a pity, though, that the compass didn't come with a directional point marked "grandfather." For the past week Vidal had been trying to locate Miquel so that he could talk to him. What should have been a simple task had turned into a frustrating game of cat and mouse. Vidal was supposed to be the cat, of course. Instead, as he traveled through the maze of back roads that connected one farm to another — always far too many steps behind his grandfather's weather-beaten blue pickup truck — Vidal had the strange feeling that someone was purposefully leading him off course and laughing at his bungled attempts to track down his prey. And who could that someone be, if not his Grandfather Miquel?

If his hunch was correct, it meant that his grandfather's mind was still as sharp as ever. That was comforting. But it didn't explain why his grandfather refused to talk to him. It also didn't make his work any easier.

Vidal reached for his water bottle and took a drink of cold water. He had one more meeting scheduled for that day, and he hoped his voice would hold out. After taking another drink, he turned the car onto the dirt road that led to the home of Joanna's parents, Luis and Regina Adarra. His watch told him that the atmospheric pressure was normal, the temperature was hot, and he was traveling southeast. As for the time, he didn't need a watch to tell him that it was running out for him, and for Peaceland.

When Regina heard Vidal's raspy voice, she ordered him to sit down and not say another word until she brought him a hot tea with honey and lemon.

"Maybe it's a sign, not being able to talk," she said as she reentered the room and handed Vidal a china teacup. "At least it happened among family. Drink your tea."

As Vidal raised the cup to his lips and took a sip, his eyes peered over its edge at Mrs. Adarra's smiling face. He wondered when he had become part of the Adarra family. It was true that they were related by marriage, but it was a distant relationship, which he had always supposed was due to Joanna's dislike for every Bonet except her husband.

"Does the tea need more honey?"

"No, it's excellent," Vidal whispered hoarsely. He took another sip, then set down the cup and opened his briefcase.

"Relax, Vidal, and finish your tea," said Luis. "We're in no hurry. Are we, Regina?"

"Not at all."

Vidal's original plan had been to keep the meeting short, since he didn't expect their support anyway, because of Joanna, but his reception had been much better than he had anticipated. He knew that the Adarras had two sons who were living in foreign countries. Perhaps they realized that they had something to gain — the return of their sons should the village be revitalized — which is why they seemed willing to listen. If that was the case, the best course of action would be to immediately go into his pitch.

On the other hand, his throat was aching and the tea was soothing. Surely there wouldn't be any harm in giving the tea a few more minutes to do its work. He took another sip and whispered, "Thanks."

Regina and Luis exchanged glances. Then Luis took up the cue.

"You know, Vidal, I was once in the same position that you're in now. I also wanted to bring an industry into Sant Joan Januz. Of course, it wasn't as ambitious as this Peaceland project of yours. It was just a small electronics factory. Still, your grandfather was against the idea."

"Really?" Vidal managed to croak. "Why?"

"I never found out the real reason. At the time, he said a lot of things. The factory would be too noisy. It wouldn't be profitable. When I showed him the numbers, he had an answer for that as well. He said that even if the factory was profitable, no one would want to work in it except foreign workers. In the end, that's how he scared off the people. He convinced everyone that Sant Joan Januz was about to be overrun by a horde of Arab invaders."

Vidal laughed. Then he remembered that it wasn't funny. His grandfather was using the same tactic to thwart his plan, only this time the invaders were Las Vegas–style gangsters and other unsavory characters.

"I guess your plan was voted down."

"That's right, Vidal. Just like your plan is going to be voted down."

Vidal took another sip of tea. He noted that Mrs. Adarra was still smiling. He vaguely remembered that Regina Adarra's mother had been related to his Grandmother Anna. They were second cousins, or maybe even first. At any rate, Mrs. Adarra had been right. They were family. Mr. Adarra, on the other hand, was not related. He was cold and calculating, like Joanna.

"I don't know about that, Mr. Adarra. I have some solid support. There are a lot of people in the village who are ready for a change."

"Mrs. Adarra and I would like to see a change, too. Wouldn't we, Regina?"

"Yes, we would." Regina said, still smiling.

"But we're realists," Luis continued. "We know that nothing happens in this village without your grandfather's approval. So in our opinion the only way to make any change is to make a complete change."

"That's very interesting, Mr. Adarra. What sort of change did you have in mind?"

"We should sell the village."

The teacup almost fell out of Vidal's hand. "Sell the village?"

"Why not? A lot of people living in out-of-the-way places have made big money from selling their homes to the government because of that new high-speed railway system the country is building."

"But we're not anywhere near where they're going to lay the train tracks."

"True, and that's our bad luck. But Spain's Muslim population is growing. Maybe you could convince that wealthy real estate developer friend of yours to buy us out and develop the village for his own people."

"Sell Sant Joan Januz to Arabs?"

"It's something to think about."

"After all, Vidal," said Regina, still smiling, "what's a bright young man like you going to do in Sant Joan Januz after your resort gets voted down?"

Clara switched off the oven and removed the freshly baked loaves of bread. Even as she noted that the loaves had turned out just right, an inner voice whispered that her mother would have waited until the next day to bake the bread so that it would be absolutely fresh for the holiday meal. But this was no ordinary holiday, she reminded herself. It was the first time that she was responsible for preparing the meal instead of just helping her mother, and she still had many other things to do. She therefore assured herself that if she wrapped the bread properly, it would be fine.

"And whoever doesn't want to eat it doesn't have to," she whispered with a smile, recalling what her mother used to say when a dish didn't come out perfectly.

Clara paused for a moment to see how that sentiment felt coming from her own lips. During the past week she had been mulling over the idea that she was now the matriarch of the family.

Although the role still felt foreign to her, she was consciously trying to sort out how a matriarch was supposed to think and act. She wondered if her mother had gone through the same process after her grandmother had passed away. It was likely, since her mother had also been shy by nature. Yet her mother had possessed an inner strength that Clara didn't know if she had. When her mother said no, no one was misled by her quiet voice. They all knew that her mother's no meant don't bother to argue, cry, or otherwise try to change her mind.

Her mother had also known how to value her work and not feel threatened by imperfection. Those were qualities that Clara wanted to work on as well. As she placed the hot loaves on an oven rack to cool, she assumed a confident manner and silently whispered, "Even if the bread isn't perfectly fresh, no one will go hungry. There will be plenty of other food on the table."

"It's getting late, Clara. The light is fading."

Clara turned to face her husband. Josep had closed the workshop early, because she wanted him to paint the kitchen's walls.

The usual custom was to give the house a fresh coat of paint in the spring. But once she decided to do as her father wished — have the meal in the kitchen, instead of in the living room — she wanted to do something to spruce up the room. This was also part of being a matriarch, she had decided. If her kitchen was now going to be the center of the extended family's life, she wanted the room to accurately reflect the tone she hoped to set for her "reign."

Josep had balked at the color of paint that she had chosen, a bright shade of yellow. "You'll have to look at it every day," he had warned her.

"Yes," she had replied. "That's what I want to do. I want to look at a kitchen that is bright and cheerful every day."

Josep had shrugged. The kitchen was his wife's domain. As long as Clara didn't ask him to paint the dark wood cabinets bright red, he could live with her choice for the walls.

While Clara moved the loaves of bread into the living room, so they could cool undisturbed by the mess, Josep got to work in the kitchen. She hoped Vidal would come home soon. If two of them were working, the paint job would go much quicker, and she would have more time to clean up the kitchen afterward.

A car did pull up the driveway while she was dusting the top of the mantelpiece, but she saw through the window that it was Joanna, and not Vidal, who was walking up to the front porch. Since Joanna never just dropped by for a casual visit, Clara assumed that something was wrong and she was at the door even before Joanna had a chance to ring the bell. To her relief, she saw that Joanna was smiling. In fact, she couldn't remember when was the last time she had seen Joanna look so happy.

"Hello, Joanna, what a nice surprise," she said, herself surprised that her greeting was actually sincere. "Come inside."

"I know you must be busy, but I was in Girona today and I thought this would be perfect for you."

Joanna handed Clara a package wrapped in expensive-looking gift wrapping. She noted Clara's hesitation. "It's to say thanks, from Arnau and me, for all the hard work you've done for the holiday. Open it."

Clara carefully undid the paper, trying not to tear it more than was necessary. Inside was a long, shiny rectangular box — another sign that the gift had come from an expensive shop. Inside the box, nestled between a piece of colored tissue paper, was a silk scarf. Clara lifted up the scarf and turned it in the fading light. The floral pattern, hand-painted in gently muted earth colors, was neither too large nor too bright. It was the sort of tastefully elegant design that would go with anything, except a bright yellow kitchen or dress.

Of course, there was no way that Joanna could have known about the transformation that was taking place in the Bonets' kitchen at precisely that moment, or about the matriarchal musings that had been occupying Clara's mind. And Clara was touched by this unexpected show of appreciation. She said graciously, and without showing even the slightest trace of disappointment that now she wouldn't be able to wear the yellow dress that she had bought for the holiday, "Thank you, Joanna. It's absolutely beautiful."

It was only later that Clara realized that Joanna had slipped away before the obvious question had been asked. What had Joanna been doing in Girona?

The drive home took just long enough for Vidal to sail through every color of the emotional spectrum. After leaving his meeting with the Adarras, Vidal's first reaction was to fall into a black bog of a mood. If that's what people were really thinking — that it would be better to sell the village than try to save it — he had just wasted two years of his life. And he had angered his grandfather for no reason.

On the other hand, it was very possible that the Adarras were espousing a sentiment that was entirely their own. If that was the case, this was just one more obstacle thrown across his already obstacle-crowded path. As the vision of that bumpy road loomed large before his eyes, he began to feel sorry for himself, and his black humor lightened into a classic case of the blues.

Yet why would the Adarras want to sell their home? Where would they go? It didn't seem likely that they would follow their two sons to whichever foreign countries they were living in. And Arnau and Joanna were firmly entrenched in Sant Joan Januz.

Or were they?

Now that he thought about it, selling Sant Joan Januz sounded like the kind of thing that Joanna would dream up, just to spite him. That made him angry, and his emotional color wheel moved to red. Just because she didn't like the village, or him, didn't mean that she had the right to interfere with a plan that would help others. And if she disliked Sant Joan Januz so much, she could leave. No one was stopping her.

Then he realized that perhaps Joanna was serious. Her share from the sale would enable her and Arnau to set up a new home somewhere else. But the idea that Al's father would want to buy the village was laughable. Al's father traveled in too rarefied a sphere to be interested in building low-cost apartments for poor Muslim immigrants. To think that the fantastically wealthy Saudi businessman was hungering to get his hands on Eduard Garcia's grocery store was too ridiculous for words. What would he do with the property? Open a falafel stand for Al to manage?

As he visualized Al frying falafels in the square of Sant Joan Januz, Vidal started to laugh, and his world was once again filled with light. He decided that he would give Al a call after the holiday and share the joke with him. It would be good to check in with Al in any case and discuss with him the difficulties he had been encountering. As a confidant Al was a pale substitute for his grandfather, who had always been the person Vidal had sought out for support and advice. But at least Al was on his side; he had an interest in seeing the plan succeed, too.

Having arrived at his home at the same time that he arrived at a successful conclusion to his thoughts, Vidal parked the car in the back of the house, near the entrance to the kitchen. When he walked through the open door his first instinct was to turn around and leave, he was so sure he had mistakenly driven to the wrong place. Then he saw his father, who was looking at the yellow walls with an equally bemused expression.

"Wow," said Vidal. "That's some color."

Clara hummed as she ran the vacuum cleaner over the rug. She loved the energy of the day before a holiday. Everyone was so busy, but they were all working together and toward a common goal. It wasn't like a regular day, when that life force was scattered.

When she was done vacuuming, she decided it was time to make a light supper. Josep and Vidal were probably starving. "Anyone hungry?" she called out as she walked into the kitchen. Then she stopped and looked.

"What do you think?" Josep asked.

"I love it!" Clara said with real joy. "It's so..." She struggled to find the right word.

"Yellow?" Vidal suggested.

Josep tried not to laugh.

"It's full of life," Clara said with satisfaction, oblivious to the reactions of her husband and son. "It's full of happiness and life. May this room always be full of happiness and life!"

Vidal glanced over at his father, who only shrugged in response.

"You'll have to wash the windows again," said Josep. "Some paint splattered on the panes."

"I don't mind," said Clara, still entranced by the bright energy emanating from the walls.

"What about the inside of the chimney, Mama?" asked Vidal. "Do you want that to be yellow, as well?"

"Don't make fun of your mother," said Josep.

"But why not paint it yellow?" asked Clara.

"Did your mother paint the inside of her kitchen chimney yellow?" Josep replied.

"No, it was always white," said Clara.

"There's your answer, then," said Josep. "Vidal, there should be a can of white paint on the back porch."

Vidal left to get the paint.

"Do you hate it?" Clara asked Josep.

Josep carefully wiped the wet paintbrush against the inside of the paint can. Then he looked at Clara and smiled. "It's not as bad as I thought it would be."

Vidal returned with the paint. As the youngest member of the family, and the one with the strongest back, he was elected to paint the inside of the chimney. He was able to complete the whitewash job quickly with the help of a roller brush with an extra-long handle that made the brush especially well suited for the task.

Years ago, when the house had belonged to Clara's great-uncle Manel and great-aunt Nuria, the task had been much harder, even with a long-handled brush. Back then the hearth had been used for cooking and to heat the room and so cleaning and painting the chimney had been a real job. After Josep and Clara moved into the farmhouse they made several changes, including putting in a heating unit and new appliances. The kitchen hearth then became a fond, rarely used, and relatively soot-free reminder of an earlier time.

"This is how we should always begin a new year," said Clara as she wiped down the kitchen counter. "I don't know why everyone waits until spring to paint their homes."

"I suppose we do it then because that's when we clean out the winter's cobwebs," said Josep. "It's natural to want to make a fresh start in the spring."

"Then why celebrate the New Year holiday now? We should celebrate it in the spring, when the rest of the world is making a fresh start."

Josep looked at her. "Really, Clara, I don't know where you get such crazy ideas."

For a moment the room went black. Clara knew, with her mind, that it was Josep who had just spoken. But when she heard those words, she had the sensation that her mother was in the room, shaking her head in dismay.

Her mother would never have painted the walls of her kitchen yellow, she knew. Yellow was fine for flowers, which were small and had a whole world to disappear into. But for people the color was too bright. Her mother had told her that, she now recalled, when she had once wanted to buy a bright yellow dress.

Clara recalled the bright yellow dress hanging in her closet, and her joy melted away. In its place was a sick feeling in her stomach, which was telling her, as she took another look around the room, that the yellow walls made the kitchen stand out too much. It invited people to stop and look. She wasn't quite sure what was wrong with that. Certainly she had nothing to hide, except perhaps some dust balls lurking behind the refrigerator. But she knew that she had made a mistake. She should have taken Josep's hint — he always seemed to know what the proper thing was to do — and repainted the kitchen the same shade of cream.

It was too late, though, to paint the room again. She would have to suffer through the rest of the family's stares and comments. At least she would be able to return the dress. That mistake could remain her secret.

Clara forced herself to smile at Josep, who was still studying her with a worried look.

"I was only joking, Josep. Of course, we have to celebrate the New Year in the fall."

CHAPTER 9

Clara's eyes shifted from the clock hanging on the kitchen wall to the sun sitting precariously close to the horizon. The hour was getting late, and none of the guests had arrived.

"Don't worry, Mama," said Vidal, noting the worried expression on her face. "They'll be here in time. Where should I put the cards?"

Clara glanced over at Josep, who was fixing a chair leg that had come loose. Everything had become so complicated. Her husband Josep was the head of the household. But her father was the elder of the family. Who took precedence? Who should receive the tokens of honor?

It took Josep only a moment to make a decision. "Put the cards near my place," he said to Vidal. Then he turned to Clara. "When the time comes for the game, I'll hand the deck to your father."

"Yes, that's the solution," Clara agreed with relief.

Vidal went to the head of the table and slid open a little drawer that was fitted into the table's apron. He placed the deck of cards inside the drawer and closed it. Meanwhile, Josep finished with the chair and went out to the tool shed to put away his tools.

"Vidal..."

Vidal waited. He knew what his mother was going to say. The meal's seating arrangement hadn't escaped his notice. She had placed his seat next to hers, at one end of the table. His grandfather would sit next to his father, at the other end. The only way they could be seated further apart was if one of them sat in another room.

"I'd like everything to be nice tonight," said Clara.

Vidal didn't say anything. In the silence, they could hear a car pull into the driveway and come to a stop. While car doors opened and slammed shut outside, they went to the front door to greet the arrivals.

"Where's your grandfather? And Uncle Pau and Uncle Biel?" Clara asked after she and Vidal exchanged greetings with Arnau and his family.

"They're following behind us."

"Why didn't you pick them up?"

"I made a sweet-potato casserole," Joanna said blithely. "Come help me bring it to the kitchen, Manel."

"You look very pretty, Mama."

"Thank you, Arnau. Joanna gave me this scarf."

"It suits you very well. Where's Papa? In the kitchen?" Arnau started to leave, but Clara stopped him.

"Why didn't you pick up your grandfather? I didn't want him to drive home in the dark."

Arnau shrugged. "He insisted on driving."

A second car pulled into the driveway. Arnau saw that his mother's attention had been diverted by the arrival of his grandfather's pickup truck, and he slipped into the kitchen. Through the living room window Clara could see that Josep had come round to the front of the house to greet Miquel, Pau, and Biel and escort them inside.

"Hello, Clara," said Miquel as he gave her a quick hug. "Let's go, everybody. It's getting late."

Miquel took Clara by the arm. As he led her toward the kitchen, the others followed after them. When they reached the doorway, Miquel stopped and stared at the bright yellow walls.

"What's this?" he asked.

"We painted the kitchen," said Clara.

"I see that."

"Did you bring your sunglasses, Grandpa?" called out Manel.

"Manel!" Joanna put her hand over Manel's mouth and pulled him close to her.

"There's no need to be embarrassed, Clara," said Miquel. "Anyone can make a mistake, and you can repaint in the spring."

"I like the color," said Vidal. "It's cheerful."

"What did he say?" Biel whispered loudly to Pau. "They got the paint on sale?"

"Everyone, the sun is almost at the horizon," said Josep, nodding toward the window.

Clara knew that Josep, in his quiet way, was trying to move the family past their comments about the kitchen and that she

88

should help him. She went over to the cupboard and took out a ceramic container. Inside the container was a small glass cup that was filled with pure olive oil.

"Uncle Biel, why don't you stand over here, next to Vidal," said Josep as he led Biel over to where Vidal was standing. The rest of the family found their places on either side of the hearth and waited.

"But why did they paint the kitchen yellow?" Biel shouted over to Pau, who was standing on the other side of the hearth.

"Because it's cheerful!" Pau shouted back.

"Sssshhh!" Miquel glared at Pau and then at Biel, and then nodded his head toward Clara.

As Clara glanced out the window one last time, the eyes of everyone else followed hers. Through the window they could see that the sun was touching the horizon. The group returned their gaze to Clara, who struck a long match and lit the wick floating in the oil.

After she was sure that the flame was burning steadily, she nodded to Josep, who silently carried the container over to the hearth and securely affixed a wire to the container's handle. The wire was attached to a pulley, which enabled Josep to hoist the container high up inside the chimney. When the container was in its place, Josep motioned to Manel to come and stand next to him.

"Look inside the chimney, Manel. Do you see the light?"

"No, Grandpa. Where is it?"

"You can't see the flame," said Josep. "You can only see its shadow flickering on the wall. Do you see it?"

"Lift up your eyes, Manel," said Vidal. "Look high up in the chimney."

"I see it!"

When Manel finished with looking at the flickering shadows, Josep invited the rest of the family members to look at the light. After they had done so, Miquel signaled to Pau and Biel to go with him out of the room.

"We have to drink a toast to the New Year," said Clara. "Where are you going?"

"We'll be back," said Miquel.

The three men went out to Miquel's truck, where a bulky object covered with a heavy blanket had been sitting in the back compartment. They carefully lifted the object onto their shoulders and brought it into the kitchen.

"What is it?" asked Manel.

"You'll see in a minute," replied Miquel, as he placed the object next to Clara's place at the table. When he was satisfied with its placement, he turned to the little group with a smile. "Close your eyes, everyone. When I count to three, you can open them. Ready? Manel, are your eyes closed?"

"Yes, Grandpa."

"One... two..." Miquel lifted off the blanket with a flourish, revealing what had been hidden underneath it. "Three!"

Clara opened her eyes and stared. Sitting in her kitchen, next to her place at the table, was her mother's chair, the one with the wildflowers carved into its back. She blinked her eyes, unsure if what she was seeing was a true vision or a trick of her imagination.

"Well, Clara?" said Miquel. "Come and sit down."

Clara slowly shook her head. "I can't, Papa. I can't sit in Mama's chair."

"Your mother would have wanted you to have it."

"But it belongs in your home, with your chair and the others."

"It belongs in the home of the matriarch of the family, and now that's you. Your mother wouldn't mind your sitting in it. I know that for a fact. She often told me what a comfort it was to know that she had a daughter who would carry on after her and faithfully preserve our village's traditions."

"Come on, Clara," said Pau, who never liked emotional scenes. "You know your father isn't going to let you sit anywhere else, and the rest of us are hungry."

Clara knew that her uncle was right, on both counts. She slowly walked over to the chair, but she couldn't yet bring herself to sit down on it. Instead, she lightly touched the top of its back, half expecting that the chair would disappear in a puff of smoke, or that a hand would appear and slap her, making it obvious to everyone — and especially to her father — that she wasn't the rightful owner. When nothing happened, she allowed herself to run her fingers over the wildflowers that her great-uncle Manel had carved into the wood so many years before. Then she took a deep breath, slipped between the chair's two arms, and sat down.

"Bravo, Clara," Miquel called out as he clapped his hands. "Now, let's drink a toast to the New Year."

90

Miquel strode over to the table and lifted up the wine decanter. He poured the wine into the tall glass goblet and was about to fill the smaller glasses when he suddenly stopped and looked over at Josep.

"Go ahead, Papa," said Josep. "No one knows how to make a speech like you."

"Thank you, Josep. I'll take that as a compliment," Miquel replied with a smile. "But just in case it wasn't, I'll try and keep my remarks brief."

Everyone laughed politely as they took their seats. Miquel filled the wine glasses and passed them around the table. Then he cleared his throat, as a signal that he was ready to speak. The gesture was unnecessary since the room was already quiet.

"Tonight we've gathered around this table to celebrate the anniversary of the founding of Sant Joan Januz. Although we don't know exactly when our village was founded − the year, as you all know, is shrouded in the mists of time − we do know that our ancestors looked upon this season as a special time. For us, it is the start of a new year, and so it is a time for making a brand new start. But it is also a time of renewal. It is a time of renewed hope for the future, a time of renewed strength for the present, and a time when we renew our commitment to preserve the traditions that have come down to us from the past.

"Now, I'm not a philosopher, and I know that everyone is hungry, so I won't go into a long discussion about why our traditions need to be preserved. All I have to say is that they should be preserved. They must be preserved. And it is up to our family − as the leaders of the village for generations − to preserve them."

"Here, here!" said Pau, as he clinked his teaspoon against his wine glass.

Miquel silently acknowledged Pau, who was sitting next to him, with a nod of his head. "But how are we to fulfill the sacred trust that we, the leaders of Sant Joan Januz, have been given? Manel, perhaps you can think of a way. What would you do if you had a favorite toy that you didn't want to lose?"

"I don't know, Grandpa," Manel replied with a shrug.

"Don't be shy. I know that you're a smart little boy. If you had a special toy and you didn't want other children to play with it and break it, what would you do to protect it?"

91

Manel thought for a few moments. "I'd hide it in the chimney!"

The others laughed, but Miquel shushed them. He took a piece of candy out of his pocket and handed it to Manel. "That was an excellent answer, Manel. It shows that you learned something tonight. Because there is only one way to preserve our traditions for future generations, and that is the way of the past. We must look to the wisdom of our ancestors and learn from their actions. And what did they do when they first came to Sant Joan Januz and settled here? Does anyone know what they did to preserve our traditions?"

When no one replied, Miquel supplied his own answer. "They erected a high wall around this village, that's what they did. Of course, this wasn't a wall built from bricks and mortar. That kind of wall can be battered down by any army. Instead, they erected a wall that was constructed from the strongest material in the world: an ironclad policy of keeping to themselves and keeping strangers out.

"This invisible wall is what preserved us in the past, and our ancestors guarded its preservation as they would their most precious possession in the world. And that's the policy that we, the leaders of Sant Joan Januz, must continue to follow today. All of us, without exception, must take upon our shoulders the burden of ensuring that this wall is never breached. And should one of us ever try to tear down this wall, because he's become blinded by selfish dreams of personal glory, the rest of us must remind ourselves of our public obligation and, without remorse, cast him out from our midst. Unless, of course, we can open his eyes and get him to admit his error.

"So, everybody, let's drink a toast to Sant Joan Januz and the New Year. May it be a year of good health and prosperity for our family, and may it be a year of true peace and abundance for our ancestral home."

Pau nudged Biel and they both stood up.

"To Sant Joan Januz and the New Year," said Pau as he lifted his glass.

"Here, here," said Biel.

The rest of the family remained seated and cast furtive looks at Vidal, who was intently studying the napkin ring that sat next to his plate.

"Clara," said Miquel, "your family is waiting for you to stand."

"But, Papa..."

"You're not being fair," said Josep. "Not to Clara and not to Vidal."

"Let's not start off the New Year with a fight," said Vidal as he rose to his feet. "The village is going to be sold, anyway. Happy New Year!"

He didn't wait for anyone else to acknowledge his toast. He swallowed his glass of wine in one gulp and plopped back down in his chair. When he noted, with not a little satisfaction, that his grandfather and great-uncles were staring at him with open-mouthed silence, Vidal turned to Clara and said, "Shall I serve the soup, Mother?"

"Please do start the meal," Joanna said to Clara. "Manel is so hungry."

"Here, here," said Manel, imitating his great-uncles. But when he tapped his teaspoon against his little wine glass, he did so with such a powerful swing that it toppled over the glass and sent the wine flowing all over the white tablecloth.

"Oh, Manel, look what you've done," said Joanna.

"I'll get a cloth to clean it up," said Arnau.

"Tell Grandma you're sorry," said Joanna.

"I'm sorry, Grandma," said Manel.

"If the stain doesn't come out," Joanna said to Clara, "we'll buy you a new tablecloth."

"Stop making a fuss about the tablecloth," Pau said with exasperation. "We want Vidal to explain what he meant about selling Sant Joan Januz."

"Apparently some people believe that selling the village is the answer to our problems," said Vidal, rising from his chair. "Did you want carrots in your soup, Uncle Pau?"

"What people?" asked Pau.

"People who would rather live somewhere else, I suppose," replied Vidal.

"So let them go. What does that have to do with selling the village?"

"They don't want to leave empty-handed," said Joanna. "They think it's unfair that they can't sell their property."

Vidal smiled as he ladled out the soup. He was now certain that the idea of selling the village had been hers.

"But that's what the village's bylaws say," said Pau. "If someone leaves, their land goes back to their family. If they don't have family, the land goes to the village."

"And that's why people are unhappy," replied Joanna. "It's absurd that people can't sell their property."

"Sell the land to who?" asked Pau.

"To whoever wants to buy it."

"You mean, to strangers?"

"If they're the only people who are interested, then, yes, sell it to strangers."

"This is all your fault, young man," Pau said to Vidal, who was passing around the bowls of soup. "If you had come back with an idea for a factory, none of this would be happening."

"And what were we supposed to make in that factory? Stickers that say, 'Made in China'?"

"Vidal..." Josep gave Vidal a stern look.

"I'm sorry, Uncle Pau. I didn't mean to be disrespectful."

"We didn't ask Vidal to come back with a factory, Pau," said Miquel, carefully choosing his words so as not to betray his emotions. "If you recall, he was supposed to find a way to take advantage of these new technologies — invisible computer technologies — so that the people could make a good livelihood without us needing to bring strangers into our home."

"It wasn't feasible," replied Vidal, trying hard to stay calm. "I looked into things like outsourcing, but salary expectations in Catalonia are too high. We wouldn't have been able to compete."

"Then you should have admitted defeat," said Miquel. "That would have been the honorable thing to do. Instead, you betrayed us."

Vidal froze, still holding the last bowl of soup in his hand.

"You tricked us into providing a public forum to present that irresponsible idea of yours. Well, isn't that right? Did you, or didn't you betray our trust?"

Without emotion, Vidal replied, "Yes, sir, I did."

"And why did you do such a low and devious thing?"

"Papa..."

"Quiet, Clara. This conversation is between Vidal and me. Well, Vidal? You wanted to talk, so talk."

Vidal was silent.

"If you don't want to tell your family why you betrayed us, I will. You did it because you don't care a bit about preserving our village's traditions. They mean nothing to you. You'd sacrifice every one of them, rather than let them come in between you and what you think is your ticket to success. Well? Am I right?"

Vidal stared straight ahead, into empty space. Then he set down the soup and left the room. A few moments later, the front door slammed shut. Clara started to get out of her chair, but Josep stopped her.

"Let him be," said Josep. "It won't do him any harm to think things over." He turned to the others. "We should eat the soup before it gets cold."

Pau nudged Biel and motioned to him to start eating his soup. Joanna busied herself with cutting up the vegetables in Manel's bowl.

"Mama, can I get you something to drink?" Arnau asked.

"No, thank you," replied Clara, keeping her eyes fixed on her soup bowl.

Miquel silently studied Arnau for a few moments, and then he turned his attention to Joanna. "I assume the 'unhappy people' you referred to are your parents. Tell them to call me after the holiday, and I'll work something out."

"Where will we get the money from?" asked Pau.

"We'll discuss that later," Miquel replied.

"It's not just my parents who want to leave," said Joanna.

"Not now," Arnau whispered to her under his breath.

"Why not?" Joanna replied in her normal voice. "They're going to find out after the holiday anyway."

"Find out what?" asked Miquel.

"I've accepted a job offer in Girona," said Joanna. "We're going to move there."

"Move?" Clara almost didn't recognize her own voice, which sounded weak and far away.

"Yes, we've found a wonderful apartment in the old part of the city. We'll invite everyone after we've settled in."

"You're leaving Sant Joan Januz?" Miquel directed the question to Arnau, who was studiously avoiding his grandfather's eyes.

"But you'll be renting?" asked Josep.

"In the beginning, Papa," replied Arnau. "But if everything works out with Joanna's job, we'll look for an apartment to buy."

"Will your parents also be moving to Girona?" Miquel asked Joanna.

"That's what we've been discussing. They won't have any reason to stay after we leave. My brothers, as you know, left the village several years ago."

"But why do you have to move?" asked Clara. "Why can't you live here and commute?"

"It would be too tiring for Joanna, Mama," said Arnau. "And besides, Manel will be starting kindergarten soon. We'll have more options for schools in Girona."

"You mean, Manel will be leaving, too?"

"Of course," said Joanna. "We're not going to leave him behind."

Everyone looked at Manel, who was happily navigating a piece of carrot through his soup with his spoon. Since no one had anything else to say, a gloomy silence fell upon the room.

"Mama, shall we serve the next course?" asked Arnau.

"Yes, let's clear the table," Joanna said to Arnau. "Manel, would you like to help? You can be in charge of the spoons."

While Joanna, Arnau, and Manel removed the soup bowls, the rest of the group remained silent. It was Miquel who was the first to rouse himself from his thoughts. He opened the drawer that was hidden within the table apron directly in front of his seat and took out a small bowl that was filled with colored tokens. He put the bowl on the table and waited.

"It's our tradition to play cards in between each course," said Miquel when he saw that no one else had followed his cue.

"I know, Papa, but I don't know if anyone is in the mood," Josep replied. "Maybe we should just get on with the meal."

"Mood has nothing to do with it," said Miquel. "A tradition is a tradition."

Josep looked across the table, to where Clara was sitting. Her head was bowed. He didn't think that she was crying, but he wasn't sure. "Clara?" he asked. "Your father would like to start the game. Is that all right?"

Clara nodded her head, but without raising her eyes. Josep shrugged. He opened the drawer near his seat and removed a small bowl that also had colored tokens inside it, while Pau and

Biel did the same. Josep took out the deck of cards that Vidal had placed there earlier.

"You deal the first hand, Papa," said Josep, handing the deck to Miquel.

"Thank you, Josep," replied Miquel.

Miquel inspected the forty-card Spanish deck to make sure it was complete. He then shuffled the cards, but without his usual banter and theatrics. When the cards had been shuffled, he silently passed the deck to Pau, and Pau cut the cards.

"Shouldn't there be a pencil and a pad of paper on the table?" asked Pau, as he passed the deck of cards back to Miquel. "To keep score?"

Josep went to get the paper and pencil. Then Miquel, who had waited for Josep to return, began to deal out the first hand. "Thank you, Pau, for reminding us," said Miquel. "We almost forgot."

As he lay stretched out on the garden swing, Vidal watched the starry night sky play hide-and-seek through the leafy branches of the ancient oak trees that stood on either side of him. The swing sat in a secluded spot in the garden, and it made an admirable berth for contemplating the mysteries of the universe. Long ago, there had been many evenings when he had sat on the swing with his grandfather, who taught him how to read the celestial narrative that was written, not with words, but with stars. On a chilly autumn evening, like this one, they would search for the seven bright lights of the Pleiades, whose return to the heavens above signaled the return of cold weather below.

The swing had also been his favorite place to go when he needed to think. In the past, no problem had been so big that it couldn't be gently chiseled down to a manageable size by the swing's rhythmic movement back and forth. On this night, though, as Vidal gazed up at the Pleiades, he wondered if the swing had lost its power. The chaos inside his head remained stubbornly out of tune with the calm symmetry of the night.

The sounds of the holiday meal breaking up interrupted his thoughts. He heard the good-byes on the front porch followed by car engines starting up. The noise from the cars became fainter and fainter, until they faded away completely. Just when it seemed that the world was ready to return to silence, he heard footsteps approaching, and he sat up.

"There's food for you in the kitchen," said Josep.

"Thanks, but I'm not hungry."

"Your mother will be upset if you don't eat something."

"I'll come inside in a little while. And I'll clean up. You and Mama can go to bed."

Josep sat down on the swing beside Vidal. "Arnau and Joanna are going to leave the village."

"I thought they might. I suppose that will be hard for Mama. Arnau in voluntary exile, me banished and cast out without remorse."

"I told your grandfather that this quarrel is really all his fault. You didn't create the village's problems. He shouldn't have put so much pressure on you to solve them."

"No one forced me to go to New York. I wanted to help the village."

"I know that. And I think your grandfather knows it as well."

"Papa, why is Grandpa so against strangers? Mr. Adarra told me that he once suggested the village build a factory, and Grandpa was against that idea, too."

"It's as your grandfather said. We're only a small village. If people with different customs started moving in here, our traditions would eventually disappear."

"Would that be such a terrible thing?"

"Sant Joan Januz is a nice place to live. It would be a shame for it to lose that quality."

"I agree. But can't it be a nice place even if we don't hide the light in the chimney?"

Josep didn't reply.

"Why do we do that, anyway? Why is it forbidden for us to look directly at the light?"

"It's bad luck. You know that."

"Then why bother to light the light at all?"

"Because we're waiting."

"For what?"

"You're not a child, Vidal. You know the answers to these questions as well as I do."

"Then that's the problem, Papa, because I don't know. I don't believe that anyone knows anymore what we're waiting for, and that's the real reason why everyone is leaving."

CHAPTER 10

Here or Girona?"

Manel looked intently at the toy typewriter that Vidal was holding. He wanted to take it with him, just as he wanted to take all of his toys to his new home. But Joanna and

Arnau were taking only the minimum to the rental apartment they had found in Girona since the apartment was furnished. Manel was also expected to pack lightly, and so he had only two boxes for toys. One of them was already full.

"Why don't you leave the typewriter here for now, Manel, until you learn how to write?"

"Or until you come to visit. You could bring it as a surprise."

"That's also a possibility."

Manel went back to sorting through his toys. Vidal was happy that his nephew had accepted his ambiguous answer. He didn't want to make a promise that he wouldn't be able to keep, and the chance of his being invited to visit Arnau and Joanna in Girona was unlikely.

The toy typewriter was still in Vidal's hands. "Manel, would you mind if I keep the typewriter at my house for the time being?"

Manel gave Vidal a quizzical look, as children sometimes do when they feel that an adult isn't acting quite up to par. "You'll give it back?"

"Of course. When you're ready for it."

Manel shrugged and returned to his toys. Vidal, who knew the gesture well from other members of the family, interpreted the shrug to mean that his request had been granted. He knew it was childish of him to feel possessive about the typewriter, especially since it had been his idea to give it to Manel. But the typewriter had once meant a great deal to him. It was part of his past, and he didn't want it to end up in some rubbish bin in Girona.

The small caravan laden with its cargo of boxes arrived in Girona in mid-afternoon. Arnau's car guided the others through the new part of the city and to a bridge that traversed the Onyar River and led to the city's medieval quarter. Standing guard above the river's banks was a long line of houses. Painted in rich, earthy shades of red, orange, and ochre, the houses appeared to signal that Girona, despite its urban status, still had its roots firmly planted in the Catalan countryside from which it had sprung more than two thousand years before.

"It is pretty," said Clara, who was accompanying her father in his pickup truck, which was carrying Arnau's canvases and art supplies.

"There are lots of pretty places in the world," Miquel replied. "That doesn't mean you have to live in them."

Since the apartment that Arnau and Joanna had rented on Carrer Sant Llorenc could only be reached on foot, the boxes were transferred to hand trucks for the final stage of the journey. Carrer Sant Llorenc was actually a narrow medieval passageway, whose pavement was a long and steep flight of stone stairs. The last section of steps was covered with a vaulted stone ceiling that cast a distinctly medieval gloom over the entire street. While some members of the group gazed uneasily into the darkness, Manel joyously dashed down the steps, thrilled with this new game.

"Won't it be too dark?" Clara asked Arnau as they watched Manel disappear into the dimly lit passageway. "How will you paint?"

"It's only a rental," said Arnau. He unlocked the front door to the apartment, which was at the top of the stairs.

"This section of the old city is very atmospheric, in my opinion," said Joanna.

As she tried to maneuver her hand truck through the front door, Joanna missed a step. The hand truck tipped over and sent the top box tumbling down the stairs.

"I'll get it," said Miquel.

Arnau followed after him. He wanted to reach the landing where the box had come to a halt before his grandfather did, but he was too late.

"What's all this?" asked Miquel, peering through a wrought-iron gate. On the other side of the gate was a large courtyard. It had a gigantic six-pointed star embedded in its stone floor.

"It's a museum," said Arnau. He picked up the box and returned up the stairs.

"A museum?"

"It's Girona's Jewish museum," said Joanna. "But there's no need to worry, Grandpa."

"Why should I worry?"

"We know how you feel about strangers. But there aren't any Jews living in Girona anymore. They were all expelled in 1492."

"*Hola!*" Manel had reached the bottom step and was waving to them.

"Manel, come back here at once!" Joanna called down to him.

"Okay." He cheerfully started the long trek back up.

While the men brought the boxes inside, Clara looked around the bottom floor of the apartment, which consisted of a living room and a kitchen. The space had been recently renovated, but the owners had preserved as much of the old as they could.

"It's certainly atmospheric," said Clara. She placed her hand on a wall of exposed stone. The stones were already cold, even though the winter season hadn't begun. "But how will you keep the apartment warm?"

"With heaters," said Joanna. "Arnau, why don't you find Manel and take everyone to that restaurant in the square? You all must be famished."

"But we want to help you unpack," said Clara, who had gone into the kitchen. She observed that it was equipped with all the conveniences, including a small dishwasher.

Josep had also noticed that the owners hadn't cut any corners when they renovated the space. "It's none of my business," he said quietly to Arnau, "but it must cost a small fortune to rent this place. Are you sure you'll be able to manage?"

"We fell into a bit of luck," Arnau replied. "The owners are living abroad for the year, and they were looking for a caretaker. We just need to pay the utilities and a nominal monthly fee. Joanna's boss arranged it."

"I see."

"Arnau, please find Manel," said Joanna, who had noticed that Miquel was also intently examining the rooms. "And after everyone has eaten, I want you to send your family straight back to Sant Joan Januz. I know your mother will want to be home before it gets dark."

"Where's the fireplace, Joanna?"

"There's a whole closet full of electric heaters upstairs," Joanna said to Miquel. "Really, we'll be very comfortable."

"How you heat the place is your business," replied Miquel. "What I want to know is how you're going to light the light every Friday evening if there's no fireplace in the apartment."

Joanna glanced over at Arnau.

"Well? Where are you going to put the container?"

"We're not going to put it anywhere," said Joanna.

Miquel looked at Arnau and waited.

"Joanna's family stopped doing it years ago," said Arnau. "We don't do it, either."

"Clara, did you know about this?"

"I never asked them what they do in their home. I just assumed..."

"You have ten minutes to get your paintings out of my truck, Arnau. Then I'm driving back to Sant Joan Januz."

On the return trip to the village, Clara once again accompanied her father. Josep was driving ahead of them, with Vidal. She wished she was with them. The silence in her father's car was starting to feel oppressive.

"They may not like it in Girona," she said quietly, just to say something. "Arnau never was a city person. And I don't care what Joanna says, it's going to be very hard to heat those rooms with electric heaters. And expensive. Stone walls get very cold in the winter. Do you remember how cold my house was before we put in central heating?"

"Why are you rambling, Clara?"

"You can't be angry at the entire family, Papa. I know our traditions are important, but..."

"But?"

"The world is a different place. It's a different generation."

"Does that mean you approve of Joanna's decision?"

"I didn't say that I approve. It's just that my family is all that I have. Can't you come to some sort of compromise with Vidal?"

"If even you're against me, it looks like I'll have to."

When they reached the square in Sant Joan Januz, Miquel signaled to Josep to park his truck. "I want to talk to Vidal," he said. "Clara, you go home with your husband."

While Vidal took a seat at the cafe table, Miquel entered the general store.

"Do you sell loose sheets of paper, Eduard?"

"How many do you need?"

"Three."

"Peace negotiations?" asked Eduard, nodding his head toward Vidal, whom he saw sitting outside.

"Something like that."

Eduard Garcia tore off three sheets from a notebook that he kept near the cash register. "It's on the house."

"Thanks. I'll return the favor someday."

Miquel joined Vidal at the table. He took out a ballpoint pen and drew a rough sketch of Sant Joan Januz on one of the sheets of paper.

"Here, and no further," said Miquel, putting a large X on a plot of land located in the southernmost part of the village that was communal property. "And I want a separate road for your resort, so that your tour buses don't drive on the road that the villagers use. I'd tell you to build a moat around the resort, too, if I weren't afraid that mosquitoes would breed in the water and give us all malaria."

Vidal scrutinized his grandfather's face, looking for something that would tell him if this was really a capitulation or just a change in tactics.

"You can relax your eyebrows, Vidal. If it were up to me, I'd let both you and Arnau leave the village. But it isn't only up to me."

Vidal nodded and studied the map. "I see that the square is off-limits."

"Think of it as being a hostile, foreign country. Build your own square for the people who want to open up a shop or restaurant."

"I accept. Thank you, Grandpa."

"Not so quick. You didn't ask about the price."

"All right. What is this going to cost me?"

"Number one, the money to pay for the land will come from that Saudi investor of yours."

103

"There's money in the budget for that."

"Number two, there will be no mention of Sant Joan Januz's traditions in your resort's promotional materials. Neither will you mention our traditions in any interviews you give to the press. We're just a village like any other village in Catalonia, and you're just a good Catholic with the same traditions as any other Catholic, although you might be a little lax in the practice of those traditions."

"Agreed."

"Number three, you have to sign this." Miquel quickly wrote out a few sentences on the second sheet of paper. When he was done, he copied the text onto the third sheet and handed it to Vidal.

"I don't understand," said Vidal after he had read the short contract. "This is why you'll let me build the resort?"

"You've won, Vidal. Even if all of our other traditions are abandoned after my generation is gone, I have to do everything in my power to make sure that this one is preserved. Spanish law gives urban developers the right to move a cemetery. Someone from our family has to stay in Sant Joan Januz and make sure that no one disturbs our dead. Arnau will never come back, not with that wife of his. So it looks like that someone has to be you."

"But what if I have to leave the village someday?"

"That's covered in the agreement. If you should decide to sell the resort — or the entire village, for that matter — there has to be a clause that the new owners can't tamper with the cemetery, even if the law permits moving it, and even if there is a profit to be had from selling the land. You will have to personally make sure that the cemetery is never touched."

"For the rest of my life?"

"Accept my terms, and you can proceed with my blessing. Reject them, and you'll build that resort over my dead body."

Vidal took out his pen and signed both copies of the document. Miquel added his name. He then gave one copy back to Vidal.

"If this is a binding agreement between us, shouldn't there be witnesses?" Vidal asked.

Miquel pointed up to the sky. "The generations are our witnesses."

PART II: HOLA!

CHAPTER 11

The important thing, Vidal, is to keep the project moving forward."

Vidal nodded, though he was talking on the phone, and Al, who was about seven thousand miles away, couldn't see him.

"I agree, Al, and the project has been moving forward. The resort was approved by the village. The people in the Girona regional council gave their preliminary approval to the architect's plans. But they're still waiting for your office to send them the final version, with the revisions."

"Okay, I'll give the main office a call. And instead of a regular museum, my father wants an indoor *La Convivencia* sound-and-light show."

"You mean, build sets and all that?"

"That's right. It will be much more dynamic, especially with the right music."

"I thought the museum was supposed to be small. Do we have money in the budget for this?"

"Don't worry about the money. Speaking of which, did you check your bank account?"

"Yes, the money was deposited. Thanks."

"Great. Now I have to go. This new resort in Bali is amazing, but there are still a million details to iron out before it's ready to open its doors next month."

"You won't forget about sending the final plans?"

"I've put it at the top of my list. And, Vidal, you should know that my father is very impressed with the work you've done so far. Once Bali is up and running, you're going to have our undivided attention. In the meantime, start thinking about a script for the sound-and-light show. We don't get overly involved with the local culture presentation, so you'll be in charge of that. Just make sure that whatever you come up with is snappy and sappy."

"Snappy and sappy?"

"You know, the ratio: twenty percent head, that's the historical stuff; forty percent heart, that's the positive, feel-good spin on said historical stuff; and forty percent gift shop. That's self-explanatory. Now I really have to run. My father's waiting for me down in the restaurant."

"Give him my regards."

"*Adeu*, Vidal. See, I'm already learning a little Catalan."

"*Adeu*, Al."

The line went dead. Vidal hung up the phone and closed his eyes. He was no longer in the small, musty former housewares store that his grandfather had agreed to rent him for use as a temporary office. Instead, he pictured Al sitting on a deck chair on some pristine beach, watching the evening sky burst into red and orange flames. "Snappy and sappy!" he could hear Al call out to the errant setting sun, which was dawdling over the clear blue waters, oblivious to the fact that it was distracting visitors from spending their money inside the restaurants and gift shops of Bali's newest luxury resort.

Vidal laughed and opened his eyes. He enjoyed talking to Al. It made him feel connected to the greater world, the world of action and accomplishment. If he was less than enchanted with Al's unabashedly twenty-forty-forty worldview, where style was more highly prized than substance, and profit margins were valued highest of all, Vidal attributed that to the fact that Al and his father were essentially nomads. They stayed in a place for only as long as it took to build their resort, and then they were off to the next destination. The only long-term communication they maintained with their far-flung empire came in the guise of monthly financial statements.

With the right people telling the *La Convivencia* story, Vidal decided that he just might succeed in slipping in more than twenty percent of meaningful content without Al and his father noticing. At the very least, finding a talented creative team would give him something concrete to do again. After the village had approved the resort, he discovered that, despite his official title and generous salary, he had quite a bit of free time on his hands. Al's company was in charge of the next stage, getting the building permits and hiring the contractors. It made sense, since the company had a corps of experts already on staff. But sometimes, such as moments like this one, when Vidal stared at the empty pages of his calendar for too long, he had an uneasy feeling that it was all a sham.

"Enjoy the quiet while it lasts," Al had said with a laugh when Vidal had voiced a mild complaint about not having anything to do. "Once the bulldozers break through that first patch of ground, it will be one headache after another."

At the time, Vidal had been reassured by Al's words. Now, when he recalled the conversation, for some reason those same words were having the opposite effect.

"I just made a fresh pot of coffee. Want some?" Eduard Garcia had popped his head inside the door.

"Thanks," Vidal replied. "I could use some fresh air."

While Vidal sat at the cafe table and slowly sipped his coffee, a car drove up the road to Sant Joan Januz and pulled into the general store's parking lot. The driver, a young man in his early twenties, walked into the square and looked around. When he noticed Vidal sitting at the table, he casually strolled over to him.

Vidal eyed the approaching stranger warily. People didn't just drop into Sant Joan Januz.

"*Hola*," said the young man with a smile.

Vidal looked the stranger up and down. "*Hola*," he replied noncommittally, stretching out the two syllables of the word. Within the greeting a trained ear could hear a whole chorus of subtextual questions: Who are you? What are you doing here? And when are you leaving?

"Mind if I sit down?" asked the young man. When Vidal didn't answer, he sat down. "That coffee sure smells good." When Vidal still didn't say anything, the young man asked, "Am I by any chance in Sant Joan Januz?"

From the way the stranger spoke and dressed, it was obvious to Vidal that he was from the United States. That, of course, made his appearance in the village even more suspect.

"Do you want to be in Sant Joan Januz?"

"Yes."

"Why?"

"My name is Charlie Green." The young man extended his hand to Vidal. "Nice to meet you."

Vidal glanced at the outstretched hand, and then returned his attention to his coffee.

"I'm a graduate student at the University of Kansas, Department of Anthropology. I'm doing my thesis on comparative farm cultures in Kansas and Catalonia. This is a farming community, isn't it?"

"Yes."

"So that's why I'm here."

"To write your thesis?"

"No, to do research for my thesis. I'll write it when I'm back in Kansas."

"What exactly do you want to research, Mr. Green?"

"Coping strategies. How rural communities that once revolved around the family farm are adapting to change in an increasingly centralized and industrialized world."

"There's nothing here that would interest you."

"Don't be so sure. I'm not necessarily looking for something grand. Several towns in Kansas are repositioning themselves as tourist sites, for example, and they're doing it based on attractions that are really small. Ever hear of Cawker City?"

"No."

"It's home to the biggest community-made ball of twine in the world — almost eight million feet and still growing. It put Cawker City on the map."

"People go all the way to Kansas to see a ball of twine?"

"I'm not saying the town needs to build an airport to handle all the incoming traffic. It's just an example of the way that farm people are using their traditional resourcefulness to keep their communities alive." Charlie paused for a moment and looked around the square. "This place sure looks dead."

"So maybe you shouldn't waste any more of your time."

"My thesis isn't just about business strategies. I'll also be studying how traditional farm culture is enabling people to transmit their knowledge and values to the next generation."

Vidal stood up. "Good luck with your thesis."

"There's really nothing of interest here?"

"Not a thing."

"That's funny. Your neighbors over at the agricultural cooperative's office told me that I'd find a gold mine of information in this village."

108

"They must have been pulling your leg."

"Why would they do that?"

"To get rid of you."

The young man took the hint and also stood up. "Thanks for the invitation to stay for coffee, but I've got to run. Have a nice day."

As the young man strolled back to his car, Eduard Garcia came out of his store. "Who was that?" he asked.

"Nobody," replied Vidal.

"He looked like a foreigner. Was he lost?"

"Apparently."

"Well, it can happen."

Instead of returning to the main road, Charlie Green drove down the narrow lane that continued further into the village. He didn't have a specific destination in mind. He just wanted to find someone who would talk to him. But before he continued any further, he decided he should first say *minchah*, the afternoon prayer.

When he saw a clump of trees that would hide his body from curious eyes, he pulled his car over onto the side of the road. He would have liked to remove the cowboy hat he was wearing, since it wasn't his usual head covering when he prayed, but he left it on. He didn't want to take the chance that someone would see the black yarmulke that he wore underneath the hat.

He took out his compass. As he searched for the southeast, so that he would face Jerusalem while he prayed, he could see fields stretching all around him, and a tingling sensation raced up and down his spine. He was finally in Sant Joan Januz, if this really was the location of the medieval village that he was looking for.

It hadn't been easy to get even this far. Most maps didn't show every tiny village, and the people at the tourist office in Girona had never heard of the place. Trying to be helpful, they came up with a few possible "Sant Joans" that were located in the area: the monastery at Sant Joan de les Abadesses, a small town called Sant Joan les Fonts, another one called Sant Joan de Mollet, but nothing called Sant Joan Januz.

They then suggested that perhaps Chaim — for that was his real name — had mistaken the name of the village. Perhaps he was looking for a Sant Jaume or a Sant Julia, or even a Sant Jordi. In the end, he had taken the map back with him to his hotel room, where he studied the tiny print until his eyes were too blurry to see. By that time, even he was starting to believe that he had made a mistake — or that the village no longer existed.

He put the map aside. If the tourist office had never heard of the place, who in the world would know where the village was located? A few minutes later the answer came to him: the income tax office. Fortunately, the city of Girona was the capital of the province of Girona, and so finding the regional tax office was easy. Trying to explain what he wanted was a different story. But several hours later he watched as a clerk drew a circle on his map and said, "It's somewhere around here."

"Thank you, G-d!" he wanted to yell. Instead, he politely thanked the clerk for his kindness. Then he hurried to find a car rental office so he could set out for the countryside the next day.

Although the circle on his map narrowed down the possibilities considerably, he still drove past the unmarked turnoff to the village a dozen times. If he hadn't stumbled on the office of the local agricultural cooperative, where one of the farmers volunteered to show Chaim where to make the turn, he probably would have still been driving up and down that same stretch of road.

No, he wouldn't still be driving, he reminded himself, because he had to say *minchah*. After that, he would try again to strike up a conversation with one of the natives. Hopefully, that unsociable young man in the square wasn't typical of the good people of Sant Joan Januz.

Clara was the first to notice the car that was sitting by the side of the road. "Do you need help?" she asked as she pulled her car alongside the one that had its hood up.

Chaim "Charlie" Green removed his head from under the hood. "Do you know where I can find a mechanic, ma'am? This engine appears to be deader than a doornail."

"I'll call my husband."

While Clara waited for Josep to answer the phone, she noted the young man's cowboy hat. Not too many Americans spoke Catalan. Although he certainly didn't speak the language like a native, she was impressed that he could speak it at all.

110

Josep arrived on the scene a few minutes later. He knew a little about car engines, but only a little. The only practical advice he could offer was to ask, "Did you call the rental company?"

"No one answered," Chaim replied. "I guess they already closed for the day."

"What will you do?" Clara asked. "Where will you sleep?"

Chaim pointed to the car. "Don't worry, ma'am. I've slept in worse places."

"We can't let him spend the night out here," Clara whispered to Josep.

"We don't know anything about him."

"He seems nice."

Josep's instincts told him that Clara was probably right. But he did wonder how the young man had strayed so far from the main road. He must have been looking for something, but what?

"Do you have family in the area?"

Chaim smiled. That was a good question. But he wasn't ready to go into all the details of why he was in the village just yet. "I'm a tourist. My name is Charlie Green. Nice to meet you."

Josep took the extended hand. "Josep Bonet, and this is Mrs. Bonet."

Chaim acknowledged Clara with a nod. "I'm a graduate student from the United States. I'm here to do research for my thesis."

"Our son went to graduate school in New York City," said Clara, glancing over at Josep.

"I'm a student at the University of Kansas. It's farm country out there, like here."

"You grew up on a farm?" asked Josep.

"Not exactly," replied Chaim. "The old-style family farms are dying out in Kansas, just like in Catalonia."

"Look, why don't you spend the night with us?" Josep offered. "Our house isn't far."

"Thank you, but will the car be all right?"

"There's nothing to worry about. Sant Joan Januz is very safe."

"What did you say the name of this village was?" Chaim asked nonchalantly as he removed his overnight bag from the back seat of the car and locked the doors.

"Sant Joan Januz," replied Josep.

111

"We're just simple country people, Charlie," said Clara, "so I hope you won't mind that dinner won't be anything special."

Chaim looked around the room where he would be spending the night. It was the "sewing room," meaning it was the room where the lady of the house stored things that were too worn out to use but too good to throw out. An old, lumpy sofa was pushed against the back wall. His hostess had apologized that it wasn't a proper bed, but Chaim didn't mind the inconvenience. He was happy to have made his first entry into the village, and a few lumps couldn't diminish that joy.

He was also happy that his hostess had accepted his story about being on a macrobiotic diet, which is why he had brought with him his own food, cooking utensils, and dishes. He didn't want to lie to the people who had so kindly taken him into their home. But he could hardly tell them that he was an Orthodox Jew who kept kosher.

After he had taken out of his bag everything he needed to prepare his dinner of brown rice and steamed vegetables, Chaim went into the kitchen. Clara was already preparing dinner for the rest of the family, and the smell of the stew simmering on the stove filled the room.

"Are you sure you can't eat this?" asked Clara. "It's just fresh cod cooked in a sauce of tomato, onions, and herbs."

"It sounds delicious, but macrobiotics is very strict. Tomatoes are absolutely..." Charlie made a sweeping gesture to demonstrate just how forbidden that vegetable was. As he did so, hundreds of grains of rice tumbled out of the open bag that he held in his hand and went flying all over the kitchen floor.

"I'm really sorry, Mrs. Bonet."

"It's nothing," said Clara, who was already at the broom closet.

"Please, let me clean this up." Chaim took the broom and dust pan and quickly began to sweep the rice in the direction of the kitchen door.

"Stop!"

Chaim looked up. "Is something wrong, Mrs. Bonet?" He noted that her face had turned white.

"I always sweep toward the center of the room," Clara said quietly. "It's the way my mother taught me."

"Family traditions are very important where I come from as well," Chaim reassured her. "Thank you for telling me."

Thank you, indeed, he thought with satisfaction. Sweeping toward the center of the room was one of the customs preserved by the *Anusim*. That was the Hebrew term for the descendents of the Spanish and Portuguese Jews who were forced to convert to Christianity during the Middle Ages. It meant the "Forced Ones." Other terms commonly used in books and research articles to describe them were crypto-Jews, Conversos, or New Christians. In the past, they were called Marranos, but since this was a Spanish word that meant "pigs" the derogatory term had fallen out of usage in modern times. The *Anusim* themselves used the term "People of the Nation" to describe their ambiguous relationship to the Jewish people.

Whatever name was used, the practice of sweeping dirt toward the center of the room was one of the pieces of evidence used to condemn them during the Inquisition. According to a seventeenth-century book called *Mishnas Chachomim*, which Chaim had come across while doing his research, the Jews of Spain had swept dirt toward the center of the room to show respect for the *mezuzah* — the small piece of parchment inscribed with biblical verses that hung on the doorposts of Jewish homes. The *Anusim* had continued the practice even after there was no longer a mezuzah to honor.

Most modern Jews put the parchment in a metal or plastic container and affixed the container to the doorpost with nails or two-sided tape. But in the past, when houses were built from stone, a small space was carved out of the stone doorpost and the parchment was placed inside it. Chaim glanced over at the kitchen door, but not because he expected the Bonets to have a *mezuzah*. He knew from the stone farmhouse's exterior that it was an old structure. If there was just one doorpost in the entire house that had retained the telltale indentation that marked where the parchment had once rested, it would be a stunning piece of evidence.

He walked over to the closed door and made a few sweeps with his broom toward the center of the room. Clara smiled at him and went back to her cooking. While the coast was clear, he reached his hand toward the doorknob, so that he could quickly open the door and check the doorpost without being detected. To his surprise, before his fingers even touched the knob, the door suddenly swung open. It took Chaim a moment to realize who it was that had opened the door from the other side. When he recognized the person, his heart sank.

"What are you doing here?" Vidal asked Chaim.

"Have you two already met?" asked Clara.

"Not formally," Chaim replied.

"This is the son I was telling you about, Charlie, the one who went to graduate school in New York." Clara turned to Vidal. "Please close the door, Vidal. You're letting in all the cold air."

"Nice to see you again," Chaim said to Vidal. "I'll get the door."

While Vidal went over to his mother, Chaim quickly ran his fingers down the doorpost. To his disappointment, it had a modern concrete finish. He closed the door and went back to sweeping the floor.

"What's he doing here?" Vidal whispered to his mother.

"His car broke down, so he's going to spend the night," Clara replied. "How do you know him?"

"I met him in the square. Mama, if he asks you any questions about Sant Joan Januz or about our customs, don't answer him, all right? I don't know who sent him here, but he's up to something."

"Mrs. Bonet..." Chaim stood with the dustpan in his hand. "Where can I toss this?"

"The bin is in there." Clara pointed to a bottom cabinet door.

As Chaim dumped the contents of the dustpan into the garbage bin, he glanced over to the stove. He saw that his hostess was whispering something to her son.

"And please tell your father that dinner is ready," Clara said to Vidal in her normal voice.

Chaim watched as Vidal disappeared through the doorway. This was an unfortunate development. But if he worked quickly perhaps all wasn't lost.

"Mrs. Bonet," he said with a smile, "I hope you don't mind my asking, but I was wondering if there was a reason your mother always swept toward the center of the room. Sometimes these simple customs have a deeper meaning. In Kansas, for instance..."

"I'm sure it was just habit," Clara replied tersely, turning her back on Chaim.

Chaim wasn't surprised by his host's chilly politeness during the meal. He assumed that Vidal had warned his father to be on guard as well. The dinner conversation listlessly focused on neutral topics, such as the pros and cons of a macrobiotic diet and the price of wheat in world markets, until it faded away entirely. Clara broke the silence by telling Josep and Vidal about her afternoon.

"I went over to Arnau's house," she explained. "A part of the fence was down."

"That rainstorm last night must have done it," said Vidal. "The winds were pretty strong."

"I would feel so much better if someone was living there. What if a pipe burst? There could be a flood, and we wouldn't know it."

"It's not that cold outside, Clara," said Josep.

"I can drive by there a couple times a week, Mama, on my way home from the square."

"I can do that, too, but it's not the same," Clara replied. "By the way, there was an article about a new book out on La Convivencia. Did you see it?"

"No."

"I saved the newspaper for you."

"Are you interested in history?" Chaim asked Vidal.

"Certain periods."

"I suppose most people in Catalonia are interested in history, since there's so much of it in these parts. But I don't recall there being Muslims in Catalonia for very long. Didn't Charlemagne drive them all out in the late 700s?"

"That's right," said Vidal.

"So I guess that means there never was a *La Convivencia* in Catalonia."

"But there will be," said Clara. "Vidal is going to build a museum about it as part of his resort."

"Really?" Chaim then turned to Vidal. "You're going to build a resort? In Sant Joan Januz?"

"Yes," Vidal replied curtly.

"And it's going to have a museum?" Chaim only partially tried to hide his ironic reaction to this news.

"That's right."

"That's very interesting. But to be honest, I don't understand it. Why build a museum about the coexistence between Muslims,

Christians, and Jews when there weren't any Muslims in Catalonia to coexist with?"

"As I recall, there weren't any talking mice in Florida," said Vidal, "but that didn't stop Disney from building a resort there."

"So it's all a fantasy?"

"There are Muslims living in Catalonia now," Clara said to Chaim. "Lots of them."

"Are there any Jews?"

"I don't know."

"There are a few," said Josep. "In Barcelona."

"Do you know anything about Muslims or Jews?" Chaim asked Vidal.

"A little," Vidal replied.

"Well, I don't know much about Muslims, but I can tell you that the Jews are a very prickly people, and so you'd better get your story right. Otherwise, your museum about coexistence is going to make your own existence pretty miserable."

"How do you know so much about Jews?" asked Vidal. "I wouldn't think there were many of them in Kansas."

"Some of my relatives are married to Jews," Chaim replied. He had chosen his words carefully. All of his relatives who were married were, in fact, married to other Jews. The family's children, who weren't married to anyone, allowed him to truthfully use the word "some."

"Maybe Charlie could help you with your museum," Clara said to Vidal.

"I don't need his help, Mama. There's a whole organization based in Girona that develops Jewish historical sites. If I need advice, I can contact them."

CHAPTER 12

The house was finally quiet, and Chaim hoped it would stay that way, at least for the next hour or so. He wanted to write down everything he had observed that evening while the details were still fresh in his mind. Taking care not to make any noise, he turned on the lamp next to the sofa that was serving as his bed for the night and then tiptoed over to his overnight bag. Stashed inside the bag was a large stack of photocopied forms — his checklist of *Anusim* customs.

He returned to the sofa the same way, on tiptoe, but this time weighed down on one side by the heavy bag. After settling into as comfortable a sitting position as the sagging cushions of the sofa would allow, he took out his first form and wrote down the words "Bonet Family." This was a moment to savor. Not only was he in Sant Joan Januz but, if his interpretation of the events was correct, he had met his first *Anusim*.

While Chaim gazed with satisfaction at his handiwork, somewhere in the house a clock chimed the hour, reminding him to get back to work. His first task was to record his general impressions of the family. After writing a few sentences about the parents, he turned his attention to the son.

"Vidal Bonet, mid-twenties, single," he wrote. Then he added, with more than a little chagrin, "MBA, New York University." That was the last thing he had expected to find in Sant Joan Januz, which in his imagination had been a village still quaintly stuck in the Middle Ages.

The list of customs came next. It had been compiled from two sources: archival records from the days of the Inquisition and testimony taken from modern-day descendents of *Anusim*. Previous research in the field had shown that no modern-day family observed all the customs on the list. Also, although there were some customs that were widely observed, the observance of others varied greatly.

At the top of the list were customs pertaining to the Jewish Sabbath, such as cleaning the house and changing into fresh clothes on Friday during the day and, of course, lighting candles. Just about all descendents of the *Anusim* lit some sort of light at sunset to mark the beginning of the holy day, which continued until nightfall on Saturday night. Since he hadn't come on a Friday, though, Chaim had to put a question mark next to those items. He also had no way of knowing if the family observed customs associated with Jewish holidays, such as lighting eight candles on Christmas to secretly commemorate the eight days of Chanukah. He therefore decided to skip down to those customs that had to do with everyday life.

"Orienting a bed's headboard toward the north or south," he silently read. The sofa was the only "bed" in the room. He didn't think he should count it as evidence, since no one usually slept on it. Next on the list was sweeping toward the center of the room. Here he had struck gold. As he jotted down his conversation with Mrs. Bonet, Chaim recalled how upset she had been. He wondered why. It didn't seem to be a normal reaction, even for someone who was aware that the source of the custom was showing respect for the *mezuzah*.

He recalled that once the *mezuzah* hanging outside his bedroom door had fallen down, and he hadn't gotten overly upset by the incident. He merely replaced the worn-out piece of two-sided tape with a fresh piece and stuck the *mezuzah* back on the doorpost. Should he have gotten more upset? Did his lack of concern demonstrate a lack of respect?

"Who's the subject of this questionnaire?" he muttered under his breath, not wanting to get sidetracked by his own issues since he had a long list to get through.

Instead of going on to the next item, though, his mind uneasily replayed the scene that had taken place in the kitchen. He was starting to feel guilty about pretending to accidentally spill the rice. For one thing, wasting food was strictly forbidden by the Torah, and he had probably thrown a whole cup of rice into the garbage bin. The other transgression he had committed was causing distress to his hostess. He could still see the look of shock on her face, as if she was afraid that something terrible was going to happen.

Chaim knew that his father wouldn't have been pleased by his little performance in the kitchen. In fact, neither of his parents was enthusiastic about his playing Sherlock Holmes in the hills of Catalonia.

"Don't get carried away by the thrill of the chase," his father had warned him. "Nothing positive ever comes out of telling lies and fooling people. The eventual loss will cancel the immediate gain."

As he recalled his father's words, he also recalled an old Jewish custom to make a *cheshbon hanefesh,* a personal accounting of one's day, before retiring for the night. This wasn't something that Chaim usually did, but since he was starting to wonder if he had said or done anything else that day that he would later regret, he decided that a quick review wouldn't be a bad idea.

Was his name Charlie Green? Not exactly. But he did have a reason for adopting an American-sounding first name, and in his opinion it was a good one. Anti-Semitism was on the rise in Europe, and so it was legitimate not to call unnecessary attention to one's Jewish identity.

Was he a graduate student at the University of Kansas? Yes. He could say with a clear conscience that he was enrolled at the KU Department of Anthropology. His family, of course, thought he was crazy. A university degree was fine, if it was in something practical, such as business or computer science. But anthropology?

He was getting sidetracked again. If he continued to drift off topic, he would be up all night.

Was his thesis really about comparing farm cultures in Kansas and Catalonia? Yes. Sort of. His interest wasn't farm culture, per se, but how social groups transmit their religious customs — or their "symbol systems," in sociocultural anthropological jargon — to succeeding generations. He did plan to study two primarily rural communities: the Mennonites of Kansas and the *Anusim* of Catalonia.

The reason for his interest in the *Anusim* was obvious, at least to him. Of course, the University of Kansas wasn't the most natural choice for pursuing that interest, since there weren't any *Anusim* in Kansas, as far as anyone knew. But he was a Kansas resident and therefore eligible for in-state tuition, which turned out to be the deciding factor when it came time to choose a school. When it came time to choose a thesis topic, his advisor would only agree to a study of the *Anusim* if Chaim found a comparable group that had settled in Kansas. The advisor had most likely thought that this would end the discussion and that Chaim would wise up and write his thesis on a more politically correct subject, such as "symbol systems" in Africa or the Pacific. The advisor was mistaken. Chaim uncovered a group in Kansas whose customs were as politically incorrect as those of religious Jews: the Mennonites.

To escape from religious persecution, the Mennonites, a Christian sect, had wandered across Europe. They eventually settled in the Ukraine, but when government reforms in the 1870s resulted in the loss of many of their rights, they decided to move on. It was a subject that Chaim was very familiar with. His paternal great-grandfather had fled the Ukraine in the early 1900s because of those repressive decrees and ended up in Kansas City. But that was another story.

The Mennonites settled in Kansas, thanks to the company that was building the Atchison, Topeka, and Santa Fe Railway. Facing bankruptcy, the company hoped to pull itself out of the red by selling off the nearly seven million acres of land it had received from the United States government. The sale of one hundred thousand acres of prime Kansas farmland to the Mennonites turned out to be a good deal for everyone. The railway company got some much-needed cash, while the Mennonites found a relatively quiet place to live. The state also benefited: when the Mennonites left Russia, they brought with them bags filled with kernels of the Turkey Red wheat that would transform Kansas into the breadbasket of the nation.

Although the Mennonites were sometimes ridiculed for their modest dress — in some old photographs the men, who had long beards and wore long black coats, could even be mistaken for Jews — and sometimes they incurred the wrath of their neighbors for their pacifism and refusal to serve in the army, they prospered economically in their new home, which they had optimistically named Gnadenau, or Meadow of Grace. But pressures from the modern world made it increasingly difficult to preserve their distinct identity. During the Second World War, for instance, they stopped using their native German and switched to English. Assimilation became an issue when the younger generation began to leave their rural communities for the city.

120

When faced with these findings, Chaim's advisor reluctantly approved Chaim's thesis topic. Of course, Chaim hadn't mentioned that the thesis was just a cover for some very different research that he intended to do in Catalonia.

"We're never going to finish this," he warned his wandering thoughts. "*Cheshbon HaNefesh*, Scene Three, Sant Joan Januz: Chaim Green's rental car is parked beside a quiet country lane."

Did his car have engine trouble? It did, after he removed a spark plug wire. The car rental company didn't answer the phone because he never called them. It was true that he "hadn't exactly" grown up on a farm, although not because of the reason that he had implied. His parents had never owned a family farm, and so they had never been forced to sell one. But his mother's relatives, who lived in New York City, did refer to all of Kansas as being "out in the sticks." In their opinion, at least, he had grown up in the country. Finally, he had pretended not to know the name of the village, even though he knew very well where he was.

Chaim took a deep breath. That was a lot of fudging. His intention hadn't been to harm anyone. He just wanted to create an opportunity for getting invited into a home. Even so, his father's image once again rose up before Chaim's eyes, and it wasn't a happy moment. But what was he supposed to do? A person couldn't just barge into these people's homes and ask, "Do you happen to have any Jewish skeletons in the closet?"

"So don't go to Sant Joan Januz," he could hear his father saying.

Chaim wearily rested his head against the back of the sofa. If the only reason he had come to Catalonia was to do research for his thesis, the story of his trip would be very different. There were organizations that helped researchers make contact with *Anusim* who were willing to talk. It was easy, and it was clean, and there was still time to switch gears. All he had to do was drive back to Girona and send off a few e-mails. He could probably have two or three interviews in Barcelona or Palma de Mallorca set up by the end of the week.

He stared up at the ceiling. Its exposed medieval-looking wooden beams added just the right touch of atmosphere, and a tingling feeling raced through his body. It was the same feeling he had experienced that afternoon out in the fields. He knew a Torah

Jew wasn't supposed to make decisions based on tingling feelings, but...

Chaim reached into his overnight bag and pulled out a nondescript looking binder. The tingling feeling grew stronger. What he was looking for wasn't in Barcelona, and it wasn't in Palma de Mallorca. If the manuscript he was holding in his hands was a faithful witness, there was only one place where he would find it, and that place was Sant Joan Januz.

He glanced around the room again. The room's thick stone walls, which were chilly to the touch, warmed his heart. He had visualized this moment so many times, sitting in an ancient farmhouse and reading the manuscript, also ancient, to the enthralled family. True, the family was asleep — tonight. And perhaps this wasn't even the family he was looking for. Perhaps they lived down the road, or on the other side of the square. But they had to be somewhere in the village. He knew it. Just as he knew that he should return the binder to his overnight bag. If he started to read what was inside it, he wouldn't be able to stop, and he would be up all night. He knew it, having turned down this path many times before. Yet even though his mind knew it, his fingers allowed the binder to fall open to a random page, and his eyes fell into the trap.

The page was a photocopy, as were all the pages enclosed within the binder's nondescript black cover. Yet even though the bland photocopied pages were but a distant relation of the old pieces of parchment that had given birth to them, and so lacked the evocative scent of history gently awakened from its drowsy, musty sleep, they still had the power to command. No, it was even stronger than that. They had the power to compel.

Perhaps, as his mother sometimes said, it would have been better if Chaim had never made the acquaintance of Nona Anna, his great-great-nobody-really-knew-how-many-greats-to-add grandmother, on his mother's side. His "bout of insanity" had begun shortly after his bar mitzvah, when his family had gone to New York to have a post-celebration of the event with his maternal grandmother, Nona Esther, who was already too ill to travel to Kansas. During that visit, Nona Esther had motioned to Chaim to come with her to the study, the tiny room where his late grandfather had kept all of his books.

"I want to show you something," she said to him. She instructed Chaim to go over to a closet and remove a cardboard box that was sitting on the top shelf, in the back corner, where no light ever reached.

It was the sort of box that grandmothers used to store their "valuables" — handmade New Year cards from the grandchildren, letters from summer camp from the grandchildren, copies of awards, prizes, and other unbiased recognitions of genius from the grandchildren — and so Chaim wasn't expecting to be unduly impressed by whatever it was that his grandmother wanted to show him. But there was a special bond between the two of them — they shared a talent for wandering slowly through a museum and creating stories about the former lives of the items trapped inside the glass display cases, as well as an immovable obstinacy that would put a block of cement to shame — and so he decided that, come what may, he would act enthusiastic.

When Chaim saw the worn and crumbling leather-bound volume sitting inside the box, he didn't have to act. Having made his first acquaintance with "the tingle," he instinctively reached for the book, as though he were extending his hand toward a long-lost friend.

"It's only to look at," said his grandmother, pulling the box away from him.

"What is it?"

"It's a diary. It tells about our family, the ones who left Spain."

"Have you read it?"

Nona Esther laughed. "Me? Read Spanish? It's enough that I learned how to read English after the war. The Germans didn't exactly set up language schools for us in the camps."

"If I learn Spanish, will you let me read it?"

"It's very old, Chaim. If you so much as breathe on it, the pages crumble. It's just to look at, so that you'll remember. This diary survived the Inquisition and it survived the Holocaust. My brother, your great-uncle Gabriel, may his memory be for a blessing, smuggled it out of Europe right before the war. I'm showing it to you so that you'll remember that you come from a family that's strong. We were tested. We were tested many times. But we stayed Jews and we stayed loyal to the Torah. That's the kind of family you come from. You should always remember that."

Unfortunately, or so some members of the family felt, remembering wasn't enough for Chaim. The diary became an obsession. Perhaps this obsession came about because no one in the family knew what was written in the diary, and details about the family's escape from Spain had been forgotten with the passage of time. The unseen, undeciphered pages became a tabula rasa, a blank slate that played the part of willing accomplice to every whim of Chaim's overeager imagination.

For an entire year he begged his parents, using every rational argument he could think of, to let him find out how much it would cost to professionally restore the book and to reproduce all of the pages so that he could get the diary translated.

"But, Tatty, maybe it's not just a diary. Maybe it's really an important kabbalistic text. It could be worth a fortune," was one argument he tried.

"If it was Torah, it would have been written in Hebrew, and your mother's family wouldn't have forgotten what was in it," came the reply.

Another time, Chaim tried a different tactic. "But, Tatty, maybe the diary mentions something about Christopher Columbus. Maybe we'll find out that he was a relation, that he was Jewish. Wouldn't that be something?"

Chaim's father wasn't impressed with that argument either. But his parents did finally agree to get an estimate from a reputable bookbinder who was based in New York. When the price quote arrived, Chaim gulped.

"I'll pay for it with my bar mitzvah money," he stoically offered.

"You don't have enough," his father reminded him. "And besides, your money will be better spent on paying for your college education."

The following summer the family made their annual trip to New York to visit Nona Esther. Chaim's parents warned him not to say anything about restoring the diary. Nona Esther had fallen in the spring. She was still weak and had to walk with a walker, and so she had enough on her mind.

But Nona Esther knew how to interpret the not-so-concealed glances that Chaim cast in the direction of the study.

"Do you want to see the diary again?" she asked him.

"I'm not supposed to bother you."

"I'll let you know when you're bothering me," she said as she escorted Chaim into the room. "Please close the blinds before you get the box. I remember now, it's not good for the diary to be in the sunlight."

After closing the blinds, which only partially blocked out the light, Chaim removed the diary from its hiding place. At first, they just looked at the closed volume that sat on the table between them. The black binding had been added to the pages during the past century, and it had been a cheap and hasty job. But in the diaphanous glow created by the faint rays of sunshine that had snuck into the room, despite the blinds, the binding took on a luminous quality, its creases and cracks having faded into the forgiving embrace of the soft, ethereal light.

Chaim looked over at his grandmother. Her pale face, which was framed by the black cloth hat that covered her hair and the high collar of her black dress, also seemed to glow. He recalled what she had said the first time she had showed him the diary, about how old parchment crumbled easily. This wasn't entirely true, he had since learned. When stored in the right conditions, a document written on parchment could last for a thousand years or more. It was people who, having reached a certain age and fragility, crumbled easily, until there was nothing left of the body but dust.

"I suppose it won't harm anything if we look at a page or two for a few minutes," said Nona Esther. "You take it out of the box, but do it gently."

Chaim lifted the book out of the cardboard box and carefully set it down. He opened the diary to the first page, which wasn't a title page that had the name of the work and the author, but was just words that began and, having begun, seemed to flow from some inexhaustible spring. This wasn't the first time that he was seeing a document written on parchment with quill and ink. Every Torah scroll was written in this way. But as the words stared up at him, close enough for him to touch them and trace their outline with his own hand, it was the first time that he seriously thought about that so common and yet so mysterious human need to defy time and death by pouring the intangible, immortal soul into the one tangible vessel that also seemingly never dies: the written word.

125

Perhaps it was actually a good thing that he couldn't understand what was written on the page. Unfettered by distractions such as style and grammar, his thoughts could focus on the pure and simple fact that many years ago a distant relation of his had sat in a room and taken a quill in her hand, and dipped that quill in ink, and pressed that quill against this piece of parchment. As the letters passed before his eyes, he thought he could almost hear the sound of the just-sharpened quill pen scratching against the page. But who was she, this Nona Anna? And what message had she wished to impart? Was it a one-way communication? Or was the message, if no longer the messenger, still waiting for a response?

"I should have had the diary professionally restored while your grandfather was still alive," said Nona Esther, breaking the silence. Chaim wondered if she, too, had felt the presence of their kinswoman in the room. "But now I'm too old and weak to do all that running around."

"I can run around," Chaim said softly. He told her about the estimate he had received from the bookbinder.

"I'll tell you what," she said to him, "we'll be partners. I'll put down eighty percent, and you'll put down twenty percent. We'll go to my rabbi, Rabbi Lavi, and have him draw up an agreement, so everything will be kosher and according to Torah law."

"I don't know if Dad will agree. He wants me to save all of my bar mitzvah money for my education."

"That's wise advice, and very practical. And that's the difference between us. When a Jew from Spain sees an apple, he dreams of the orchards that will one day grow from its seeds. A Jew from Eastern Europe thinks about how to slice it into as many pieces as possible to feed his family. Don't get me wrong, Chaim. This is not a criticism of your father or his ancestors. People starved in the Ukraine. Feeding a family was no joke, and what a grandfather remembers gets passed on. But maybe I can convince your father not to be so practical, just this once."

Then she added, "A person's name is no accident. There's a reason you're named Chaim. With G-d's help, you'll be the one who will reclaim our family's history and give it a new life."

Nona Esther did succeed where Chaim had failed. She had age on her side. A person only had to look at her to understand that the request had about it something of a last wish. After a few more inquiries were made, the family decided to entrust the diary into the hands of the first bookbinder. Several weeks later Nona Esther got back the original pages, which were now housed between the sturdy boards of their handsome new binding. Chaim received a high-quality reproduction of the original and a simple photocopy of the entire work, which he intended to use for the next phase of the project: translating the small, hastily written cursive script.

Chaim's family was already packing their things for the return trip to Kansas when they received the news that Nona Esther had been rushed to the hospital. She passed away a few days later. When the seven days of mourning came to an end, the extended family gathered to hear the reading of the will. Chaim's mother left the room holding a cardboard box.

"It's yours, Chaim," she said to him, as she placed the diary into his hands.

"It's not Spanish," said Rabbi Lavi, as he and Chaim sat in the rabbi's study and examined the first of the diary's photocopied pages.

While Rabbi Lavi waited for Chaim to say something, he noted that the teenager looked a little lost, which was to be expected so soon after his grandmother had passed away. Still, he wasn't sure how to interpret Chaim's silence. It was possible that Chaim's interest in the diary would come to a quick end now that he didn't have anyone to share it with. But it was more likely that this was just one more piece of news that Chaim didn't know how to process.

Rabbi Lavi returned his attention to the page. He was something of an expert in Judeo-Spanish history, and the diary's strange language puzzled him. Finally, a familiar word caught his eye. "Chaim, do you know where your grandmother's family came from?"

"Spain."

"Yes, but where in Spain?"

"I don't know."

"Did your grandmother ever mention a city called Girona?"

"I don't think so. But I don't think she knew."

"Well, if that's where your family did come from, this diary is written in Catalan."

"Is that a dialect of Spanish?"

"No. Catalan and Spanish are both Romance languages, and so there are similarities. But there are many differences, as well. You'll need to find someone who is familiar with medieval Catalan if you want to get this diary translated."

Chaim was silent. Too much had happened during the past two weeks, and all of a sudden he felt like crying. He knew it would be stupid to cry just because he had never heard of a language called Catalan, and he doubted if anyone else in Kansas had heard of it either, and so he didn't.

"Have you heard of the *Anusim?*" asked Rabbi Lavi.

"Sure. I learned about them last year, at my day school."

"I was at a conference on the *Anusim* a few months ago. If you like, I'll contact some people who were there and ask if they know of anyone in Kansas who can help you. I'll also look into translation services here in New York."

"Thanks! I mean, are you sure you don't mind? I don't want to bother you."

"It's no bother. I'm curious myself to see what's in the diary."

"Rabbi Lavi, what was the name of the city that's in the diary?"

"The Catalans call it Girona, but we Jews know it as Gerundi," Rabbi Lavi said as he wrote the name on the back of one of his business cards, which he handed to Chaim. "The city was an important center of Torah and Kabbalah during the Middle Ages. The Ramban lived there. You've heard of him, of course? Rabbi Moshe ben Nachman, also known as Nachmanides?"

Chaim's eyes lit up. "Sure. Do you think my family might be related to the Ramban?"

"No, Chaim. The Ramban was one of the greatest rabbis and scholars that the Jewish people ever produced. If you were related to the Ramban, you would know it."

A few weeks later Chaim received a letter from Rabbi Lavi that contained the price quote from a translation service. Chaim wasn't unduly disappointed to learn that a professional translation would cost more than he could afford to pay. He had already made up his mind to learn Catalan and do the translation himself.

Rather than wait for Rabbi Lavi's next letter, Chaim made some telephone calls to the colleges and universities in the area to see if anyone on their staff knew Catalan. He wasn't disappointed when the second letter did arrive, since he already knew what was in it. Rabbi Lavi's inquiries hadn't turned up any leads.

When Chaim wrote back, it was to ask for help in locating a book that would teach him Catalan. A bulky package arrived a few weeks later. Both his father and mother were there as he opened the package and removed the two books that Rabbi Lavi had sent him: a teach-yourself-Catalan book and a Catalan-English dictionary.

"Remember, Chaim, your schoolwork comes first," said his father.

"I know, Tatty."

As Chaim carried the books out of the room, he overheard his mother say to his father, "He'll grow out of it. You know how boys are. One day they absolutely have to learn how to play the keyboard, and the next month they've forgotten all about it."

But he didn't grow out of it. It took him four years to master the grammar of modern Catalan and build up his vocabulary, but he enjoyed learning languages — Hebrew had always been one of his best subjects at school — and the diary gave him an incentive to keep going. Two years and several translation attempts later, the project was completed.

If his parents had hoped that this would be the end of Chaim's fascination with the diary, they were once again disappointed. The text raised more questions than it answered, but that wasn't the fault of the writer, Nona Anna. She had managed to flee across the Mediterranean to Salonika. As for the others, the family members who had been forced to stay behind, Nona Anna never learned if they succeeded in escaping from what was supposed to be only a temporary refuge, an abandoned farming village hidden in the hills of Catalonia that they called Sant Joan Januz.

The chiming of the clock brought Chaim back to the Bonets' farmhouse and reminded him that another hour had passed. "If only the walls could speak," he whispered as he pressed his hand against the stones of the rough wall that had stood guard in the room, protecting the inhabitants from the outside world, for perhaps centuries.

He knew it was a trite thing to say. But it would certainly make his search easier if a stone would suddenly fall out of the wall and reveal the hiding place of an ancient document — the cousin and companion of the diary he held in his hands. It would also be very convenient, as long as he was thinking along these lines, if this ancient document would verify that the modern village of Sant Joan Januz was, indeed, the same village that had existed in medieval times. And as long as he was formulating a request, he decided to add that this document should also help him determine if any of the current residents of the village were his relatives, or if they were all latecomers who had arrived in the village after his own ancestors had left Catalonia for more hospitable shores or, G-d forbid, perished in the flames of the Spanish Inquisition. Finally, and this really was his final request, the ancient document should solve the other puzzle, which was the real reason he had come to out-of-the-way, off-the-beaten-track, and so-obscure-that-it-wasn't-even-on-the-map Sant Joan Januz.

Sant Joan Januz. Chaim still didn't know what to make of those people, his great-great-etcetera relatives, even though he had read through the diary more than one hundred times. There was no such person named Sant Joan Januz — or Saint John Januz, as he would have been called in English. Why then, when it came time to give their little hideaway a Catalan name, did they come up with the idea of naming the place after a nonexistent Catholic saint? Was it because they had a healthy dose of chutzpah and wanted to thumb their noses at the institution that was making their lives so miserable? Or was it because they were desperate to provide some sort of legitimate cover for their precarious, clandestine existence?

The diary didn't say. He glanced again at the wall that stood behind him, which had surely been witness to more than one whispered communication. The wall remained stubbornly silent, though, like the stone that it was, refusing to divulge even the tiniest bit of information. Well, if that was how things stood, there were only two things to do, Chaim decided: go to sleep or continue filling out the form with the list of *Anusim* customs. Although he was exhausted, he picked up the form and began to read.

Did they avoid eating pork? Did they avoid eating shellfish? Did they avoid mixing milk and meat? Did they wait between a meat meal and eating a meal that was dairy?

Chaim's tired eyes tried to focus on the page.

Did they slaughter their own cows? Did they slaughter their own chickens? Did they cover the blood? Did they soak the meat?

Did they salt it? Did they check their egg yolks for a speck of blood? Did they wash their hands before eating? Did they wash their hands after? Did they boil their dirty dishes? Did they accept food from outsiders? Did they have separate sinks, one for "clean" and one for "unclean"?

The list went on and on, and that was just the section pertaining to food. Burial customs came next and there, as well, the questions sniffed out their prey. Did they bury the deceased as soon as possible? Did they clothe the deceased in a white linen shroud? Did they cover the mirrors? Did they tear their garments? Did they spill out any standing water? Did they sit on the floor and did they mourn for seven days? Did they? Did they? Did they?

The words began to swim in front of his closed eyes, where dark waters had formed somewhere, in there, out there, he wasn't sure exactly where, except that they weren't on any map, at least not on any map that he had ever seen. As the words dove into those dark waters and disappeared, a list of his own bubbled up and began to take form.

Did they recover from the strange illness that broke out when they were supposed to flee? Did they escape from the Inquisitors, who were sniffing out anyone even remotely connected to what had happened in Saragossa on the night of September the fifteenth? If they did escape, did they take with them the Torah scroll that Nona Anna's father had written with his own hand? Or was the Torah scroll still there, in Sant Joan Januz, like the people — his relatives — waiting, hiding, in fear, maybe even in terror, all this time?

The last page of the diary floated up before Chaim's still-closed eyes. It looked different, though, unfinished. Then he noticed that he wasn't alone. There was someone else in the room, a middle-aged woman dressed all in black. The woman sat at a table, writing, quickly, her jabbing strokes making a scratching sound as the quill pen flew across the page. With a few deft strokes of the pen a drawing of Sant Joan Januz, in rough outline form, had emerged.

The woman suddenly stopped and turned her head. Perhaps someone she was hoping to see had unexpectedly appeared at some unseen doorway, or perhaps she was just thinking. Chaim held his breath and waited. He knew that map like he knew the plan of his own room. Two strokes were still missing. Why didn't she continue?

"Nona Anna?" Chaim heard himself asking from a place that was very far away.

The woman looked in his direction and smiled. She dipped her pen into the ink, and, with one quick and inky stroke, a farmhouse was severed into two unequal parts and a false wall was constructed. Behind this thick black line was a tiny room, the synagogue, which was really nothing more than four walls, a ceiling, and a floor. The last stroke of the pen, a small O, showed the spot, the recessed space in the stone wall, where a Torah scroll was hidden. This was her father's Torah scroll, which he had left in the village to serve as a segulah, a protection, for those who were being left behind. Her work done, the image of Nona Anna faded away. A few seconds later, or maybe it wasn't seconds but hours, or maybe it was even hundreds of years, the face of another person took its place.

It was the face of his father, who was looking at him with eyebrows raised high. "A treasure map, Chaim? That's why you want to go to Catalonia?"

With those words echoing in his head, Chaim drifted into an uneasy sleep.

CHAPTER 13

Chaim watched as Josep Bonet's truck disappeared down the dirt road. The family had treated him with the same chilly politeness in the morning that they had shown him the night before, and so he was happy to bring his stay with them to an end. This he accomplished by removing the spark plug wire from his overnight bag and reattaching it to the spark plug. Not surprisingly, the car's engine made an instant recovery. He could continue on his way, but where should he go?

It was a real pity that he couldn't return to the village's square and try again. He was sure that a few of the old-timers had already gathered around the little cafe table, where they were enjoying a morning cup of coffee. These were the people he really wanted to meet. Not only would they have a wealth of information, but they would have the time to share it. But the last thing he wanted to do was run into Vidal Bonet a second time, so the square was out. Where should he go?

"Wherever I go, I'm going to the Land of Israel," Chaim sang softly as he took out his compass and surveyed the lay of the land. He couldn't recall if these words, which had been said a few hundred years earlier by the chassidic master Rabbi Nachman of Breslov, had ever been put to music, but it didn't matter. He didn't have an ear for music and so even when he tried to sing a well-known song it ended up sounding like something he had made up.

As he pondered which path to take, he knew what he hoped to find at the end of the road: An elderly couple who would take him into their home, which just happened to be the old farmhouse that had the synagogue hidden behind the false wall.

Unfortunately, the map in the diary could only help him find the false wall. It couldn't help him find the farmhouse, itself, since it couldn't tell him how the village had developed over the last five hundred years. So where should he begin his search? If he were to follow the advice of his song, he would travel east. But an easterly route would once again take him past the square and the Bonets' farmhouse, and those were two places that he wanted to avoid.

"*Wherever* I go, I'm going to the Land of Israel," Chaim reassured the large E on his compass, and he turned his attention to the other three cardinal directions.

He didn't need a compass to tell him which way was north. The Pyrenees Mountains, which loomed in the not-so-far-away distance, marking the border between Spain and France, were hard to miss. He was almost tempted to turn in their direction — they were a beguiling sight for someone from Kansas, which was famous for its seemingly endless acres of perfectly flat corn and wheat fields — when he recalled some chilling words from the prophet Jeremiah: "Evil comes from the north." And an evil had come to Catalonia from the north. Two hundred and fifty years before the Spanish Inquisition, an Inquisition was established in Languedoc, a region in southern France, to put an end to a Christian sect called the Cathars.

He had first heard about the Cathars while studying the Catalan language. Catalan was closely related to a medieval language that was sometimes called Provencal and sometimes known as Langue d'oc, the latter of which lent its name to the Cathars' home. The similarity between the two languages wasn't coincidental. Although Catalonia and Languedoc were separated by a mountain range, they were very alike. Both regions were situated on the shores of the Mediterranean Sea, and during the Middle Ages they were both prosperous commercial centers that jealously guarded their political independence. Both regions were also home to important Jewish communities. While the Jews of Catalonia could boast of their Torah centers in Girona and Barcelona, Languedoc's Jews could point to Montpellier and Narbonne with equal pride.

Neither Catalonia nor Languedoc made it through the Middle Ages with their wealth and independence intact. As for the Jews, Languedoc's Jewish community was expelled from France in 1306 with little more than the clothes on their backs. Catalonia's Jews were expelled, along with all the other Jews of Spain, in the year 1492. The cause of the descent into bad times was the same for both regions, at least on the surface.

The Catholic Church considered Catharism to be heretical. When the Cathars refused to be convinced of their errors, the Pope called for a crusade. French rulers from the north, eager to increase their wealth, enthusiastically took up the cause in the year 1208. They continued to slaughter whoever they found — whether they were Cathar, Catholic, or Jew — throughout a twenty-year war known as the Albigensian Crusade. By the time the carnage had ended, much of the once-independent region of Languedoc had been conquered by the Kingdom of France. To the Church's chagrin, some Cathars survived the massacres. The Church set up an Inquisition in the year 1229 to hunt them down and destroy them.

By the 1330s, the Inquisition against the Cathars had completed its work. But what happened in Languedoc could be seen as just the first act in a tragedy that would, after a brief intermission, continue in a new location: the Iberian Peninsula. The second act began in 1391, when a peasants' rebellion turned into a rampage that destroyed most of Spain's Jewish communities. Of those who survived the slaughter, tens of thousands of Jews were forcibly dragged to the baptismal font. A series of repressive edicts soon followed, which led to further despair and more conversions.

Both Jews who were forcibly converted and Jews who converted in an attempt to save their lives and property were known as New Christians. Some of them severed all ties with their former religion, but there were others, the *Anusim*, who continued to practice Judaism in secret. They were all ruthlessly targeted for their "heretical" practices by a second Inquisition, which was established in 1478 by Ferdinand and Isabella, the joint rulers of the newly unified Spain. By the time the Spanish Inquisition was abolished in 1808, hundreds of thousands of people had been hauled before its courts, and tens of thousands were condemned to death.

"Wherever I go, I go to the Land of Israel," Chaim chanted softly, and he turned his back on the mountains in the north and the gloomy thoughts they had aroused.

His compass reminded him that there were two candidates left for him to choose from: south and west. South was associated with wisdom in the Jewish tradition because the Menorah, the seven-branched candelabra that symbolized wisdom, had stood in the southern part of the Temple in Jerusalem. Wisdom was certainly an important quality to possess. But he had come to Catalonia to find a Torah scroll, and not to learn Torah from these

135

people. On the other hand, the Shechinah, the Divine Presence, rested in the west. That was why the Temple's western wall was the only wall that hadn't been destroyed when the rest of the Temple was razed to the ground by the Romans. Since Chaim was looking for a wall of his own, the false wall of the old farmhouse, he wondered why he hadn't thought of west from the very first. Having come upon it at last, he turned his car in that direction.

The rural scene that scrolled past his car window was a pleasant one, but it only partially engaged his interest until a rambling stone structure, which he assumed was a farmhouse, came into view. He turned onto a dirt road that was even bumpier than the one he had been driving on before, and within a few minutes he arrived at the farmhouse's front door.

The main house, which had two stories in some places and three stories in others, had been added to over the years in a haphazard fashion. The rough, rustic appearance of the building was further enhanced by a sloped red-tiled roof that drooped more on its right side than its left, an effect that made the farmhouse look like it was wearing a slightly embarrassed, lopsided smile. Although an appraiser from a mortgage bank might not approve of the way the structure was slowly sinking into the ground, Chaim was gladdened by the sight. Sinking walls surely meant that at least some parts of the building were very, very old — just as the tightly shuttered front door and windows testified to the farmhouse's abandoned state.

As he continued his tour of the property, Chaim saw that a large barn was attached to the back of the house. The barn's wide roof sloped all the way down to the ground on one side, and under its drooping wing was a cavernous opening that allowed the farm's animals to meander in and out. No animals meandered anywhere on that particular morning, since the barn, like the house, was empty of inhabitants.

Continuing his circuit, Chaim saw that off to the side of the main house were two smaller structures, which were also constructed from stone and crowned with sloped red-tiled roofs. The smaller of the two looked like it might have been used to store tools or produce, while the larger one might have provided additional living quarters. They both would have been perfect for hiding a secret synagogue, but the same could be said of the barn and the main house, and as Chaim contemplated the sprawling estate the enormity of his task began to dawn on him.

Back in Kansas, he had done some research on how to find a false wall. Detector kits that made use of things like ultrasonic waves and fiber optics did exist and could even be purchased — if one happened to be a member of the police or armed forces. For the average person, though, he had discovered that technologically speaking this particular area of human endeavor still lagged far behind, and its techniques were the same ones that had been used for centuries: tap on a wall and listen for a hollow sound; yank on a coat hook or bell cord to see if it will activate the spring mechanism that will cause the wall to swing open and reveal the hidden room, passageway, or staircase on the other side; and, finally, the oldest chestnut of them all, crash through the false wall by accident. With only such imprecise methods of discovery as these at his disposal, he figured that it would take all day to examine just this one farmhouse.

His thoughts whispered to him uneasily that perhaps he should have chosen south instead. He would need a healthy dose of wisdom to successfully complete his mission. But he decided against changing course. It was better to stick to a decision rather than waste time zigzagging back and forth because of indecision.

He further decided to postpone conducting a more thorough investigation of the farmhouse until a later time. First, he had to establish a base in the village. Not only did he need a place to sleep, but he also needed friends, and the latter were as important as the former. He could be arrested for trespassing on private property if he were discovered, unknown and friendless, inside the abandoned farmhouse, and he certainly didn't want that to happen.

"Wherever I go, I go to the Land of Israel," he sang cheerfully, picking up the tune somewhere within the vicinity of where he had last left it. He got back into his car and once again set off down the dirt road.

Chaim's path took him past more prime Catalan farmland, but unlike the fields he had passed earlier, these fields were unplowed and he wondered why. It was possible that the fields belonged to whoever it was who owned the abandoned farmhouse. It was also possible that they had been left fallow over the winter because they would be planted with corn in the spring. But a very different

137

possibility presented itself several minutes later, when his road ended at the entrance to a field that was in use, but not for agricultural purposes. He had stumbled on the village's cemetery.

Though he did want to do research in the cemetery at some point, this was an unwelcome development. His goal for that particular day was to meet a kind, elderly, and still living couple. Studying the headstones of the dead wasn't on his agenda.

He had already put his car in reverse when a new thought occurred to him: perhaps his agenda was out of synch with a wider agenda in the world. He recalled that some chassidic rabbi, maybe it was even Rabbi Nachman again, had said that each day has its own set of thoughts, words, and actions. Maybe he was exactly where he was supposed to be, after all.

A quick glance at his watch told him that the morning was only half over. Even if he worked until lunchtime, he would still have the entire afternoon to find a place to sleep. He therefore dug out his digital camera from his overnight bag and locked his car, which he left parked by the side of the road.

As he took a few overview shots of the cemetery's grounds, Chaim noted that the grass was more than ankle high, but it was new grass that had sprouted up after the winter rains. He further noted that all of the headstones were modest in size and simple in design, as though they didn't want to attract too much attention. Although some of the headstones had partially sunk into the ground, and so the grass practically hid them from view, on the whole it was a very orderly final resting place.

Instead of taking the time to study each headstone, he decided to photograph as many as he could, as quickly as he could, and analyze the inscriptions later — unless, of course, he happened to find some headstones that dated from the late 1400s. The truth was that he didn't know if markers from that era still existed. Until the 1500s, wood was more commonly used than stone, and wood decayed. Even if the original wood markers had been replaced at a later date with stone ones, bad weather and the passage of time might have rubbed away the engraved inscriptions and left, in their place, just blank stone.

He focused his camera on the headstone that was nearest to him, which was a fairly new one. He observed that its inscription was very brief, just the name of the woman — Regina Rodriguez — and her date of death. The name didn't mean anything to him, but he did see that it was written with Latin, and not Hebrew, letters. He also saw that not a single religious symbol or sentiment appeared on the headstone.

This lack of anything even remotely connected to Judaism was a disappointment, but it was the inscription's brevity that saddened him even more. There was no way to know if the person had died young or lived a rich and full life. There was also no way to know what values she had held dear. For an outsider, her life was a total blank. But perhaps that was the point. If this was a burial ground for *Anusim*, perhaps they didn't want to leave behind any evidence that would incriminate their descendents.

After photographing the first headstone, he went on to the next one and then the next one, and before he knew it his camera's memory card was full. A thorough check of all his pockets informed him that his supply of memory cards was tucked away in his camera bag, which was packed in his overnight bag, which was stowed in his car. The car wasn't terribly far away, but sometimes a thing can be close at hand and still be unattainable. This particular insight only occurred to him after he got his foot caught in a hole in the ground, not far from the cemetery's main pathway, which had been masked by a tangle of overgrown grass.

In the meantime, he was losing his balance. Before plunging to the ground, his body swung around, and he lurched forward, an action that sent his free leg crashing into the back of one of the headstones. The next thing he knew, although he didn't know how, he was falling backward, onto the path, and he did think to protect the back of his head with his left hand — his right hand was desperately holding on to his camera — but it was still an unpleasant meeting between a fast-moving body and a patch of unyielding earth.

The camera emerged from the accident unharmed. The same could not be said for Chaim. When he recovered enough to realize what had happened, he was aware that his legs, his arms, and his head were all frantically exchanging SOS signals in a dialect he could only describe as the language of exquisite pain.

As he lay there without moving, since he couldn't move, he wondered what he should do. Then he realized that he couldn't do anything. His cell phone was safely locked away in the glove compartment of his rented car. The only call he could make was to the One Above, and so his lips sent out an SOS message of their own, using the language of prayer.

While he stared up at the sky and waited for a reply, he had plenty of time to think. Or at least it seemed like an eternity. Each jab of pain, and there were plenty of them, seemed to last forever. Even the act of thinking was painful because he realized, in his fallen state, that he wasn't one of those giants of Torah who could focus his intellect under any circumstances and use this unexpected gift of free time to unravel a particularly knotty problem in the Talmud. Instead, he found his mind drifting to the topic of seeing stars. He had had his share of tumbles during his life, but he had never achieved this particular state of being. He therefore had sometimes wondered if such a thing really existed, or if it was just poetic exaggeration, and he decided that this was a good opportunity to discover the truth of the matter.

A careful examination of the cloudless blue sky that stretched above him like a huge, blank computer screen revealed a decided absence of stars. He did note, with more than a little surprise, that this sky, or screen, seemed to have divided itself into ten or twelve sections, which, one by one, were turning black. As the number of black squares began to seriously outnumber the number of blue squares, he wondered if he should be worried.

Then he overheard someone thinking, and he supposed it was him, and this person was saying, "Stars!"

"Look! He opened his eyes!"
"Are you all right?
"Can you hear us?"
Chaim blinked his eyes a few times. He could see that an elderly man had bent down beside him.
"Can you talk?" asked the man.
"Yes," Chaim replied. He wondered what the question was. After all, he wasn't a little child. "What happened?"
"That's what we'd like to know," replied Eduard Garcia.
Chaim looked from the man to the woman who was standing beside him. She appeared to be about the same age as the man, and she was looking down at him with a very kind and very worried expression on her face.
"I guess I fell," said Chaim. "But I'm all right now."

He started to get up. A severe pain that shot up from somewhere around the bottom of his leg and radiated throughout his entire body made a convincing argument for staying where he was.

"You'd better not move," said Eduard. "You might have broken something."

"The ambulance should be here any minute," said Joya Garcia, Eduard's wife. "It's a good thing I decided to pay a visit to my mother's grave today. Otherwise, who knows how long you would have been lying out here."

The ambulance did arrive a few minutes later. As the crew lifted him onto the stretcher, Chaim suddenly remembered that he had left something behind.

"My camera."

"I have it," said a third person, who had also been there, but out of Chaim's view.

"Great," said Chaim, looking to see who had spoken.

The doors to the ambulance swung shut and the engine started up.

"Wherever I go..." Chaim silently grumbled. The person who had his camera was Vidal Bonet.

CHAPTER 14

The X-rays confirmed Eduard Garcia's diagnosis. Chaim had broken something.

"You're lucky that it was just your ankle," said the doctor. "And it's not the worst break in the world. You'll need a splint and plenty of rest during the next few days. If you don't try walking on it too soon, your ankle should be healed in six weeks. Are you a relative?"

The doctor had posed the last question to Vidal, who had followed the ambulance to the emergency room in his car since Eduard Garcia had to return to his store.

There was a longish silence.

"Would you like me to leave the room?" The doctor looked from Vidal to Chaim.

"Yes, doctor," Vidal replied, "if you don't mind."

After the doctor had closed the door behind him, Vidal removed a black yarmulke from his pocket. Chaim took the yarmulke — it must have slipped off when he fell — and, after removing the cowboy hat, put it on his head.

"Who are you?"

"My name is Chaim Green. But I am a student at the University of..."

"What were you doing in the cemetery?"

"Taking pictures."

"Why?"

Since Vidal now knew that he was Jewish, Chaim figured that he had nothing more to lose. "I'm looking for my relatives."

"Who told you to look for them in Sant Joan Januz?"

"My grandmother."

"She's Jewish?"

"She was."

"Why would she think there were any Jews buried in Sant Joan Januz?"

"Is that really so impossible?"

142

"Yes, it is."

"Why?"

"You sound well enough to travel to me. I'll tell the doctor to put you on the first plane back to Kansas."

Vidal turned to leave the room.

"Wait a minute, Vi — Mr. Bonet. There's another reason I'm interested in Sant Joan Januz, and I think it will interest you, too."

Vidal stopped, but the look on his face warned Chaim that whatever he had to say had better be good.

"My grandmother also told me that there's a Torah scroll hidden somewhere in your village. It was written in the fifteenth century, before the Jews were expelled from Spain. Do you have any idea what that means?"

Actually, Vidal did. Although Vidal was only nine years old in 1992, when the craze for uncovering Spain's Jewish history began, he remembered that year very well. The most exciting event had been the big to-do over Christopher Columbus and the five hundredth anniversary of the discovery of America. At the time there were those who believed that Columbus hailed from Catalonia, and so pride in the supposedly native son was high. Even the doubters had to admit that Catalonia had a special claim to that historic discovery; when the explorer returned to Europe after his successful voyage, he landed in Barcelona, where he was received in triumph by Ferdinand and Isabella.

However, there was a second event that year that had also caused a stir — namely the king of Spain's very public commemoration of the five hundredth anniversary of the expulsion of Spain's Jews. Suddenly everyone was interested in the country's Jewish past. The news even reached Sant Joan Januz via the local newspapers, which were filled with photographs of King Juan Carlos and of Girona's lost Jewish Quarter.

Those were the photographs that had captured Vidal's attention, as well as the accompanying story about how a Girona restaurant owner had accidentally uncovered the Jewish Quarter's main streets — which had lain forgotten under layers of debris and dilapidated buildings for hundreds of years — while doing some renovations to his restaurant. Although the newspaper articles about Columbus were inspiring, Vidal knew that he was too young to set out on a sea voyage of his own. But discovering a lost

143

Jewish Quarter seemed possible, and he could already see the photographs in the newspapers of him standing beside the king, with family standing behind them. They were all beaming at him, yet another Catalan native son who had discovered a new world, with tremendous pride.

Vidal had taken a shovel to the square in Sant Joan Januz and started digging. When the store owners objected, his grandfather suggested that Vidal move the site of his archeological explorations to his grandfather's backyard, where Vidal could dig without being bothered. When he got tired he could take a break in Grandma Anna's kitchen, where a special treat would be waiting for him. To further sweeten the deal, his grandfather presented him with a typewriter — it was a toy, but it looked very grown-up — so that Vidal could record his finds for posterity.

Vidal accepted his grandfather's offer. He worked hard, and at the end of every day's work, he sat down at his typewriter. Unfortunately, there wasn't much to record, and so after a few weeks he abandoned the project. His grandfather planted vegetables in the dug-up plot of land.

Later Vidal suspected that this had been his grandfather's plan all along, especially when his grandfather pointed out, after the fact, that Jews weren't farmers. They lived in cities and towns, like Girona and Barcelona. Vidal's hastily conceived adventure had been doomed from the start. After digesting this lesson, along with his grandfather's jokes about the Jewish vegetables growing in his back yard, Vidal was sufficiently shamed to never again bring up the topic of Jews in Sant Joan Januz.

So, yes, Vidal did know what the discovery of a lost Jewish Quarter, or even an artifact such as a Torah scroll, meant. If you found it, you were a hero. If you went searching in the wrong place, you were a fool. And he wasn't about to be made a fool by some Jewish cowboy from Kansas.

Chaim, not being a mind reader, interpreted Vidal's silence as a signal to forge ahead. "Very few Torah scrolls written in Spain survived the Expulsion and the Spanish Inquisition. There's one that was written in Toledo in the 1300s..."

"Toledo is in Castile, and Castile is not Catalonia. No Jews ever lived in my village."

"Maybe not permanently. But maybe your ancestors were nice people and they gave my ancestors a temporary refuge. And maybe your ancestors agreed to hide the Torah scroll until my ancestors could come back for it. Those were turbulent times. Not everything that happened was recorded. If walls could speak, your farmhouse could probably tell you quite a few things about the history of Sant Joan Januz that you don't know."

The American had made an interesting point, Vidal had to admit. People had been fleeing across the Pyrenees for one reason or another since there were people to flee. It was plausible that a small group of Jews had temporarily found refuge in Sant Joan Januz. And if their stay had been brief, there was no reason why his grandfather, or anyone else in the village, would have known about it. So maybe, when he took that shovel, he hadn't been so foolish after all.

An image of a newspaper's front page began to form before Vidal's eyes, followed by glimpses of televised newscasts, SMS news alerts, blogs, articles in glossy popular magazines, and serious academic journals.

"What I am trying to tell you, Mr. Bonet, is that if you'll help me, I'll help you. Find my Torah scroll and it will put Sant Joan Januz — and that resort of yours — on the map."

Chaim blinked. For the first time since they had met, he saw a smile appear on the Catalan's face.

A few hours later, Chaim was presented with a wheelchair and a large envelope filled with X-rays and told that he could leave. Since Vidal had agreed to let him return to Sant Joan Januz, and Clara had agreed to let him convalesce at the Bonets' farmhouse, there was no longer a question about where he was going. There was, though, one last thing to do in Girona before he and Vidal set out for the village. Chaim's suitcases were still stored at his hotel, and he needed to pick them up.

"What's in here?" asked Vidal, as he struggled to lift the largest suitcase into the trunk of his car.

"My stuff."

After the morning's events, Chaim didn't have the energy to explain that for an Orthodox Jew a long-term stay in a place like Catalonia, where kosher food was practically nonexistent, required the same kind of advance logistical planning that armies used when supplying their troops for an overseas invasion. He and his mother had spent an entire afternoon at the Hen House Market in

Overland Park, Kansas, which had the best supply of kosher food in the area, buying up just about everything that was nonperishable and had a reliable kosher certification.

It had taken him a whole day to figure out how to fit it all into his suitcases. When he arrived at the Kansas City International Airport, his credit card was out of his wallet and waiting before the clerk, who observed his approach to the check-in counter with a wary eye, had a chance to say, "How would you like to pay for your overweight and excess baggage fees, sir?" Only one thing had consoled him as he signed the credit card charge form: He wouldn't go hungry while he was in Catalonia.

Clara was waiting for them when Chaim and Vidal arrived at the Bonets' farmhouse. She wheeled Chaim into the sewing room, with Vidal following after them with the suitcases. Since the sewing room was small and Chaim would need room to maneuver his wheelchair, Clara decided that the bulky suitcases would be in the way and needed to be unpacked as quickly as possible. Chaim would have preferred to wait until he had rested and was able to unpack the bags himself and in private. But he didn't have the strength to object, and so he surrendered the keys to Clara.

Whether it was due to their innate politeness or a preplanned decision not to show any reaction, neither Clara nor Vidal said a word when they saw what was inside the first suitcase. The shelves of the room's wardrobe were quickly emptied to make room for Chaim's belongings, which included several dozen cans of tuna; dozens of tins of canned fruits and vegetables; a generous supply of vacuum-packed, precooked salmon and tuna steaks; several large bags of brown rice and whole-wheat pasta; a bottle of olive oil; a large assortment of "just-add-water" instant oatmeal, soups, and mashed potatoes; several jars of peanut butter and a good supply of crackers to go with them; a few packages of cookies; many, many packages of potato chips and pretzels; a very large plastic bag filled with an assortment of chewing gum, toffees, and candy bars; three jars of instant coffee, two boxes of tea bags, and one large can of instant cocoa mix; and individual packets of sugar, salt, and pepper.

In addition to the foodstuffs, there was an impressive supply of plastic plates, cups, and cutlery; paper goods such as tissues, napkins, and disposable tablecloths; and several boxes of Ziploc containers in various sizes. At the bottom of the suitcase were the metal items: utensils such as a spatula, a can opener, a vegetable peeler, and a corkscrew; a large thermos; a medium-sized pot; a small frying pan; and a one-burner portable stove.

"Guess you're all set in case there's a nuclear war," said Vidal after the last item had been put away.

Chaim smiled at the joke. "There's another bag."

The contents of the second bag caused a momentary hitch in the operations, since the wardrobe was already full and the boxes of matzah — the special unleavened bread eaten during Passover — that were packed in that suitcase were not only numerous, but also bulky. Clara solved the problem by clearing out a bookcase, which quickly took on the appearance of a supermarket aisle before the holiday.

Since there was some room left on one of the shelves, Clara put Chaim's books there — a pocket-sized version of the five volumes of the Torah; a volume of the Talmud, his prayer book for every day, and his prayer book for Shabbos and the holidays.

His Shabbos travel kit was placed on top of the dresser. The smallish kit was deceptive. Tightly packed within it were the essentials for the holy day: a set of small silver candlesticks and a supply of candles and matches; a lightweight silk cloth to cover the challah loaves; a small silver cup for Kiddush and a small bottle of wine; a small bag of cloves and a miniature multi-wicked candle for the Havdalah service that marked the end of the day; an electric timer for a lamp; and a roll of masking tape to tape the light switches, so that he wouldn't manually turn the lights on or off by mistake.

As for his changes of clothes, which were few in number since he had run out of space in his suitcases, they found a home in the hanging space of the wardrobe.

The last thing to unpack was his overnight bag. When Clara reached for the bag a warning signal went off in Chaim's head. He didn't want Vidal and Clara to discover the diary and the *Anusim* forms. But before he could say a word, Vidal mentioned that Chaim looked tired, and so perhaps the bag, which wasn't terribly bulky, could wait.

Clara acquiesced, reluctantly. After Vidal stored the empty suitcases on top of the wardrobe, they left the room. And because Chaim actually was very tired, he soon drifted into a deep sleep.

147

While Chaim was being examined from head to toe at the hospital, his case was being dissected in a very different venue: Eduard Garcia's general store. The news about the young American who had taken a tumble in the cemetery spread quickly — neither Americans nor ambulances were common in the village — and so Joya Garcia had no choice except to graciously yield to the entreaties of the small crowd and give a full account of what had happened.

"The first thing that made me think that something was amiss was the rental car."

"Did you look inside it, to see if there was anything suspicious?" asked Carme Rodriguez, who was a big fan of mystery stories.

"Well, I did have to pass by the car to get into the cemetery, and so I took a quick look. Sitting on the back seat was a big black overnight bag."

"You're giving me the chills!" Carme exclaimed. "The same thing happened in the book I've just finished reading. Only the bag wasn't black, it was green."

"What was inside it?" asked Aster Lunel, who had just graduated from high school the year before and often borrowed the mystery stories in Carme's collection.

"I'd better not tell," Carme solemnly replied. "It might give you nightmares. All I can say is that if it had been me, I would have been much too afraid to go into that cemetery alone."

"Then it's a good thing I don't read mystery stories," Joya said, redirecting the crowd's attention back to her story. "Otherwise, that young man would still be lying where I found him."

"Where did you find him?" asked Miquel, who was standing by the checkout counter.

"Stretched out on the path right Aster's relatives are buried, may they rest in peace."

"My family? Why?"

"I'm sure I don't know."

"He had a camera," Eduard whispered to Miquel.

"Who has it now?" asked Miquel, also in a whisper.

"Vidal."

148

That day there was a steady stream of visitors to the Bonets' farmhouse. Needless to say, they didn't arrive empty-handed. Clara had to explain to each one that the invalid was on a special diet, so gifts of food, while appreciated for the sentiments they represented, couldn't be accepted.

Most of the villagers received this information without making a fuss, but Joya Garcia wasn't about to be put off so easily. As the person who had found the young man, she felt she had both a special responsibility and special privileges.

"It's only vegetable soup, Clara. It can't possibly hurt him."

"It's not a question of hurting him," Clara replied. "He just can't eat it."

"Let me talk to him. Is he awake?"

"No, he's still sleeping, and the doctor said it's very important that he gets plenty of rest."

"What can I do then?"

Chaim, who had been dozing on and off throughout the afternoon, had been vaguely aware of people talking on the front porch since his room had a window that overlooked the front yard. He thought he recognized this woman's voice, but he couldn't remember from where.

"I do need eggs, and some fresh garlic," said Clara. "If Josep hadn't driven to Barcelona this morning to deliver an order, I'd have gone to the store myself. And now Vidal has taken the car again, to develop some photos or something, and I don't know what time he'll be back."

"Don't say another word. I'll be back in a jiffy."

"You don't have to drive all the way back here. If you could just pick up the groceries for me, I'll tell Vidal to drop by your house before he comes home."

"You'll do no such thing. Really, Clara, you're just like your parents. There's nothing wrong with letting a neighbor do you a favor. Besides, I'm only offering because I want to help the young man."

Chaim suddenly recalled who this woman was. She was the kind-looking woman who had found him in the cemetery. Inadvertently, it looked like he had accomplished all of his goals for the day. He had a place to sleep and he seemed to have found an elderly friend.

149

He was about to close his eyes again when he heard a telephone ringing somewhere in the house. For a moment he hoped that it might be his parents calling. It wasn't likely that they had heard about his accident, but there was a chance that the hospital had contacted them. He strained his ears to hear what was being said on the other side of the closed door.

"Can you be home by eight, Josep?" Chaim heard Clara say. "Papa wants to have a family meeting."

Since it wasn't his parents, Chaim lost interest in the conversation. But the words "family meeting" settled into the landscape of his half-asleep state of mind, and his thoughts drowsily traveled back to his own family.

They had family meetings as well, and the best were the ones that took place several weeks before Passover. His parents would heat up a large frozen pizza — it came from New York — and the entire family would sit around the kitchen table and divvy up the pizza while they divvied up the cleaning jobs. One year, he recalled, he had gotten off easy, because his tonsils had been taken out. Instead of helping with the cleaning, all he had to do was take pictures of everyone else at work and make a photo album, which they looked at, and laughed over, during the holiday.

"That must be Vidal's job, too," he mumbled sleepily. "When he gets back from the mall, they'll have a meeting and they'll eat pizza and they'll look at my pictures."

Chaim's formerly closed eyelids opened wide. He reached out his arm as far as he could without falling off the sofa and dragged over his overnight bag. As he rifled through the bag's contents, he saw that the items he had used the night before to make his dinner were all there, as were his alarm clock, toiletries bag, and a two-handled cup for the ritual washing of his hands. His passport and airplane tickets were still in the small zippered compartment; the diary and the stack of *Anusim* forms were still in the large one. Only two things were missing: his camera bag and his camera.

Joya Garcia came back as promised. In addition to the eggs and garlic that Clara had asked for, she brought a large sack filled with vegetables. These she would personally deliver to "the sick room," she informed Clara, since she planned to help "the invalid" make vegetable soup for his dinner.

150

Of course, a vegetable soup made in "the sick room" wasn't the same as one that came from the Garcia kitchen, whose therapeutic qualities were famous in the village. But she made peace with the situation once she saw that the soup was simmering nicely on the one-burner stove. She then set up the rest of the makeshift kitchen so that everything could be conveniently reached by a person in a wheelchair. By the time she had to leave, "the invalid" had not only eaten his dinner, but had everything he needed to prepare a simple breakfast in the morning.

"So don't worry about his meals," Joya Garcia commented cheerfully as Clara escorted her to the front door. "Everything is now properly organized, and I'll come every day to help out."

"That's very kind of you," said Clara, hoping she had successfully masked the ambivalent feelings that this news stirred up.

While on her way back to the kitchen, Clara glanced down the hallway. The door to the sewing room was closed, but there was a light shining out from under it, which spilled onto the dark hallway's wood floor.

She was glad to provide the young American with a place to recuperate. Her mother had always said that a person would never regret doing a kindness. They would be repaid for it in full in the end. Still, there was something about the light — and the young man — that made her uneasy.

CHAPTER 15

I don't like it."

Vidal's laptop computer sat on the kitchen table, and Vidal, Miquel, and Josep sat around it. A photograph of a headstone that belonged to a person named Belhom Lunel, who had passed away in the year 1917, was displayed on the screen.

"He had to go somewhere, Papa," said Clara, who had dragged her mother's chair close to the door that led to the hallway. She had given their guest a little bell that he could ring in case he needed anything, and she wanted to be sure she would hear it.

Clara still felt uncomfortable when she sat in her mother's chair, but her father had laid down the law: she was the family's matriarch. Abdication wasn't an option, since there wasn't anyone else who could fulfill the role. She had to learn to be more confident, which was why she had to sit on the heavy wood chair with a field of wildflowers carved into its back during the family meeting instead of on a less conspicuous seat. She also had to learn to be more assertive and express her opinion on family matters, which was why she had spoken up even though she would have preferred to remain silent.

"Clara, I'm not criticizing you and Vidal for doing the neighborly thing," said Miquel. "But in my opinion that young man's story doesn't add up."

"With all due respect, Papa, I think you're reading too much into this." Josep was tired after his long trip to Barcelona and badly wanted to retire to the living room with his newspaper and a cup of coffee. "The young man was sent on a wild goose chase for some reason, but that's his problem. Surely there's no harm in it for us."

"If it's true that he was just looking for relatives, why didn't he photograph just their headstones? Why photograph half the cemetery?"

When no one said anything, Miquel continued, "I'll tell you why: because he isn't looking for relatives and he isn't looking for a

Torah scroll. He's looking for a Cathar connection here in Sant Joan Januz. And he's doing it because he wants to start a rumor. He wants to trick people into believing that the Cathar treasure, or at least part of it, is buried in our village."

There was a long silence.

"I know what you're thinking," said Miquel. "But before you pack me off to the loony bin, give me a few minutes to explain. We all know that this region — and I'm talking about both sides of the Pyrenees — is a magnet for schemers and crazy people because of the Cathars and the big treasure that they supposedly hid away in their fortress at Montsegur."

"Papa," said Josep, barely concealing his irritation, "according to the legend, if you believe the story, after Montsegur fell to the French, the Cathar treasure was taken to Rennes-le-Chateau and hidden there."

"True, according to some people. But remember, according to the schemers and the crazy people all sorts of things were hidden at Montsegur: gold, esoteric manuscripts, even the Holy Grail. Anything and everything was supposedly at that fortress, except maybe Cinderella's kitchen sink. So there was a lot of loot to carry off when a few of the people escaped. Who's to say that they all went to Rennes-le-Chateau? Maybe they scattered, and each one went in a different direction, taking with him a part of the treasure."

"But why would one of them come to Sant Joan Januz? The idea is crazy," Josep insisted.

"I agree with you. But there's only one explanation for why that American fellow wanted to photograph all the headstones. He was looking for evidence to back up his scheme. He must have jumped for joy when he found the graves of the Lunel family."

"Maybe that's how he fell and broke his ankle," said Vidal.

Vidal's alliance with the American had been short-lived. Contrary to his expectations, when he telephoned Al to tell him about the American's theory, Al hadn't been thrilled to hear that there might be a Torah scroll buried somewhere in Sant Joan Januz.

"It would upset the balance," Al had said.

"In what way?"

"What about the Christians? And the Muslims? You'd need to dig up something authentic for them too. Otherwise, it wouldn't be fair. It would look like Peaceland is favoring the Jews."

153

"But if no Muslims ever lived here, and the medieval Christians didn't leave anything behind..."

"Think about it, Vidal. A real medieval Torah scroll in a modern sound-and-light show would stick out like a lemon in a bushel full of apples. It's better to let it remain where it is, buried under the ground, if it really does exist."

"But I promised the American I would help him. What am I supposed to tell him?"

"You don't have to tell him anything. Just tell your grandfather about the Torah scroll, and he'll take care of the rest. Now I've got to go. The accounting office is paging me."

And so when his grandfather asked him about the American, Vidal told him everything — or almost everything. He skipped the part about agreeing to help the American find the Torah scroll and, instead, said that his reasons for wanting to house the foreigner in their home had been strictly humanitarian. If Al didn't see any value to the Torah scroll, he wasn't about to risk upsetting the fragile peace that had been established between him and his grandfather because of it. To his relief, his grandfather seemed to accept his story. The peace had held.

Miquel acknowledged with a nod of his head the little joke Vidal had made. Then he became serious again. "Maybe that's the reason he fell and maybe it isn't. But he surely knows that Lunel was a Cathar town way back when and that people sometimes took the name of the town they lived in as their family name. With a little imagination, he can easily fabricate some story about how one of our Lunels was at Montsegur during the siege and managed to slip across the Pyrenees during the dead of night with part of the Cathars' treasure hidden under his cloak."

Vidal smiled. His grandfather hadn't lost his touch when it came to telling a story. He always knew when to lower his deep voice to a whisper, to heighten the mystery of what had happened long ago on some dark and moonless night.

"Have I said something that amuses you, Vidal?"

"No, Grandpa," Vidal replied, looking serious again.

"But what about the Torah scroll?" Clara asked. Her head was starting to ache. It made sense to her that a young Jew would be interested in finding an old Torah scroll. But all this talk about the Cathar treasure was getting her confused.

"Vidal can answer you. I asked him to find out just how rare a Torah scroll from Spain really is, didn't I, Vidal?"

"That's right."

"How long did you spend on the Internet this afternoon?"

"An hour, maybe ninety minutes."

"And how many old Torah scrolls from Spain did you find in that short amount of time?"

"Half a dozen, at least. The information on some of the web sites wasn't precise."

"Half a dozen. At least!" Miquel said slowly, emphasizing each word. "And if you had spent another hour looking, you would have found half a dozen more, which means there must be a few dozen of these Torah scrolls still around. And if that's the case, finding another one isn't going to be an earth-shattering event. No, the Torah scroll was just a ploy to get that American into our village. Spreading Cathar fairy dust is what he's really after."

Miquel paused and fixed his eye on the little group. "Now, I didn't come here tonight to cast blame, but we have to face the facts. A first-class scoundrel has set up camp in our village, and he has to be stopped."

"Papa," Josep interrupted, "even if we assume for the moment that the young man is a schemer and a scoundrel, you still haven't answered why he would say the treasure is buried in Sant Joan Januz."

"Can I get you a coffee, Josep?" Clara had noticed that her husband was about to explode.

"Please," he replied tersely.

"My theory is like this," said Miquel. "That fellow was hanging around in Girona for a few days before he turned up here. Somehow he must have heard about Vidal's resort. Now, building a resort means bulldozers knocking down old buildings and uncovering foundations. In other words, it's the perfect opportunity for slipping a fake medieval document into some hole in the ground when no one is looking. Then he'll 'discover' this amazing document, which will describe how the Cathars buried part of their treasure in Sant Joan Januz. He'll call up the newspaper and TV people, and in no time he'll have enough publicity to sell his book and whatever else he's planning to do to make money off this scheme."

Josep wearily shook his head. "People aren't so gullible."

155

"They aren't? Maybe you should ask your son about that. Surely Vidal, of all people, hasn't forgotten how that buried treasure nonsense got started in Rennes-le-Chateau."

Vidal shifted uneasily in his seat.

"Back in the 1950s, there was a man living in Rennes-le-Chateau who had a little hotel that he wanted to turn into a big hotel," Miquel continued. "The only problem was that tourists weren't interested in coming to this out-of-the-way town in Languedoc. Clara, the kettle is whistling."

Clara, who had been too absorbed in observing the knot of tension growing in her stomach to notice, quickly turned off the gas.

"So what did this hotel owner do? He started a rumor that a priest, who had died a few decades earlier, had found a treasure buried inside a church in the town. The newspapers picked up the story, two other scoundrels added a few more embellishments — including the discovery of a medieval document that listed more treasures supposedly buried in the town — and today tens of thousands of tourists visit little Rennes-le-Chateau every year. The myth-spinners and unscrupulous businessmen are making a fortune from —"

"Papa, please," said Clara, glancing over at Vidal.

"Clara, I am willing to be convinced that Vidal acted as he did for purely...how did you phrase it, Vidal? Humanitarian reasons? And I will even go further and say that I'm sure that he hasn't allowed himself to be hoodwinked by that American adventurer you've got stashed away in your sewing room — at least not yet. However, just in case the thought should enter Vidal's mind during the next few weeks to join forces with that anthropologist, I do want to remind him that an attempt to promote his resort through cashing in on this crazy Cathar business would be unworthy of his talents and beneath the dignity of our village."

There was another long and uncomfortable silence.

"So what are we supposed to do?" asked Vidal. "Turn him out of the house?"

"No one is telling you to drive him to the main highway and leave him sitting in his wheelchair by the side of the road," said Miquel. "This is what I suggest we do: once he feels up to going exploring, I'll be his guide. And by the time I'm through with him, he'll wish he'd never heard of the Cathars or Sant Joan Januz."

The clock ticking on the wall was the only sound that disturbed the quiet of the night. Miquel sat at his kitchen table, doing nothing. It felt good to be quiet after such a day. And he could have sat there for a long while, doing nothing except be quiet, if the telephone hadn't rung.

"How did it go?" asked Pau. He and Miquel had agreed beforehand that the uncles wouldn't attend the family meeting.

"Josep gave me some trouble, but I managed to convince them," replied Miquel, forcing himself to sound more energetic than he felt. "Did Carme Rodriguez say anything when you borrowed the book?"

"She was too busy talking on the phone about some overnight bag to care. And I borrowed a few other mystery novels, so it wouldn't be so noticeable."

"Good. I'll return the book to you tomorrow."

"There's no rush. It's not like it's a regular library."

"I don't want a mystery novel about the Cathar treasure lying around the house. Someone might drop by and find it."

After hanging up the phone, Miquel turned off the light in the kitchen and went to his bedroom. Before retiring for the night he had gotten into the habit of taking a look at the photograph of his wedding that hung on the wall. It made him feel less lonely when he saw all the old faces, and as he stood in the bedroom and heard nothing but the silence of the night, he did feel very, very alone.

"Sssh! I hear the car. Vidal must be back."

"He was in the kitchen tonight, too, Clara."

"It's because you're tired, Josep. We should have had the meeting another night."

"Clara, you have to face the facts. Your father needs to see a doctor."

"I'm not putting my father in a nursing home."

"Why do you always jump to conclusions? All I said was that your father's obsession with strangers is getting out of hand."

"Can we please talk about this tomorrow? I've had a long day, too."

"Fine."

Josep walked out of the kitchen. Clara wiped the last coffee cup and put it in the cupboard. The kitchen was tidy again. It was bright and cheerful, too. If she would have seen a picture of such a kitchen in a magazine, she would have said to herself, "A happy family lives there."

The door opened. Vidal and a cold blast of night air entered the room. Clara forced a cheerful smile onto her face. "Well, Vidal, you certainly did a lot of driving today. I hope you know how much I appreciate it when you drive your grandfather home. Can I fix you a snack or a hot drink?"

"No, thanks."

"That was quite a family meeting we had tonight, wasn't it?"

"Yes, it was."

"Your grandfather always did have a vivid imagination. When you were a child, you used to love his stories. You'd grab his leg, and you wouldn't let go until he sat down and put you on his knee. And while he was telling you the story, you'd pester him with all sorts of questions. You two were quite a pair. But you probably don't remember."

"I remember."

"I suppose there's a good and bad side to everything," Clara continued. "When a person is telling a story, I suppose that a good imagination is a very good thing to have. But when a person uses that imagination for other things..."

Clara knew that she was rambling on, as her father would say. Since Vidal was looking at her in a funny way, she concluded by saying, "I just don't want you and your grandfather to fight again."

"I don't want to either. That's why I told him about our guest and the Torah scroll."

"Yes, that was the right thing to do."

"You look tired, Mama. Why don't you go to bed?"

"I will. Soon. I thought I'd make some tea. Are you sure you don't want a hot drink?"

"Positive. Good night, then."

"Good night. Pleasant dreams."

As Vidal walked down the hallway, he noted that the light in the sewing room was off. Their American adventurer must be asleep.

"The Cathars," he whispered with a laugh. "Our village should be so lucky."

CHAPTER 16

T here are times when you know that you are dreaming. You're walking down a street in this dream, and your dreaming self whispers to you that the street is in Girona or Barcelona, and you say, "Yes. I believe you." Then your waking self pipes up and says, "No! I know what the real city looks like, and this dreaming city doesn't look like it at all."

For a moment, you are confused.

Your dreaming self knows that what your waking self has said is true. But it doesn't care.

"My friend," your dreaming self tells you, "why the fuss? Relax. This is, after all, a dream."

And so you do. You tell your waking self to be quiet, because you want to dream.

This was the kind of dream that Vidal was dreaming after the family meeting. He was walking down a street in Barcelona, only it wasn't Barcelona. He was talking to Al, only it wasn't Al. It made perfect sense, only it made no sense. Because, after all, it was a dream.

There are other dreams, though, where you don't know that you are dreaming. The street is the street. The faces are the faces. What is happening did happen, every time you dream it. That was the kind of dream that Miquel was dreaming after the family meeting.

Miquel, nine years old, sat in the back of the family's old pickup truck with his older brother, who was thirteen. A light-brown suitcase sat between them. Their job was to guard the suitcase and make sure it didn't fly off the truck. It could happen, even though everyone knows a suitcase doesn't have wings. His father, who was sitting in the truck's cabin with Miquel's mother, had said so.

Miquel watched the suitcase, waiting to see it fly. The truck hit a big hole in the road — an occurrence that happened frequently in Catalonia in 1943 — and the truck jumped into the air for a few seconds before it landed on the road with a thud. When the truck jumped up, the suitcase jumped with it. And when the truck landed with a thud, the suitcase jumped again.

"It's flying!" he yelled to his brother.

"That's not flying," said his brother. "That's jumping."

Then the truck drove over a little stream. Miquel looked so far over the side of the truck that he almost fell overboard. "Help!" he called out.

His brother grabbed him by the back of his suspenders — and he did it just in time every time Miquel dreamed the dream — and so Miquel didn't fall into the stream. And so the truck continued to drive. And so then they were in Sant Joan Januz.

Pop!

That was the front tire. Just as they reached the square, the tire went *pop!* and lost all of its air. They all got out of the truck. Someone from the village went to find their cousins. Someone else came to look at the tire.

"You're lucky you're here and not there," that someone said as he pointed to somewhere down the road.

Then the square filled up with people. His mother hugged the lady cousins. His father shook hands with the men cousins. Everyone was happy, because it was the fall holiday and the Allied Forces had invaded Italy.

A grown-up cousin pushed Miquel toward a girl cousin, who was younger than him. "Say hello to Anna," said the cousin. "Say 'How do you do' to your future bride."

The grown-up cousins laughed. When no one was looking, Miquel yanked one of Anna's long braids. She stuck out her tongue. That was how they said hello.

Then it was time to climb into the cousins' trucks, to go to the farmhouse where they'd be staying. But before they could do so, another truck pulled into the square. This truck didn't belong to cousins. There were soldiers in the truck, or at least they looked like soldiers because they were wearing uniforms. There was also a priest in the truck. The priest jumped down from the truck and strode into the square. He glared at Miquel's parents and the cousins.

"I know why you're all so happy," said the priest. "It's your New Year, and you think the Germans are going to lose the war. But you're wrong. The Germans are going to win. And when they do, it will be the end of you Jews."

160

Everyone was quiet. Then a young man, his cousin Manel, called out, "You'd better watch what you say, Father."

Some elders of the village tried to hush Manel. Maybe because the Allies had invaded Italy, Cousin Manel wouldn't be hushed.

"The Church sprinkled a whole lot of holy water over our ancestors. So if you're saying that we're still Jews, you're saying the Church is a lie, and you can get into some pretty hot water for saying a thing like that."

The priest turned red in the face, and his lips started to move, but he was so mad that he couldn't get out a word. Everyone knew that the priest wanted to hit Cousin Manel, but Manel was bigger than the priest. So instead of hitting Cousin Manel, the priest searched through the crowd with big, wild eyes.

Miquel saw the priest coming toward him. He wanted to run, but his legs were like two blocks of ice. Then the priest grabbed him and he was flying. He was as high as the priest.

"The Germans have a special oven for boys like you!" the priest screamed into Miquel's face. He shook Miquel hard. "They're going to throw you into the fire! Do you hear? They're going to throw you into the fire!"

His father and Cousin Manel rushed toward the priest. The priest let go of Miquel and ran back to the truck. Miquel fell to the ground. He wasn't flying anymore. But he was still shaking.

He heard the truck drive off, but he was still shaking. He couldn't stop. His Papa said, "It's all right now, son. They're gone." But he was still shaking. He couldn't stop. Even when he woke up, he was still shaking. Even when he turned on the light and looked around the room and told himself that the war was over and he was grown up and the priest was dead, he was still shaking. He couldn't stop.

That was his dream.

While Anna had been on this earth, she would go to the kitchen to make him a cup of chamomile tea to help him stop shaking. She had done it quietly so that Clara wouldn't wake up. It was important that Clara stayed asleep. That had been the decision, after the war.

During the war, they hadn't really understood what the priest had been talking about. After the war, they understood. The fires of the Inquisition hadn't been put out after all. They had simply been moved to another place, a place called Auschwitz. And if that was so, even if this war was over, the fires could be moved somewhere else again.

They decided not to tell the new generation anything about being descended from Jews. Not that they had ever openly said anything about it. But somehow the children had always learned the secret, and once they learned the secret they were taught how to keep it. But after the war, if the children asked about the customs, they were only told that this was how things had been done in the village for as long as anyone could remember.

He didn't know who it was who first got the idea to tell the children that they were descended from a people who were "like the Cathars." But that's what some people started to say. "A long time ago our ancestors had some practices that got them into trouble with the Church. Like the Cathars," they told the children. "But it all got worked out, and now we're just like everybody else."

As for the customs, no one asked too many questions, because the village was their world and no one knew any different. Food could be a problem when a child went off to the regional school. But there was an answer.

"Why can't I eat pork, like the other children?" "Pork isn't healthy. It gives people a stomachache."

"Why can't I put a slice of cheese on my chicken, like the other children?"

"Eating cheese with chicken isn't healthy. It gives people a stomachache."

The children got the idea.

As time went by, more and more of Miquel's generation began to believe that they were Catalans "like the Cathars" and forgot that they were really *Anusim* "like the Jews." The elders had thought of that, too, though. It was decided, after the war, that there would be one family in the village who would keep the secret. The matriarch of the family would tell the eldest daughter, at the right time. They would pass it on from generation to generation, until the Messiah came and the fires were put out for once and for all. Then they would tell everyone.

That was the plan. And it worked very well for a while. But then things started to fall apart. The village was no longer the world. Anna died without telling Clara. And a young Jew had appeared in the village to reveal the secret to everyone before it was time.

162

CHAPTER 17

I t was frustrating. He was in Sant Joan Januz. He was in the Bonets' home. But he was in the sewing room, in a wheelchair. And the only Jewish customs Chaim could observe were his own.

A few days had passed since his accident, and the worst of the pain had subsided. He would have welcomed some company to help him pass the time, but apparently the village had lost interest in him. His interactions with the Bonet family were also few and far between. Therefore, Chaim's boredom was alleviated only when Joya Garcia came to visit him, which she did every day.

His first impression of her had been correct. She was a kind lady. He enjoyed the way she made a fuss over him, always making sure that he was eating properly and wasn't doing anything foolish that would hinder his recovery, such as putting weight on his ankle while he practiced hopping around the room on his crutches.

Yet there were times, and perhaps it wasn't right of him to be suspicious of someone who was being so kind to him, when the thought entered his mind that there was something strange about the way she had commandeered the sewing room. While she was with him, it was as if there was a big sign on the open door that said, "Caretaker at Work: Do Not Disturb." When she wasn't in the room, there wasn't really a need for any of the Bonets to drop in, because there was nothing for them to do there. And so, as the days passed, he increasingly had the feeling that he was being kept a prisoner in the sewing room, and that Joya Garcia was his jailer.

Even if his suspicions were correct, there wasn't anything he could do about them. But he could make the best of the situation. By using his little prison cell as his laboratory and Joya Garcia as the subject of his experiments, he could use his convalescence to do some research for his thesis.

"You probably think it's odd that I brought all this tuna," he said on the Thursday afternoon after his accident as she removed a can from the wardrobe's shelf.

"Not at all," she replied. "Many people are vegetarians today."

"I'm not a vegetarian. At home I eat meat and dairy products. But not together."

"That's very wise. A person shouldn't eat too many different kinds of food at the same meal. Would you like rice with your tuna or noodles?"

"Noodles, please. But you were about to say something."

"I was?"

"Yes, about why you don't eat meat and dairy products at the same meal."

"I was?"

"Yes. Why it's not wise to do it."

"Oh, yes, because it can cause obesity. Of course, a young man like you doesn't have to worry about counting calories. But Mr. Garcia and I are at an age when we do have to watch our weight, and studies have shown that people tend to overeat when they have too many choices. It's called the 'buffet effect.' "

"The buffet effect?"

"Yes."

"That's very interesting. I thought you were going to say it can cause a stomachache."

The bright smile faded from Joya Garcia's lips. Then a faint cousin quickly took its place.

"Is that what happens to you when you eat too many different kinds of food?" she asked with a concerned tone of voice.

"Sometimes."

"Then that's another good reason for eating simply," she said triumphantly, having regained her customary cheerfulness.

He had to be content with her partial admission about not eating milk and meat together, since she left the room once the noodles were cooking. When she returned, she came armed with a newspaper. Although Chaim said that he would much rather learn about the history of the village, she dismissed this comment by happily informing him that Sant Joan Januz was the most boring village in the entire world and nothing of interest had ever happened there.

While he ate his meal, she read him the news. He noted that she skipped some of the international news stories — for instance, those that had to do with the Middle East — and concentrated instead on the local news, since he was "so interested in Catalonia." As his interest didn't extend as far as the local soccer teams and political intrigues, he let her read without interrupting. After he finished his meal, though, Chaim saw an opportunity for further research and said, "You sweep the floor the same way that Mrs. Bonet does."

"Do I?"

"Yes. You both start at the door and sweep toward the center of the room."

"That's very perceptive of you to notice. I can't say that most young men would."

"I noticed because Mrs. Bonet got very upset when I swept some dirt the other way, toward the door. I don't want to offend anyone while I'm a guest in your village. I'd really appreciate it if you'd explain what I did wrong."

"I'm sure Mrs. Bonet has already forgotten the incident."

"Then I did do something wrong?"

"Yes, you did," she said quietly.

During the pause that followed, Chaim had a slight hope that she was about to trust him with her secret. Although this was rare, it did sometimes happen. But when she spoke again, she only said, while looking at him intently, "You brought bad luck into the house."

"What?"

"When a person sweeps toward the door, he sweeps out all the good fortune that's in the home. Of course, it's just an old superstition, and today most people don't take it seriously. But some of us still cling to the old ways, even though our children and grandchildren laugh at us. Does that answer your question?"

"Yes, thank you, it does."

In his eagerness to unearth *Anusim*, Chaim had forgotten about this particular superstition, which he now remembered turned up in some form or another in many cultures.

He was about to admit defeat when an opposing voice warned him not to be so easily convinced. If all Spaniards believed in it, the Inquisition couldn't have used it to trap the *Anusim*. Many

165

people counted calories, but few refrained from eating meat and dairy products at the same meal to lose weight.

"Since you're so interested in the way we do things," Joya Garcia continued as she went back to tidying up the room, "I'm warning you in advance that tomorrow we're going to be very busy. Friday is the day we clean the house."

Before he could make a comment — for this was yet another *Anusim* custom — she again looked him in the eye and said, in a tone of voice that brooked no argument, "Women do all the housework on Friday so we can enjoy the weekend with the family."

The next day was a busy one, for both of them. While Joya Garcia cleaned his room and took charge of his laundry, Chaim organized his meals for Shabbos. As he stared at his cans of food, he envisioned his mother's kitchen in Kansas on a typical Friday morning: the chickens baking in the oven, the chicken soup and gefilte fish simmering on the stove. For a few moments, he felt sorry for himself. But only for a few moments, because there wasn't time to brood. Sundown would come all too soon, and he had dozens of details to sort out. After planning his menu for the traditional three meals, he turned his attention to setting up a Shabbos table in his room and asked Joya Garcia to bring him one of the white paper tablecloths that were stored in the wardrobe.

"Does your mother use a paper tablecloth when she sets her table?" she asked as she looked unhappily at the package.

"No."

"I didn't think so."

She returned the package to the wardrobe and left the room. A few minutes later she returned with one of Clara Bonet's white cotton tablecloths, which had just been freshly laundered. She also let Chaim know that she didn't approve of using disposable dishes for special occasions. Since he refused to use the Bonets' dishes, she had to make peace with the floral-patterned paper plates with matching cups and plastic silverware that Chaim had saved for Shabbos. But it was only after he placed his silver Kiddush cup and the silk challah cover on the table that she reluctantly gave her approval to the set table. Then it was time for her to go home, and Chaim made the rest of his preparations alone.

166

"How's the invalid doing?" Miquel asked after the soup course for the traditional Friday night meal was served and Clara had returned to her seat at the table.

"Fine," replied Clara.

"I hear that Joya Garcia is helping out."

"Yes, she is. She's doing everything really."

"Aren't there any croutons, Clara?" asked Uncle Biel.

"Of course there are. I'll get them." She was about to push back the heavy chair with the wildflowers, when she stopped and listened intently. "What was that?"

"What was what?" asked Miquel.

"I thought I heard something. Outside."

They all listened. A faint howl was heard in the distance. It was answered a few seconds later by another howl, which sounded closer.

"It's probably some dogs from the next village," said Miquel. "They must have gotten lost."

"You don't think they're wolves, do you, Papa? So many ouses in the village are empty now."

"A wolf hasn't been spotted in Catalonia in seventy years," said Uncle Pau.

"Still, it won't hurt to scare off whatever it is that's out there," Josep commented, glancing at Clara. "Vidal, do you want to come with me?"

"Sure, Papa."

"As long as you're making a party of it, I'll come along, too," said Miquel. "Pau, you stay here and guard the croutons."

Clara forced herself to smile at her father's little joke, but her eyes followed Josep, who opened a cupboard and took out his shotgun.

Josep and the others went outside and circled the house, beginning at the back and working their way around. They reached the front lawn without seeing or hearing anything unusual.

"Whatever they were, they seem to have moved on," Josep commented.

Miquel stared into the distance, still listening. "I wonder what attracted them to these parts."

"We can take another look around in the morning. I'll fire the gun once to calm down Clara."

167

"Maybe you should walk to the end of the drive so it doesn't scare our guest," Vidal suggested.

"A good idea," Miquel agreed. "We don't want him falling out of his wheelchair from fright and breaking his other ankle."

Josep and Vidal started to walk. When Vidal noticed that Miquel wasn't with them, he turned to see what had detained him. Miquel was standing still and staring at the house.

"What's wrong, Grandpa?" asked Vidal, coming up beside him.

Miquel was silent, and so Vidal looked in the direction where he was staring. A moment later Josep joined them. All three stood on the lawn, in the dark, and stared at the window that belonged to the sewing room. Shining in the window were two lights.

"I'll take care of it," said Vidal.

"Is everything all right?" asked Clara. Vidal had reentered the house through the kitchen door, since the front door was already locked for the night.

"Yes, Mama. I'll be back in a minute."

Vidal quickly walked out of the kitchen and down the hallway. When he reached the sewing room he knocked, but he didn't wait for a reply. Instead, he opened the door and walked straight over to the window, where two lit candles were sitting on the window's ledge.

"Hey! What are you doing?" Chaim asked, as Vidal blew out one of the flames. "Those are my Shabbos candles!"

Vidal blew out the second candle and yanked the curtains shut. "Candles in the window are bad luck," he said coldly, and then he strode back to the door. "Good night."

CHAPTER 18

The rain beat down on the car's roof with a steady, relentless rhythm. It was deafening, and a little scary, the way the raindrops hurtled themselves against the metal shell, like fists pounding to get in. This unsettling impression was made even more intense by the view from the fogged-over windows, which, in eerie contradistinction to the racket going on above, reduced the passing landscape to a somber reverie in gray, all sad and ghostly. With a little imagination, and Chaim had more than a little, a person might think that the car had entered a strange world of angry, shadowy spirits.

The truth was more mundane. Chaim was seated in the backseat of the Bonets' car, on his way to Girona, where he had an appointment to see his doctor. If the examination went well, the doctor would take off his cast, for the weeks had passed, and according to the calendar, if not the weather, spring had arrived.

In front of him sat Joseph Bonet, who was navigating the car through the torrential downpour. Vidal sat in the passenger seat beside his father. A heavy silence sat upon them all.

One could, if one wanted to fool oneself, blame the silence inside the car on the rain outside; the pounding on the roof did make conversation difficult. But Chaim knew the truth. After the incident with the Shabbos candles, his status had been elevated, not to one of happy kinship, but to the unenviable state of pariah-hood.

When he asked Joya Garcia what he had done wrong this time, she had solemnly informed him that a lit candle in a window was an invitation for a departed spirit to visit the home. He had lit two — two candles! — and didn't everyone know what had happened next on that fateful Friday night? Hadn't everyone heard, or at least heard about, those two — two! — spine-chilling, bloodcurdling, otherworldly howls?

Chaim had tried not to smile at this ridiculous explanation, with its implied suggestion that he had willfully conjured up a pair

169

of werewolves from the grave. He knew the real reason behind their fears, even if they didn't. During the days of the Inquisition, if a passerby had noticed lit candles in a window on a Friday night, it would have meant certain arrest for the unfortunate family.

He didn't say anything about this. The time wasn't yet right to do so. Instead, he mentioned that he thought — actually, he was sure, but he didn't want to contradict his benefactress outright — that he had heard four or five howls that night, and not just two. Joya Garcia refused to admit the existence of conflicting evidence, or that the village could possibly be mistaken in its interpretation of the events.

Since the court had already decided the facts of the case, the only thing he could do was try to lighten the sentence. His intentions had been pure, he explained. He had only wanted to set the candles in a safe place so that he wouldn't burn down the house. He had assumed, innocently, that no one — neither living nor dead — would see them other than himself.

This wasn't one hundred percent true. He had wanted the family to see the candles, but not for malicious reasons. He had hoped that the candles would start a conversation that would close the gap that existed between the sewing room and the rest of the house. Apparently, though, the opposite had happened. If Joya Garcia was correct, he had committed a transgression so severe that it ruled out any possibility of repentance or hope that he would be welcome in any other home after his ankle had healed.

Seeing how things stood with the living, Chaim devoted the next few weeks to studying his photographs of the village's cemetery. His camera bag had mysteriously appeared in the wardrobe one afternoon while he was sleeping and, to his relief, the photographs were still saved on his camera. As he had suspected, the information on the headstones was too sparse to construct any sort of family history for the village. But his work had not been entirely for naught. Although there weren't any obviously Jewish names on the headstones, the photographs strongly suggested that the people of Sant Joan Januz were descendents of *Anusim*.

He based his conclusions on the fact that a few dozen personal names appeared again and again as one generation gave way to another. Since these names were apparently Catalan names, and therefore unfamiliar to him, he had dared to ask for computer

170

privileges, despite his pariah status, so that he could research their historical origins.

His request was granted, although it was limited to the hours when Vidal wasn't home. Perhaps Joya Garcia wiped down the keyboard with alcohol after he was done to remove any pariah impurities he had left behind. He didn't know. But he found what he was looking for. The first names on the headstones were names that regularly appeared in historical records pertaining to medieval Catalonia's Jews.

The names Josep and Vidal were included on his list of names, and for a moment Chaim had an urge to break the silence in the car and say, "Guess what? You both have Jewish names. Wouldn't it be something if it turned out that we were related?"

He decided against it, though. If he was going to be thrown out of a speeding car, he wanted it to be done after his cast had been removed.

Before his trip, it had never occurred to Chaim that he might be disappointed by what he would find at the end of his journey. He had imagined that discovering long-lost relatives would be like completing the unfinished parts of a colorful tapestry or filling in the blanks of a haunting piece of music. Never did he imagine that he would find, instead, an impenetrable wall of silence, whose mute presence heralded a shifting, unclearly defined border between the lands of indifference and hostility.

But there they sat, silent as three stones, and so Chaim had plenty of time to think, time which he used to think about the names and about how even when the living have nothing to say to one another, the dead have plenty to say to everybody.

He removed his list from his pocket. The names, at least, "talked" to him. In fact, every time he studied his list, he uncovered more associations, and so he once again engaged the names in conversation.

Catalan Names with Biblical Equivalents:

Anna — Hannah, the Biblical woman associated with sincere prayer. The name means "gracious" or "merciful." Perhaps a reference to the prayers of the *Anusim* that G-d be merciful to them.

Aster — Esther, the heroine of the Purim holiday. After the destruction of the First Temple, she went into exile and married the

171

king of Persia and was instrumental in saving the Jewish people from a plot to annihilate them. Perhaps because she had to keep her Jewishness a secret from the king — the name Esther is similar to the Hebrew word that means "hidden" — she had a special meaning for the *Anusim*. In any event, Aster was always a very popular name.

Biel — Short for the archangel Gabriel. He's associated with strength of character and the ability to stand firm — important qualities during the years of the Inquisition.

Carme — Short for Carmel. A mountain in Israel associated with Elijah, the prophet who will herald the Final Redemption.

Joan — Masculine form of the name Yochanan. Perhaps a reference to Yochanan ben Zakkai of the Talmud, who kept alive Torah study and its observance after the Romans conquered Jerusalem and the majority of the Jews went into exile.

Joanna — Feminine form of the name Yochanan.

Josep — Joseph, son of the patriarch Jacob. Betrayed and imprisoned, he eventually became second-in-command to the King of Egypt. Like Esther, he concealed his identity (from his brothers).

Manel — Short for Immanuel, which means "G-d is with us." Probably refers to the hope that G-d is still with them, even though they were forcibly converted to Christianity.

Miquel — Catalan version of Michael. He is the archangel who is a powerful advocate for the Jewish people.

Zach — Short for the prophet Zachariah, which means "G-d has remembered." The prophet was author of the words "Return to the stronghold, you prisoners of hope; even today do I declare that I will pay you double." (Nona Anna mentions this quote in the diary. Perhaps the name expresses a hope that G-d will remember them — the Inquisition's "prisoners of hope" — and reward them for clinging to their Jewishness.)

Catalan Names That Embody Jewish Concepts:

Arnau — From the German name Arnold, which means "eagle power." It could refer to the hope that they will be taken out of Spain like the Jews were taken out of Egypt — "on eagle's wings."

Astruc — A Catalan word meaning "lucky." They would need *mazel*, good fortune, to stay out of the clutches of the Inquisition.

Beatriz — From the Latin, it means "voyager," as in through life. Perhaps it was a hope that the bearer of the name would "sail through life" without harm. Or it could suggest the transient nature of this world, as compared to the eternity of the World to Come.

Belshom — Perhaps means a "good name," as in the Hebrew name Shem Tov. If so, it could be a hope that a person with this name will have good fortune.

Blanca — Means "white." A symbol of purity, white is also sometimes associated with *chesed,* kindness. Perhaps it refers to the purity of their hearts and/or a desire to be a recipient of G-d's kindness.

Clara — A Catalan word meaning "clear" or "bright." It could be a reference to the kabbalistic work *Sefer HaBahir* (*The Book of the Brightness*). A fourteenth-century commentary on this book was called *Ohr HaGanuz* (*The Hidden Light*). (*Ganuz* — Januz. Is there a connection?)

Durant — A Catalan word meaning "enduring" or "steadfast." Like the name Gabriel, it probably refers to their clinging to Judaism.

Ferran — From the name Ferdinand, which means, in rough translation, "brave peace." This could refer to their need to remain brave until they found peace.

Joya — A name from medieval French that means "joy." Perhaps this has to do with the Jewish imperative to be happy no matter how bitter the situation might be.

Regina — Catalan for "queen." A popular name in the cemetery, probably because of its association with Queen Esther.

Pau — The Catalan word for "peace," an obvious desire.

Vidal — Catalan for "life." The Catalan equivalent of the Hebrew name Chaim. Vidal has been a popular name in Catalonia since the medieval period for Jews and non-Jews alike. The *Anusim* may have used it to refer to both life in this world and eternal life in the World to Come.

Catalan Names with No Known Jewish Connection:

Bernat — Bernard, from the French. It means "brave bear" or a "brave warrior."

173

Eduard — Edward, an Old English name popular throughout Europe that means a "blessed guard."

Luis — Louis, a French name derived from the German name Ludvig. It means "famous warrior."

Nuria — Name of a village on the Catalan side of the Pyrenees. Perhaps someone from the village originally came from there.

Perhaps it was because of the rain pounding on the roof like fists, or perhaps it was because of the fog that clung to his window like some forlorn phantom, but as Chaim continued to stare at the names he was suddenly back in the cemetery, standing among the headstones, which at first had seemed so blank and silent. Now the cemetery wasn't quiet at all. Each headstone was one word of a communal prayer, and together they were pleading, "*Have mercy, G-d. Stay with us. Grant us peace. Grant us life. Remember us. Redeem us. Carry us on eagle's wings to Your Holy Land. Pay us back with double portions of joy, Your prisoners of hope, for our clinging to You, in secret, while in our double exile, in exile from our land and from ourselves.*"

As these words echoed in his head, he wanted to cry, too. But he didn't. He remained silent, like a stone, as the car drove though the blinding, deafening rain. Yet he wondered, as he stared at the two figures sitting in front of him, if the moment would ever come when he would be able to say to them, "Hey, do you want to hear something amazing? We're all part of the same Jewish prayer."

While Chaim was deep in his thoughts, Vidal was thinking about the events of the past few weeks. Were someone to have asked him a month ago if he believed there was such a thing as bad luck, he would have laughed. Worrying about sweeping dirt in the wrong direction or candles burning in the window was his mother's department, not his. Yet even though Vidal still had trouble comprehending how two small candles could cause so much trouble, it was hard to ignore the fact that an ill wind had blown into the Bonet home during the American's first Friday night in Sant Joan Januz.

When the family was once again seated around the dining table, after the unsuccessful search for the source of the mysterious howling, his grandfather had treated them to yet another lecture about the harmful effects of strangers. No candle had burned in a window for centuries, they were informed. Yet what had happened just a few days after the stranger's arrival? The village's windows were "ablaze" with light!

Vidal was used to his grandfather's unapologetic preference for the grandiose when speaking in public. Yet he knew that this time his grandfather wasn't exaggerating. His grandfather really had seen danger in those two candles.

He, on the other hand, hadn't seen anything, except an unintentional breach of a quaintly archaic tradition. If he had reacted, it was to prevent others from being upset and not because he felt in any danger. He was sure that his was the rational reaction.

Yet the thought suddenly occurred to him that strict rationalism could sometimes be as blind as unfettered superstition. Folk medicine was a case in point. Although the brews conjured up by the medieval apothecary weren't as precise and effective as modern remedies, there was a kernel of truth in their work. The ancient herbalists were neither the simpletons nor the charlatans that modern science had once claimed them to be. So before he dismissed his grandfather's overblown reaction as being totally irrational, he wanted to know if there was actually something behind this fear of candles "blazing in the window." Was there a spark of truth hidden behind all the smoke?

As he looked at the three elderly faces seated around the table, Vidal was painfully aware that the time for asking a question like this was running out. And so even though he knew from hard-earned experience that the best thing to do, when his grandfather was in one of his sermonizing moods, was to eat his soup and keep quiet, he once again allowed a spirit of folly to lift him up and dump him in a place he didn't want to be: within the direct path of his grandfather's wrath. He innocently asked what harm had been done by the two flames, which were, after all, tiny and barely visible.

Perhaps it would have been wiser to leave out the bit about the flames being tiny and barely visible. Or perhaps it didn't matter, since any question was bound to be interpreted by his grandfather as a renewed call to battle. In any event, the counterattack to Vidal's insurgence was quick in coming.

175

But before the battle could really get going, it veered off into an unexpected direction. His father — who in the past had always remained serenely oblivious during family quarrels, due to his self-prophetic belief that they would eventually resolve themselves without his interference — interrupted Miquel in mid-sentence and demanded, "Answer him. What harm did the candles do?"

If Miquel was caught off guard by this rebellion from another quarter, he didn't show it. Instead he eyed Josep coolly and replied, "Do? I should think everyone in this room knows what lit candles in a window do."

"That's not an answer," Josep answered just as coolly.

"They bring bad luck," said Pau, irritably leaping into the fray. "That's what they do."

"Bad luck?" Josep raised an eyebrow. "My son is being attacked because of a superstition?"

Josep wasn't normally a stickler for clearly enunciating his words. But when he said the word *superstition*, he pronounced each syllable slowly and distinctly, the way people sometimes do when they're speaking to a foreigner and they want to make sure that they've been understood. When the final letter was reached, it continued to vibrate in the air, where it hung suspended, as it were, upon a very large question mark.

Miquel and Pau exchanged quick glances. Biel knew something was up, but a nod from Pau told him to keep quiet. Miquel looked over at Clara, who didn't meet his gaze.

Vidal, who had noticed the looks and nods, knew that the family was walking through a minefield, and he didn't want his mother to be the one who got hurt.

"Actually, Papa, I meant something a bit different. If you don't mind, I'll rephrase the question so it will be clearer."

Josep shrugged.

"I know that they're bad luck, according to our traditions," Vidal continued, emphasizing the word *traditions* in the hope that this word would pacify his grandfather without angering his father. "But do candles in the window attract a particular kind of bad luck? Is something specific going to happen now?"

He persisted because he really did want to know. This one question had brought to mind all the other questions that had come up in New York while he was working on his Peaceland proposal — questions about the village's customs and its history and, of course, its location. It had also opened a door in his mind to the memory of his roommate's reaction to his lack of knowledge.

"How can you know so little about your village's traditions?" Al had asked him.

Vidal hadn't known what to answer.

When he was young and he had a question, he would go to his Grandma Anna. For some reason, she was always the "address." She would sit him down at her kitchen table and place a plate of cookies before him. While he talked, she would smile at him, with a big smile, as though she was so proud of him for asking such good questions. And then she would say...

The truth was that he couldn't remember what she would say. All he could remember was her smile, and the cookies, and the feeling, while sitting in her kitchen, that their little world, with its traditions and customs, was a happy place that made perfect sense.

"But how can you not remember?" Al had persisted.

At times like these, when Vidal felt like he was a specimen being studied under Al's ironic microscope, he was sorry he had brought up the topic. The only reason he had shared information about the village's customs was because Al, as a Muslim, also observed customs that other people might think strange. That had created a bond between them early on.

But Al knew why he didn't eat pork. People could disagree with his reasoning, but he had a more-than-thousand-year-old tradition to back him up. The only justification Vidal could give for his dietary habits was that pork gave people a stomachache. Even Al had laughed when he heard that one.

It was too bad that he couldn't ask his Grandma Anna now, when he was older and would remember her answers to all his questions. But he had returned too late, and so now he was posing his question to the others — his grandfather and great-uncles. Surely one of them had to know. An entire family — an entire village — couldn't forget their history. Someone had to remember where their customs and traditions came from, and what they meant, and why their roots were in this particular place. Because if no one remembered, where were they? If bad luck really was going to come — if that forgotten spark still had a glimmer of truth in it — what could they do except close the curtains and wait?

Clara, meanwhile, was stealthily glancing from her father to Vidal. She assumed they were waiting for her to say something.

177

She silently repeated Vidal's question a few times, concentrating on it as though it was a question on a test for which she had insufficiently prepared: *Do candles in the window attract a particular kind of bad luck?*

She knew that hidden high up in the chimney was a ceramic container, and inside this container was a flame. This flame, doubly hidden from strangers' eyes, didn't attract bad things. It brought good things into the home: the qualities of patience and kindness and hope. Her mother had explained this to her when she was a little girl.

Her mother surely also had explained what happened when the light wasn't hidden. Because Vidal was right. It couldn't cause just a general kind of bad luck. A general kind of bad luck was everywhere in their little world. But a candle in the window was special. It brought its own special kind of bad luck into the home. But what kind?

Clara suddenly had the feeling that her mother was in the room and that she was looking at Clara. Or, rather, that she was looking past Clara and at the chair with the wildflowers.

"I'm only asking," Vidal added, still speaking quietly, "because if we know what the bad luck is, perhaps we can do something to prevent it from happening."

"Really, Clara, I don't know where your children get such crazy ideas," she could hear her mother saying to her. "Certainly not from your great-uncle and me."

Clara suddenly remembered. It wasn't her mother who told her. Her mother never told her the reason for a "never." It was her great-uncle Manel who had whispered the secret in her ear.

"Candles attract ghosts," she blurted out. And then she burst into tears and fled from the room.

Vidal looked over at his father. Josep had already stood up and begun to clear the table, having once again retreated into his serenely oblivious mode.

"I think I'll get some fresh air," Miquel said to no one in particular.

"Where's everyone going?" Biel asked Pau. "Isn't it time to play cards?"

They didn't play cards that night and Vidal didn't ask again about the candles. Even without his questions, though, similar scenes were repeated with unnerving frequency during the next

178

few weeks. One minute the family was gathered around the dining table talking calmly. Then, out of the blue, an innocent remark was misconstrued, and a new skirmish began. Sometimes his grandfather was the instigator. Sometimes, surprisingly, it was his father who flared up first. They had become almost used to seeing his mother flee from the kitchen in tears.

Who could they blame for this ill wind of discord? Because they were all, at least on the surface, rational people, ghosts weren't an option. And yet — and perhaps it didn't make sense, according to the rules of logic — after the storm calmed down, somehow the trail of incriminating evidence always led back to the sewing room, the American, and those two candles.

Vidal did suggest, once, that since their guest was already much better, they could send him back to the United States. His mother, horrified, refused to even consider turning out their guest until his ankle was completely healed. Vidal supposed her obstinacy was due to some sort of international code of honor for mothers that she was afraid to transgress, and so he added their guest's early departure to his growing list of topics to avoid. The result, though, was that the fights and tears continued, and the American continued to be blamed for them. Even the blame for the unsettling, howling winds and the unseasonably heavy rains that had taken up residence in the village was placed at his doorstep.

The strange weather not only rattled everyone's nerves, it also delayed the groundbreaking ceremony for Vidal's resort. Al wasn't happy to hear this news. He informed Vidal that postponements, which were in their very essence the antithesis of "sappy and snappy," were never a welcome guest in his father's organization. Fortunately, the main office gave Vidal a new start date. Peaceland, it seemed, had been only slightly battered by the destructive forces created by the American's presence in the village.

"Where do you want to be dropped off?"

Vidal had been so wrapped up in his thoughts that he hadn't noticed they had already reached Girona, or that the rain had tapered off.

"Anywhere near Independence Square is fine," he said to his father.

Vidal rolled down his window and took in the sights and sounds of the city waking up to another morning. Girona was tiny, as cities went, but it was alive. The sheer energy of it, so welcomingly different from the lethargic yawn that greeted him every morning in Sant Joan Januz, made him smile.

"Be optimistic," the city seemed to be telling him as a gust of air blew into the car, fresh and clean, after the rain. "Delays aren't necessarily a bad thing. If the American is a lightning rod for bad luck, it's actually a good thing that the groundbreaking ceremony will take place after he's gone."

His father pulled the car over to the side of the road. Vidal, filled with a new spirit of magnanimity, which extended even as far as the backseat of the car, cheerfully called out to their passenger, "Good luck at the doctor's office."

"Thanks..." Chaim started to say.

But before Chaim could finish the word, the car door had already slammed shut.

PART III: THE ART OF "IT"

CHAPTER 19

J osep hadn't come to Girona with a specific agenda other than to play chauffeur for his son and their guest. When he learned that the American's doctor had been delayed, though, Josep decided to use the opportunity to drive to a residential area of the city, where a nursing home was located. Again, he didn't have an agenda, he assured himself. He was going there only because he was in the area and he had some extra time on his hands. And it wouldn't hurt to see the place, which was considered to be one of the best in the area. For informational purposes.

It wasn't hard to find the nursing home. It was located on a major thoroughfare, which meant cars, concrete, and geraniums in window boxes to remind a person how far they were from authentic country life. The building, built in the functional style, had all the charm of a cardboard box. It lacked even the geraniums. But since he was there and he had the time, etcetera, it would be foolish not to take a quick look inside. For informational purposes.

A guide was summoned to show him around. Their first stop was a sparkling clean public room used for social gatherings. The concrete walls were painted a bright yellow. The polyester mats on the floor were dyed a bright red. The chairs were upholstered with a fake leather fabric that was a bright blue. The relentlessly childish cheeriness of it all gave Josep the feeling that he had stumbled into an oversized box of crayons.

"Each of our residents receives personalized attention," his guide assured him as they walked to the next room. "A whole team of doctors, nurses, therapists... And here's the dining room."

Josep looked around the room, which was filled with tables already set for lunch. He had forgotten about this part. Residents would have to eat their meals with strangers. They would have to

181

use the nursing home's dishes. They would have to eat the food prepared by the nursing home's kitchen.

"I assume you serve meat here," he said.

"Oh yes. Our residents enjoy well-balanced meals that are prepared by a team of nutritionists and..."

"Thank you," said Josep. He left the dining room and walked quickly toward the main door.

"But, sir, you haven't seen the gym..."

"It's going to be a showcase for the entire region."

Vidal smiled. Jordi Martinez was not only a high-ranking official at the Girona Regional Council, but he was also a rising star on the Catalan political landscape. To have his support was essential. To have his enthusiastic support was exhilarating. But to have him call your project a "showcase for the entire region" was practically a surefire guarantee of phenomenal success.

Martinez had liked the idea of the Peaceland resort from the moment the proposal had landed on his desk, which was why the resort had gotten building approval so quickly. And despite his busy schedule, he had taken a hands-on interest in the development of the *La Convivencia* sound-and-light show. At his request, three of the top creative agencies in Catalonia were invited to develop a concept for it. The results of their creative efforts were going to be presented to Martinez and Vidal that morning.

"Of course, it's going to be much more than a rural resort for socially minded tourists," Martinez added as he escorted Vidal to the conference room.

Vidal nodded his head in agreement. He assumed this was all that was expected of him while they walked down the hallway.

"I see it becoming another Davos," Martinez continued, growing expansive.

Vidal, taking a cue from Martinez, nodded his head more expansively. Davos was huge, at least in comparison to Sant Joan Januz. The Swiss town was host to international conferences and seminars, including the annual meeting of the World Economic Forum. It also had a full range of winter sports, spas, cultural festivals, and shopping venues. In other words, it was the real thing.

"I see it..." and here Martinez stopped in the middle of the hallway and focused his gaze on a large abstract painting that was

When he noticed that this time Martinez was waiting for a reply, [Vi]dal steadied his reeling thoughts enough to say, "We're [b]rothers."

"Interesting," said Martinez, who was already ushering Vidal [ou]t of the conference room. "I assume you'll be coming to the [co]nference tomorrow on 'Creating New Models for Individual and [Cu]ltural Identity in Multinational Catalonia.' "

"Yes, I'm looking forward to it."

"Good. The title is a mouthful, but I understand that some of [the] presenters have some original things to say."

They were once again standing in front of the abstract [pa]inting hanging in the hallway. Vidal now realized, from the [pa]inting's style, that it had been done by Arnau. He also noticed [tha]t Martinez was giving him another quizzical look.

"Al did tell you, didn't he, about the new plans for your [res]ort?"

"No, he didn't," replied Vidal. "It must have slipped his mind. [He']s a very busy guy."

"Well, then, that explains it."

hanging on the wall, as though he was seeing "it" within the painting. Vidal also stopped and looked at the painting, as though he was seeing "it," too.

Martinez, who was about fifteen years older than Vidal, returned his gaze to his younger colleague and gave Vidal one of his famous smiles. "But I don't have to explain it to you."

The first presentation was so disappointing that there was little for Martinez and Vidal to discuss. After a short break, the second company appeared. When their presentation had also come to an end, Jordi Martinez turned to Vidal and remarked, "It lacked something, didn't it?"

"Yes, I thought so, too," Vidal replied truthfully.

There wasn't time to say more. Martinez had to return to his office to take an important phone call. Then the third company arrived. They set up their equipment, Martinez returned to the conference, and the presentation began.

Their concept was daring, warned the final presenter, as the opening image of the company's PowerPoint presentation appeared on the screen. It was abstract as the open seas, evocative as the starry skies.

Vidal glanced over at Martinez. He saw that the rising star of the political scene was intently gazing at the abstract, evocative painting — perhaps it was of the heavens or perhaps it was of the seas — and smiling.

"After all," the presenter continued, "isn't this the essence of what *La Convivencia* was all about? What was it, if not a celebration of the triumph of the human spirit? A time when everything was possible; a time when science flourished and poetry soared; a time when the seas were tamed, and the imagination was set free. A time of peace! Coexistence! Brotherhood!"

The presentation continued. More abstract, evocative paintings appeared on the screen. There was music as well. It was inspiring, energizing, and Vidal could visualize the masses marching out of the hall and heading straight for the gift shop, where the *La Convivencia* T-shirts and tote bags were on display. And he was surprised at himself for feeling so cynical. After all, didn't he want his resort to inspire people to aspire for peace? And buy the T-shirt?

"What did you think?" whispered Martinez as the final notes of the music faded away.

"I thought it lacked something," Vidal replied.

Martinez gave him a quizzical look. "Did it? I didn't notice."

"It didn't say anything about the *dhimmis* — the second-class citizens."

"You thought it lacked that, did you?"

"Christians were second-class citizens when the Muslims ruled over Spain. So were the Jews. Both groups were considered to be *dhimmis* under Muslim law."

"Every society has its second-class citizens," said Martinez, eyeing Vidal with the same quizzical expression.

"But discrimination isn't written into law, at least not in modern Western countries. Don't we have an obligation to say something about that? All three presentations completely ignored it. In fact, they entirely ignored the religious beliefs of the people. How can you talk about coexistence between Muslims, Christians, and Jews without mentioning anything about what it means to be a Muslim or a Christian or a Jew?"

Instead of replying to Vidal's question, Martinez asked, "Was there anything else you felt was lacking?"

"There was that big massacre of the Jews in Granada in 1066. And the deportation of the Christians to Morocco in 1126."

"You think we should mention that as well?"

"Massacres and expulsions were part of the narrative."

"What narrative?"

"The historical narrative."

"Vidal," and here Martinez smiled, like a parent smiles at a beloved but not terribly bright child, "who cares about the historical narrative?"

It was Vidal's turn to assume a quizzical expression.

"Every epoch has its good and unpleasant sides," Martinez continued. "Violence is a part of life. I think people are smart enough to figure that out."

"Without us saying anything?"

"What would it add to the narrative? Our narrative."

"Which is?"

"You of all people should know that."

The people who had made the presentation [packing up their equipment and were waiting to say Martinez.

"Thank you, gentlemen," he said warmly, s hands. "We'll be in touch."

After the others left, Martinez returned his gaze wasn't so good for the Jews and the Muslims after took control of Spain."

"No one ever claimed that the Inquisition wa peaceful coexistence."

"I don't understand you, Vidal. This project v What's the problem?"

"I don't believe in rewriting history."

"Neither do I. But we're not going to rewrite going to write the future. By the year 2050, Europe twenty percent Muslim. We're all going to have to l along. We're going to need a vision for how to d class citizens and massacres are not part of that v together to create a new sociocultural dynamic f Europe is, and the Peaceland International Center going to play a starring role in making this new d By the way, what did you think of the artw presentation?"

Vidal stared at Martinez's smiling, sphinx-li to read in it when and how his Peaceland resort ha international center for EuroIslam. His dumbstru seem to concern Martinez, who apparently was u his own questions.

"I thought the artist did a very good job concept," Martinez continued. "Not everyone is art, and I can see why the average person wants a boat and the sea to look like the sea. But what Bonet's work is that it's totally ambiguous. A pe it whatever he likes. Is he a relative of yours? I'v ask."

The mention of his brother, whom Vidal since Arnau moved to Girona, caught Vidal c time. Although he couldn't explain why, he feeling that he was on board one of Martinez' where he was being tossed about by a mob of

CHAPTER 20

After leaving Martinez's office, Vidal quickly headed north, toward the gardens located near the city's Archeological Museum. The gardens, like most of Girona's small historic center, were pretty without being self-consciously showy. Groves of tall majestic cypress trees modestly invited the visitor to look past them and instead enjoy rooftop views of the jewel-like medieval city. Further on, the ruins of the Gironella Tower, which had once been a fearsome, heavily armed fortress, returned the compliment by docilely playing the role of silent backdrop to an evergreen parade of trees, shrubs, and exotic plants. In short, the gardens were the sort of place that invited respectful, even reverential recreation. Chattering was best left to the birds.

But Vidal wasn't interested in silently communing with nature as he dashed up the steps that led to what had once been a lookout point on top of the tower's outer wall. Nor did he notice the commanding vista of distant, tree-capped hills spreading beneath his feet as he punched a long string of numbers into his cell phone. As for the chattering birds, they only provided a counterpoint harmony for the staticky noise hissing loudly on the line when Al, who was somewhere in the Ecuador Cloud Forest scouting out locations for a new resort, finally answered the phone. And so in this place that was all peace, Vidal found himself striking the lone discordant note as he shouted into the phone, "*American* tourists! *That's* my target market!"

"Take it easy," Al replied reassuringly from somewhere beyond the clouds. "You have to be nice to the local politicians. If Jordi Martinez wants to talk like a Euro big shot, I let him talk."

"But he's talking about turning Sant Joan Januz into another Davos."

"What's wrong with that?"

"The place will be swarming with..."

"Arabs?" Al said with a laugh. "Don't tell me that the executive director of the Peaceland resort is a bigot."

"I'm not a bigot. But this resort is supposed to be for tourists."

"You mean nice people who will quietly take the tour, buy a few souvenirs, and go home?"

"Yes!"

"As opposed to those pesky Arabs who'll riot and tear down the place if they don't like what you serve them for breakfast?"

"You know what I'm talking about."

"Unfortunately, as an Arab and a Muslim, I know all about the intolerance you're talking about. I just didn't expect it from you."

"I'm not intolerant!"

"Then what do you have against creating a pleasant space where like-minded Muslims and Christians can come together to discuss ways for their two peoples to live together in peace and harmony?"

"I don't have anything against it. But it's...it's not what I envisioned."

"What didn't you envision? The pleasant space? Or Muslims and Christians living in harmony?"

"I thought we had a plan."

"We did."

"So why did you make a separate deal with Martinez?"

"I don't know what you're talking about. You're both in Catalonia. How was I supposed to know that Martinez wasn't keeping you informed?"

When Vidal didn't answer, Al asked, "Vidal? Are you still there?"

"Yes," Vidal replied after a short silence.

"Vidal, this is what happens in the real world. You start with Plan A and end up with Plan G. And since there's no guarantee that Martinez is going to get the okay from Barcelona, we might be back to Plan A tomorrow. But honestly, I don't understand what's bothering you. It would be one thing if Martinez wanted to scale back the project. But he's talking about developing the entire area around Sant Joan Januz. There's no downside in this for you. In fact, if you play your cards right, you're going to be the tourism king of Catalonia."

188

Vidal wanted to be reassured by Al's words, which continued to flow as soothingly as a gurgling stream in a shady glen. There had been an unintentional breakdown in communication. Government officials and academics, including Arab officials and academics, spend money — good money! — at international conferences. There was no rational reason for objecting to the expansion of the resort's original concept. In fact, the concept's transformation from being generally about peace in the Middle East to being specifically about EuroIslam was actually a stroke of marketing genius on Martinez's part. Sant Joan Januz would become in actuality, and not just in peace tourism babble-speak, a modern-day Cordoba — that fabled center of *La Convivencia* that had been renowned throughout medieval Europe for its academic, scientific, and artistic achievements. But while Cordoba's influence was felt only in Spain, Sant Joan Januz would spread its light over all of Europe, and from there to the rest of the world.

By the time Vidal hung up the phone, he was convinced that the new concept really wasn't all that different from the vision he had presented to the villagers several months earlier. The target market had shifted a bit. The scope had grown larger. But in its essence the idea was still the same: Peace and Profits.

A small part of him, though, must have stubbornly held onto its doubts, because that night Vidal wandered restlessly from one disturbing dream to another.

First he was walking through a large, multistoried department store. A policeman suddenly blocked his path and accused him of stealing something. Vidal saw someone run to the emergency exit.

"There's the thief!" he called out. "Catch him!"

The policeman ran after the man, and Vidal ran after the policeman. When they all reached the street, they discovered that the man was actually a woman. The policeman searched through her shopping bags, Since he didn't find anything unusual, he let her walk away, free.

"How dare you place the blame on an innocent person!" the policeman shouted.

"She's lying!" Vidal yelled back. "It's a disguise. Or she's a decoy for the real thief, who's still hiding in the building."

They were still arguing when the scene suddenly shifted, and Vidal found himself in a small and empty room with a real estate agent, who was persuading him to rent the space. When Vidal

189

expressed his reluctance, the agent led him into a larger room, which was elegantly furnished with antique pieces of furniture. This was more to Vidal's liking. Vidal then noticed two closed doors.

"Are those the bedrooms?" he asked.

"One door goes to your room," the agent replied. "The second door is for the other family."

"What other family?"

"The other family that lives here. You won't mind sharing the apartment with them," the agent assured him.

They went into the kitchen, which was very large. Vidal saw that he would have his own sinks and cabinets. "You'll have to share the oven," the agent told him as he led Vidal to the room where the oven was located. "But you won't mind."

The old-fashioned, wood-burning oven was built out of bricks. It was large enough for several families, or even an entire community. A loaf of bread was baking in the oven. The agent took it out and cut off a slice, which he handed to Vidal.

"Take it," said the agent.

The bread looked delicious, and Vidal was tempted to take it. But just as he was about to tell the agent that he wanted to rent the apartment, a voice inside him warned, "Don't be fooled. Who needs such a large oven to bake one loaf of bread?"

Vidal returned to the other room, but the antique furniture had disappeared. The real estate agent had disappeared as well. A group of people were sitting around a nondescript table, playing cards. One of the men looked over at the doorway, where Vidal was standing.

"What are you doing here?" asked the man.

"I'm here to play cards."

"To know when to pass is to know how to play," said the man, quoting an old Spanish proverb.

Then it was morning and Vidal was back in Girona, where the conference on "Creating New Models for Individual and Cultural Identity in Multinational Catalonia" was going to take place. The lobby of the conference hall was already crammed full of people by the time he arrived. As he looked over the crowd to see if he knew anyone, Vidal heard a familiar voice say quietly, "I hear you spoke to Al."

Vidal turned. Martinez was standing next to him, smiling. "Everything all right now?"

"Yes," said Vidal. Martinez gave him another smile and disappeared into the crowd.

Vidal went to sign in at the hospitality desk, and the clerk handed him his name tag. He saw that he had, indeed, become the executive director of the Peaceland International Center for EuroIslam. As he read the words, a vague memory of his dream floated past his eyes, bringing with it a feeling of uneasiness. Before he could give the matter further thought, a bell announced that the conference was about to begin. Vidal hastily put on his name tag and followed the crowd into the hall.

After he found a seat, he still had a few minutes to study the people in the room. If he had hoped to see Arnau there, and he wasn't entirely sure that he did, those hopes were dashed. He thought he recognized a few people from his student days at the University of Girona, for the conference had attracted a motley group of academics, cultural types, local politicians, and people like Vidal, who were there mainly to curry favor with

Martinez, whose office had organized the event.

The conference was supposed to create "beacons of light in an increasingly dark and anxious world," but someone apparently forgot to convey that message to the first speaker. His talk on identity was so filled with opaque, technical jargon that it promptly put most of the audience to sleep.

"The next speaker will wake everyone up," the man sitting next to Vidal said with a grin. "He's quite the new sensation on the academic scene."

Vidal glanced at his neighbor, whose gray hairs suggested that a long time had passed since anyone had referred to him as a "new sensation."

His eyes moved down to the man's name tag, which said: Tomas Domenech, District Supervisor, Department of Antiquities, Catalonia. It was impossible not to note the contrast between the elderly man from the Department of Antiquities and the next speaker, a young professor from a well-known university in Barcelona, who had already taken his position on the stage.

The professor dove straight into his topic, which was "Halloween: A Universalistic Holiday for a Multinational Era." He made his first splash when he reminded the audience that this

191

holiday, which had only recently been imported from the United States, had been embraced by Catalans with — pardon the pun — frightening speed. The crowd laughed appreciatively, but the professor cut them off with a gesture that suggested that there was more fun to come. And so the audience waited expectantly as the professor developed his theme, which was that Halloween should be the prototype for creating a new calendar of universalistic holidays suited to the new cultural identity needed for a new multinational Europe. The professor went on to inform the crowd that, unlike some timid souls, he wasn't afraid to spell out what this brave new holiday would look like.

"One, the holiday's roots must come from a universally accepted, culturally neutral space, such as the Hollywood film studio or the greeting card factory. Two, its primary activities will involve a high level of community-building consumerism that everyone can engage in, such as gift-giving, eating, and the like. And three, its sole purpose will be to have fun; the holiday will be totally devoid of any meaning so as not to offend anyone."

It's a joke, Vidal assured himself, as he glanced over at his neighbor, who was still grinning. But a quick look at Jordi Martinez, whose eyes were closed in deep concentration and whose lips had assumed a position of what could only be described as beatific bliss, made him realize that in some quarters the talk was being received with a seriousness that was, in a word, scary.

The crowd was still enthusiastically discussing the professor's talk on Halloween as they filed into the dining hall, where lunch was served. Vidal's new acquaintance found them two empty seats at a table that was already occupied by the young director of an important museum in Girona and a few other people whose ties to the event were as nebulous as Vidal's. Domenech seemed to know the museum director well, since they were soon engaged in a heated discussion about the lecture.

"He took an extreme position to make a point," said the museum director. "There's not a single country in the European Union that has a homogenous society. The old calendar — the one that was dominated by the religious cycle — has to be replaced by one that's culturally neutral so that all of Europe's citizens can participate and celebrate."

"But celebrate what?" asked Domenech.

"Life."

"A life devoid of meaning is something to celebrate?"

"People today aren't interested in meaning." The museum director glanced over at Vidal, as if to say, *We young people know what's what, even if this old man doesn't.* "At my museum we ignore the meaning aspect entirely. Our cultural activities revolve around food or music, and the events are packed. No one seems to mind that all we've offered is a good time."

"It sounds a bit empty."

"Perhaps to you, but today's generation no longer has a need, or even an ability, to find meaning in an artificially imposed shared past, or in the holidays and rituals that came along with it. Instead the individual is in control. The person chooses which holidays or life cycle events to celebrate, how to do it, and what sort of meaning to attach to the experience, if any."

"So one can still find meaning in life? That's a relief. I'd hate to think that everyone has to waste their brief time on this earth on trivialities."

And here it was Domenech's turn to give Vidal a knowing glance.

"But there's no obligation," the museum director insisted.

"I understand. And if you'll pass me some of those culturally neutral potatoes, I'll try not to find any meaning in life for the next fifteen minutes."

Despite Domenech's halfhearted promise, just a few minutes later he and the museum director were once again wrangling over weighty topics. Vidal, who felt a bit depressed by all the talk, was glad when the meal came to an end. He decided to skip the afternoon sessions. He slipped out the door and quickly walked down the street, hoping that no one would notice. But the sound of fast-approaching footsteps told him that his mutiny had been observed.

"I see you've had enough," said Domenech.

"Some of the lectures aren't relevant to my business."

"Yes, I noticed from your name tag that you're Martinez's EuroIslam man. What got you interested in the topic, if you don't mind my asking?"

"Building a resort is my interest."

"I see. You're building the empty vessel, which others will fill."

"It was nice to meet you," Vidal said curtly, and then he started to walk away.

"Sorry if I've offended you," said Domenech, following after him. "I'm not a big admirer of Martinez and his crowd, as you might have noticed. In my opinion, the old religion, for all its faults, made the world a more civilized place. And even if secular humanism does manage to stave off the Islamic threat here in Europe, what kind of life will it be without any grand idea to inspire it? Mind you, I'm not just talking about the degradation of Western culture. It's modern society's contempt for values that were once... But I see you're impatient to be rid of me, and so I'll come to the point. I've received an e-mail from an American by the name of Chaim Green. Do you know him, by any chance?"

Vidal stopped and turned to face Domenech. "Yes, I know him. Why did he contact you?"

"He seems to think that his ancestors lived in your village for a short time, during the early days of the Inquisition, and left behind a synagogue and a Torah scroll. I tried doing some research on the history of Sant Joan Januz, but there's absolutely nothing about it anywhere."

"It's a small village."

"That's why I was curious to hear what you think about all this. I ask because I need to decide if my office should help Mr. Green with his search. There's an interest, you know, in these old synagogues. And it would be quite a feather in my department's cap if we found an old Torah scroll. But I can't waste money on a wild goose chase."

"I've never heard anything about it."

"I thought as much. Ever since this craze for rediscovering Catalonia's Jewish past started, my office has been inundated with claims about 'lost' Jewish Quarters that have just been found. Needless to say, the vast majority of these claims are based more on wishful thinking and greed than on anything even remotely resembling a true archeological find. The people just want their town to be the next Girona and rake in the Jewish tourism dollars. That's why I find your village so remarkable. I looked through all the files and didn't find a single inquiry from Sant Joan Januz. Either the people in your village are scrupulously honest or you've all been fast asleep."

194

"From what I understand, the Jews usually lived in cities and towns. Since Sant Joan Januz is a farming village, there's no reason to believe that Jews ever lived there."

"You raise a valid point, but history isn't always so neat. And so before I close Mr. Green's file, I would like to ask one more question. Are there any people in your village who have customs that could be considered unusual? Or have you ever heard your relatives − perhaps your older relatives − talk about such people?"

"Country people have a whole slew of customs and superstitions that city dwellers might find amusing."

"It wasn't my intention to offend you, although I see I've done it again. But I was actually referring to the customs of a specific people: the *Anusim*. That's the Hebrew term for the Jews who were forcibly converted to Christianity during the Middle Ages. You've heard of them, of course?"

"I've heard of the New Christians. But I thought they assimilated into the mainstream culture a long time ago, like the Cathars."

"Many of the New Christians did. But the *Anusim* didn't. They've retained some of their Jewish customs, and they still consider themselves to be connected to the Jewish people."

"And Mr. Green told you that there are *Anusim* living in Sant Joan Januz?"

"No, he didn't say that."

"So where did this crazy idea came from?"

"I thought of it myself. When I receive an inquiry, I do feel it's my duty to consider it from all the angles, which in this case includes the *Anusim*. I didn't mean to suggest that you might be one of them. But if the thought gives you offense, I won't apologize this time. Surely in today's multinational Catalonia there's no need to be embarrassed about being descended from Jews."

"There are no *Anusim* in Sant Joan Januz. Good afternoon."

Vidal walked away. But before he had gotten far, Domenech called out, "Mr. Bonet!"

Vidal stopped and turned, although just halfway.

"At the risk of offending you one last time, might I offer you a word of advice? I imagine it must be quite exciting to travel in the same circle as a person like Jordi Martinez. But there's an old Spanish proverb that's useful to keep in mind, whether you find yourself traveling in the company of card players or politicians: 'To know when to pass is to know how to play.' Good day."

Domenech walked briskly toward the direction of the conference hall. Vidal watched him disappear down the narrow street, and snatches of his dream floated past his eyes for a second time. He recalled that one of the men in the dream had quoted the same proverb, and the feeling of uneasiness returned.

He didn't want to feel uneasy. He wanted to feel good about himself and Martinez and Al and EuroIslam and everything else that had to do with his Peaceland resort, and he resented Domenech's interfering with his attainment of those feelings. He continued to walk, hoping that his troublesome thoughts would be chased away by the exercise.

Apparently, though, it was his thoughts that were leading him, because without his being aware of it, his path led him to the entrance to Sant Llorenc Street. The covered passageway, with its stone steps that disappeared into the darkness, looked gloomy even in midday. Yet he knew that the steps led to Arnau's front door, and he decided that a visit with his brother might be just what he needed. After all, despite their differences, he and Arnau were family. And if Martinez was Arnau's patron, then his brother surely would have some unique insights into the politician.

It was odd that Arnau had kept his work on the sound-and-light show a secret, and Vidal did wonder about that as he stepped into the shadowy passageway, which seemed to hide more than it revealed. On the other hand, Arnau must have known that he would find out about it at some point. It was possible that Arnau was actually hoping that Vidal would turn up at his door.

CHAPTER 21

V idal knocked loudly on the heavy wood door. When no one answered, he knocked again. A man passing by stopped and looked him up and down.

"What do you want?" asked the man.

"My brother," said Vidal. "Do you know where he is?"

The man silently motioned for Vidal to follow him. When they arrived at a small building, which Vidal assumed was Arnau's studio, the man shouted, "Bonet! A man here says he's your brother."

The door opened slightly. Arnau stood in the doorway, neither opening the door wider nor slamming it shut.

"Can I come in?" Vidal asked.

Arnau didn't answer at once. While Vidal waited for what seemed to be a very long time, and all the while very conscious of the stranger who was watching them with undisguised curiosity, he wondered if he hadn't made a mistake in thinking that he and his brother would ever be able to have something resembling a normal conversation. After all, his first question had been a simple one. Either Arnau didn't mind being disturbed at that moment or he did. Yet instead of responding to the question in a simple manner, Vidal had the feeling that Arnau was turning over every detail of their shared past history, every resentment and misunderstanding, before making a decision. That wasn't a promising beginning to what he had hoped, however briefly, would be a new stage in their relationship. But because he did want to talk to Arnau, Vidal decided not to become irritated, as he usually did, by his brother's ponderous ways. He forced himself to silently count backward from ten to one while he waited for the verdict to be pronounced.

The silence was broken not by a word, but by a creak as Arnau opened the door wide enough for a person to slip through it. Vidal accepted the unspoken invitation and stepped inside.

The air inside the studio was heavy with the smell of paint. The fumes made Vidal feel a bit sick, and so he tried to focus his attention on the paintings leaning against the walls. Unlike Martinez, who seemed to know something about these things, Vidal had no illusions about being a connoisseur of modern art. An abstract painting made him feel like a man lost in the wilderness without a compass. Perhaps the art was leading somewhere, but he didn't know if it was anywhere that he wanted to go.

The silence was becoming noticeable, and Vidal knew that Arnau was waiting for him to start the conversation. Saying something like, "That's a nice shade of blue," or an equally inane comment would end the discussion before it began. His eyes therefore bounced from one canvas to another, searching for something to latch on to. But wherever he looked, he saw only gaping holes throbbing with color — deep red wounds, puddles of blue, eerie patches of silvery white light, and, in many of the paintings, small black rectangles that seemed to be frozen in an eternal "Oh!" The strange energy of it all, combined with the heady smell of the fumes, made his heart race.

Finally, Vidal spotted a canvas propped up against an easel that seemed more welcoming than the others. He walked over to the painting and studied it, as if he understood what he was looking at. What he could see was that the painting was divided into three sections. So far, so good.

The right side, he noted, was a kind of abstract landscape painted in shades of gray. Perhaps it depicted a dark castle sitting on a hill. Or maybe the castle was a cat sitting in a crouched position, ready to pounce. Whatever it was, the middle section was obviously some sort of lunar landscape. The gaping holes — craters, he supposed — couldn't be anything else. Unless, as Vidal looked more closely, it was meant to represent a face carved out of wood, like in an ancient totem pole.

Well, whatever the rest of the canvas was about, it was the left side that had attracted his eye in the first place. A cascade of white streaked with ribbons of honey-yellow tumbled down the canvas like a waterfall tumbling down onto the rocks below. In the center of the waterfall was a swirling bouquet of reds and pinks and greens, although what a bouquet of flowers was doing in the middle of a waterfall he didn't know. And when he looked more closely, he saw that the bouquet wasn't composed of flowers, but

198

stars — quickly drawn stars that seemed to have been caught at the moment when they were bursting onto the scene, like the lights in a fireworks display that cover, for a moment, the night sky with an explosive shower of color and light.

Yes, that was it, Vidal decided. The painting meant to show some sort of contrast, or even a conflict — yes, a conflict — between the heavy mute figure on the dark hill and the whirling swirl of light dancing in the water.

"That one interests you, does it?" Arnau had come up behind Vidal.

"Yes. What's it called?"

"Brothers."

Vidal continued to stare at the canvas, hesitating to speak or to move. Whether it was because of the fumes, or the colors, or the feeling that he was trapped between the easel standing before him and his brother standing behind him, the picture seemed to take on an ominous tone. The heavy brooding figure on the gray hill was definitely a cat, he decided — a cat that was waiting for the right moment to pounce on the bouquet of starry flowers and rip it to pieces.

"I see," he said finally, not knowing what else to say.

"That's all an artist asks," Arnau replied noncommittally, as he returned to the canvas he was working on.

Vidal wasn't sure if he had just been dismissed from the studio, or if Arnau's retreat was simply his way of protecting himself from what was an uncomfortable intrusion into his private world. He chose the latter interpretation. He also decided to dismiss from his mind his perhaps too hasty interpretation of what was, after all, an abstract work of art. Contrasts didn't always have to mean conflict, he convinced himself. Just as there was a time and a place for quick bursts of insight and dazzling displays of creativity, there was a time and place for quiet contemplation and slow, careful analysis. That was the trick, really, to be able to respect the other, one's opposite — as opposed to being contemptuous or afraid or envious — and recognize the world's need for a wide variety of qualities and ideas and talents.

Looking at the painting with fresh eyes, Vidal saw that Arnau had achieved a remarkable balance between the opposing forces of darkness and light, movement and rest. A further flash of insight told him that Martinez had been right: in this work, which was so aptly named "Brothers," Arnau had captured on canvas the animating spirit of peaceful coexistence that was behind *La Convivencia*.

It was easier to think these thoughts in the abstract than express them to his brother, especially when Arnau was keeping himself very busy behind his easel. And so Vidal said, in what he hoped wouldn't be a too obvious attempt at flattery, "Jordi Martinez is a very big admirer of your work. I'm starting to see why."

Arnau shrugged.

"He was very impressed with the presentation," Vidal continued. "We saw it yesterday. Your group will probably get the job, and I'd be very happy if we were to work together on this project. That was always my hope, that the resort would provide both of us with a good livelihood."

"I have no intention of working with you or for you," Arnau replied without raising his eyes from the canvas. "If I accept the commission, it will be because of Martinez."

Vidal once again counted slowly from ten to one. Yes, it was definitely easier to express a concept like coexistence in art or a PowerPoint presentation than to put it into practice. Yet if he couldn't coexist with his own brother, what could he hope to achieve with Peaceland? He ignored the reference to himself and said, "I assume Martinez is a good person to know, in terms of helping one's career."

"Why are you here, Vidal?"

Vidal decided to lay his cards on the table, since it was obvious that a roundabout course was leading him nowhere. "I've come to ask for some advice."

"From me?"

"Yes. You are my older brother."

Arnau shifted his gaze from the easel and looked at Vidal. In the afternoon light, which was already starting to fade, Vidal thought he saw a mocking smile appear briefly on his brother's face. It disappeared as Arnau returned his gaze to the easel and asked, "Well?"

"I was at that conference on identity that's going on today, and someone there advised me that I might want to keep my distance from Martinez."

"Did this person say anything specific?"

"No."

"So what's the problem?"

"I don't know. That's my problem. I just have an uneasy feeling."

"Then stay away from Martinez."

"You don't seem to mind working with him."

"I paint pictures and he buys them. That's the extent of our relationship."

"And you're not at all curious about who he is, and what he's up to?"

"No."

"But wouldn't you be disturbed, as an artist, if he saw something in a painting of yours that was diametrically opposed to what you meant to convey?"

"My only concern, as an artist, is that a person does see. What he sees is his own business. There's no right or wrong in nonobjective art."

"What kind of art?"

"Nonobjective. That's what this type of art is called."

"You mean it has no point?"

Arnau gave Vidal an icy look, before once again retreating behind his easel.

"It's a question, Arnau, not a criticism. I know nothing about this. But I'd like to know."

"All right. Nonobjective means that there are no identifiable objects in the painting. It's totally abstract. It's the antithesis of realism."

"Is realism bad?"

"I didn't say that. But they're two different journeys. Realism gives you an appreciation for the material world. Nonobjective art takes you on a journey to what's beyond that world, or inside it, if you prefer. It depicts the world of the emotions, the world of the spirit. If one were religious, I suppose it would be called the world of the soul. Some people would say that this is the real world, or at least that it's the world that really matters."

Vidal nodded noncommittally, while he tried to make a connection between Martinez and the world of the soul. Either Martinez was deeper than he thought, or he didn't understand what Arnau was saying.

The latter seemed more likely, since Arnau, noting his confused expression, continued, "I'll give you an example. Let's say an artist paints a realistic painting of a field of yellow daffodils juxtaposed against a blue summer sky. When most people look at such a painting, they feel happy. But why? Is it because of the daffodils? I say no, and what's my proof? If you were to stick a bunch of daffodils in a dark room they wouldn't make you happy. In fact, they wouldn't make you feel anything. So it's not the daffodils that make you feel happy. It's their bright yellow color. And that's what the artist gives you in non-objective art — just the yellow. It's an experience of pure emotion, after it's been freed from the constraints of corporeality."

"I see," Vidal said slowly. "But shouldn't art be more than just the experience of an emotion? Shouldn't it also elevate the viewer and make him a better person?"

"You mean a more moral person?"

"Yes, that's what I was trying to say."

"I don't think anyone today cares much about that. At least, not any of the people I know."

Arnau stole a quick look at Vidal, who was slowly nodding his head up and down. Vidal was only vaguely aware of what his head was doing as he said, for the third time, "I see."

Vidal supposed that his conversation with Arnau ended politely, but the truth was that he was so absorbed in trying to decipher his brother's words that he wasn't aware of much except his own thoughts. It was only when he was back on Sant Llorenc Street and happened to glance through the wrought-iron gate that led to the courtyard of the Jewish Museum that he became aware of his surroundings. The sight of the Jewish star embedded in the courtyard's tile floor reminded Vidal that Martinez wasn't his only problem.

The American, who had contacted the Department of Antiquities as if he owned Sant Joan Januz and could do as he pleased, had committed an act of treachery that would have to be dealt with. When Vidal got home, he would demand that their guest make a plane reservation that evening. And unlike some people, who cloaked their true intentions in ambiguous phrases that could be interpreted in multiple ways, he would state his demand in words that were plain and simple and impossible to misconstrue.

He was already feeling more at peace when the sound of something screeching made him tense up again. He looked down to where the sound was coming from — the bottom of the steps — and saw a small boy standing in the covered passageway playing a very tiny violin. Between the screeches, which were loudly amplified by the stone walls, and the pauses, which were numerous since it took the novice violinist as much time to find the wrong strings as the right ones, Vidal thought he could discern a note or two from that children's concert hall classic, "Twinkle, Twinkle, Little Star."

"Manel?" Vidal called out when he thought it was safe to assume that the performance had come to an end.

Manel raced up the steps and gave Vidal a hug. "Did I surprise you?"

"You certainly did."

"Do you know what song I was playing?"

Vidal pretended to think for a moment, and then he said, "Could it be a song about a star?"

"I knew you would know it! I played it for Mama and Papa's friends and they didn't know what it was."

"Not everyone is as smart as your Uncle Vidal."

Vidal wasn't surprised to see that Joanna had followed Manel up the steps. He'd assumed that the child wasn't wandering through Girona alone.

"Hello, Joanna," he said, making an effort to sound like he was glad to see her. "I was just over at the studio, talking to Arnau."

"Are you going to have dinner with us?" asked Manel.

Since Vidal knew that Manel was the only one in the family who would be pleased if he joined them for the meal, he replied, "I'd love to, but I have other plans."

"Mama, can I tell him our secret?"

Vidal saw that Joanna wasn't returning Manel's smile. But before he could think of a tactful way to end the uncomfortable silence, she said, "We were going to tell your parents in a little while, anyway, so I suppose there's no harm in telling you now. We're going to buy the apartment that we've been renting. The owners decided to stay in the States, so it's all worked out very well."

"That's wonderful," said Vidal, trying not to show his surprise. "I'm sure my parents will be very happy to hear the news."

"You know as well as I do that they won't be at all happy. So would you mind telling them? It will save us and them an unpleasant phone call."

"All right, I'll do that. They'll ask about the finances, though. Should I tell them that you have everything under control?"

"Please do. Arnau has had a bit of luck here in Girona. We should have made the move years ago. Let's go, Manel. It's time for your bath."

"Bye, Uncle Vidal."

"*Adeu.*"

As Vidal watched them walk up the steps, he silently disagreed with his sister-in-law's assessment of Arnau's relatively short sojourn in Girona. The apartment had to cost a small fortune, and he couldn't imagine that Joanna earned much money from her office job. Arnau's relationship with Martinez had most certainly brought him more than "a bit of luck." Arnau had to be selling a lot of paintings. That wasn't entirely surprising since politicians usually had an entourage of wealthy friends, each one richer than the next. But why hadn't Arnau been more forthcoming about the advantages of having Martinez as a patron? he wondered.

When Joanna and Manel reached the top of the stairs, Joanna disappeared inside the apartment. Manel, sensing that he still had an audience, turned and waved to Vidal. Then he lifted his violin and began to play an encore of his song.

Vidal assumed that not too many people were being disturbed by the concert. The stone walls in the passageway were thick and windows were few. But the twinkling star that Manel was serenading did disturb Vidal, whose thoughts had gone back to the painting in the studio. His first instincts had been correct, he decided, as he recalled Arnau's mocking smile. His brother was still jealous of him. Arnau would probably be overjoyed if Vidal did sever his connection with Martinez and, in the process, throw away the opportunity of a lifetime.

"Brothers," he muttered under his breath. He had been to ask Arnau for advice! And while he was at it, he decided that he had been a fool to let himself be disturbed by that fellow Domenech. After all, once one got past the high-sounding sentiments, which also contained their fair share of ambiguous meaning, wasn't it obvious that Tomas Domenech was just a bitter old man who was envious of anyone who was on his way up?

Feeling very grateful that he hadn't fallen into either one of their traps, he gave Manel a final salute. Then he bounded down the steps, certain that the waves of relief that were spilling over him must be similar to what a drowning man must feel after he realizes that his ordeal is over and he's safely back on the shore.

CHAPTER 22

C haim stared at the computer screen, where a message was staring back at him. "We regretfully must decline your request, etcetera, etcetera. Thank you for contacting us, etcetera, etcetera. Best wishes, Tomas Domenech, etcetera, etcetera."

The message was a disappointment. Without help from anyone in the village, or an outside source such as the Department of Antiquities, he didn't see how he could look for the synagogue. It was a fitting climax to his stay in Sant Joan Januz, which, regretfully, had been full of disappointments. And so although he was in Vidal's room, a place where he usually didn't even breathe too deeply so as not to disturb anything in it, Chaim lifted his cane and gave the stone wall beside the computer table an angry whack.

"Practicing?"

Chaim quickly lowered his cane and turned toward the door. He recognized the voice; he had heard it in the house many times. But this was the first time he was seeing the person who went with it.

"I'm Miquel, Vidal's grandfather."

"Nice to meet you, Mr. —"

"You can call me Miquel. I don't mind."

"And you can call me Chaim."

"Thank you. And now that we've taken care of the introductions, we can get down to business. I understand that your ankle is healed."

"Yes, it is."

"Then is nine o'clock tomorrow morning all right?"

"For what?"

"Hunting for your synagogue."

"With you?"

"I'm not as decrepit as I look."

"I didn't mean to imply anything of the sort. I'm just surprised that you're going to help me."

"I hope it's a pleasant surprise. See you tomorrow."

206

Instead of returning to the kitchen, where Clara was preparing the family's evening meal, Miquel went to the front porch. After the long and rainy winter, it was a pleasure to sit outside and enjoy the sweet-smelling air that had only just recently drifted into the village, bringing with it the first hints of spring. It also wasn't a bad idea to relax for a half-hour or so, since tomorrow was going to be a busy day.

Miquel had already decided that the "search" would start at his house, in his cellar. He assumed that the American wouldn't protest. A cellar was as good as any place to look for a synagogue that didn't exist. He, of course, had his own reasons for the plan. The spring holiday was coming up, and so it was time to start with the spring cleaning. Every year about this time, Anna would ask him to clear out the cellar, reminding him that if he hadn't needed something during the past twelve months — especially something that had been accumulating dust and rust for decades — it was highly unlikely that he would need it in the future.

He had protested, year after year, that the past wasn't always an accurate indicator of the future. Now he saw that she had been right, as usual. And it wasn't because he was feeling morbid or maudlin. It was just a fact that a person never knew when he was going to leave this world. He shouldn't go up to heaven leaving behind a house full of broken, worn-out things for others to throw out.

A car pulled into the driveway. It was Vidal, coming back from Girona. Vidal waved and Miquel waved back. Then the car disappeared around the side of the house. Miquel wondered if Vidal recalled the time that Vidal had gone digging for a lost synagogue. From his own experience, Miquel knew that it was a mystery what a person remembered and what he forgot. But that incident he remembered very well, and so if the American wanted to continue looking for his synagogue after they finished with the cellar, Miquel would give him a shovel and put him to work in the backyard. Homegrown watermelons would taste very good in the summer.

Vidal didn't get a chance to tell off the American because his grandfather, for a reason that he wouldn't divulge, wanted their guest to be in a good mood when they set off on their adventure the next morning. And Chaim was in a good mood when Miquel's pickup truck appeared at the Bonets' door precisely at nine o'clock.

"The oldest part of the village is the group of houses just north of the square," Miquel explained as they drove along a back road that led to his home. "That includes my daughter's house, the property that belongs to my two brothers-in-law, and my house."

"The square was built after these houses?"

"Yes."

"How do you know?"

"Sant Joan Januz has always been a small farming village. The idea of a square and shops came much later."

"I thought that the focal point of a square was usually the church."

"And I thought you were looking for a synagogue."

"I am."

"So what do you care about a church?"

"I don't. I just think it's interesting that your village doesn't have one. That's the anthropologist in me. We're always snooping around communities, trying to make sense of their culture and beliefs."

"What made you choose that particular field of study?"

"There was an anthropologist named Ruth Benedict who once said, 'The purpose of anthropology is to make the world safe for human differences.' I would like to use anthropology to make Judaism safe for young assimilated Jews."

"I don't understand. If your interest is Judaism, why aren't you studying religion?"

"Because the young Jews I'm talking about wouldn't be caught dead taking a course about the Jewish religion. But they might sign up for a course in the Anthropology Department about different symbol systems in traditional Mediterranean cultures."

"And one of those symbol systems would be traditional Jewish religious culture?"

"You guessed it. So, where are we going to start the search?"

"I thought we'd begin at my house. In the cellar."

"That sounds like a plan."

Miquel smiled. "I'm glad you think so, too."

They continued down the country road and passed a meadow where a few horses were nibbling on the fresh blades of grass, oblivious to the show being put on by a long border of red poppies that were dancing on the breeze. As Chaim took it all in, he wondered if his Nona Anna had also ridden past this particular meadow on a spring morning and admired its beauty.

"I suppose this all looks pretty much the same as it did five hundred years ago," he commented.

"I wouldn't know about that. But I do know that in a little while the countryside is going to look very different. The yellow broom will be in bloom, and there will be yellow blossoms everywhere."

Chaim glanced over at Miquel. It was odd that he had mentioned the shrub so casually. Either the elderly man wasn't aware of its significance, or he assumed that Chaim couldn't possibly know the secret.

"Is that good?" asked Chaim, returning his gaze to the window so it would look like he was just making conversation.

"Is there a reason why it wouldn't be?"

"In Kansas it's considered to be a weed. You folks must see something in it that — "

"Here's my farmhouse." Miquel swung the pickup truck onto a dirt road that led up to a large, solidly built stone building.

Chaim smiled. He had hoped Miquel would change the subject.

Miquel parked the truck close to the steps leading up to the farmhouse's front porch. Chaim would have liked to take a look around the outside of the building first, but Miquel was already unlocking the front door and so he joined Miquel on the porch. He quickly searched the right doorpost for a sign of an indentation. There wasn't one, of course.

After depositing his coat and backpack in the vestibule, Chaim hurried after Miquel, who was already walking down a hallway. With a guide to lead the way to the cellar, there wasn't any need for Chaim to tap with his cane along the stone walls to find a hidden doorway. And when they were standing in the brightly lit underground space, which was filled with old furniture and appliances that were past their prime but still too young to evoke a faraway age, Chaim felt a bit let down by the total lack of mystery.

Then he reminded himself that it wasn't the cellar he was interested in, but the false wall that might be in it. Since he knew from Nona Anna's map to look in the north, he took out his compass to get his bearings.

"I thought we could start by looking for a trapdoor," said Miquel, coming up beside Chaim to see what he was doing.

"Wouldn't a false wall be a more likely way to conceal a secret passageway?"

"Perhaps, but in my opinion this room only dates back to the seventeenth century. If your synagogue is here, it would have to be underneath this floor."

Chaim didn't say anything, even though he did wonder why the elderly man seemed to think there was a trapdoor in the cellar. Miquel hadn't moved into the farmhouse the day before yesterday. If a trapdoor existed, at some point over the years some adventurous child would have surely found it while playing hide-and-seek, or some other game. A false wall, especially one hidden behind a piece of furniture, would have been harder to discover. But it was Miquel's farmhouse, and Chaim didn't want to start the day with a disagreement.

"So let's get to work," said Chaim. Then, recalling the incident with sweeping the floor, he added, "Do you want to move the furniture to the side of the room, or to the center?"

"Why don't we clear everything out so we'll have a clean space to work in?"

Chaim stared at Miquel. "You mean lug all this stuff up the steps?"

Miquel smiled sweetly, as though it was the most reasonable thing in the world to do.

Chaim didn't need a trapdoor to unexpectedly open under his feet and send him hurtling down to a dark dungeon to make him realize that he had been tricked. As he quickly considered what to do next, two good reasons for angrily storming out of the room came to mind: he didn't like being made a fool of and he didn't want to reinjure his ankle. But there were also reasons for agreeing to do this favor, despite the deception. After all, he had been the family's guest for several weeks, and this could be a way to repay the debt. And if he helped out Miquel, he might gain the trust of the elderly man.

"Okay," Chaim said after he finished his deliberations. "But first I want to get a bandage for my ankle. I'll be back in a minute."

"Where are you going?"

"I left my bag upstairs."

"I'll get it. I don't want you to make more trips than necessary."

Chaim tried not to laugh. Since he would be making dozens of trips up and down those stairs, one more wouldn't matter. But Miquel was already gone.

While he waited for Miquel to return, Chaim gravitated toward the bookcase. Though it sat against the room's eastern wall, it looked like the perfect thing to hide a secret passageway. And so, just in case his Nona Anna had been mistaken about the false wall's location, he tested the wall around the bookcase by giving the stones a knock with his cane.

After listening carefully for the telltale sound of a hollow space — and not hearing one — he changed tactics and gave the bookcase a shove. It didn't budge. He pressed against the bookcase with all his weight and shoved again. The bookcase still refused to give way.

He knew there was a spiritual concept known as "storming the gates of heaven," but he didn't think it could be applied to this situation. No one, not even the most zealous master of prayer, would shove aside such a heavy piece of furniture three times a day for very long. If the bookcase was concealing a secret doorway, there had to be a hidden lever, so that the bookcase would be swung aside in an instant.

While searching for the lever, he also took a look at the things gathering dust on the shelves. He passed over a collection of novels written by Catalan authors he had never heard of and turned to a pile of old magazines. They would have been fun to look through if there had been more time. But there wasn't, and so he turned to another shelf, where an old-fashioned record player and a stack of records were sitting.

He gave the dust-covered turntable a spin. Once his grandmother, Nona Esther, had showed him how a record player worked, and he remembered how he had tried not to laugh at the way the cumbersome machine unceremoniously plopped a ridiculously large black disc onto the slow-moving turntable. When the machine's arm went into motion, creaking as it moved upward and then collapsing into place with a thud, he could conceal his amusement no longer. "Nona Esther, your record player is Jewish!" he had called out with mock surprise.

211

"What do you mean?" asked his grandmother, her eyes twinkling.

"It *kvetches*! Didn't you hear it? When it lowered its arm it said, '*Oy!*'"

"It's probably got arthritis, too," Nona Esther had replied, also laughing. "But I'd rather listen to my old record player than one of those new squawkmen."

"Walkman," he had said with a laugh, correcting her intentional error.

Now even a Walkman was ridiculously awkward and out of date, he thought as he turned to the albums sitting beside the record player and flipped through them. He supposed that someday he would be showing his grandchildren how an MP3 player worked and telling them that it was good enough for him. And would that be such a terrible thing?

"What's important is to know what's important," his Nona Esther had advised him more than once. "Time is the most precious commodity there is. Waste it on trivialities and you'll waste your life."

He glanced at his watch. More than a quarter of an hour had passed, and he wondered what was delaying Miquel. He was about to turn away from the stack of records, which held as much interest for him as the Catalan novels, when he spotted a recording of medieval music that seemed to beckon to him to take a closer look. When he lifted up the album, he was sorry that he had disturbed its musty sleep. The bottom of the cardboard cover suddenly split apart and a black disc, followed by a small book, tumbled out. Chaim instinctively reached out to save the book, and the record fell to the floor.

After determining that the record had survived the accident unscathed, Chaim returned it to its cardboard cover and turned his attention to the slim volume. It was a collection of medieval troubadour poems, and from the look of its frayed cloth binding it was even older than the records. Since the book, like the record album, seemed out of place in what was essentially a collection of modern popular culture, Chaim opened it to see if its owner had left behind a clue as to his or her identity.

He had.

Chaim stared at the name, wondering if he was really in Miquel's cellar, or if he was actually back in the sewing room, where he was experiencing the odd sensation of watching himself dream this entire scene. It would be too trite, he decided, to pinch his arm to determine if he was asleep or awake, and so he opted to hum a tune instead. If he could feel the noise vibrating in his head, that would mean he was awake. If not, he was dreaming. Having established the rules for his experiment, he took a deep breath and hummed a few bars of a chassidic melody.

The air tickled the inside of his nose. He was really there. The book was really there. And so the name, whose letters he gently traced with his fingers, was really there as well. "Manel Esperandeu," he whispered softly.

"Found something interesting to read?"

Miquel stood at the foot of the stairs, holding the backpack.

"Yes, Mr. Esperandeu."

"What makes you think that Esperandeu is my family name?"

Chaim handed the volume of poetry to Miquel. When Miquel didn't say anything, Chaim added, "I found it in the bookcase, with the records. Shall I put it back?"

Miquel shook his head. He handed Chaim his backpack.

"Thank you, Mr. Esperandeu."

"I told you to call me Miquel. It's not good manners to disobey your elders."

"All right, Miquel, but would it also be bad manners if I were to ask if Manel Esperandeu was a relative of yours?"

"It's not necessarily bad manners, considering that you're an American and Americans are known for talking freely about themselves, even with strangers. But I wouldn't exactly call it good manners, at least not according to the rules of Catalan etiquette."

"So was he your father? I'm from Kansas. It's known as the 'Heart of America.' A person can't be much more American than that."

"Manel was my older brother. He died from tuberculosis when he was seventeen. He was the scholar of the family, and my parents gave him this book just a few weeks before he passed away."

"I'm sorry."

"It happened a very long time ago."

"Still, a brother is a brother."

Miquel slipped the book into his pocket. "Shall we get started?"

"Sure." Chaim didn't want to hurt the elderly man, but he had to pursue this clue to the end. While he wound the bandage around his ankle, he said, "You didn't ask why I was so interested in knowing about your brother."

"I'm not from Kansas."

"That's true. So I'll tell you, without your asking. I also had a relative named Manel Esperandeu."

Chaim raised his eyes from his bandage and looked over at Miquel. As he suspected, the elderly man had turned very pale.

"My relative named Manel Esperandeu lived a very long time ago," Chaim continued, as he kept his eyes on Miquel so he could see the elderly man's reaction. "He was probably born around the year 1462, because his sister — who was my direct ancestor, on my mother's side — was born in the year 1466."

"How can you be so sure about the dates?"

"This ancestor of mine wrote a diary. She managed to escape not long after the Inquisition arrived in Catalonia. But her brother Manel wasn't so lucky. He and his wife had to stay behind, in a little farming village called Sant Joan Januz."

"I hear it's a nice place," Miquel said quietly. "Or at least it was."

"I didn't come here to cause trouble."

"Then why are you here?"

"Like I told Vidal, I came here to find a synagogue and a Torah scroll. And some family, if there's any still around."

"The synagogue is mentioned in the diary?"

"Yes."

"Is what happened in Saragossa mentioned, too?

"Yes."

"And you've actually seen this diary? With your own eyes?"

"The original belonged to my grandmother. Now it's in a safety deposit box in Kansas. But I do have a few photocopies of it back in the sewing room, if you'd like to read it."

"I'm not much of a reader."

Miquel slowly walked back toward the staircase and began to climb up the steps.

"Miquel?" Chaim called out. "Don't you want to get started on clearing out this room?"

Miquel turned. There was an empty look in the elderly man's eyes that made Chaim feel uneasy.

214

"There isn't any synagogue in Sant Joan Januz. If there ever was one, it disappeared a long time ago. I'll take you back to my daughter's house."

They were both silent during the drive. Clara was surprised to see them back so soon, but Chaim said that his ankle was hurting him. The bandage was his witness, and Clara was in too good a mood to be unduly worried about her guest's minor relapse.

"Look, Papa," she said as she handed Miquel a small bouquet of bright yellow flowers. "It's the first yellow broom of the season. Vidal found it over by where he's going to build his resort. He said one bush is already full of color."

"You keep it, Clara," said Miquel. "There will be plenty more for me in a few weeks."

"I wish Mama were here to see it."

"I do, too."

Miquel suddenly remembered that Chaim was with them. "I'll take your bag back to the sewing room," he said as he grabbed the backpack from Chaim's hand. "You need to be careful with that ankle."

When they reached the sewing room, Miquel quickly shut the door behind them. "I've changed my mind. I would like to read that diary of yours."

"No problem."

Chaim went over to the cupboard to get one of the photocopies out of his overnight bag. "I hope you'll be able to decipher my great-great-grandmother's handwriting."

"I'll manage. Does anyone else in the village know about this diary?"

"No."

"Let's keep it that way, at least for now. The same goes for the book you found in the cellar. All right?"

"Doesn't your family know you had a brother?"

"They know I had a brother, and they know his name was Manel. But they don't know that our family name is Esperandeu."

"How can they not know?"

Miquel looked at the American. He wondered if he should telephone the authorities to inform them that a visitor from outer space had taken up residence in Sant Joan Januz. How else could a

215

person explain this strange phenomenon of two people standing in the same room and being universes apart?

But instead of saying what he was really thinking, Miquel said only, "We'll talk later."

PART IV: ANNA

CHAPTER 23

Miquel stood at the window, debating whether or not to close the curtains. He wanted privacy, but shutting out the light on a beautiful spring day would look suspicious.

"I'll leave them open," he whispered, and he sat down at the kitchen table, where the diary was laying. But he didn't open the diary. Instead he just sat for a very long time and stared at the troubling object.

Written documents were dangerous. Of course, the American couldn't be expected to understand that. For him, the diary was probably just a colorful piece of family history, just as the search for that old synagogue was a supposedly harmless adventure. How could he know that the past was still a minefield, ready to explode at any moment? Or that it was cruel, and not a kindness, to awaken fires that had been so carefully extinguished?

But Miquel did understand. That was why he knew that he had to read the diary, even though reading it was going to be upsetting. He had to know everything that was in it so that he could prevent it from harming his family.

He picked up the diary, but not to read it. Not yet. With his other hand, he reached under the wood table and felt for the lever hidden underneath it. A drawer slid open.

The drawer wasn't deep, but it was large enough to hold a large serving plate. The old-timers — the villagers who had been old-timers when Miquel was still a newly married man — had said that the secret drawers built within their dining tables were a remnant from the bad times. The villagers would always have a plate of pork and vegetables hidden inside a secret drawer, just in case an unwelcome visitor turned up at their door by surprise during mealtimes. Some tables had smaller drawers as well, to store the playing cards. The cards were used when they were surprised during their meals on the Sabbath or holidays. Moments after an unexpected knock on the door, the drawers would slide open, and the men of the family would instantly become absorbed in an enthusiastic game of El Tresillo. After the visitor departed, the cards were returned to the drawer, and the Sabbath peace returned to the table.

No one prepared a pork dish anymore in Sant Joan Januz. But for some reason the tradition of playing cards at holiday meals had been kept, though it was observed in a somewhat altered form. That, too, would probably die out in a few years, after his generation was gone, Miquel thought as he slipped the diary into the drawer to make sure that it would fit inside — just in case. It did.

He removed the diary and put it back on the table. Then he remembered the volume of poetry that was still sitting in his pocket. It was also a problem. He had forgotten about the book's existence, and he wondered what other incriminatory pieces of evidence were still down in the cellar. He could have kicked himself for not clearing out the room when he was younger and could have done the work by himself. But he had been so sure that there wasn't anything down there.

Miquel took the book out of his pocket and placed it beside the diary. He didn't have many tangible remembrances of his brother, but this was no time to start feeling sentimental about the dead. If he had to destroy these two talebearers from the past, that's what he would do. It was the living he had to concern himself with. He had to keep his mind focused on that.

And yet he wasn't a stone. He couldn't be totally unmoved by the sight of the diary and the volume of poetry sitting side by side on his kitchen table. After being separated for so many years, Manel Esperandeu was finally reunited with his sister Anna.

It was only an imaginary reunion, of course; a meeting of pen and ink and letters written on a blank page. His mind wasn't so far gone that he didn't see that. Still, it was something. And so even though he knew it was a foolish, sentimental thing to do, and most likely a sign of early dementia (he would have to watch himself more closely; talking about yellow broom to an outsider had been a careless mistake), he opened the volume of poetry to the page where the name Manel Esperandeu was written. Then he turned to the first page of the diary and began to read:

With the Help of Heaven

The 1st day of the month of Iyar, the Month of Radiance, in the year 5276, also known as the year 1516,

I, Anna, the daughter of Rabbi Isaac and his wife, Regina, may their memories be for a blessing and protect us from harm, belonging to the exiled Jews of Jerusalem, express my thanks to the G-d of Heaven for all the acts of loving-kindness that He has bestowed upon me and my family, without any merit of my own, but in the fullness of His mercies.

Even as my eyes turn to the holy city of Jerusalem and the land of our forefathers, and my heart yearns for the fulfillment of the prophecy that we, the remnant of this long and bitter captivity, will be returned to our homeland — may it be soon! — so do my thoughts return to the land of my birth and the loved ones I left behind.

I am like the one who roams through the town, through the markets and the squares, seeking the ones I love, and asking, "Have you seen them?" My steps take me every day to the place where the ships come to rest — would that my scattered people would also know rest! — and always this question is on my lips: "Have you seen them?"

"Have you seen them?" For thirty long years I have asked this question of those who have fled from that land which has repaid our kindness with cruelty. During this time, the number of our people who have found refuge from the fires of the Inquisition in this gracious city of Salonika where I now live — may the G-d of Heaven repay the Sultan with long years and good health! — has grown numerous as the sands of the shore, may their numbers increase. During this time I have seen brother reunited with brother, sister with sister, parents with their children. Yet I, Anna, return every day to my home without having found the ones I seek, for no one has seen them.

Do not think that I write these words as a complaint against the One Above, whose judgments are perfect and whose ways are merciful. The G-d of Heaven has been gracious to me and provided me with a loving husband and children and grandchildren, may they be blessed with a good and long life and merit to follow in the ways of our ancestors. We have been privileged to find a safe haven in a city that is G-d-fearing and as full of good deeds as there are seeds in a pomegranate. We have been blessed with prosperity and all good things. I am all gratitude. I have no complaints.

And yet now, as my strength begins to fail me and my eyes grow dim, my thoughts journey to a future day when perhaps my dear brother and sister-in-law — may the One Above be gracious to them and protect them from harm! — will arrive at this port and search the pier for a familiar face, hoping to be reunited with their family in joy and gladness.

So that their hopes will not be disappointed, should I no longer be in this world to greet them, I will write down my family's history for my children and my children's children. I hereby entrust them, my descendents, with the sacred trust of remembering those who have been so cruelly severed from our midst, so that their memory will never be forgotten. And I ask of those who may read these words long after the hand that writes them has returned to dust, to take my place at the port, and the market, and the square. Never grow tired, do not despair, but always keep this question in your hearts and on your lips: "Have you seen them?"

With the help of Heaven, I will begin my task. May I have the merit to complete it.

I begin my story not at the beginning, for I do not know how it began. When did the Jews first come to Catalonia? How can one pretend to speak with certainty about something that occurred so long ago that it is lost in the mists of time, like the rains of former years? Perhaps, then, it is easier to say when the Jews first arrived in Girona, the city of my birth? Here, as well, the years have leapt by, not in the tens or twenties, but in the hundreds, and so who can gather up the days and put them in a scale and say,

"This is an honest reckoning"?

What can I say then? I will tell you that the Jews lived in Girona for more than six hundred years before that bitter day when they were exiled from their adopted home. During many of these years they lived in peace with their neighbors, and the entire city prospered. Some worked quietly at their looms or their potter's wheels. Others were entrusted with matters of finance and trade and the public administration of the city. Still others, and my family was fortunate to count themselves among their numbers,

220

spent their days studying our holy books and guiding the community in spiritual matters.

Our community was a community of kindness. We supported synagogues and schools, a hospital, and a home for the poor. Scholars from throughout Catalonia and Languedoc came to our houses of study to learn the secrets of the Kabbalah, and to sit at the feet of our greatest leader, Rabbi Moshe ben Nachman, the Ramban. Those were the good days, when the joyous song of the bride and bridegroom filled our streets, when the sweet melody of Torah was heard in every courtyard, when the name of Girona inspired pride and awe.

When recounting the tale of this happy time, I would be remiss if I did not mention our good King Jaume. I leave it to others to sing of his military adventures and how he tamed the waters of the Mediterranean Sea, bringing prosperity to all of Catalonia and gaining renown throughout the world. Instead, I say this: King Jaume was good to the Jews and he protected us. Let that be his praise.

We paid a price, of course, for the king's favors, in the form of taxes and, when this was not enough, even more taxes. However, we did not complain, because we were allowed to live in peace.

But then, in the year 1263, the king commanded our Rabbi Moshe ben Nachman to appear before the royal court in Barcelona and debate the merits of the Jewish faith against a wicked man who had forsaken the ways of our fathers and taken on the faith of our gentile neighbors. When our wise Rabbi Moshe was declared the victor of this disputation, the people of Girona expressed their displeasure by attacking the Jewish Quarter.

King Jaume's men put an end to the rampage, but after the king's demise, more unrest followed. The new king was despised by the noblemen, and they did not listen to his edicts. The clergy also grew bold. Murder and plunder of the Jews became a common occurrence, and there was no one to save us.

And then, in the year 1348, the Great Plague came. It swept through all of Catalonia

— entire villages were emptied of their people — and I have been told that it devastated many other lands as well. Although we suffered along with the others, and buried our loved ones just as they did, a terrible rumor spread throughout the land. They said that we Jews caused it — They said we poisoned their wells! — and in Girona our homes were once again attacked by angry mobs. Yet still this was not the end.

1391. I write these numbers with a trembling hand, knowing that my pen, a frail servant, cannot adequately describe the misery and destruction that befell my people during this one year. A troubadour, perhaps, would know how to weave together verses that would cloak the eyes of his readers in tears. I, however, am no poet. I raise my hand, but fine words defy me. They flee or hang their heads in shame, refusing to heed my call. Therefore, let me tell the woes of this year in the only language I am able to command, the language of a broken heart.

It was a time of unrest throughout the land. Political intrigues were rife, prices were unstable, and no one knew what the next day would bring. Then an accuser arose in Seville who demanded the destruction of that city's synagogues, our pleasant places of worship. His ranting fell upon receptive ears, and in the spring a mob stormed Seville's Jewish Quarter, killing and destroying everything in its path.

Once started, the riots spread throughout the land. The Jewish quarter of Cordoba was sacked, its people slaughtered. Toledo did not escape. All that spring the killing continued, until the Kingdom of Castile overflowed with gushing streams of innocent Jewish blood. Yet this was not all. Our eyes wept hot tears and our mouths cried out in pain as we heard the terrible news: thousands of Jews — perhaps tens of thousands — were dragged through the jeering crowds to the baptismal font, where they were forced to convert under pain of death.

The terror spread further north. In Valencia, that once-pleasant kingdom by the sea, only one Jewish Quarter was spared. Majorca was laid waste, and still the madness continued. By summer's end the people of Catalonia had also become infected, and the holy community of Barcelona was no more.

When this news reached Girona, we stormed the heavens with our prayers, pleading for a miracle to save us. But the day came when we at last saw with our own eyes what we had heard described, but could not fully imagine.

It was a holy day for the Christians, dedicated to the memory of Sant Llorenc. They celebrated his martyrdom at Roman hands by setting the Jewish Quarter on fire. When we tried to flee the raging flames, the peasants came after us with knives and bludgeons and whatever else they could lay their hands on. To escape from the fury, a few souls fled to the church and, in their panic, converted to save their lives. But many of us were killed, cruelly.

As for my family, we fled, along with a few others, to an ancient fortress, the Gironella Tower, that stands at the city's edge. The mob followed us even there, screaming for our blood! But thanks to the mercies of Heaven, we reached this place of refuge and the councilors of the city, who were loyal servants of the king, closed the heavy gate in time.

We remained in the tower until the revolt was stamped out, and in this way we survived the slaughter. But when we returned to our homes there was very little left to return to. So many friends and neighbors were dead. The synagogues were destroyed. The workshops of the weavers and potters were empty and silent. The splendor of Girona was no more.

The days when we could depend upon the protection of the king had passed. The blame for every misfortune that fell upon the city was laid at our door. To restore the peace, or so the rulers said, many streets where we lived and worked were suddenly forbidden to Jews. My family was among those who were forced to leave their homes. We moved to a different street in the Jewish Quarter, which had now become so diminished in size that it could scarcely contain us all. However, this was but a passing problem. By the time I was born, in the year 5226, also known as the year 1466, it had been sadly resolved. The once-proud Jewish community of Girona numbered no more than two hundred heartbroken souls.

Yet if times were bad — and today I know they were — my young and innocent eyes did not see it. My family's home was always filled with light and gladness, and so I still recall that little world of narrow streets and dark passageways with fondness.

In the morning, my brother Manel and I would wake up to the melody of our mother's song. Then, after being coaxed out of our cozy beds by the warmth of her smile, we would chant together the ancient words of the new day's first prayer, Modeh Ani — "I am thankful!" This is how we would start our day, happy and thankful to the One Above for returning our holy souls to our small bodies for another day of life and service to our eternal King. This was our mother's gentle instruction.

223

My father, Rabbi Isaac, a man for whom our holy Torah and its commandments were truly the life and length of his days, was our other kind and patient teacher. He taught us to engrave the words of the Torah upon our hearts and obey the directives of our Sages.

Manel, four years my elder and a promising scholar, was the pride and joy of our entire community. With such a one as him, we all thought proudly − we did not say such thoughts aloud − the day would surely dawn when Girona's Torah would once again illuminate the world.

However, the cup of bitterness had not been fully drunk. Laws were passed with one purpose in mind, to humiliate us and impoverish us, so that our will would be broken and we would desert our faith. My father and his learned colleagues did their best to keep up our spirits, but the sweet sound of Torah learning became harder and harder to hear. It was drowned out by the sound of the bells.

The bells! Who can understand who did not hear them? Not far from our homes was that other place, whose tower rose up so proudly, in such contrast to our weary and downcast heads; whose bells rang out so strongly, when our voices were hushed and fearful.

Although so many years have passed, I can still hear their ringing. Sometimes, when they summoned us to enter their place of worship and listen to their lies, or forfeit our lives on their altar, they frightened me with their angry peals. But sometimes, when all was dark and everyone else was asleep, they seemed to call to me like a loving friend. Gently, so gently, they awoke me, singing, "Come here. Come here. Anna, come here. Life will be good. You will wear fine dresses, live in a fine house. People will smile at you. They will like you. Come here. Come here. Anna, come here."

I would throw the blankets over my face, to shut out their singing. Trembling, I yearned for morning. And when day finally came, I frantically scrubbed the clothes, the dishes, whatever needed to be cleaned, hoping and praying that I could also wash away the wicked thoughts that clung to me, staining my soul. But the bells found me even there, in the daylight, as they called out the hour, the half hour, and even the quarter hour, just to torment us.

The years passed by, and with each passing year our little community grew even smaller. Now, however, our people were not dragged to the baptismal font by their hair. They walked there willingly. Because a few drops of water could change a Jew into a Converso, and a Converso could walk down the street with his head held high. He could become a wealthy merchant or a powerful councilor. Or he could become a respected scholar.

My brother saw it all, and his eyes lost their sparkle.

One morning, when my brother Manel had already reached the age of marriage, the place in the synagogue where he usually sat was empty. My father, upon opening his prayer book, found a letter waiting inside. Manel had allowed himself to be baptized. He would not stay in Girona and embarrass my father, he wrote. He was already on his way to Saragossa to start a new life.

It has been said that a person cannot know what sweet is until he has tasted something bitter. I can vouch that this is true. The sweetness was gone from our lives, and we knew it.

My parents never uttered my brother's name. I knew I must banish thoughts of him from my heart as well. But how I secretly hoped that just as a seed sometimes drifts on the wind and lands in a neighboring field, so too would word of Manel travel to Girona and reach my ears.

One day my prayers were answered. I learned that Manel had found favor with a wealthy Converso family named Esperandeu and married one of their daughters. He had taken their name and their way of life, and, in return, his new family had provided the young couple with every good thing that money could buy.

"But is he happy?" I asked, even though I was afraid to hear the reply.

"Oh yes," said the messenger. "There is no lack of good things to enjoy in a city like Saragossa."

When I heard this, I was sure that I would never see Manel again. I had forgotten that everything can change in the blink of an eye. But that is what happened. With just a few brush strokes of the royal pen, King Ferdinand of Aragon and Queen Isabella of Castile, who jointly ruled over the entire land, brought forth an ill-begotten child that was to change all of our lives: the New Inquisition.

The Old Inquisition, which had been established many years before to punish Christians who held beliefs considered to be

225

heretical, was not unknown to those of us who lived in Catalonia. There was an Inquisitor's court at Barcelona, over which our good Fray Joan Comte presided — "good" because he saw nothing and he did nothing, which everyone in Catalonia agreed was the best way for an Inquisitor to fulfill his solemn duties.

This New Inquisition was very different — at least, according to the rumors, for at this time its courts were still confined to the cities of Castile. Not only was it zealous, but its wrath was directed at the very people that the church had labored so long to win: the Conversos!

"The Conversos?" we asked. "Why?"

Apparently many of these former Jews had been deceiving the Church all this time and were secretly practicing the faith of our forefathers! Now they were to be punished for their betrayal! Once-powerful families were being stripped of their wealth and position! Some were even being burned at the stake! The terror was so great that families were fleeing by the thousands! Children were denouncing their parents, brothers were betraying brothers, and neighbors were turning upon their former friends in desperate attempts to save their own lives!

Or so we heard.

In the beginning, we listened to these rumors with disbelief. If they had spoken of some new persecution of the Jews, we would have accepted them without question. But the Conversos? They were councilors of state and advisors to princes! They were the architects of the cities' wealth and the foundation of the land's prosperity! They could even be found in the upper echelons of the Church! How could their fortunes change so suddenly? Surely these messengers from Castile were merely overly excitable prophets of exaggerated doom.

But as the months passed, new reports only confirmed what we had heard before. A destroying force had been set loose in the land, and even though the New Inquisition was still only in Castile, the tension in Catalonia increased. Catalan noblemen, who guarded their political independence as jealously as their wealth, talked openly of opposition should the royal couple try to replace our good Fray Joan Comte with someone else.

The cynics among us said that this talk had little to do with sympathy for the Conversos and everything to do with the noblemen's concern that the wealth of the land would be

226

transferred out of Catalonia and into the royal coffers in Castile. Yet even if their reasons were selfish, we hoped that their talk would turn into action. We Jews were safe, for the moment. But who among us did not have someone dear who was in danger?

Our hearts were gladdened when we heard that the New Inquisition was as welcome in nearby Aragon as it was in Catalonia. There was even a happy rumor that the noblemen of Aragon — or perhaps it was the Conversos — had defied the king and risen up in bloody revolt!

But then one day, while we were having our midday meal, a neighbor knocked at our door. "Excuse me for disturbing you, Rabbi Isaac," said the man, "but I have just heard news that you might want to know."

"Speak."

"The Inquisition has set up a court in Saragossa."

My mother raised her hands to her mouth to stifle her cry. My father said nothing. The neighbor left and we were left alone to contemplate this terrible news. And think about it we did, for by this time the reports and rumors were coming so quickly that it was impossible to think about anything else. But who should we believe? Who was a reliable source?

Some said that the world had never seen such a terror before. Innocent people were being dragged to prison cells where the sun never showed its face. If they did not confess willingly, they were tortured by men who had forgotten the meaning of mercy. And no interrogation was considered complete until the accused soul had not only confessed his guilt, but had also accused at least a dozen others.

There were others, though, who said that these stories of terror and torture were an exaggeration, the product of idle people with too much time on their hands and too little sense in their brains. Yes, many were called in for questioning. Yes, the Inquisitors recorded all the details of a person's family and circle of acquaintances. And, yes, only the Conversos were singled out for suspicion, even though they did not own a monopoly on laxity in religious observance. And, yes, yes, yes, it was the wealthiest of the Conversos who were being especially singled out for arrest and condemnation and confiscation of their wealth. But those who could prove that they were good Christians, loyal to the Catholic faith, were released without being harmed. And the proof was that although thousands were being arrested, only a handful had been burned at the stake so far.

These words were but a cold comfort to us. In our hearts, we hoped that Manel was still inwardly loyal to his Jewish faith. Yet that same heart trembled at the thought of what might happen to him if he actually was.

We anxiously waited for even the tiniest scrap of news from Saragossa. It was too dangerous, of course, for Manel to send us word. We, as well, were cautious not to do anything that might pin upon him the dreaded accusation of "Judaizer." Then one spring evening my father rushed into our home and told us to come to the synagogue at once. A Converso from Saragossa had arrived in Girona.

Only a few candles had been lit in the room, because the fugitive, whose face was hidden by a veil, wished to keep his identity concealed. And so, in this shadowy darkness, we listened in hushed silence to the words of one who had seen with his own eyes this thing called the New Inquisition.

The city's troubles began when the Grand Inquisitor, the dreaded Tomas de Torquemada, appointed a church official named Pedro Arbues to head the Inquisition in Saragossa. To demonstrate his zeal, this Arbues quickly arrested many of Saragossa's wealthiest Conversos. Not long afterward Saragossa saw its first auto-da-fe.

The Act of Faith. We had heard of it before, but we did not know exactly what it was. There had been so many rumors about this as well, and so we listened eagerly as our witness continued his testimony.

The ceremony, which the entire city attends, begins when the accused Conversos are escorted into the city's main square. Barefoot and dressed in the "sanbenito" — a coarse robe that is yellow in color for those who are repentant, and black in color for those who refuse to express remorse for being a secret Jew — they are paraded in front of the jeering crowd. Next there is a long sermon, whose purpose is to further increase their humiliation. Only then comes the reading out of the sentences, for in their cruelty the Inquisitors have left the accused in suspense. Not one of them yet knows if he will be proclaimed innocent or guilty, if he will be returned to life or delivered to the grave.

One by one, each name is called out, in cruel mockery of the Day of Judgment. With what fear and trembling each of the accused steps forward — men, women, the gray-haired elder along with the youth of tender years — and bows his head before his earthly tormentors!

Those whom the court deems sincerely reconciled to the church receive a "light" sentence: flogging or a short term of exile and a heavy fine. Others are sentenced to life imprisonment and required to forfeit a large part or all of their property to the crown. The rest — those whom the Church has deemed irreconcilable — are relaxed to the secular authorities.

Relaxed? We eagerly seized upon this word. Were they let go, to return to our people?

No, explained the Converso from Saragossa. The sensibilities of the Church are too delicate for it to become directly involved in the gruesome work of executing irreconcilable heretics. The prisoners are therefore relaxed — turned over — to the secular officers of the crown, who carry out the order to burn these secret Jews at the stake.

When I heard these words, I was sure I would go mad if I did not find out what had happened to Manel. But then, as though already knowing what was in my heart, and the hearts of others who were sitting in the room, the man continued, "I can say no more. Do not ask me about the fate of specific people. In times such as these, when lists of names are being compiled even as I speak, the true friend is silent."

I do not know what became of this fugitive, if he made it to safety or if he was captured by the king's officers. The Inquisition's concern for saving the Converso's soul had led to a new edict forbidding the escape of his body. Therefore, just as it was forbidden for a Jew to leave the land — or even leave the city of his birth — so too was it now forbidden for a Converso to leave the kingdom. Shipowners were warned they would pay a heavy price should they disobey the edict and secretly carry Conversos to foreign shores. Therefore, only one alternative remained: flee to the Pyrenees. Seek refuge in the Kingdom of Navarre or disappear into the hills of Languedoc.

In the weeks and months that followed, other Conversos quietly slipped into Girona and just as quietly slipped out, on their way across the mountains, careful to avoid the larger cities, such as

Barcelona, where the courts of the Inquisition were situated. My mother and I joined the other women at the communal oven, where we baked extra loaves of bread. Like our good Fray Joan Comte — who had been relieved of his duties when the New Inquisition replaced the old one in Catalonia — we did not ask and we did not see. We left the bread by the door of the synagogue at night. In the morning it was gone.

Yet how I yearned to ask just a word of those shadowy figures passing through the midnight streets of Girona, like phantoms in a disturbing dream! "Have you seen him? Have you seen my brother?" But I did not dare ask, for I knew they dared not speak.

One night, when the hour was already very late, I heard a soft rap, as if someone was knocking. Was I dreaming? All was silent. Yes, it must have been a dream. No! There it was again. Someone was at our door!

By the time I lit a candle and hurried down the stairs, my father was already escorting some people into our home. There were six of them, all heavily bundled up in thick cloaks, even though it was fall and the nights were still pleasant. I had no idea who they were.

My mother, who also had come into the room, surveyed the little band with a hopeful glance. But after determining that they were strangers, for their dress and behavior did seem very strange, she motioned to me to come over to the hearth and help her make the fire. The strangers would surely be hungry. They would need beds to sleep in, if they were planning on spending the —

"Mama!"

My mother froze. When she finally spoke, the word caught in her throat. "Manel?"

The next moment Manel was hugging her and tears were flowing down her cheeks. But there was no time for us to shower Manel with our hugs and kisses. A young woman nearly fainted, and Manel rushed to her side and helped her to sit down.

"This is my wife, Beatriz," Manel said to us as he gently helped the young woman remove her cloak. My mother sat down beside her and took Beatriz's hand in her own.

Beatriz. So that was her name. How many times I had tried to envision Manel's bride and guess her name. It was a nice name, and she had a nice face. But when I smiled at her and looked into

230

her eyes, I became frightened. It was as if she did not see me. It was as if she did not see anything.

"Is she blind?" I whispered to Manel.

"No. She is very, very frightened."

I took my mother's place at Beatriz's side so that my mother could prepare the meal. I took her hand, as my mother had done, and let it rest gently in mine. Her hand trembled so that it felt like a little bird beating its wings against my fingers.

"Beatriz?" I whispered softly. "I am Anna."

At first she did not respond. Then she slowly turned her head. She looked at me, but she did not see me. "Anna?" she whispered weakly.

"Yes, Anna. Manel's sister."

Her hand continued to tremble. Then a terrible sob suddenly escaped from her lips. Tears flowed from her eyes, and she jerked her hand away from mine to cover her face. And this was a good sign. Her terrified soul had returned to her frail body.

Of course we wanted to know what had brought Manel and Beatriz to our home and we were curious about the others — a company that included another young married couple and two young men.

"We will talk later," Manel whispered, "after Beatriz and her cousin have gone to sleep."

When the two young women were comfortably settled in my room, I returned downstairs, where the others had gathered around the large table. One of the men looked up at me with hatred — or perhaps it was just fear — in his eyes.

"Go upstairs," he snapped.

"She is my sister," Manel replied.

"Go upstairs!"

"She can be trusted," Manel insisted.

"Manel," said my father, "perhaps it is best if Anna does not know."

"Papa!" I cried out. "Mama?"

"We are wasting time. None of us can be trusted," said another member of this strange company with a bitterness that seemed too old for his young years. "No one knows who will be caught, who will break, who will betray."

With those words, the bitter young man took out a deck of cards and moved over to a corner of the room, where there stood a

231

little table and a bench that my mother and I used when we did our sewing. The husband of Beatriz's cousin joined him. However, the angry one strode over to the hearth and stared into the fire.

"Wine!" the angry one suddenly called out, and then he took out a long dagger and stirred up the flames with its tip. "Bring me wine! Or are all the vats in Catalonia as dry as a dead rat's throat?"

I saw my mother glance over at my father, and then my father cast his stern gaze upon my brother. "I am willing to give you and your friends a place of refuge, Manel. But I will not turn my home into a den for gamblers and drunkards."

"It is a show, Papa, to protect you," Manel said softly. "If officers come here, you must tell them that we are bandits who forced our way into your home. You must give us over into their hands gladly, as you would the real gamblers and drunkards that we only pretend to be."

We glanced over at the young men. The angry one had joined his friends. The young man with the cards was dealing them out, and despite their exhaustion, they forced themselves to look engrossed in the game.

"I am sorry," said my father. "I apologize to all of you. Regina, please bring some wine for our guests."

The wine was served, along with some of my mother's hearty stew. Then we could finally sit quietly with Manel. His face looked so pale. Dark circles rimmed his eyes, which were red from lack of sleep. It was so clear that something terrible must have happened. But Manel was silent. And he just looked down at the food that my mother had placed before him without tasting it.

"We are your family, Manel," my father said quietly. "You may tell us everything."

Manel raised his eyes and looked at us with an expression that was very sad. "Forgive me for coming here, Papa, and putting all of you in danger. But I am in trouble, serious trouble, and I do not know where else to turn."

After that brief introduction, this is what he told us, from the beginning to the end.

Saragossa was full of wonders, as befitting the capital city of a prosperous kingdom like Aragon. Its squares were lined with beautiful houses. Its markets were filled with the bounty of the local produce and delicacies from faraway places. There was no lack of fine clothes and furniture either, for the craftsmen were eager to please their wealthy customers, who were more than willing to lavish their extensive fortunes on luxuries.

In such an atmosphere of abundant wealth and ease, it was perhaps not surprising that religious piety was in scarce supply. For Old and New Christians alike, ignoring religious teachings was considered a virtue, and dedicating one's life to the enjoyment of pleasure was considered a mark of distinction.

Although many Conversos embraced this life with all their hearts, there were others who took advantage of the city's permissive culture to practice the rites of their former faith. They did not openly gather in synagogues, of course. Everything had to be done in secret. But because the upper classes held all religions in low regard, no one cared if, for sentimental reasons, someone performed his family's ancient rites. And so secrecy was observed, but the secret was carelessly guarded.

Manel had been in the city only a few days when a prosperous Converso invited him to his home for a meal. While he feasted his eyes upon the rich furnishings, a servant held before him a silver cup and laver so that he could wash his hands. Frightened, for this ritual of washing the hands before eating bread was in accordance with Jewish law, and so forbidden, Manel glanced over at this host. The wealthy man smiled, and in that moment Manel discovered the openly undisguised truth: Manel's benefactor was a secret Jew.

The Esperandeu home, for that was the name of the family, was a little island of goodness and purity in that worldly city. The wealthy merchant was so pleased with Manel that he offered his only daughter, Beatriz, in marriage, and Manel gratefully accepted the proposal. Introductions to other wealthy and important families who were secret Jews — the Sanchez family and the Santangels, to name just a few — soon followed. And so before long Manel found himself happily married and part of a congenial, well-connected community.

The New Inquisition changed everything. Prominent members of the Esperandeu family were among the first to be arrested. The Sanchez and Santangel families were not spared either. Panic about the present mingled with fear of the future. Then came the first auto-da-fe, the first burnings at the stake. Something had to be done, quickly, to stop this beast before it devoured their loved ones and destroyed them entirely.

Manel did not know who first uttered the word, for he was not a member of that clandestine group who met in a hushed chamber not far from where the flames of the funeral pyre were still smoldering. But the word was said, and once it was said there was no turning back, for to say it — and to hear it — was a crime as severe as the actual doing of it.

"Assassinate..."

Ssshh! No need to say more. Everyone understood. Assassinate Saragossa's Inquisitor. Assassinate Pedro Arbues.

A desperate plan, you say? Remember, these were desperate times. And the plotters were not alone. There were many Old Christians who hated the Inquisition as much as the Conversos. They gave their word that they would help. After the post of Inquisitor became "vacant," they would sound the alarum and arouse the common folk. The mob, whipped up to a heated frenzy, would fill the streets with their shouts for blood and rebellion. By the time the roaring crowd arrived at the court's door, the frightened flock of secretaries and wardens and interrogators would be on their knees, begging for mercy. And they would find it, for the citizens of Saragossa would let the Inquisition's henchmen flee. They would let them run all the way back to Castile, to deliver a message to the crown and the church from the angry, defiant people: Leave Saragossa alone!

Armed with this support, the conspirators calmly set about their work — for this was to be no hastily devised plot spoiled by rash decisions and avoidable mistakes. With everything to lose, they could not fail. Everything must be planned, down to the smallest detail.

Assassins were found. Joan Esperandeu, whose father had been arrested by the Inquisition, had volunteered for the task of finding them and he fulfilled his duties with filial devotion. The Inquisitor's movements were carefully studied, until his daily rituals were as well known to the conspirators as their own. In short, everything was prepared. All that was needed was the right moment to strike.

In the spring of 1485 the assassins were summoned. They quietly made their way to the Inquisitor's house. The signal was given. They waited. When the signal was not returned, they realized that something had gone wrong and slipped away as quietly as they had come.

The months passed.

The cool breezes of September brought relief from the summer's heat, but not from the fear. There were more arrests. Another auto-da-fe. Nerves were taut. The tension was becoming unbearable. So far the secret had been kept, but for how much longer?

The assassins were summoned again. This time they were instructed to go to the cathedral. There they would find Inquisitor Pedro Arbues kneeling in prayer.

A blow to the neck, the side, the arm, and the deed was done. The Inquisitor fell, the assassins fled, and then...

The bitter young man threw his cards down on the table. "You win, Sanchez," he said to the young man who was married to Beatriz's cousin.

"To know how to pass is to know how to play," the man called Sanchez replied grimly.

"Too bad Joan Esperandeu is not a card player," said the angry one, as he glanced over at Manel with an angry look. "Even a country fool knows not to spill blood in a cathedral!"

"Yes, he should have waited," said Manel. "But what is done is done."

"And because of what your cousin did, we are all as good as dead," said the angry one. "All of us!"

We did not understand. A crime had been committed. But what did it have to do with Manel and his friends? And what about the uprising that the Old Christians had promised to start? What had happened with that?

The angry one laughed. "Yes, Manel, tell your family about Joan's friends."

"That was not Esperandeu's fault," said Sanchez. "We all boasted of our connections. Your family was no different."

"We are wasting time." The bitter one shuffled the cards and dealt out a second hand.

Despite their great caution, in the end the conspirators miscalculated. Badly. For the common people, the cathedral was a sacred place, and prayer was a sacred time. To violate them both with an act of bloodshed was an outrage, an insult to everything that was holy. And so, as the news spread, an angry mob did assemble. But instead of protesting the excesses of the Inquisition, the crowd ran though the streets shouting, "Burn the Conversos!"

This tactical mistake was compounded by one that was even more severe. Far from being cowed by the murder of one of his Inquisitors — especially since the mob was on the church's side — King Ferdinand made it known that he expected justice to be done or the city councilors would pay. To drive home his point, the outraged monarch lost no time in sending a new Inquisitor to Saragossa.

Pressured thus by both the king and the mob, the Old Christians' resistance to the Inquisition crumbled. Large rewards were offered to those who came forward with information about the plot. Excommunication was threatened for those who did not. The people acted accordingly. The names of the conspirators became known: Esperandeu. Santangel. Sanchez. Moras. Almazen. Santa Cruz. Perez. Ram. Manas. The list went on and on. There was hardly a powerful Converso family in Saragossa who was not supposedly involved. When the officers came to make their arrests, however, they were disappointed. The conspirators directly involved in the plot had fled.

The people were reminded that a reward of five hundred ducats was waiting for whoever helped the authorities bring the criminals to justice. Thus encouraged, more people came forward and new testimony was given. Close relatives of the conspirators were dragged to the interrogation cells. As the weeks passed and the confessions piled up, even cousins three times removed had become implicated in the plot.

Esperandeu. Santangel. Sanchez. Moras. Almazen. Santa Cruz. Perez. Ram. Manas. Names that had once been considered a great honor to bear now only entitled their owners to arrest, torture, and even death. And so whoever could — old and young alike — fled.

Manel wanted to flee, too. But Beatriz, who had never strayed far from her father's house, was afraid to go. Joan Esperandeu was a distant cousin, she said to Manel, trying to calm her own fears as much as his. Surely the Inquisition would understand that they were innocent.

And so they stayed. Then one night there was a loud knock at the door. Beatriz's mother and father were arrested.

Manel and Beatriz escaped that night. They had been warned to keep their traveling party small, and so at first their number was only four: Manel, Beatriz, her cousin Nuria, and Nuria's husband, Luis Sanchez. At the last minute two brothers from the Santangel family — Martin, the angry one, and Gabriel, the bitter one — asked to join them. Their parents had already fled, with their younger sisters. They were afraid to remain in Saragossa.

And so they set out, with the Santangel brothers impatiently leading the way. Their original plan was to ride north, straight to the border. However, all the roads leading to the Pyrenees were heavily guarded. It was Manel who suggested that they take the long way to the border and first travel east, to Girona. The journey from Saragossa to Girona took them four nerve-racking days, but the ruse was successful.

"And from here you hope to escape across the Pyrenees?" asked my father.

"Yes," Manel replied.

"But the roads north of Girona may be guarded as well."

"What else can we do?"

"You can do as the prophet Isaiah suggests. 'Hide for a little while, until the rage passes.' "

"We cannot remain in Girona and put the community in danger."

"I agree, but there may be someplace else to hide."

"Where?"

"I will tell you more in the morning. For now, you must all get some sleep."

"Sleep?" Martin, the angry one, had been listening to our conversation, along with the other young men, and now he came over to where we were sitting. "I did not flee Saragossa to wait in this hovel until the king's officers come to arrest us. You mean to betray us, to save your own lives."

"He is tired, Papa," Manel said hurriedly. "Please do not pay attention to what he says."

"No one is being forced to stay here against his will," my father said to Martin. "But the border is far away. You will not reach it before dawn."

"I am willing to take a chance."

"So am I," said Gabriel. "We have eaten. The women have rested. We are wasting time."

"Do not be fools," my father said. "Do you really think I would betray my own son?"

Under ordinary circumstances, we would not have minded if Martin and his brother left. But unbridled anger is a sign of weakness, as our Sages have taught us. Since all our fates were now bundled together in one uneasy sheaf, we knew it was best to keep the brothers under my father's watchful eye.

In the end, sheer exhaustion, that most eloquent of persuaders, accomplished what my father's arguments could not. While Manel and his companions slept, my parents and I kept watch. I must have dozed sometime during that anxious night, for I was suddenly awakened by a woman's cry.

It was Beatriz. I rushed to her side. She was staring vacantly into a place that I never wanted to see with my own eyes.

"The fires," she whispered hoarsely.

I wanted to calm her down, but as I clasped her cold hand her terror became my own. I am also an accomplice, I realized with horror. As I stared into the darkness, I saw a city square emerge from the shadows. I heard the jeers of the crowd. And then I saw it. A body, small and delicate, writhing in agony in the —

"Do not think about it, Anna," I heard another voice say. It was Nuria. "We must be strong. We must have faith that G-d will help us get to safety. We must have faith in His kindness."

When I heard these words, I was ashamed. It was I who should have been comforting them. Yet there I sat, too frightened to say a word.

The next day my father gathered all of us around the table and told us his plan. In Girona there was an Old Christian of noble birth who owned some land in the Catalan countryside. Long ago tenant farmers had worked the fields, but the Great Plague had taken their lives. Since the land was situated far from the king's roads, and because it was rumored that the ghosts of those farmers sometimes visited the place, no one had wanted to settle there. And so the village was still deserted.

Once, my father did this nobleman a very great kindness. Wishing to repay the debt, the man had offered to give the village and its lands to my father. There, in the forgotten hills of the Catalan countryside, our family and a few close friends could live our lives in peace, far away from the church and Girona's angry mobs.

My father declined the offer. He would not desert Girona's Jewish community and leave its people to fight their spiritual battles alone. But that was yesterday. Today we were as dangerous to others as if we were infected by the plague. We had to leave before anyone in the community knew about Manel's visit, or guessed the reason for our sudden departure. And so early that morning my father paid a visit to his noble friend. If we wished it, horses and a guide would be waiting for us that very night.

"But how long will we stay there?" asked Luis Sanchez, glancing nervously at his wife. "We are townspeople, not farmers. How will we live?"

"My advice is that we remain in the village for two or three months, until the worst of the wrath has passed. As for supplies, my friend has promised to be the faithful ambassador of the One Above and provide us with our needs during this short time."

"But can he be trusted, Papa?" Manel asked the question politely before Martin could put it to my father in his brusque way.

"If his intent is to betray us, we will discover it tonight. Once he helps us flee, he becomes the same as us, an accomplice to the crime."

Even Martin and Gabriel agreed to my father's plan. I believe they were all so exhausted and wracked by fear that they would have agreed to any plan my father suggested. And so my mother and I went to work, packing a few belongings and preparing food for the journey.

There was no time to say farewell to my favorite corner in the courtyard, the place where a worn stone bench sat underneath the branches of an almond tree. There was no time to think about how I would never again sit in its shade and share secrets with my friends. Nor would I ever again see the tree's white blossoms and gather up its fruits — a springtime reminder of those other almond trees that sat in courtyards in our beloved Jerusalem and dotted the hills of our longed-for Holy Land. No, there was no time to think upon the very thing that should have been foremost in my mind: like so many Jews before us, my family was once again going into exile.

After darkness had fallen and footsteps could no longer be heard in the street, I quietly accompanied my father to the synagogue. I held a small candle while he approached the Holy Ark and pushed aside its cover. Inside the ark was a Torah scroll that he had written with his own hand many years ago, in thanksgiving for when Manel was born. He had given the Torah scroll to the community on loan. Now it would come with us.

There was nothing more to do except lock the door of our little home one last time. Then we hurried to where the horses were waiting. I did not bother to look back as we rode past the city's gates. Girona was dark and dreaming, and I doubted that it would miss us.

The journey was not easy, since none of us were experienced horsemen. However, the One Above smoothed our way and removed all obstacles from our path. Toward morning, a few other fugitives joined us. They were members of the Sanchez family, and they had chosen an indirect route, as well. Not long after sunrise we all arrived at a small stream.

"It is not much further," our guide informed us.

The trees had become so numerous that their tangled branches blocked out the warming rays of the quickly rising sun. I shivered. It all looked so gloomy and forlorn. "It is good, the gloom," Manel whispered to me. "This place looks like a hidden garden that has not been disturbed for hundreds of years. No one will suspect that anyone lives here."

I tried to smile. But as we traveled further, I recalled my almond tree and I grew sad. And then our guide pointed to a few broken-down stone structures that were nearly hidden from view because the wild grass around them had grown so tall.

"This is the village," he said.

We stared. The guide, who was a simple man, saw our despair and tried to comfort us. "The grass has many uses. It can feed your horses. It can be bundled tightly and used for fuel."

"You are right, my friend," said my father. He turned to the rest of us and said, "The men will cut down the grass and clear some pathways. The women will make the structures inhabitable."

My father's words rallied our flagging spirits. By the end of our first week in Sant Joan Januz — for that is what we decided to call the village — the roofs had been repaired and the hearths rebuilt. And once a cheerful fire is glowing in the hearth, even the most humble room becomes a home.

After everyone had a place to live — a few more fugitives had found us, and our community had grown to almost twenty souls — my father turned his attention to the Torah scroll. It also needed a home. However, some objected to having a synagogue in the village. They said that if the synagogue was discovered, the Inquisitors would send everyone straight to the fires.

Others were on my father's side. They wanted to use these three months to prepare spiritually for their full return to the Jewish people. A synagogue would give them both comfort and a place to meet for instruction. And if our village was discovered, we would all be sent to the fires, in any case, because of the assassination.

In the end, we reached a compromise. We constructed a false wall in one of the structures so that the synagogue would be hidden from sight. My father and Manel carefully carved out a niche in the building's eastern wall to serve as the synagogue's ark. Then, with much singing and gladness, our Torah scroll was joyously escorted to its new home.

It was not an easy winter. Rain and cold were plentiful. Food was scarce. Many of us were afraid. We heard soldiers' voices in the howling winds. The pounding rain was mistaken for the sound of hoofbeats. Once someone thought they saw torches approaching and terrified us all.

The news brought by the nobleman's messenger, along with fresh supplies of flour and vegetables, was not good. Many fugitives had been caught and carried back to Saragossa. But there was good news as well. Some had made it across the border. All the Inquisition could do was burn their bodies in effigy.

The winter was coming to an end, and the wrath of the Inquisitors had not abated. They were determined to hunt down every last member of the accused families, no matter how long the hunt took. There was no longer a reason to remain in the village. We chose Rosh Chodesh Adar, two weeks before the holiday of Purim, for the day of our escape. This was the time of the new moon, when the dark night sky would cloak our movements. And was not Purim the holiday when, during the days of the First Exile of our people from Jerusalem, the Jewish people had received a miraculous salvation? Just as the Jews of that long-ago time had been delivered from annihilation, so did we hope that we would live to see a similar happy resolution to our people's present misfortunes.

Once again the nobleman came to our aid. He would send us a guide to take us over the mountains, to Navarre, which was an independent kingdom at that time and beyond the reach of the Inquisition. Our plan was to settle in the city of Tudela, where

241

there was a Jewish community. Spirits were high as we anticipated our freedom. We even joked that we would miss our little Sant Joan Januz.

And then disaster struck.

It started when Nuria said she did not feel well. Not long after she went to rest, Gabriel complained of a violent sore throat and a fever, and he, too, took to his bed. Several others also complained of strange aches and pains. Then Beatriz's face became flushed. A few hours later her body started to shake violently.

The guide came. He would not wait. A decision had to be made.

"Go," said Manel. "We will follow later, when everyone is well."

We did not want to leave, but Manel insisted. "This, too, is from G-d," he said quietly.

My father gave Manel the Torah scroll, which he had carefully wrapped for the journey. "Keep it,

Manel. And may it keep you."

"We will wait for you in Tudela," said my mother. "We will all be together for Passover. I know it."

Manel accompanied us part of the way as we rode toward the mountains. Then it was time to say good-bye. I would not cry. Not when everyone else was trying so hard to hold back their tears. Besides, we would see each other again — and soon. Passover was only six weeks away.

But then I cried out, "What if you cannot flee? How will we know that you are still alive?"

Manel reached down and plucked off a stem from a shrub that grew wild in the Catalan countryside.

"This will be our sign, Anna. When you receive a sprig of yellow broom from a messenger, you will know that I am alive. You will know that I still hope to be reunited with you and Papa and Mama, and with the Jewish people."

We reached Tudela safely. But we celebrated Passover alone. A few sprigs of yellow broom sat on our table, which was set for the traditional holiday meal. They were dry and the flowers had lost their bright color, but we treasured them all the same.

Tudela was a pleasant place, but we could not enjoy it. The news was too distressing. Joan Esperandeu was finally caught. His body was horribly mutilated before it was thrown into the fires. One of the assassins, a man by the name of Vidal Durango, suffered the same fate.

We also heard that King Ferdinand had requested permission from the king and queen of Navarre to enter their kingdom and hunt for the fugitives that had found refuge there. We did not wait to hear the royal couple's decision.

I did not ask my parents how Manel would ever find us again, after we left Tudela. If we were meant to be reunited, it would come to pass. When the One Above decrees a thing, no power on earth can prevent it.

And so my parents and I once again took up the staff of the exiled wanderer. Once again G-d was good to us. He led us to green pastures. We did not want. Our steps eventually took us to Salonika, where we were joined by other Jews who had been exiled from their homes in Catalonia, Aragon, Valencia, and Castile.

We never again heard from Manel. But does not our prophet Zechariah tell us, "Return to the stronghold, you prisoners of hope"?

And so I return to the pier every day. And even though I return home alone, I still have hope that our family will be reunited tomorrow — if not tomorrow in Salonika, then tomorrow in Jerusalem. For those who sow in tears will reap in gladness.

That is a promise.

The telephone rang. It was Clara, wondering where he was. Dinner was ready. They were waiting for him.

"I'm leaving now," Miquel told her.

But there was still one more page of the diary to look at. It wouldn't take long. It was just a crudely drawn map of the village. The map was useless, of course. Five hundred years was a long time. Those first structures were probably knocked down and replaced with better ones not long after the decision was made to stay in the village. Those, in turn, had either been torn down or added to as the village grew.

He supposed, though, that he couldn't blame the American for wanting to find the synagogue. In his younger years, he also would have been tempted by this sort of adventure. Then there was the question of what had happened to Manel. He could understand why the American would be intrigued by that, too.

243

He didn't know why Manel and Beatriz stayed in the village. Several members of the Esperandeu family did make it to Languedoc. Some still lived there, although most of them were full-fledged Christians. His family had also settled in Languedoc, but they kept the secret about their being "People of the Nation." They also kept their ties with Sant Joan Januz and a few other villages where descendents of the fugitive families had settled. That was why his family had spent the war years in Spain. They had been visiting relatives when France fell to the Germans in 1940. When forced to make a choice between the dictatorships of Franco and Hitler, they chose Franco. Sometimes those were your choices: bad or worse.

Perhaps that was why Manel stayed. As the group's leader, he felt he had to remain until everyone could escape. But there weren't any written records. They were too dangerous. According to the unofficial history of the village, the stories that were passed down orally from generation to generation, they made the right choice. The village was shielded by a special protection. The Inquisitors never found them.

It had to do with some words Manel had used to describe the village, how it was a *gan ganuz* — Hebrew words for "hidden garden." And that had something to do with the *ohr haganuz*, the great spiritual light that was seen during the six days of Creation and then hidden away until the day when the Messiah would finally come. When a person refrained from saying something that could harm another person, they were rewarded by seeing a glimpse of this light. That was what his parents had taught him. If Miquel kept their family's secrets, one day he would see this light.

Of course, his parents never would have told him about Saragossa. But in every generation there's someone who always has his nose in a book. In his generation, that person was his older brother, Manel. He was always reading about the history of this or the history of that. It was inevitable that one day he would read about the Inquisition and what happened in Saragossa and triumphantly announce at the dinner table, "We're related to a murderer!"

In France, it didn't matter. But then the family was back in Spain, and Esperandeu wasn't a common name. On the other hand, his mother's family name was Sanchez. That name was so common in Spain that it could never prove a connection with the murder, unless they knew that the mother of his French-speaking mother had been born in Sant Joan Januz. And so his family took the name Sanchez. One could do that in Spain, because people often kept their mother's family name.

But his mind was wandering. There was a point he wanted to make, but what was it?

It was something about the name. Just as the name gan ganuz was hidden within the name Sant Joan Januz, so too was the village hidden within the Catalan countryside. It was like the Hidden Light. As long as they were careful to hide their differences — to speak well of one another and stick together and strive for peace — they would merit to remain hidden from their enemies. They would have a safe haven. Until the Messiah came.

Or something like that. It had made sense to him when he was young. But after he found out about what happened to the Jews in World War II, he didn't believe there could ever be a place that was totally safe. He had kept up a pretense for the others. But behind his false wall there wasn't any synagogue. There was just a gaping hole.

"Why are you sitting in the dark, Grandpa?"

"And why didn't you knock, Vidal?" Miquel hoped his grandson didn't notice how startled he was by Vidal's voice. Or see him slide open the drawer and slip the diary inside it.

"I did, but you didn't answer. I'll turn on a light."

"I must have dozed off. Is your mother worried?"

"You know Mama. She's a Sanchez through and through."

"You'd better call her, to let her know I'm all right."

While Vidal was on the phone, Miquel slid the drawer shut. That was the problem, in a nutshell. They were Esperandeus and Sanchezes and Santangels through and through. Somehow he had to convince the American to destroy the original of that diary.

PART V: TERRA INCOGNITA

CHAPTER 24

Miquel barely tasted the vegetable soup that Clara had prepared for the family's dinner. His eyes kept wandering in the direction of the doorway that led to the hallway that led to the sewing room. He had to persuade the American to give him the original copy of the diary so he could destroy it. But what tactic would work best?

He could try to scare the American. The fact that the American's family lived in the United States didn't mean they were safe forever. Everything can change in the blink of an eye. On that point he and the Anna of the diary were in complete agreement. And today it was easier than ever to track people down thanks to computers and all that other new technology.

On the other hand, Jews never were very good at seeing danger coming, even when it was just around the corner. How could they be expected to take seriously a threat that was vague and only simmering beneath the surface of ordinary, everyday life? Maybe no one could.

"Is that all right with you, Grandpa?"

Miquel looked blankly at Vidal. He hadn't been following the family's conversation. He saw Josep give Clara a look. It was easy for Josep to feel superior. He sat in his workshop all day. He didn't carry the burden of the community on his shoulders. But he would show Josep that he could still outsmart them all.

"Why wouldn't it be all right?" There, now the ball was back in Vidal's court.

"You know how it is on the first day at a construction site. The road to the village will probably be a mess. I wanted you to know, in case you were planning to drive to the cooperative."

Ah, so that was Vidal was talking about. Vidal was going to start building that resort of his. "I don't see that Thursday will be a problem."

246

"Wednesday."

"That's what I meant to say. Just make sure the other people in the village know. If I were you, I'd put up a sign at Eduard Garcia's store."

"That's a good idea."

Miquel nodded his head, both to show that the topic was closed and that he was still in charge. "How's the American doing?" he asked Clara. "Is his ankle better?"

Josep gave Clara another look.

"He left for Barcelona this afternoon," said Clara.

"Clara mentioned it a few minutes ago," Josep added.

"Are you feeling all right, Papa?" asked Clara.

"I could be coming down with a cold," Miquel replied. If Clara was going to throw him a lifeline, he might as well grab it. "I was feeling tired all afternoon."

"It's the change in the seasons," said Clara.

"But what's this about the American? Why did he go to Barcelona?"

"He said he had a meeting there. And since there's some Jewish holiday in a few days — I think he said it was called Purim — he decided to stay in Barcelona."

"He's gone for good then?"

"No, he took just one bag. I told him I didn't mind if he left the rest of his things in the sewing room."

"You should have told him to pack up everything," said Vidal. He was still angry with the American for contacting the Department of Antiquities' branch office in Girona. Then the thought occurred to Vidal that the American's meeting in Barcelona might be with the department's main office. Perhaps the American had found something in the village after all.

"How did your search for the synagogue go, Grandpa?"

"Fine."

"I thought he said he hurt his ankle," said Clara.

"He did. That's why it was fine. We finished not long after we began."

"So he didn't find anything?" asked Vidal.

"What could he possibly have found?" Miquel hoped he didn't look troubled by the way the conversation was going. To his relief, Vidal let the subject drop and the conversation turned to something else.

247

A small army arrived in Sant Joan Januz on that Wednesday and proceeded to set up camp. After selecting a spot for an on-site office, the next order of business was to find a place to erect the large sign announcing the project. The sign had a full-color picture of what the resort would look like when completed, and it said, in gigantic letters, "Peaceland International Center for EuroIslam." Underneath that, in smaller letters, was written: "City of Sant Joan Januz. Girona Regional Council. Government of Catalonia."

It was an impressive-looking sign, but Vidal wasn't sure why the crew's foreman was investing so much time in finding a location for it. No one traveled on the rural road except the villagers and, now, the construction crew. In his opinion, it would have made more sense to put the sign someplace near the highway, where people could see it and then get on with the real work.

"It's for the groundbreaking ceremony," the foreman's assistant explained. "We don't want the sun to be in the eyes of the television crew when they film it. After the ceremony, we'll move the sign to a spot where it will be seen from the highway."

Vidal felt foolish for having asked the question. Of course, the public relations event had to be carefully planned. Jordi Martinez and Al, who were both coming to Sant Joan Januz for the ceremony, would expect everything to be perfect. Vidal was glad the foreman was on top of things — and that it was only a low-ranking assistant who had witnessed his blunder.

At least he could now sound knowledgeable when he explained the crew's actions to the villagers who had come by to see the work begin. It was a big day for the village, and a small crowd had gathered by the road.

"City of Sant Joan Januz," said Ferran Rodriguez, as he admired the sign. "Yesterday we were a village that was dying and today we're a city. That's quite an accomplishment, Vidal."

"Let's hope the Regional Council doesn't raise our taxes," said Eduard Garcia, and everyone laughed.

The assistant ran up to Vidal. "The foreman needs to speak with you, Mr. Bonet. He's in the office." The assistant ran off before Vidal could reply.

"We'd better get going and let you do your work," said Miquel, who had been standing with Pau and Biel and Eduard Garcia.

248

The little crowd took the hint. They said their good-byes to Vidal and began to disperse.

"Good luck," said Miquel.

"Thanks."

Everyone left, except Josep.

"I guess I'd better go see what he wants," said Vidal.

"Nervous?"

"A bit."

"You'll do fine. Just remember that a construction crew asks only two things of an executive director: Don't hit your head and don't fall into a hole."

"Thanks. I'll try to remember that."

Then it was Josep's turn to drive off, and Vidal went over to the caravan that served as the crew's office.

"We're going to start by demolishing that old farmhouse that's sitting on the property," said the foreman.

"Great."

"What do you want to do with the rubble? Salvage what's still usable or cart it all away?"

When Vidal didn't reply immediately, the foreman said, "It'll be faster if we dump it. But some people have a fondness for old stones and like to reuse them in new structures. It's up to you."

"Cart it away," said Vidal.

The assistant popped his head into the office. "The groundbreaking ceremony is rescheduled for tomorrow. I just got the call from Martinez's office. The Saudi investor has been delayed."

"Did the office give you a new time?" asked the foreman.

"Not yet."

"Tell the crew to get ready to demolish that structure."

The assistant left.

"I personally prefer to get all the showbiz over with on the first day," said the foreman. "But what can we do? It's the Saudis that are paying our salaries, and so we have to dance to their tune."

Vidal didn't say anything. It was true that Al's company was paying him his salary, but Al was also his friend. He didn't like the way the foreman had put himself and Vidal in the same category.

"We'll give you a call when we know the new time for the ceremony."

249

The foreman left and walked over to the abandoned farmhouse. Vidal knew he had just been given a not-so-subtle hint to leave the site and let the crew work in peace, but he lingered at the door to the office. Even without the groundbreaking ceremony, this was an important day for him. A year ago he had been a student in New York working on his business plan. Today he was about to see that plan be put into action. He didn't want this moment to just slip by, unmarked and unnoticed. He wanted to be aware of it: the color of the sky, the coolness of the breeze, the way he was feeling. He glanced down at his watch, the one he had bought in New York for a graduation present. To his surprise, the LED screen was blank. He took off the watch and shook it a few times, but apparently the battery had died.

All right, these things happen. There was no need to feel uneasy about a dead watch. He shifted his glance instead to the abandoned farmhouse. It was no accident that his grandfather had given him this particular tract of land. No one had wanted to live in that house or farm this land, at least not for as long as he could remember.

The village's children had believed that the building was haunted. He couldn't remember where they had gotten that idea from. Perhaps it had come from his Grandpa Miquel. At any rate, someone had told them that the ghosts of the people who had once lived in the farmhouse still came to visit their former home from time to time. Being children, they naturally wanted to see a real ghost. That desire would lead them as far as the road's edge. A few of the braver children would even walk across the field. But as soon as they heard a noise — even if it was just the noise of their own feet snapping a small branch into two — they would run as fast as they could back to civilization. No one had dared to go inside the farmhouse. That was why he watched with fascination as the foreman and the workers went in and out of it. Since they didn't know the story about it being haunted, they weren't afraid.

Vidal felt a twinge of envy. He also wanted to go into the building, like them, without any fears. But he recalled the foreman's hint and his father's words, and he knew that the best thing for him to do was keep out of the way. At any rate, the moment was gone. The foreman and the workers came out of the building, and the assistant called for everyone to stand clear.

A bulldozer and an excavator pulled up alongside the farmhouse and got into position. The excavator slowly raised its arm. Vidal thought it looked like a salute, a kind of farewell gesture to the building about to be demolished. He smiled when he saw it. Soon there would be one less haunted house in Sant Joan Januz.

He waited, expectantly, to hear the crash. Instead, a man shouted. The foreman and his assistant ran inside the building. The excavator's driver looked over at the bulldozer's driver. The driver of the bulldozer shrugged. After a few long minutes, the foreman's assistant came out of the building and ran over to Vidal.

"The foreman would like to speak with you."

"Is something wrong?"

"That depends on you."

As Vidal walked over to the farmhouse, he recalled the old adage "Be careful what you ask for." He assured himself that he wasn't afraid to enter the building. He wasn't a child anymore. Yet as he stepped across the threshold and gazed inside the dark, cavernous room, a shiver went up and down his spine.

It took a few moments for his eyes to adjust to the gloom. When they did, he saw that the room was empty. Only a large hearth bore witness to the fact that the farmhouse had once been filled with life. Its blackened walls, which were heavily caked with soot, were a remembrance of the countless meals that had been cooked over its open fires.

"It's through there," said the assistant, who pointed to a doorway at the northern end of the room.

The door had disappeared long ago, and so Vidal could see into the room beyond. He suddenly had a memory of his visit to his brother's studio. In a painting he had seen there, a long and slender boat was sailing in a sea of gray clouds toward a patch of light that appeared to be some sort of doorway to a tunnel in the sky. That tunnel, in turn, led to another shadowy doorway. Where that doorway led, he didn't know.

"Terra Incognita," he whispered as he walked toward the doorway in the abandoned farmhouse. That was the name he would have given to Arnau's painting. It was the name that medieval cartographers used when they knew there was something beyond their known world, but they didn't know what. The irony, of course, was that large parts of their maps of the "known" world were as inaccurate as their depiction of this "unknown land." But that couldn't be avoided, Vidal supposed, as long as there were doorways and rooms behind those doorways that hadn't yet been explored. The real problem was what to do once the error on the map was discovered.

The second room was smaller. The foreman was standing in front of the room's hearth, quietly talking to one of the workers. When Vidal entered, they both turned to look at him.

"Do you know anything about the history of this building?" the foreman asked Vidal.

"Only that it's very old. Why?"

"Enric, show Mr. Bonet what you showed me," the foreman told the worker.

Enric stepped into the large hearth as though he was stepping onto a darkened stage. "One, two, three!" he called out.

A rectangular patch of dim light suddenly filtered into the hearth through its back wall. Then, just as quickly, the light disappeared.

Enric had vanished.

The foreman glanced over at Vidal, who was staring into the darkness. "It's a false wall," said the foreman. "Come and see."

He stepped into the hearth and pressed down on one of the stones in the back wall. A door swung open. The foreman passed through the opening, and Vidal followed. On the other side of the hearth was a long, narrow, windowless room. Light came in through a hole in the roof, where the tiles had blown off.

"Clever, isn't it?" said Enric. "It's like fighting fire with fire, if you get my drift, Mr. Bonet."

"No, I don't."

"It's as though they were thumbing their noses at the Inquisition, hiding their synagogue behind the fires of the hearth. Of course, the fire wouldn't have been blazing away when they snuck in here to say their prayers. In fact, they probably didn't use this hearth that often. You can tell by the layer of soot. There is much less here than in the hearth in the main room. They probably built this hearth just to hide their synagogue. It's much cleverer than hiding the doorway behind a bookcase."

"How can you be so sure this is a synagogue? Maybe this is where they hid their valuables."

"Look over here." Enric went over to the room's eastern wall. A wood door, about four feet tall and two feet wide and rotting away from damp and neglect, signaled that there was some sort of storage space behind it. Enric carefully opened the door and held on to it so that it wouldn't fall off its hinges.

"See this niche that has been carved into the wall?" Enric said to Vidal. "It's empty now, but that's where they put their Torah scroll."

Vidal stared into the empty space. "How do you know?"

"I'm a bit of a history buff. I know something about these things. I had a hunch we would find a synagogue out here once I discovered that there's no Catholic saint named Joan Januz. And when I saw two hearths in what's only a simple, country farmhouse — which is not at all common in these parts — I said to myself, 'Enric, there is definitely something fishy about this village.' "

"Thank you, Enric, that will be all," said the foreman.

"No offense intended, Mr. Bonet. I personally don't care if a person is a New Christian or an Old one, as long as he has a good heart."

Enric left. After the door swung back into place, the foreman turned to Vidal and said, "You have to make a decision."

"About what?"

"Whether or not to notify the Department of Antiquities."

"Don't I have to? Isn't that the law?"

The foreman didn't reply.

"You mean some people don't say anything?"

"Let me know what you decide."

The foreman "disappeared," and Vidal was left alone. He knew what he should do. He should phone Tomas Domenech. The Antiquities man would be delighted to hear the news. So would the American.

But where would that leave him? It would have been one thing if the synagogue had been discovered in another part of the village, but the location of this farmhouse couldn't be worse. It was right in the middle of the construction site for his resort. The entire site would be cordoned off for months while the archeologists were digging around, looking for the missing Torah scroll or who knew what. Al and his father wouldn't be happy about another long delay. They might even decide to cancel the project. And for what?

253

Vidal glanced around the room. There wasn't anything special about it. It wasn't as if there were murals or sculptures in it, or anything else that had artistic value. It was just an empty room where some Jewish people had once gathered to say their prayers. How many people in the world would care about that? Certainly no one in the village would. They didn't even go to church.

The muscles in his throat began to tighten. Yet there was absolutely no reason to panic. New Christians, Old Christians — that was all a thing of the past. And hadn't the American — the Jewish American! — given him a perfectly logical explanation for the existence of a synagogue in the village? The villagers had given temporary refuge to the American's Jewish ancestors. That was the reason. Case closed. So who cared if people like Enric — people who too quickly jumped to erroneous conclusions — were whispering behind his back?

His eyes darted about the room, which had become oppressively narrow. All right, so maybe Enric was right. He and his family were New Christians. That would explain the village's funny customs. And the whispers and looks that some of the other farmers in the region gave them when they had business to do at the agricultural cooperative. When he had been young, his grandfather had let him accompany him in the truck. That stopped once Vidal was old enough to notice the whispers and ask about them.

His grandfather hadn't been able to stop him from hearing the whispers when he went off to the regional school. But he knew how to fight. When a classmate called him a dirty Jew, he pummeled the boy's face until it was covered with blood. That was the last time anyone taunted him with that name.

But the farmers, and their children, were country folk. Prejudice thrived in isolated places. Everyone knew that. Things were different elsewhere. In places like Barcelona, or even Girona, who would care?

There had been an incident when he was a university student in Girona. Another student — he had been from Montblanc, a town in the wine country south of Barcelona — had defended some action of the Israeli army, saying that the Jews had a right to defend themselves against people who wanted to kill them. The professor had responded by asking if the student ate pork or if pork gave him a stomachache. All the other students had laughed.

254

Everyone knew that Montblanc — the wine country — was filled with New Christians. For months afterward people continued to whisper and laugh and point out the ostracized student, some more openly than others.

But that was school. Students, even professors, could be immature. In the real world — the business world — who cared? No one cared about what a person believed or didn't believe. Certainly Al wouldn't care if he was from a New Christian family. Al and his father probably wouldn't even have to find out, unless someone told them. And even if the Saudis did find out, what did it matter if his ancestors had been Jewish? Surely what mattered was that the person was intelligent and hardworking and a man of principle. Honesty, integrity — those were the qualities that mattered.

But if that was the case, he would have to call Tomas Domenech. There was a law about not destroying historical sites. Only the Department of Antiquities could decide if this room was worth preserving or not. That was his answer then. He was out of the tunnel.

Then the secret door swung open, and Jordi Martinez stepped into the room.

"Sorry for intruding into your monk's cell, Brother Vidal," said Martinez. "I hope I didn't disturb you while you were at prayer."

"I thought you weren't coming today."

"Surprise visits keep the crew on its toes."

"That's the evidence," said the foreman. As he led Martinez over to the niche. "And the false wall."

"Well, well, well. This is an interesting development." Martinez turned away from the niche in the wall and began to slowly circle around the room, as though he was in deep thought. When he came to false wall, he stopped abruptly and asked, "And what if this is a hidden synagogue?"

"This farmhouse becomes a historical site," the foreman replied.

"A historical site...a historical site..." Martinez continued to pace. When he next stopped, it was in front of Vidal.

"Is that what you want, Vidal? A historical site? Before you answer, let me explain to you what a historical site means. It means that instead of having an internationally renowned resort in your village that will generate millions of euros every year, your village will become a fifteen-minute stopover on a 'Jewish Roots' tour, and you'll be the manager of a kiosk that sells postcards and cold drinks. That's what a historical site in a small village means. But it's your property, so it's your decision. Here's my cell phone. I've already punched in the number for the Department of Antiquities. All you have to do is press 'Call.' "

Vidal looked down at the cell phone. Its blue screen, glowing faintly in the dim light, also looked like the illuminated doorway in Arnau's painting. It was amazing, really, how many doorways and tunnels there were in the world when one knew how to look for them. But this wasn't the time for philosophizing. He had a decision to make.

Vidal looked at the foreman. The man had turned away and was intently studying some stones in the wall. A glance at Martinez revealed the politician staring up at the hole in the ceiling in apparent commune with the cosmos. He, too, could look away, he realized.

And so he did.

Martinez slipped the phone back into his pocket. Then he told the foreman to call for Enric, who quickly entered the room.

"I hear you are an amateur historian."

"That's right, Mr. Martinez."

"On this job you're being paid to be a construction worker. Understand?" Martinez took out of his wallet a fat wad of bills and stuffed them into Enric's shirt pocket. He strode out of the room, and the foreman followed.

"But...I don't understand," Enric said to Vidal.

"Out of the building, everybody!" they heard the assistant shouting outside. "Stand clear! Everybody, get out of the way!"

"We'd better get out of here," said Vidal, and he pushed the worker toward the secret door.

It didn't take long to demolish the building. The driver of the excavator had obviously done this type of work before. The long metal arm rammed into the building's eastern wall, and the building gave a shudder. With the second punch several stones became dislodged and tumbled to the ground. After the third hit, a large section of the wall gave way. Tiles flew from the roof like a flock of birds, Vidal noted. But they didn't sing.

And when they fell to the earth, it was with a thud. Vidal also noted that Martinez seemed to take pleasure in watching it all. Enric, on the other hand, looked like he was going to cry.

When all the walls had been demolished, the driver of the bulldozer deftly scooped up the rubble and tossed it into the back of a truck. The truck drove off toward the highway, and the area's dump. Martinez got into his car and drove away.

Vidal knew that he should leave the site, too. He didn't want the crew to think that he had nothing better to do than watch them work. But he couldn't leave. Not just yet.

He stared at the vacant space where the building had stood. Already a butterfly was flitting about the site. Then two birds — real birds, this time — swooped down and pecked at the earth. A moment later they were joined by a few others. It was as if the building had never existed.

He wanted to leave. He really did. But he couldn't, not when a voice was screaming inside him, "Where are you?"

CHAPTER 25

Vidal didn't say anything to his family about the destroyed synagogue. Instead, the main topic of conversation at the dinner table was the upcoming press conference, since it wasn't every day that television crews came to the village. Naturally the family had ambivalent feelings about such attention, but Vidal did his best to convince them that the attention would be on the resort and not the village.

"You'll have to take a backseat tomorrow, Grandpa," Vidal promised. "Martinez is too much of a politician to let anyone steal the limelight from him." To Vidal's relief, his grandfather laughed.

The next afternoon they all went out to the construction site, which had been spruced up for the occasion by the Girona Regional Council's public relations office. Flags had been placed along the road from the highway to the village so that the invited guests would be able to find their way. A neat row of matching folding chairs sat underneath the big sign. Opposite them were more matching chairs for the press and guests. The area where the ground was to be symbolically broken had been cordoned off with a festive banner of streamers that flapped happily in the breeze. The brand new shovel was ready and waiting. The sun was sitting off to the side, where it wouldn't shine in anyone's eyes.

The television crews arrived and began to set up their equipment. Jordi Martinez drove up a few minutes later, accompanied by a few other politicians and a battery of assistants. Vidal was surprised to see that Arnau and Joanna had also come, along with Manel. But then he remembered that it was Manel's birthday, and the family was going to have a special dinner afterward.

The only thing missing was Al. After some telephoning back and forth, a black limousine finally came lumbering down the dirt road. Al jumped out of the car, cell phone in hand, even before the limousine came to a complete stop. He was still talking on the phone while he shook hands with the politicians. When he saw

Vidal, he gave his former roommate a hug and whispered, as he nodded to his cell phone, "Ecuador. Amazing."

They took their seats under the sign. Vidal didn't have to make a speech; that honor was reserved for the politicians. All he had to do was hand the shovel to Martinez and pose for a picture. First, though, the politicians had to talk. A high-ranking official from the Girona Regional Council gave the welcoming remarks. Vidal saw one of the journalists yawn. The official was followed by a minister from Barcelona. Then it was Jordi Martinez's turn to speak.

Martinez was clearly in his element as he spoke about his vision for the resort. They were going to bring prosperity to Catalonia and peace to the world. They were going to provide a showcase for local artistic talent, like Arnau Bonet — and Martinez asked Arnau to stand up and enjoy two seconds of TV time. They were going to build multinational bridges between dynamic young entrepreneurs like Catalonia's Vidal Bonet — and here Vidal felt the lenses of the TV cameras on him, before they moved on to "their esteemed investment partner from Saudi Arabia." Al was invited to say a few words, which he did, in his usual charming way. Then it was time to go over to the shovel for the next round of photographs. But before they did, Martinez asked if there were questions.

"I have one, Mr. Martinez."

For a moment, Jordi Martinez looked surprised. His call for questions had been a formality. He hadn't expected anyone to take him up on it. Vidal noted that the journalist who had the question was the same one who had yawned during the speeches.

"Yes, Mr. — I don't believe I know you."

"Jeremy Fisher, Associated Press. I understand that a medieval synagogue was destroyed here yesterday and you bribed one of the workers to keep quiet. Would you care to comment?"

The world suddenly became very quiet. Even Al stopped whispering into his cell phone.

"Are you new to Catalonia, Mr. Fisher?" asked Martinez.

"I arrived last week."

"That explains it. The Catalan accent can be tricky. You must have misunderstood your source. Now, ladies and gentlemen, let's move on to the next photo op."

A public relations assistant showed Vidal where to stand and how to hold the shovel. He felt like a fool. It didn't help that Martinez was seething with anger under his false show of enthusiasm. The mood went from bad to worse when Al refused to participate in the photo op, citing a sudden allergic reaction to too much publicity. The politicians from Girona and Barcelona had already quietly slipped away. That left only Vidal and

Martinez to pose with the shovel. For a moment, Vidal thought Martinez was going to hit him on the head with it.

The press got their photos, and then they packed up their equipment and left. The chairs were folded and loaded onto the back of the van, along with the streamers, the flags, the cold drinks, and the shovel. Then the public relations people were also gone.

Vidal saw Martinez talking to the foreman, who was nodding his head. Al was already in his car and, as usual, talking on his cell phone. Vidal went over to him, and Al snapped shut his phone.

"What's up, Vidal?"

"Can I invite you to have dinner with my family? They'd really like to meet you."

"I'd love to, but I have to get back to my hotel and do some work. How about lunch tomorrow, in Barcelona?"

"Great. Just let me know when and where."

"I will."

"And, Al, about that synagogue..."

"I don't want to know about it."

The limousine drove off. Martinez came up to Vidal and watched Al's car disappear down the road.

"Don't take any calls from the press until I've straightened this thing out," Martinez told him. Then he, too, was gone.

As Vidal drove home, his mind felt gray and empty. He supposed Joanna would make some snide comment about the fiasco that had just happened, but he hoped the others wouldn't ask too many questions.

The birthday party was in progress when he arrived. Josep had set up the barbecue in the backyard, and he was grilling the chicken cutlets. Clara and Joanna were preparing the salads. Above the patio Miquel had strung up a homemade banner that said, "Happy Birthday, Manel!" Manel was now at an age when he could remember something like that.

The guest of honor was busy with one of his presents, a digital camera for young children. It turned out to be the perfect gift. Manel called his own press conference and, with Arnau's help, photographed Miquel and the great-uncles while they answered his questions and made speeches.

As Vidal watched the scene, still unnoticed, he wondered if it wouldn't be better if he turned around and left. He didn't want to spoil the party. Then his mother saw him, and he had no choice except to join them.

The meal was devoted to Manel, who clearly enjoyed being the center of attention. He regaled them with the latest jokes from his preschool and shared his wisdom about the best places to play in Girona. His eyes were starting to close, though, by the time the birthday cake was served. And so while the rest of the family lingered over their cake and coffee, Manel went over to the chaise lounge and fell asleep.

At first no one spoke. No one even bothered to turn on a light, though the sun had already set and the trees bordering the yard were draped in shadowy darkness. When the silence became too uncomfortable, Miquel cleared his throat and said, "So, Vidal, do you want to tell us about that synagogue?"

Vidal didn't want to. But he knew he had to offer an explanation for what he had done, and so he said, "One of the workers found a false wall in that old farmhouse that was on the property. It led to a room that he claimed was a synagogue. But that was just his opinion. There wasn't anything in the room, no murals or inscriptions. It was just an empty room. So I gave the crew the okay to demolish the building."

"Are you sure there wasn't anything in the room? If that worker went to the press, he must have felt pretty confident about what he saw."

"There was a niche carved into one of the walls. He said that was where the Jews kept their Torah scroll. But in my opinion, that room could have been used for a lot of things. The niche could have been where they locked up their money, for all we know. It was an empty room."

"But why didn't you contact the Department of Antiquities?" asked Clara.

"Once you start with these government offices, there's no end to the red tape," said Joanna. "They're always asking for financial information."

Arnau coughed.

"Of course, they have to," Joanna continued, glancing quickly at Arnau. "They need to know how many people visit a historical site for their statistics. But it can be annoying. They always phone up at your busiest time."

Vidal glanced from Joanna to Arnau and then back to Joanna. He wondered why she was defending him.

"That's not a reason to destroy a place that's of historical importance," Clara protested. "Why did you do it, Vidal? You're not an expert in these things. Why did you give them permission?"

Vidal looked at his mother with surprise. He was used to his grandfather demanding explanations, but not her.

"Well?"

Things change. The words jangled in his head.

"Answer me."

"I'll tell you why he destroyed it," said Miquel. "He destroyed it because he didn't want people to know that we're descended from Jews. I would have done the same thing, if I had been in his place."

Josep set his coffee cup down on the table with a crash. "This is no time for another one of your ridiculous theories! No one knows who built that synagogue, or when. It could have been built a hundred years before our ancestors came to Sant Joan Januz."

"You're wrong, Josep, on both counts. The synagogue was built by our ancestors, and there is someone who knows it. Your houseguest has a diary that dates back to the Inquisition and explains the whole story. I read it the day we went to my house to look for the synagogue."

There was another silence.

"It doesn't matter," said Joanna. "The newspapers can say what they like. We're not Jews."

"But this does matter," said Clara. "Vidal destroyed a synagogue. Isn't that against the law? Won't he go to jail for what he's done?"

"We don't know the law," said Josep. "We might just have to pay a heavy fine."

"Or we can convince the American to keep quiet and destroy that diary of his," said Miquel. "Without the diary, it's just that worker's word. There's no evidence."

"But there is evidence. Enric took some very nice photographs of the entire farmhouse, including the synagogue. The press already has them."

The family turned to see who had spoken, though they already knew who the speaker was from his accent.

"I've come to get the rest of my things," said Chaim, who had been standing in the shadows, near the edge of the patio. "Is it all right if I go to the sewing room, Mrs. Bonet?"

"Of course. The door is open."

"I'd like to pay for whatever expenses I've incurred while staying in your home," Chaim added. "If you don't want to make up the bill now, you can e-mail it to me and I'll send you a check."

"You don't owe us a thing," said Clara. "Does he, Josep?"

"No," said Josep.

"I'll leave my e-mail address in the room, in case you change your mind."

Chaim walked toward the door, but Vidal got there before him and blocked his way.

"It was an empty room!"

"You've got it wrong, Vidal. You're the one that's empty."

Chaim went into the house. There was another silence. Then Biel commented, "I hope that American doesn't expect any of us to give him a ride back to Barcelona."

Vidal closed his eyes for a moment. Then he ran to the driveway, where an unfamiliar car was parked. Tomas Domenech was sitting in the driver's seat. Enric was sitting beside him.

"I have nothing to say to you, Mr. Bonet," said Domenech, "except get a good lawyer."

CHAPTER 26

I t didn't take long for Chaim to pack his things. He took one last look around the room to be sure he hadn't forgotten anything. The stone walls stared back at him as impassively as on that first night he had spent in the village. No, he wasn't leaving anything behind. After loading the suitcases into the trunk of Domenech's car, he got into the backseat and they drove off.

During the drive to Sant Joan Januz, Domenech had explained to Chaim that Enric had done some work for the Department of Antiquities in the past. That was how they knew one another.

"When Enric mentioned he had been hired to work on the construction site at Sant Joan Januz, I remembered your e-mail. I told him to keep his eyes open and bring a camera, in case he found something. It was a lucky break that he was there. At least we have some record of the synagogue, thanks to the photographs."

Chaim had agreed. It was an amazing stroke of Divine Providence. The photographs were proof that he hadn't been on a wild goose chase. They did make him furious, though, every time he looked at them, since they were also a reminder of how the synagogue had been so callously destroyed.

He was still thinking about the photographs when they left the village behind and turned on to the main highway that would take them back to Barcelona.

"Do you think anyone in the village knew the synagogue was there?" he asked Enric.

"Even if someone did, I don't think the room had been used in a very long time. It had that smell of history about it, if you know what I mean."

Chaim did know what he meant, and the rage returned.

"Is the story going to be in the morning newspapers?" Enric asked Domenech.

"Front page, according to what I've been told." Domenech glanced in the rearview mirror and said to Chaim, "Do you read the Catalan newspapers?"

"Yes."

"Be sure to get to the newsstand early tomorrow morning, before all the papers are sold out."

"So many people will be interested in the synagogue?"

"The synagogue is just the tip of the iceberg."

"What iceberg?" asked Chaim.

"The iceberg that is going to sink Mr. Jordi Martinez."

The house was quiet. Josep and Vidal were asleep. But Clara was wide awake. Of course. She supposed a nuclear war could break out and it wouldn't disturb the sleep of anyone in the house but her.

Her mind kept wandering back to the events of the day: the news about the synagogue that had been destroyed, the realization that her son might go to jail. And then there was the diary. After the American left, Vidal drove her father over to his house to get it. Her father read the story to them. She was still trying to sort out what it all meant. She didn't know how the others could sleep.

If she made herself a cup of chamomile tea, it might make her drowsy. But she didn't want to go into the kitchen. She didn't want to look at her mother's chair. Even without the chair to accuse her, she knew that she had failed. She had failed to protect her son from danger.

She wondered how long it would take for the government to press charges and decide what to do with Vidal. She hoped it wouldn't take long. Both Josep and her father had assured her that they would hire a good lawyer. And it was just stones that had been destroyed. It wasn't as if a person had been harmed. But their words didn't reassure her. They had tripped over the little piece of wire, just like her mother had said they would if they didn't keep their eyes open.

But how was she supposed to have known what to look out for if nobody told her? And why hadn't her mother told her, if her mother had known the whole story? She could also point the finger and accuse. If she had known — if they had all known — maybe Vidal wouldn't have destroyed the synagogue.

Stop! This isn't the time to start placing blame.

The family had to stick together and help Vidal. She knew that, just as she knew that she she should go to bed and get some sleep. But she couldn't sleep, and so she decided to get a head start on the spring cleaning. It would feel good to sweep out the debris that had accumulated during the winter, and she knew exactly where she wanted to begin: the sewing room.

The American had been careful to leave the room in order, she noted, but after a long occupancy the room needed to be properly cleaned and aired out. She opened the window and went to work on the closet. Since the shelves were empty, they were easy to wipe down. She moved on to the dresser. The note with the American's e-mail address was sitting on it. In the morning, she would ask Josep what to do with it. The bookcase came next. She saw that the American had left behind the English-Catalan dictionary that Joya Garcia had bought for him. When there was nothing else to dust, she washed the windows. After that, she swept the floor.

As she was sweeping around the closet, she noticed the edge of something white sticking out from underneath it. When she pulled it out, she saw that it was some kind of form. The writing was in English, and so she assumed that it must belong to the American. It must have fallen out of his bag without his noticing.

She had learned a little English in school, and she had been good at languages, but that had been a long time ago. After so many years, she couldn't make out any of the words. Some of them, like the word at the top of the form — *Anusim* — didn't even sound like an English word.

She went to the dictionary to look it up. It wasn't there. She felt a twinge of pride. She had known it wasn't an English word.

But the foreign word made her suspicious. Perhaps the form had something to do with the synagogue. If so, the form could be important, even though it was blank. With the help of the dictionary, she just might be able to translate enough of it to know what it was about. And if it turned out to be nothing, at least the work might put her to sleep. That would also be an accomplishment.

It took her almost an hour to translate the explanatory paragraph at the top of the form. The minute she realized what the words "customs of crypto-Jews" meant, her blood began to boil. Their guest hadn't come to their village just to look for the synagogue. He had been spying on them!

266

Now that she was furious, the work went much quicker. The next section was about "Customs Pertaining to the Jewish Sabbath." Did they clean the house on Friday? Did they do laundry? Did they change into clean clothes? Did the family gather for a meal in the evening? Did they light a candle? Did they put the lit candle in a cupboard? Or did they hide the candle in a chimney?

As she read over the list, becoming angrier and angrier, she silently informed the form that she could ask questions, too. Whose business was it what they did? she wanted to know. And what did it matter if her family had a special meal on Friday nights and they hid the light in the chimney? They weren't bothering anyone. Why did other people need to know this information? To laugh at them, because they thought that the village's customs were funny, even stupid?

How could outsiders possibly understand, from a few words on a piece of paper, how special that moment was when the family gathered around the hearth and silently watched as the light traveled up the chimney? The form couldn't possibly convey the feeling of closeness, the feelings of peace and hope. If even someone like Joanna, who had grown up in the village, didn't understand, how could an outsider?

Then her anger was replaced was a different feeling, a feeling of uneasiness, and her hand began to tremble. This whole business about the Inquisition and the assassination was troubling. She could understand why the secret Jews had been afraid, why they had done something desperate to defend themselves and their families. On the other hand, she had a vague memory of that cathedral in Saragossa. There was a chapel in it that commemorated the memory of the slain Inquisitor. A painting in the chapel depicted his reward: an angel hovered above his head, holding a wreath, ready to crown him with the crown of martyrdom. For some reason, the painting had touched her. Perhaps it was the simplicity of its message. Or perhaps it was the hushed grandeur of the cathedral. But she had accepted that the man looking up toward heaven was a holy man, a martyr, a person who deserved to be bathed in a golden light and admired. She hadn't given any thought as to why he had been assassinated, or to the lives that he had wanted to destroy.

And she supposed that most people who entered the cathedral were like her. They didn't think too deeply about things.

267

They just accepted the narrative that was presented to them: The Jews had murdered an innocent man. They deserved the punishment they received.

But now that she had been presented with new information, what was she supposed to do with it? She felt some sort of response was expected from her, from her family. But what?

She would ask Josep about this as well, in the morning. He always somehow knew the right thing to do.

It was too bad that Vidal hadn't inherited that quality from his father. But there was nothing to do about that now. It certainly wouldn't help to dwell on it.

She went back to translating the form.

The next section had to do with the Jewish holidays. There was a list of customs for the New Year. Some she had never heard of, such as blowing a ram's horn. She was sure her parents never did such a thing. She couldn't recall them making a spiritual accounting and confessing their transgressions either. Perhaps they did that behind closed doors. But they did celebrate their New Year in the fall, like the Jews. And then there was the food. Like most people, the Jews had traditional foods for each holiday.

"Mama, why don't we make a lemon cake this year?"

"Lemon cake? In the fall? Who ever heard of such a thing? Really, Clara, I don't know where you get such crazy ideas. Certainly not from Papa and me."

Well. Now she knew. Jews never ate sour things at their New Year's holiday meals. They ate only sweet things, like honey cake, so they would have a sweet year. That was one less question to ask, she supposed, as she burst into tears.

The house felt like someone had died. That was the only way Clara could describe it as she entered the kitchen in the morning and saw Miquel and the great-uncles huddled around the kitchen table with Josep. Vidal was there, too, at least in body. But his face was so pale that Clara wondered if he hadn't come down with something during the night.

She wished she had gotten more sleep the night before, so that she could understand what Josep was saying to her. It wasn't like him to take an interest in the laundry. But for some reason that was what he was talking about, of all things, and she didn't understand.

"Not clothes laundering, Clara," said Josep, trying to be patient. "Money laundering."

"Let her read the newspaper article," said Miquel.

Josep handed her the morning's newspaper. There was a big picture of Vidal and the politician, Jordi Martinez, on the front page. It was a good picture of Vidal. He looked very handsome. There was also a nice picture of Arnau, although it was much smaller.

The headline was another matter. It sounded serious. But she couldn't understand what such words could have to do with her two sons. So she read it again, slowly, as if she was translating a difficult phrase from a foreign language: "Corruption Charges Rock Girona Regional Council."

She looked up at the others, but no one said a word. So she looked back down at the newspaper. The silence continued as she read the article. But even without any interruptions, it was hard to comprehend what the article was saying. She went over the article a second time, so that she could better understand its main points.

Someone was claiming that Jordi Martinez was involved in several money-laundering schemes. One of them involved the Peaceland International Center for EuroIslam, which was being financed by Saudi investors. The Saudi investors possibly had links to terrorist organizations such as al-Qaeda.

She felt a panic attack coming on. *Breathe*, she whispered. *These are charges. Nothing has been proved yet.*

Another charge had to do with accepting bribes from building contractors. Some of the money Martinez received from them was laundered through small businesses, such as interior design companies. And some of the money was laundered through the bank accounts of local artists. One of the artists mentioned was Arnau Bonet, who happened to be the brother of Vidal Bonet, who was involved with the Peaceland scam.

These are just allegations. Breathe.

The story continued on an inside page. It was too early to know if there was enough evidence to indict Martinez. The big break had occurred a few days ago when a medieval synagogue had been demolished illegally on the Peaceland construction site and Martinez bribed a worker to keep quiet.

There was a quote from someone from the Department of Antiquities, who commented that the destruction of the synagogue was a great loss, both for Catalonia and the Jewish people, since not too many of these medieval synagogues still existed. The article ended with a quote from an anonymous source, who surmised that Martinez had wanted the synagogue destroyed so that the Peaceland center could continue to operate as a privately owned company. If there wasn't a historical site, the government wouldn't snoop around while overseeing its maintenance and the money-laundering scheme wouldn't be detected.

Clara carefully folded the newspaper and set it down on the table.

"Vidal says he didn't know about the money-laundering scheme, Clara," said Josep. "We believe him."

"Of course he didn't know," she whispered.

"Mama, these are just allegations," said Vidal. "Al is my friend. He wouldn't involve me in something like this. He and his father wouldn't be involved either. They're legitimate. They build resorts all over the world. Someone is just out to get Martinez, and so they're spreading rumors about everyone who has a connection with him."

"That's right," said Miquel. "They're casting a big net in the hope of catching at least one little fish."

"Has anyone spoken to Arnau?" asked Clara.

"No," said Josep. "We tried calling him, but no one answered the phone."

"I should make breakfast."

"No one is hungry," said Josep.

"You still need to eat. Are cheese omelets all right with everyone?"

The telephone rang and startled them all.

"I'll get it," said Josep. "Maybe it's Arnau."

It wasn't Arnau. After a moment, Josep handed the phone to Vidal.

"It's Al."

Vidal took the telephone from his father. He turned away from the family and whispered, "Al?"

"Is that you, Vidal? You sound so glum."

"Shouldn't I be?"

"Don't tell me you've already forgotten lesson number one?"

"I guess I have."

" 'Think good and it will be good.' Repeat it one hundred times. Doctor's orders. But do it on the way to Barcelona. What time can you be here?"

"I can leave in ten minutes. Where should we meet? At your hotel?"

"No. Let's meet at the top of that statue that you like so much."

"The Christopher Columbus Monument?"

"That's right. And bring your passport."

It was one of those rare in-between times in Barcelona. As Vidal walked down La Rambla, he noted that he had never seen the normally busy street so quiet. It was almost like a dream, or a nightmare. Barcelona wasn't Barcelona without its crowds of people, just as La Rambla wasn't La Rambla without its street musicians serenading the throngs of office workers and tourists with their music and the vendors hawking their wares.

But this morning the street musicians and sellers of cheap flowers and cheaper souvenirs were silent. They just followed him with their eyes as he walked by them, and it made him feel uneasy. He knew it had nothing to do with the picture in the newspaper. They were just waiting for the slow period to pass and for the lunch crowd to descend upon the sidewalk and fill the place with life. Still, he wished that the city would wake up from this empty dream that it was dreaming so that he wouldn't be so conspicuous.

The Columbus Monument loomed ahead, marking land's end. Christopher Columbus had his back to him; as always, the explorer was pointing out to sea. For a moment, Vidal had the urge to take the statue's advice and flee the country. But where would he go?

He had reached the end of La Rambla. The monument was across the street. He wondered if Al was already on the observation deck and looking down at him, observing his movements. It suddenly occurred to him that his meeting with Al might be a setup. Maybe he would find the police on the observation deck instead of Al.

He glanced around. The street was almost empty. A newspaper seller was dozing in his kiosk. A few pensioners were gathered around a cafe table, playing cards.

To know when to pass is to know how to play, a voice whispered to him.

271

He wondered if the American had given the diary to the press, as his grandfather feared. It was possible. But it was absurd to think that he would punished for some crime that had taken place hundreds of years ago. Things like that didn't happen today. And he had enough to worry about without the burden of history weighing him down.

He glanced up again at the observation deck. This couldn't be a setup, he decided. The police knew where he lived. That, at least, was no secret.

A few people were standing in line at the ticket seller's booth and he joined them. After they all had their tickets, they were shown to the tiny elevator that traveled up to the observation deck. Vidal let the tourists exit the elevator first, so they could make their circuit around the narrow observation deck ahead of him. Al was already there. He was staring down at La Rambla, which stretched out below him. Al had probably seen him.

Vidal came up beside him and waited. Al glanced down at a guidebook that he had brought. They stood in silence until the tourists went back into the elevator. Then Al shifted his gaze back to the city and said, "This guidebook says that La Rambla was once a river."

"That's right."

"You Catalans are a crazy people, turning water into stone."

"It happened a long time ago."

"But you're still a crazy people. This could have been a very sweet deal for all of us, if some of us hadn't been so greedy."

"So it's true?"

"Don't play dumb, Vidal. You had to know."

"I didn't."

"You mean you didn't want to see it. But let's not waste time on arguing. There's a flight to Ecuador in a few hours, and I want to be on it."

"Have a nice trip."

"I would, except I have a slight problem. The police have invited me to stay in Catalonia and answer some questions. My father, on the other hand, wants me to get out of here as quickly as I can. Being a dutiful son, I naturally would prefer to obey my father's wishes. I'm sure you understand, since you also come from a traditional family."

"What do you want, Al?"

"Your passport."

"What?"

"It's risky, I know. But the police haven't contacted you, have they?"

"No."

"So it's very possible that airport security doesn't have your name yet. And we look enough alike that I might be able to pass for you."

"You don't speak Catalan."

"I'll pretend I have laryngitis. Vidal, if you do me this favor, my father and I won't forget you. We'll get you out of here, I promise. I can't offer you the top job in Ecuador, but we'll find you something."

"I don't want to go to Ecuador."

"And I don't want to go to jail. Why didn't you tell me that your brother was on Martinez's payroll?"

"I didn't know."

"What? Your brother never mentioned that he was getting half a million euros per paint splash to decorate the walls of Martinez's office?"

"I didn't know."

"You mean you didn't want to see it. Who does your brother think he is anyway? Picasso's nephew?"

The elevator doors opened, and a small group of tourists emerged. Vidal and Al moved over to the other side of the observation deck, where they had a view of the sea. Al had come to their meeting prepared. He gave the guidebook to Vidal and took out a camera. While the tourists circled around the platform, he snapped photographs through the dirt-splattered pane of glass. When the group left, Al put away the camera.

"I'm not blaming you, Vidal, for what your brother did. But you have to understand that I feel betrayed."

"You feel betrayed?"

"If we'd kept the project small, like we talked about back in New York, this never would have happened. You should have warned me about Martinez."

"Al, you're the one who said that turning Peaceland into a center for EuroIslam was a brilliant idea."

"And it was a brilliant idea, which is why I'm so shocked that Martinez turned out to be so stupid. Bribing that worker! Couldn't

273

you two have found a smarter way to get rid of that synagogue? You've let me down, Vidal. You've let me down big time. My father is furious. I had to beg him to give you a second chance. But I told him that our relationship isn't just business. We're friends. Good friends. And friends don't let each other down when one of them needs a favor."

"I'm not giving you my passport."

"Martinez won't help you, Vidal. He hates Jews. And don't tell me that you didn't know that your people are secret Jews. Anyone can look into your sad eyes and see who you really are."

While Al waited for the elevator to arrive, Vidal gazed down at the sea. He heard the elevator doors open and then he heard them close. And then he was alone.

CHAPTER 27

Chaim tapped his fingers on the diary's black binder as he waited for the rabbi to return. He felt uncomfortable, the way he always did in a rabbi's office. Even if he hadn't done anything wrong, the shelves lined with books written by the Jewish people's greatest scholars and ethical masters — and all rabbis' offices had shelves lined with books written by the Jewish people's greatest scholars and ethical masters — reminded him that he could do better.

"Sorry for the interruption," said the rabbi when he returned. "Where were we?"

"I was explaining about how I was having second thoughts about giving Domenech the diary," said Chaim. "That's why he offered to drive me to Sant Joan Januz. So I could get my bags and give him a copy. He wants to give the diary to the press to keep the story on the front page of the newspapers."

"Right," said the rabbi, nodding. "I'm with you."

Chaim would have preferred to talk things over with his father. But his family had gone to New York for the long Shabbos and Purim weekend, and Chaim had mistakenly deleted the e-mail that had the information where his parents were staying. So he had contacted this rabbi instead.

He didn't know much about him, except that the rabbi was one of the leaders of Barcelona's Jewish community. Chaim therefore offered a quick prayer that the rabbi should be granted wisdom to give him good advice, and then he continued with the background information that pertained to his question.

"Like I explained earlier, there was something about having the diary publicized in the newspapers that made me feel uneasy, especially since I didn't know what Domenech meant by this 'iceberg' business. So when we got to my hotel, I made up an excuse and told Domenech I would send him the diary after Purim. He wasn't happy, and he warned me that I could get into trouble for obstructing justice, but he finally left."

275

To say that Domenech had been unhappy was an understatement. The man had been furious. Not that Chaim could entirely blame him. After all, Domenech had spent the entire evening chauffeuring Chaim around. First they had made the trip together from Girona to Sant Joan Januz. Then Domenech had driven Chaim back to Barcelona, which took even longer. So he could understand why Domenech would be angry about returning to Girona empty-handed. Still, Domenech's abrupt change from the coolly rational academic to a mean-spirited child throwing a temper tantrum was unpleasant to see. And as he stared at Domenech's features, which had contorted into a frightening, angry mask, Chaim had wondered if that was how his own face had looked when he first saw the photographs of the destroyed synagogue.

The rabbi glanced down at his watch. It was a small movement, but Chaim took the hint. Shabbos would begin in just a few hours. They both had to prepare.

"So I don't know what to do," Chaim said in conclusion. "Should I give Domenech the diary or not?"

Chaim was almost hundred percent sure he already knew what the rabbi would say. A person doesn't act based on uneasy feelings. A person who has respect for the law doesn't keep silent when he has information that will be useful. So he was surprised when the rabbi asked, "Why do you think this man Domenech needs the diary if he has the photographs?"

"My Nona Anna describes the false wall and the niche in the eastern wall. That's additional proof that the room was a synagogue."

"She only mentions that there was a false wall. She doesn't say where the wall was."

"She does say that they rebuilt the hearths."

"But she doesn't say that the false wall was in the back of one of these hearths."

"Couldn't a person put two and two together? There's that line in the diary..." Chaim flipped through the pages until he found what he was looking for. " 'And once a cheerful fire is glowing in the hearth, even the most humble room becomes a home.' "

"So?"

"Fire is a metaphor for Torah. We use it all the time, right?"

"And so?"

"The Hebrew word for 'home' is *bayis*. That could refer to the synagogue, the *beis knesses* — the 'house of assembly.' If you put it all together, the sentence could be saying to look for the Torah scroll in the hearth, which will change the room into a synagogue."

The rabbi smiled. "Tell me something, Chaim. Did you come up with this novel interpretation before you knew the synagogue was behind the hearth, or after?"

"After. Why?"

"It's clever, but sometimes it's better to stick with the simple reading of the text. And according to the simple reading, there's no conclusive proof that the synagogue in the diary is the same one this Bonet fellow destroyed."

"But the room was a synagogue. Domenech is sure of it."

"And so?"

"Vidal Bonet destroyed a synagogue."

"And so?"

"Shouldn't he be punished?"

"If indeed, he did do something illegal, you're right. He should be punished. The question, though, is by whom."

"I don't understand."

"Look, the Department of Antiquities has a full set of photographs of the farmhouse and the room. They have people on their staff who are knowledgeable about medieval synagogues. So they should have everything they need to prove their theory that the room was a synagogue, even without the diary. Correct?"

"I guess so."

"The only information that your diary adds to the discussion is Vidal Bonet's family history, which is problematic, to say the least."

"Didn't the Spanish Inquisition end two hundred years ago?"

"Yes and no. If you're talking about the arrests and the auto-da-fes, yes, that's over. But if you're talking about the hatred that led to the Inquisition, I'm not so sure. It's impossible to know how people will react when it's revealed that the Bonets are distantly related to the *Anusim* who assassinated a Catholic clergyman. If the press plays up all the gory details, which they probably will, old passions could be reignited."

"But aren't I obligated to hand over evidence that could be important to the case?"

277

"But to whom? And is the diary important evidence? In law, there's something called inadmissible evidence. One reason why a court of law won't allow a piece of evidence is because its value is outweighed by the inflamed passions it will cause. So it could be that the diary will be rejected. But if everyone has already read the diary in the newspapers, the damage will have already been done. It's easy to say, 'Ignore what you read.' But the brain doesn't come with a delete button. It's not so easy to erase prejudices from the human mind. So let's say that when this case is reviewed that Vidal Bonet gets a judge who is prejudiced against him because of the diary. It could mean the difference between his being slapped with a fine and being sent to jail."

"What if he does get the heavier sentence?" asked Chaim. "Isn't that also from G-d?"

"Everything is from G-d. But G-d uses messengers to mete out His justice. So you have to ask the question: Do you want to be one of those messengers? Are you sure that your motives are pure? Have you volunteered for the job of avenging angel because you truly believe that justice won't be done without you – or do you have another motive for taking up the sword?"

Chaim didn't say anything. From somewhere down the hall he could hear the sound of someone typing on a computer keyboard.

"You don't have to rush to make a decision, Chaim. This inquiry will take months. You have time to go back to Kansas and think things over."

The person was typing quickly, as though in a hurry to finish what was being written.

"But remember, Chaim, one day you're going to reach one hundred and twenty and go up to heaven. You're going to meet all of your relatives, including your Nona Anna. Isn't that right?"

Chaim nodded his head.

"What are you going to say to her if you use her diary to destroy her family?"

Clara took the baked chicken out of the oven. It was a new recipe and it smelled delicious. She glanced at the clock. There was still time to bake a cake if she hurried. As she took out her baking utensils she wondered if she should ask Vidal for his preference. She decided not to. He had looked so tired when he came home after his trip to Barcelona. And he had gone straight to his room without saying a word.

That wasn't like him. It was Arnau who always retreated to his room when he had a rough day at school. That's why they weren't entirely surprised that no one answered at Arnau's home. She had wanted to invite them to come to the village for the Friday night dinner. They could have stayed all weekend. But no one picked up the phone.

Josep came into the kitchen through the back door just as the five o'clock news came on the radio. They both listened as the news announcer said that the son of the Saudi investor had disappeared. The police thought the young man might have fled the country, but they weren't sure. Clara glanced over at Josep. He just shrugged and left the kitchen.

An hour later her father and the great-uncles arrived. Josep had picked them up since Vidal was still brooding in his room. Clara poured the oil into the container. She got the wick and stuck it into a piece of cork so that it would float on the oil.

"Shouldn't someone call Vidal?" asked Miquel.

Josep went to get him. A few minutes later he returned with Vidal, and the little group stood around the fireplace. Clara glanced out the window. The sun was at the horizon. It was time to light the flame.

After the wick was lit, Josep carried the container over to the hearth and attached it to the pulley. He hoisted the container up into the chimney. When he had secured the wire, he stepped back so everyone could look at the hidden light. Pau and Biel went first, followed by Miquel and Clara. Josep motioned for Vidal to step forward, but Vidal didn't move.

"Vidal?" Josep said quietly.

When Vidal didn't react to that hint, Miquel cleared his throat. When Vidal still didn't move, Miquel said, "We're waiting."

Vidal turned and stared at his grandfather. "You're waiting? And what about me? I had to wait twenty-five years to find out the truth."

Miquel closed his eyes. He seemed to see those years fly by like pictures in an old family album. There was Clara in the hospital, with the new baby. There was Vidal at his birthday party, proudly holding his typewriter. There were the two of them on the swing, talking about life while they looked up at the stars on a

279

summer night. Then there was the trip to the airport, before Vidal left for New York. Everyone was smiling. No one else had known about his secret hope that Vidal would find a good job in New York and get married there and never come back. Not even Anna.

"Well, Grandpa? You're the one who always has an answer for everything. Maybe you can explain why everything you told me was a lie?"

Miquel looked at Vidal, but only part of him was there, in the room. The other part was in the square, many years ago.

"I didn't want them to throw you into the fire."

CHAPTER 28

C lara decided that she couldn't wait in the house and do nothing any longer. She thought it was cruel that the police still hadn't contacted Vidal to let him know if he was under suspicion, though Josep thought the silence might be good. At any rate, she didn't have to take the silent treatment from her own son. So after the weekend, she packed up some food and took the train to Girona.

No one answered the door at Arnau's apartment. But Vidal had told her where Arnau's studio was, and she found it easily enough. She couldn't tell if Arnau was surprised to see her or not. He escorted her back to the apartment, explaining that the studio was small and stuffy, and he didn't want the fumes to make her feel unwell.

She bit her lip. She refused to let the words fly out: If he was so concerned about her health, why had he agreed to take the money from that politician and bring shame upon the family? Instead of saying that, she asked, "Why didn't you call, Arnau? Don't you think your father and I want to help you?"

"I'm fine. There's no need to worry."

"No need to worry? Aren't the police going to question you?"

"They already have. This morning."

"And?"

"I answered their questions."

"You told them about the money?"

"They had copies of my bank statements. It wouldn't have done any good to lie. I'm following the advice of the lawyer Martinez got for me. He's one of the best."

"I'm glad to hear that."

"That's why I didn't call. He advised me not to have contact with the family, to protect Vidal. So far Vidal hasn't been implicated in the money-laundering scheme."

"He hasn't?"

"His Saudi friend watched out for him, apparently. The only money that went into Vidal's bank account was his salary. It was high, considering that Vidal didn't do anything. But if the police arrested every manager who was overpaid, there wouldn't be room in jail for anyone else."

Clara smiled. She was relieved to hear the news about Vidal. She wondered, though, how Arnau could make jokes when he was still in trouble.

"But what's going to happen to you?"

"I'll have to return the money. And I'll probably have to spend some time in jail. The main thing is to make a deal as quickly as possible. Martinez will help me once I get out. He promised."

"Won't he have to go to jail, too?"

"He'll wriggle out of this. But let me fix you a cup of coffee, Mama. And I see you've brought a cake."

Arnau filled the kettle with water and put it on the fire, and he put the cake that Clara had brought on a platter. Clara again wondered how he could be so unconcerned. And unrepentant.

A week later Vidal was questioned by the police. The investigators were very polite. They seemed to accept his testimony that he didn't know about the money-laundering scheme. His bank account statements supported what he said. So did his e-mails. They had confiscated both his computers and read them all.

The police had thought it odd that he didn't know anything about Arnau's involvement. But when Vidal explained that he hadn't been on good terms with his brother for years, they seemed to understand and accept that as well. The questions about Al were more difficult. The police found it very hard to believe that Vidal didn't know anything about the shady dealings of Al and his father.

"Let them believe you're stupid or naive," his lawyer had advised him. "This is a police interrogation, not a job interview."

And so Vidal stuck to his story. He hadn't seen. He really thought that he and Peaceland would do some good in the world.

One of the police officers rolled his eyes, while another one hid a smile behind his hand. Vidal wondered if that was how he would go through the rest of his life, always aware that some people believed he was a crook and the rest thought he was a fool.

Then it was time to tell the police about the meeting in the Columbus Monument. His lawyer had advised him to do so. Although it was unlikely, there was a chance that his movements had been watched. And so he told the police about Al's request for his passport. He learned that it was a good thing that he hadn't given it to Al. If he had done it, he would have been in serious trouble. The police weren't at all happy that Al had fled the country. They still didn't know how he'd slipped through their fingers. But since Vidal's name didn't appear on any airline passenger lists, the police put a line through that charge as well.

Vidal noted that the police weren't terribly interested in the synagogue. His lawyer had guessed correctly that the synagogue was just a footnote to the case. And since the American hadn't given the diary to the press and wasn't planning on doing so in the future — his mother had e-mailed the American, who was back in Kansas, and that was the answer she had received — the public also quickly lost whatever interest they had had in it.

At some point, when all the other charges had either been proved or dismissed, the police would get back to the synagogue, his lawyer had told him. But when they did, his cooperating with the police on the big charges would surely work in his favor. And so Vidal was free to return to Sant Joan Januz.

When he arrived in the village, he decided to drive by the construction site. He parked the car and walked around. The crew had done a good job of cleaning up their debris. The only thing they had left behind was the full-color sign, which was still standing. Somewhere between the overblown International Center and the empty tract of land was his original vision for bringing Sant Joan Januz back to life.

He decided that the cartographers were wrong. The world was flat. And sometimes,

people did fall off the edge.

He walked over to one of the yellow-broom shrubs — they were all in bloom — and he snapped off a few branches for his mother. Then he remembered the diary, and he let the branches fall to the ground.

The weeks went by and spring was over. Then it was summer — and it was a hot one. There was plenty of work to do in the fields, and so Miquel and the great-uncles set out early every

283

morning. But Clara was worried. Her father had seemed to age overnight. She didn't want him, or the great-uncles, to overexert themselves in the scorching weather.

Vidal knew that he should volunteer to help out. He wasn't doing anything except moping in his room. But he needed that time to mourn. He had pinned all his hopes on the resort. It wasn't so easy to manufacture a new supply.

One morning he decided, finally, that he had had enough of staring at the same four walls. He put on his old work clothes and drove out to the fields. When he arrived, he saw that his grandfather and great-uncles were tying the branches of the grape vines to stakes. He gave a nod to his grandfather — it was a small gesture, but the unspoken gesture of reconciliation was both understood and gratefully acknowledged — and silently joined them. He had spent many summers out in the fields, and he knew what to do.

The clusters of grapes were still tiny. They looked like the little bright green sprinkles that his mother would sometimes use to decorate one of her cakes. But with each passing week there was a noticeable difference. Soon the little grapes turned into clusters of pearl-sized opaque plastic beads, and the branches started to droop under their weight.

As the grapes grew larger, the number of lines in the daily newspapers devoted to the corruption scandal grew smaller. Vidal therefore wasn't surprised to read, at summer's end, that the police didn't have enough evidence to indict Martinez.

Arnau and a few other people were going to have to go to jail. But he would be out in less than a year, Arnau had assured Clara. Once again Clara waited for some sign of remorse, in vain. Arnau had already moved on to a new topic, the new apartment that he and Joanna were moving to. It was located in the new part of Girona, and it was more comfortable. Clara had been right. It was hard to heat those old drafty apartments in the winter.

Clara wondered if the move had something to do with Arnau and Joanna not wanting to live in the former Jewish Quarter, now that they knew the family was descended from Jews, but she didn't feel she could ask. She was meeting enough resistance in her own family every time she brought up the topic of their Jewish ancestry. She didn't know why no one wanted to talk about it. In her opinion, the subject was very interesting.

After Josep and Vidal went to work in the morning, she would sit at the computer for a few hours and read about the history of the Jews in Spain. Because of the diary, she felt her family was a chapter in that story. True, it was a story that had a sad ending. But at least they were no longer a tiny bubble floating alone in the universe. They came from somewhere. But where were they going? She found herself thinking about that a lot. It seemed odd to go on as though nothing had changed. She felt they should do something, even something little, to acknowledge their family's history.

One night, at the dinner table, she announced that she was thinking of going back to school. Not full-time, of course. But the Jewish Museum in Girona was offering a beginners class in Hebrew, and she wanted to sign up for it.

There was a long silence.

"Why?" Josep asked.

"I always enjoyed learning languages," Clara replied.

"But why not learn something useful?"

"Maybe Hebrew will be useful."

In the end, nothing came of it. The classes were at night. She couldn't ask Josep or Vidal to pick her up at the train station at a late hour, not when they were both working from sunup to sundown to help her father and great-uncles harvest the grapes. They both had to help out, because the older members of the family weren't able to do all the work anymore. That was another change.

So she went back to reading about the Jews on the computer. Once a week she did go to Girona, to visit Arnau. But she went during the day, during visiting hours. She always felt horribly embarrassed when she had to pass through the gates of the prison, but Arnau was her son and so she did it. Since it was the season, she would bring him grapes. He commented that the grapes were very sweet. She just nodded. She didn't understand how he could enjoy them so much, under the circumstances.

Then the last of the grapes were picked, Josep returned to his workshop, and it was time to think about the New Year. One night after dinner, Clara got down her mother's recipe book and leafed through it. It was still too early to do the cooking and baking, but half the fun was planning the meals. Or at least it had been, when she had sat with her mother.

285

"Does chicken with orange sauce sound good to you?" she asked Josep. "Or should I save the oranges for a cake?"

Josep didn't say anything. Clara couldn't expect Josep to take the same interest in holiday meals as her mother, but it wasn't like him not to reply. She tried again.

"I think I made the chicken with orange sauce last year. Do you remember if you liked it?"

"Clara, why don't we skip the holiday meals this year?"

"What?"

"I don't see the point, now that we know where the custom comes from. We're not Jews. So it's not our New Year. Why should you do so much work for nothing?"

Clara stared at Josep. This wasn't the change that she had in mind. If he had said that he wanted to repaint the kitchen, she would have agreed to his suggestion without a problem. She now understood her mother's aversion to too much yellow. In the world that G-d had created, yellow was a beautiful color. It was the color of joy and optimism and warmth. But humans had a way of turning everything upside down. Yellow was the color of the sanbenito, the Inquisition's robe of shame. It was the color of the star that the Jews were forced to wear during the Holocaust. And so she was ready to return her kitchen to a neutral color, like off-white, so that her family wouldn't have to be reminded of all those unpleasant associations. But she couldn't imagine giving up all the family traditions, not when they were the very things that had added so much joy and warmth and color to the family's life.

Clara didn't have a chance to say any of that because Josep had already taken his coffee cup to the living room to read the paper. She supposed that meant the discussion was over, and she didn't think that was fair. It was her home, too. There were also Vidal and her father and the great-uncles to consider. Surely before they all took such a drastic step and cut themselves off from their traditions they should at least discuss it.

It would be better, though, if it didn't look like the idea for a family meeting had come from her. She didn't want Josep to think that she didn't respect his opinion. But if it didn't come from her, where could the suggestion come from? There had been tension between Josep and her father for months. And it wasn't right to involve Vidal in a dispute between his father and mother.

286

No, the idea would have to come from her. And what was so terrible if it did? Her mother hadn't been afraid to open her mouth and suggest things where the family was concerned. Of course, her mother had always done it in a respectful way. So she would also find a way to respectfully suggest to Josep that everyone should have a say in such an important decision.

But there was another problem. She wasn't sure if anyone else would agree with her about preserving the customs. Friday nights had become awkward. They still lit the light, and Josep still hoisted the container up into the chimney, but most weeks neither Josep nor Vidal bothered to look at it. Even her father and great-uncles just took a quick glance. She was the only one who really took the time to look at the shadows of the flames.

It suddenly occurred to her that Joanna might become an ally in the fight. It must be hard for Joanna, with Arnau in jail. And she didn't know what they had told Manel. Whatever excuse they had come up with, it must have caused Joanna to do some soul-searching. Their cutting themselves off from the village and its traditions hadn't done them much good. Perhaps Joanna could now see that. She might even be willing to come back, for the sake of Manel. Her daughter-in-law could be abrupt, but Clara knew that she cared about Manel more than anything else in the world.

All wasn't lost yet. There was still hope.

Joanna shut the door, but not completely. It was the hour when Manel practiced his violin. The screeching got on her nerves, but she consoled herself with the thought that all beginnings were difficult, even for great violinists. And if Manel didn't improve, he could always drop it.

As she returned to the main room, Joanna wondered why her mother-in-law had come to see her. She hoped Clara wasn't going to shower her with pity.

"Manel sounds like he's improving," said Clara when Joanna re-entered the room.

"He is, but I don't think the neighbors will miss us when we leave."

"Why don't you move back to the village, Joanna?"

Joanna's smile froze on her face. Clara knew she had made a mistake by broaching the subject so quickly. She should have waited until they had drunk their cups of coffee at least.

287

"Of course, I know you won't," said Clara, trying to salvage the situation. "And I don't entirely blame you. Girona is starting to grow on me, now that I come here more often."

Clara didn't have to look at Joanna to know that she had made another mistake. The only reason she was visiting Girona more frequently was because Arnau was in jail. Joanna certainly knew that. On the other hand, why pretend that this wasn't the truth of the situation?

"It must be lonely for you and Manel on the weekends," said Clara, forging ahead. "We'd love to have you stay with us, and it would give you a break. You wouldn't have to look after Manel every minute."

"We'd feel lonelier in the village. Manel's friends are here in Girona. And so are mine."

And what about your family? Clara wanted to ask. *Don't they count for anything?* But Clara reminded herself not to judge — Joanna might be too embarrassed to come back to the village and face everyone — and so she said, "It must be nice for Manel, having so many friends to play with."

Clara saw Joanna look over at the clock. She supposed that soon Joanna would have to get dinner for Manel. She had better get to the point. "Are any of his friends like us?"

Joanna shot her a look. Then Joanna quickly returned her eyes to her coffee cup and blew on the coffee a few times to cool it down.

"I really don't know. But I assume that most of the families we know have their roots in Girona."

"I meant, does he have any friends who also have their roots in the Jewish people?"

"I don't believe in looking through people's closets for skeletons, just as I hope that people will do me the courtesy of not looking through mine."

"But it's part of our heritage. You were there when my father read us the diary. Why be ashamed of it?"

"Arnau and I will make the decision about what's part of our heritage and what isn't. Not some diary."

Joanna suddenly realized that Manel was standing in the doorway. "What is it, Manel?"

"Another string went pop."

"I'll fix it after your grandmother leaves."

"Who has skeletons in their closets, Mama? Are they real ones?"

"We'll discuss it later. Now give Grandma Clara a kiss, and tell her good-bye."

Clara heard the door slam shut behind her. She forced herself to smile. The visit hadn't been a total loss. One thing had been accomplished. She knew she couldn't count on Joanna for support.

But it wasn't wise to read too much into what people said, she reminded herself. She mustn't be influenced by stories she read in magazines, where family members were always feuding and not speaking with each other. Joanna surely didn't mean that Clara would no longer be welcome in their home. Did she?

The train station wasn't far away, and so Clara decided to walk. She liked to walk. Like cleaning, it helped her to think. But she arrived at the train station before her thoughts could really get going, and so she didn't mind that she had to wait a little bit until her train arrived.

The Girona station was small. Only two tracks were used, one for the northbound trains and one for the trains going south. As she looked down at the two sets of train tracks, she had a sudden moment of clarity. She was moving in one direction. Her family was moving in the opposite one. Who was traveling down the right path?

Their ancestors had had a reason for hiding the light in the chimney. They had wanted to preserve their connection to the Jews, and to G-d. That's what a *mitzvah* — a commandment — was. She had learned this through her searches on the Internet. It was something that bound a Jew to her G-d, and to the Torah, and to the Jewish people. It kept them all connected, close. But if she and her family weren't interested in any of that, why should they bother with the customs? Why do it for nothing?

True, the special family dinners were nice. But she could still prepare special food, even if it wasn't on a Friday night. Other families got together on Sunday afternoons. Her family could do that, too, especially if it would maintain the peace. And that was the main thing, to keep the peace in the family. Peace had always been very important to her mother. She recalled that her parents rarely fought, and whenever there was a feud brewing in the

289

village, her parents were always the ones who ran to make peace between the neighbors.

And if maintaining a connection to their Jewish past had been important to her mother, surely her mother would have said something to her. Even if her father had wanted to keep it a secret, her mother would have called for a family meeting. In her quiet way, her mother would have convinced the others that the connection had to be passed on to the next generation — to Clara and Josep — so that they wouldn't forget. But if her mother hadn't said any of this, who was she to insist? Her mother must have decided that maintaining the connection wasn't as important as maintaining peace.

While she was still engrossed in her thoughts, Clara gradually realized that something strange was going on around her. People were standing on the edges of the platforms — both of them — and shouting. Catalan people usually didn't behave like that. Something was wrong. She looked around the platform to see who they were shouting at. Then she looked down and saw that there was a woman standing on the tracks.

What was the woman doing there? It was dangerous — very dangerous — to be on the tracks like that. Clara supposed that the woman, who was middle-aged and should have known better, was taking a shortcut. She must have taken the wrong escalator, and now she wanted to get to the platform for the train traveling north, the train Clara was waiting for. But that was foolish. And that's why everyone was yelling at her. The southbound train was coming. Hadn't they just now heard the whistle? It would pull into the station any minute.

They heard the second whistle of the approaching train. Everyone was still yelling, only now more frantically. Clara wanted to yell, too. But the words stuck in her throat. The woman was standing on the tracks and smiling at her, and she didn't know why.

Don't smile! Clara wanted to yell. *Move! Walk forward! Don't stay where you are! You'll die!*

The woman didn't move. She just stood there, smiling at Clara.

The whistle blew a third time. This time it was even louder.

Clara shut her eyes tight. Everything was quiet for a moment.

290

Then pandemonium broke out again. Clara slowly opened her eyes. A woman on the opposite platform was shrieking. A man was holding his head with his hands and moaning. Everywhere Clara looked people were sobbing. One woman had fainted, and a few of the train station's workers were splashing water on her face to revive her.

Clara was afraid to look at the train tracks, but she forced herself. When she did look, oddly enough there wasn't much to see. The southbound train, the train to Barcelona, had stopped a few feet before reaching the passenger area of the platform. Some railway workers, dressed in their fluorescent green vests, were kneeling down on the tracks and peering underneath the train.

Several minutes later, Clara's train arrived. She got on and took a seat by the window. The train pulled out of the station. In the seat behind her, a woman was crying. A few people had gathered at the back of the compartment.

"She's at peace now," Clara heard a woman say.

Peace. Clara felt the word echoing inside her head. Instead of feeling comforted, she began to cry.

PART VI: *ADEU,* SANT JOAN JANUZ

CHAPTER 29

I f his parents were surprised by Chaim's reticence about his trip, they tried not to show it, at least not at first. But as the days turned into weeks, and Chaim continued to bury himself in his thesis work, his parents' questions became more pointed.

"Why do you have to do telephone interviews with *Anusim* in Mallorca if you were in Catalonia for two months?" asked his mother.

"I'll pay for the phone calls."

"It's not a question of money. Your father and I are just curious to know what happened. Why don't you want to talk about it?"

Chaim didn't know if he could trust himself to reveal the truth. He was still too angry about the synagogue. At first, when he returned to Kansas, he had hoped that distance would bring him a sense of calm. But then he received an e-mail from Clara Bonet. He had opened it eagerly, thinking it must be an apology from the family, an admission that they had done something wrong and that they were sorry about what happened. When he realized that her only reason for writing was to ask him not to publicize the diary, the anger returned in full force. He could barely say the word *Catalonia* without choking on it.

He also couldn't look at the diary anymore. Just the sight of it made him feel sick. So one evening he put the black binder in a box and stashed it on the top shelf of his closet. Chaim supposed that his mother had noticed the empty place on the desk and told his father, because the next Shabbos, when the family was sitting around the dining table, his father commented, "You know, Chaim, you don't have to be embarrassed about not finding the synagogue. People have been looking hundreds of years for the Menorah that stood in the Temple, and no one has ever found it."

"No one has found the Menorah because it's still not time for the Temple to be rebuilt."

"And maybe that's why you didn't find your synagogue, because it wasn't the right time."

Chaim didn't mention that the synagogue had been found – and destroyed. Or that if there had been a right time, now that moment would never come.

"At least the synagogue wasn't turned into a pub or a dance hall," his mother said. "People sometimes do things like that with old buildings."

Oddly, his mother's comment gave him some comfort. He hadn't thought about that possibility. At least the synagogue hadn't suffered such an ignominious fate. Perhaps there was a reason it had been destroyed, after all.

"If anyone in the village did something that hurt your feelings, Chaim," his father continued, "or you did something to hurt them, remember that Elul begins tomorrow. Yom Kippur is in forty days. That's all the time we have to repair what's been broken and restore peace."

Chaim nodded. It was the custom to use the month of Elul, the last month of the Jewish year, to make a cheshbon hanefesh and review one's actions during the previous year. People you had wronged had to be asked for forgiveness. People who had wronged you had to be forgiven. Yom Kippur, the Day of Atonement, couldn't cleanse a person of his transgressions if that person was filled with anger and resentment. Chaim knew all that, and the Elul reminder made him realize that his parents had intuited most of the things he had tried to conceal.

After Shabbos Chaim went to his room and sat down at his desk. He couldn't help but recall the last time he had made a cheshbon hanefesh. It had been his first night in the village. As he had done that night, he wrote the same words at the top of the sheet of paper: *Bonet Family.*

He stared at the piece of paper for several long minutes, but not because he wanted to savor the moment. Reluctantly, he came to the conclusion that he should send Clara and Josep Bonet a letter to apologize for taking advantage of their hospitality and using it to spy on them. So next to their names he wrote: *Write a letter.*

Next came Vidal Bonet. Chaim could feel a hard knot of anger form in his stomach as he wrote down the words. He hated Bonet.

He had hated him from almost the first moment he had laid eyes on him. But why?

Chaim looked around his room, which had been decorated in a style that was stubbornly American-suburban. It was between these four characterless walls that he had first dreamt up his plan. This was where he had plotted out everything he had hoped to accomplish in Sant Joan Januz. First, he was going to find the synagogue and the Torah scroll. Then he planned to gather the villagers in the synagogue and read them the diary. Then, when everyone was overcome with emotion, he had planned to deliver the coup de grace and reveal that he was their long-lost relative, a descendent of Nona Anna. And then, when everyone was really crying and totally overwhelmed, he was going to mention — in a few gentle words — that the door was open. They could come back. They could return and be Jews. He would help them to do that, if they wanted, which of course they would.

None of that had happened, and he knew who to blame. If Vidal Bonet had stayed in New York to get a Ph.D., Chaim was sure he would have had more success.

Or would he? Was it really Vidal's fault that the villagers had refused to play the part that Chaim had written for them?

Or, Chaim wondered, had he temporarily forgotten that there was a G-d in the world? He was the One who wrote the script. He had His reasons for why the synagogue was destroyed so soon after it had been discovered, why the villagers had rejected Chaim's attempt to reunite the family.

But his father was right. That rejection didn't make him a failure. It just hadn't been the right time. When the time was right for Nona Anna's family to be reunited with the family of Manel Esperandeu, it would happen. It had to. His Nona Anna was stubborn. She would continue to storm the Gates of Heaven until the promise was fulfilled.

Chaim went over to the closet and brought the diary back to his desk. He opened the cover and traced the first few words with his finger.

"Prisoner of hope," he whispered, thinking about his Nona Anna and how she waited at the pier in Salonika for all those years. "Me, too."

Clara switched the setting on the oven to warm so that the fish and the vegetables wouldn't dry out. The salad was already made. The table was set. Everything was ready, except it was too early. She couldn't expect Josep to close his workshop at this hour just because she was terrified to be in the house alone when she had nothing to do.

She had tried to forget the train accident. Josep didn't believe her, she knew. He accused her of being like her father — always imagining things, letting her thoughts run wild, not having any self-control. But what could she do? Wherever Clara looked, she saw her. She couldn't stop replaying the scene in her mind. Over and over again she saw it. The woman. Her smile. As though she was laughing at Clara, mocking her.

"Stop it!" Clara whispered. She put her hands over her eyes and shut them tight. "I don't know you. Leave me alone."

"Mama? Is something wrong?"

Clara quickly lowered her hands and reached for a sponge and began to vigorously clean the countertop. She hadn't heard Vidal open the back door. She wondered why she could hear the train whistle but not that.

"Of course nothing is wrong."

"I thought you might be upset."

"Why?"

"Papa just told me that we're not going to have a special meal for the New Year."

"Will you be disappointed?"

Vidal shrugged.

"Don't, Vidal. Life is too precious. Don't waste it on being angry, or indifferent."

Vidal looked at her quizzically. She knew what he was thinking. *Don't waste it on being afraid either.* But he was too polite to say what he was really thinking.

"I'll be all right," he said. "It just takes time to decide what to do next."

Vidal left to change his clothes and wash the dirt of the vineyards off his face and hands. It still pained Clara to see her son dressed like a common farmhand. She would be glad when the cleanup work in the vineyard would be over. And she would be glad when Vidal finally pulled himself out of the dumps and decided what he wanted to do. Then she remembered that she had forgotten to ask Vidal what he wanted for dessert. If he wanted a piece of lemon cake, she wanted to take it out of the freezer so it could thaw.

"Lemon cake? Really, Clara, I don't know where you get such crazy ideas. We'll have honey cake for dessert, after the holiday meal, just like every year."

Clara dropped the sponge, and quickly turned around. Sitting in her mother's chair was a woman, who was staring at her and smiling. Only it wasn't the woman at the train station. And it wasn't her mother. It was a woman from a long time ago. She was dressed in a long black dress. Her hair was covered, too, with some kind of old-fashioned black hat. The woman held a sprig of something yellow in her hand, which she was holding out to Clara.

"Take it, Clara."

"I can't."

"Your mother would want you to have it."

Clara knew the woman was right. Her mother had tried to tell her, before she died, about the yellow broom. She remembered that now. But so much had happened since then. Arnau was gone, and Manel. Vidal would probably leave, too. What was she supposed to do? Sit at the kitchen table all by herself, with no one to keep her company except the family's ghosts?

"I can't. I can't fight everybody."

The woman was still smiling. "Oh yes, you can."

Everyone was seated around the table, and for the first time in many days Clara felt she could relax. She had settled the issue of the holiday meal by sticking on the refrigerator door her planned menu: a vegetable soup for starters, chicken with orange sauce for the main course, a string bean and potato casserole for the side dish, salad, and honey cake for dessert. Everyone saw it. But no one — not even Josep — had said a word.

She noted with further satisfaction that her family was having a normal conversation. Her father was calmly speaking to her husband about some new trellises needed for the vineyard. They were discussing measurements and different types of wood. Even Vidal appeared to be interested in the topic and had offered his opinion. Yes, it was a normal conversation. No fights. No tears. And there weren't even any ghosts at the table to distract her. *This is life*, she decided. *This is how a family should be.*

They were still passing around the salad dressing when they heard a knock at the kitchen door. Josep went to see who was there, and Eduard Garcia came inside.

"Sorry to disturb everyone."

"You're not disturbing anyone, Eduard," said Miquel. "Come to the table and have a seat."

"Vidal, get Mr. Garcia a cold drink," said Josep.

"Thank you, but it's not necessary. I'm here on business. Someone was looking for you, Miquel, from the post office. I signed for this registered letter."

Eduard Garcia handed Miquel an envelope. Miquel looked it over slowly. Then he raised his eyes and said, "It's from Madrid."

While the others took in this news, he carefully slit open the envelope with his dinner knife and took out the letter that was inside it. They waited in silence while Miquel read what was written.

"Bad news?" asked Eduard. They had all seen Miquel's face go pale.

"The government has decided to change the route of that new high-speed railway system they're building, the one that's going to connect Spain with the rest of Europe. The tracks are going to go straight through Sant Joan Januz."

"What? The government is going to take our land?" asked Eduard.

"You can read the letter for yourself." Miquel handed it to him. After Eduard read it, he gave the letter to Josep.

"How can the government do such a thing without asking us for permission?" asked Clara.

"We'll be paid for the land," said Josep, after he finished reading the letter. "It says so in writing. This could be a blessing in disguise. The village is dying. Everyone knows that."

"But where will we go?" asked Clara, glancing over at her father and uncles.

"The government will pay us a good price, probably a better one than we could have gotten if we tried to sell the land to a private developer. We'll make sure," Josep added, "that everyone has a new home."

"What about the cemetery, Josep?" Miquel's face was still pale. "I refuse to let some politicians from Madrid dig up the cemetery."

"You won't be able to stop them. They'll lay the tracks wherever they want to. But we can ask them to move the bones to a municipal grave someplace else."

"That's not good enough for us, and you know it," Miquel replied. "According to our traditions, the cemetery is a House of Eternity. It has to exist, untouched, until the Messiah comes and all the bodies are resurrected."

"You'll be wasting your time if you try to stop them."

"We should at least try, Josep," said Clara.

"It is the graves of our parents that we're talking about," added Eduard. Then he looked over at Vidal. "And our grandparents."

After dinner, Vidal went to his room to write some letters. Like his father, he wasn't optimistic. He couldn't imagine the government officials becoming sentimental over some graves of New Christians. But he would try. He had made a promise to his grandfather and the "generations," as his grandfather had called them on an afternoon that seemed like it took place an eternity ago.

But it wasn't just the promise that had made him take on the project. He also felt bad about having to uproot the cemetery. His Grandma Anna was buried there. So were the wives of Uncle Biel and Uncle Pau. He didn't remember them, they had died before he was born, but he knew that disturbing their graves would upset his great-uncles. Then there were the ancestors of the Garcias. And when the news got out, the entire village would be at his door, begging for his help and praying for his success.

The irony of the situation didn't escape his notice. He had wanted to save the village for the living. Instead, everyone was counting on him to save the dead. Maybe his father was right, and this was a blessing in disguise. Perhaps he could not only save the present cemetery, but also convince the government to let him keep some more of the land so that he could expand the cemetery and turn it into a luxury burial ground for the entire country. He already had a name for the new project: At Peace Land.

He tried to laugh, but since there was no one to share the joke with him he found it difficult. Al was presumably somewhere in the Ecuador rainforest, talking on his cell phone, making plans. Martinez was doing whatever politicians do when they're not looking at abstract paintings and making oblique statements.

Domenech would have missed the humor entirely, since he spent his entire life digging up the past. That left the American. He might have gotten the joke, but he didn't matter. The American had been laughing at him the entire time.

Vidal got up from his desk and walked over to a mirror and studied his reflection. His face was sunburned from all the weeks spent in the vineyard, and he needed a haircut. But it was the lines that had formed on either side of his downturned lips that held his attention. He thought of Luis Adarra. He, too, had suffered an early disappointment, and Vidal wondered if this was why the man was so cynical and cold.

"Please, G-d, don't let me become bitter," Vidal silently prayed, not quite sure who he was praying to now that he was a New Christian or a secret Jew, or whatever name people used when they joked about people like him.

He wished he could ask his Grandma Anna about that — about who she had prayed to, and what she had called herself when she did it. The American had used a different term: *Anusim*. The Forced Ones. In an odd way, that seemed like the most appropriate name for his family. First they were forced to admit they were descended from Jews. Now they were being forced out of their home. But why? And where were they supposed to go? And why did their ancestors have to have their eternal rest disturbed?

Why were they being forced out of their graves, too?

He didn't have an answer. But he did suddenly have the strangest idea: Sant Joan Januz wasn't dying. For the first time in five hundred years, it was waking up. Suddenly he could see, reflected in the mirror, a vision of a long and elegant tall ship, its white sails billowing in the wind. It was the ship that had haunted him whenever he had tried to puzzle out the mystery of Sant Joan Januz. Before, the ship had drifted aimlessly, lost in a hazy dream. Now it was going somewhere. Where it was going, he didn't yet know. He only knew, as the vision faded, that something had changed.

Josep didn't say anything as he watched Vidal send out his letters and make his phone calls. He was too busy making his own inquiries. As it turned out, most of the village's older residents had children they could go to. Ironically, it was his family that was going to be the hardest to resettle. He couldn't see all of them living together in the same house. It was one thing to have Miquel and the uncles over for meals, and quite another to have them around every minute of the day.

"I suppose we could buy a farmhouse somewhere else," he had said to Clara. "Then we could convert one of the structures into a home for your father and the uncles."

"We could. Or we could all move to Girona. That way we would be close to Arnau and Manel."

And Clara did want to be close to Manel. After all, her grandson was named after her great-uncle. She wanted to take him on trips to the countryside and tell him the names of all the flowers. Joanna wouldn't like it when she found out that Clara had told Manel about the yellow broom. But if she could help it, Manel wouldn't have to ask, twenty years from now, why no one had ever told him.

"What about Vidal?" Josep asked. "Don't you want to live near him, too?"

"Of course I do. But I don't think Vidal knows yet what he wants to do, or where he wants to live." What she didn't say, although she was thinking it, was that she believed that whatever lay in store for Vidal, he was going to be all right.

Josep, on the other hand, was uncomfortable with the changes he was seeing in his son. He was glad to see Vidal enthusiastic about something again, even though he was surprised to see his son so concerned about the cemetery. Young people usually weren't sentimental about such things. But he didn't like it that Vidal was starting to do some research into Jewish customs, or that Vidal and Clara would sometimes sit in the kitchen until late at night talking about the topic. Josep was therefore relieved when Vidal ran out of people to call and government offices to petition. He hoped that after admitting defeat, Vidal would direct his newfound energy toward a more useful endeavor.

Of course, they couldn't let the matter of the cemetery drop just because Vidal had received a pile of rejection letters from the various offices. Josep knew the family better than that. To no one's surprise, Miquel called for another family meeting. Clara suggested that Eduard and Joya Garcia be invited to attend, too. It seemed like the right thing to do since it had been Eduard who had brought them the news. The others agreed.

Once everyone was comfortably seated around the kitchen table, Vidal made his report and gave them his assessment of the situation: the government didn't care. It refused to make any guarantees about the cemetery.

"That's our answer then," said Josep.

"Your answer, Josep, not ours," said Joya Garcia.

Clara was glad that she had thought to invite the Garcias. Joya was the perfect ally. She was stubborn, like Clara's father, but she could contradict Josep without causing offense.

"Who else is there to contact?" asked Josep.

"The American. The people buried in the cemetery are his ancestors, too."

"I don't think he'll care about this, Mrs. Garcia," said Vidal. "I'm sure he doesn't have fond memories of Sant Joan Januz."

"He might forgive us when we tell him that the whole village is going to be destroyed," Joya Garcia replied. "If you hadn't found the synagogue, it might have disappeared in the rubble without a trace. At least now he has photographs of it. A person could even say that you did him a favor."

"You might say something like that, Mrs. Garcia, but he'll never forgive me for destroying the synagogue." Vidal looked over at his mother and added, "I can't say that I blame him."

"Still, it can't hurt to write him," said Clara. "All he can do is tell us no."

"But how can it help us?" asked Josep. "What can he do that Vidal hasn't already done?"

"He can contact one of those Jewish organizations that fight to protect Jewish cemeteries in Europe," said Joya Garcia.

"This isn't a Jewish cemetery." Josep looked to the others for support.

No one said anything.

"I'll e-mail him if you don't want to," Joya said to Vidal.

"It's not that I don't want to. But he's not going to help us."

Joyce smiled. "Oh yes, he will."

301

CHAPTER 30

T he square looked as empty and forgotten as it had looked in the winter. The only difference was that this time the people gathered around the cafe table were smiling at him. But he hadn't promised them anything. The truth was that he didn't know if he would be able to help.

After they had gotten the greetings over with, the Garcias led Chaim into the general store. Miquel, Clara, Josep, and Vidal followed. The great-uncles entered last, and Pau turned the key to lock the door.

Eduard Garcia motioned for everyone to follow him to the storage room that was behind the checkout counter. The room was a jumble of grocery and hardware supplies, and he cautioned them all to watch their step. Then he went to the back of the room, where four large wooden kegs were sitting.

Chaim glanced at the others. He assumed that this room was just a meeting point. Perhaps Eduard Garcia had a map of the village, which he would use to point out the location of the object of their search. Yet, Chaim noted, no one else seemed surprised to see Eduard Garcia pick up a chisel and hammer and begin to gently tap on one of the kegs, and so he waited patiently to see what would happen next.

When the sides of the keg swung open, Chaim stared. Sitting inside the keg was the Torah scroll.

He was too stunned to say anything. Joya Garcia had sent him photographs, which he had looked at dozens of times, and so he knew the scroll was in the village. But he had expected it to be hidden away in some attic or field, or anywhere else but in a pickle barrel sitting in the back room of Eduard Garcia's general store. Yet there it was, and he reached out his hand to touch it.

The parchment bore the signs of years of neglect. Large dark spots showed where the damp had left its mark, and it had the smell of history about it. But that only made the scroll dearer in Chaim's eyes. Each sign of age was a witness that the scroll was a tangible link to his Nona Anna and her father, Rabbi Isaac, and her brother, Manel — his ancestors, the villagers' ancestors. He wondered if anyone else was experiencing "the tingle" or if they all thought he was crazy for being so emotional.

"No one except Mrs. Garcia and me knew about it," said Eduard, finally breaking the long silence. "I don't know why my family was chosen to keep it, but that's what was decided during the war. There's a lot that's been forgotten. But it's yours now. You're family. You can decide what to do with it."

Chaim tried not to smile. If he was suddenly part of the family, it was because they needed him. The Torah scroll wasn't a free gift. He was expected to do something for the village in return. He knew all that. But he didn't mind. Although he had come to Sant Joan Januz to find the synagogue and the Torah scroll, it was the cemetery that had had a hold on him from the start. Literally. And it had "talked" to him when no one else in the village would. He couldn't turn down the village's request to try to save it.

"I'm flying to Jerusalem in three days," he told them. "I have a meeting set up with someone who says he might be able to help us. But you'll have to keep your story straight. You have to say that your ancestors were *Anusim*, who were descended from Jews. 'Like the Cathars,' won't score any points with my crowd."

"We know that," said Miquel. "Don't we?"

The others nodded in agreement, except Josep, who shrugged.

"And I still think it would be more effective if someone from the village came with me," Chaim said to Miquel. "It will show that it's not just me who cares about the cemetery. It's important for these people to know that you'll continue to look after it if we do manage to save it."

"We'll let you know what we decide."

Three days later Vidal and his mother and grandfather were waiting in the departure area of the Barcelona airport. Chaim was also there, standing a little off to the side. While the El Al security people roped off their check-in area, Miquel glanced over at the five Catalan policemen, distinguishable by their red caps, who were standing nearby and silently watching the movements of everyone who came close to the area.

They were there to prevent a gunman from opening fire on the Jewish passengers, Miquel supposed, or to stop a suicide bomber from blowing everyone up. In his excitement over saving the cemetery, he had forgotten about that. The fires of the Inquisition had moved again, this time to the Middle East. Although that Bin Laden fellow was worrisome, his wife Anna had been most troubled by the madman from Iran with the long name. He was always talking about how the Jews of Israel had to vanish from "the page of time." Some might say it was just talk, but that's how it began in Spain and in Germany — with one crazy man and a lot of crazy talk. And now, because of him, his grandson was walking straight into the line of fire.

Clara also looked over at the policemen. Then she glanced at the check-in areas of the other airlines, where people were waiting in line without all the fuss. "I hope that someday the Jews will be able to check in like normal people," she said to Chaim.

He laughed.

"Aren't you afraid?" she asked.

"When the Jews were wandering in the desert, G-d gave us a pillar of cloud to lead us during the day and a pillar of fire to lead us during the night. That's to show us that a Jew can never be afraid to serve G-d. Whether its day or night, whether the times are god or they're dark, a Jew always has to go forward."

Clara nodded. That's what she wanted to tell Vidal. Go forward. Confront the darkness. Make peace with the hidden light. That sounded much more inspiring than "Watch out for the little piece of wire." But she knew she would tell her son to do that, too. She was her mother's daughter, after all.

The El Al staff had finished setting up, and the first few passengers in line had started the security process.

"They're going to ask you a long list of questions," Chaim warned Vidal. "I'll wait for you at the check-in counter."

Chaim walked over to join the line, while Vidal turned to his family to say good-bye.

"Be careful," Clara whispered as she gave him a hug.

"You can change your mind," said Miquel, nodding toward the policemen.

"You know I can't do that, Grandpa. I made a promise."

"I release you from it."

"But I didn't make the promise just with you. I also made it with the generations. Remember?"

Vidal left his grandfather and mother and walked over to a security person who was free, an Israeli who was about his age.

"*Hola,*" said the young man, as he held out his hand for Vidal's passport.

Although the Israeli was smiling, Vidal could see that the young man was carefully studying him — and he didn't like it. He wasn't used to being the one under the microscope. Being suspicious of strangers was his family's specialty. Then he remembered — the Israeli was family — and he handed over his passport.

"*Hola.*"

THE END

Historical Note

The year was 1917. Samuel Schwarz, a Jewish mining engineer from Poland, was on assignment in Portugal when he stumbled upon a small, isolated village called Belmonte – and a group of people with some unusual customs that were suspiciously similar to Jewish rituals. Certain that he had discovered descendents of *Anusim*, crypto-Jews who had hidden their Jewish origins during the Spanish Inquisition, Schwarz proudly announced to them that he was also Jewish. The villagers, who thought that they were the last Jews in the world, didn't believe him. No one who was really Jewish would dare to admit such a thing so openly. It was only when Schwarz recited the *Shema Yisrael*, one of the holiest prayers in the Jewish liturgy, and came to the word *Ad-onoi*, one of the names of G-d that the *Anusim* recognized, that the villagers accepted him as a fellow Jew.

Schwarz remained in Portugal, where he continued to study the *Anusim*. His findings were published in the 1920s in his book *The Crypto-Jews of Portugal*. As might be expected, his discovery made quite a stir in the Jewish world, which had previously assumed that all the *Anusim* had already either converted back to Judaism or assimilated into their non-Jewish surroundings.

After all, people had no reason to assume otherwise, since the history of the *Anusim* wasn't unknown. The tragic events of the year 1391, when most of Spain's Jewish communities were annihilated and many of the survivors were forcibly converted to Catholicism, were well documented. Court records from the Spanish Inquisition, which had mainly targeted the *Anusim*, had been preserved in Spanish archives. The flight of some of the *Anusim* to France, Italy, Flanders, Turkey, and other European countries also was well known, since the fugitives established flourishing communities wherever they were allowed to openly congregate.

When the *Anusim* dropped out of Jewish history during the nineteenth century, there was a ready explanation. The Spanish

306

Inquisition came to an official end in the year 1821. The Emancipation movement in Europe made it easier for both the *Anusim* and the Jews to freely assimilate into European society. With nothing to stop them from either coming forward as Jews or assimilating, the *Anusim*, it was assumed, made their choice. Their separate communities were disbanded. The doors to their synagogues were shut. Their story was consigned to the history books. Or so people thought.

Schwarz's discovery of a community of *Anusim* in Belmonte did create a brief flurry of interest, but subsequent world events, including the destruction of European Jewry during the Holocaust, moved the *Anusim* back into the shadows. It wasn't until the 1990s – a decade that saw the 500th anniversary of the Jewish Expulsion from Spain - that the story of the *Anusim* truly captured both the interest and the imagination of the Jewish world. University professors, researchers, and world travelers began to actively seek out *Anusim* communities not only in Spain and Portugal, but also in South America, Mexico and the southwestern United States. Suddenly, it seemed that everyone knew about those Shabbos candles hidden inside clay pots or cupboards.

Yet despite the number of books, academic papers, and magazine articles that have been written about them – and the fact that a few of them, including the *Anusim* of Belmonte, have returned to Judaism – there is much about the modern-day descendents of the original *Anusim* that still remains a mystery. No one knows for sure how many of them there are. No one knows for sure where all their communities are located. But according to Rabbi Isaac Abarbanel, the Torah scholar and diplomat who was expelled from Spain in 1492 along with the rest of Spanish Jewry, one day the mystery will be solved. The *Anusim* will return to the Jewish people, and together we will rejoice in the rebuilding of the Temple in Jerusalem, may it come speedily and in our days.

If you enjoyed this book, please consider leaving a review at your favorite online bookseller.

About the Author

LIBI ASTAIRE is an award-winning author who often writes about Jewish history. In addition to her Jewish Regency Mystery Series featuring Ezra Melamed, General Well'ngone and the Earl of Gravel Lane, she is the author of *Terra Incognita,* a novel about modern-day descendants of Spain's crypto-Jews, and several volumes of Chassidic tales. She lives in Jerusalem, Israel.

For updates about future books, visit her website at www.libiastaire.weebly.com

Read more about the *Anusim* in this two other great books
by Libi Astaire

The Banished Heart
"A surprisingly GREAT read." – Goodreads.com

For Paul Hoffmann, a Jewish student at the University of Berlin, life would be sweet if he could write poetry and, of course, graduate. But since the year is 1933, his life is about to take a very different turn — one that leads him back to Elizabethan England, where his idol, William Shakespeare, is having a crisis of his own. Shakespeare's theatre company expects him to write an anti-Jewish play that will incite the public against Dr. Rodrigo Lopez, a crypto-Jew accused of planning to poison Queen Elizabeth. But there is a problem: Shakespeare knows that Lopez is innocent.

Will Shakespeare remain loyal to the truth and his friends in London's crypto-Jewish community or sacrifice Dr. Lopez to further his own career? As Shakespeare struggles over his rewrites of the play that will be known as "The Merchant of Venice," questions are raised for Paul Hoffmann, as well: in a world where he can no longer be a German, can he find the courage to rewrite the "script" and be, first and last, a Jew?

Day Trips to Jewish History
"Her descriptions of her discoveries in Spain and Portugal are fascinating." – Amazon.com

Who was the New World's first Jewish author? Why did some medieval moneychangers cover their hair? Which Jewish woman became queen of a North African people? And what's the truth about the story that claims Hebrew almost became the official language of the United States?

Join journalist and historical novelist Libi Astaire for a fascinating journey down some of the less-traveled roads of the past in her latest book, *Day Trips to Jewish History*.

GET COZY WITH A
JEWISH REGENCY MYSTERY

There's trouble afoot in Regency London's Jewish community, and no one to stop the crimes — until wealthy-widower-turned-sleuth Mr. Ezra Melamed teams up with an unlikely pair: General Well'ngone and the Earl of Gravel Lane, the leaders of a gang of young Jewish pickpockets.

Tempest in the Tea Room
"For anyone who loves Jane Austen, Georgette Heyer, or who enjoys cleverly plotted mysteries dressed in period costumes." — *Kansas City Jewish Chronicle*

When a young doctor newly arrived in London is accused of attempting to poison his patients, Mr. Melamed must discover the true culprit before it's too late.

The Moon Taker
"Intriguing from beginning to end" — Amazon.com

When General Well'ngone and the Earl of Gravel Lane set out to discover who murdered a colleague of theirs in the secondhand linen trade, their quest takes them from their East End slum to an elegant country house where a group of distinguished astronomers are meeting — one of whom has a secret darker than the night sky.

The Doppelganger's Dance
"Another great read by Libi Astaire" — Amazon.com

David Salomon, a young violinist and composer, seeks fame and fortune in Regency London. But someone is stealing his compositions before he can perform them and soon he is the laughingstock of the beau monde he had hoped to conquer. He turns to Ezra Melamed for help, but the deeper Mr. Melamed looks into the violinist's story the more jarring notes he finds, making *The Doppelganger's Dance* one of the most discomposing mysteries in his career.

Made in the USA
Middletown, DE
06 April 2017